Secrets & Thyme

A Witches & Immortals Sequel

Stephanie Vorwald

This book is dedicated to my parents for always encouraging me to keep writing and to my little family for letting me write when inspiration starts to flow. The Mississippi River will continue to have my heart and be my home away from home.

Thank you for the continuing support in my magical journey of Crystal Rock, WI.

<u>Witches & Immortals Series</u>
Book 1: Witches & Immortals
Book 2: Secrets & Thyme (Sequel)
Book 3: Eric & Izzy (Prequel)
Book 4: Bonds & Bones (Finale)

Stephanie
VORWALD
ESCAPE FROM REALITY
YA FANTASY

Chapter One

Freya Chamberlain

Journal Entry: October

It's been three months...

I could feel the pen lift off the paper as I hesitated going any further. Thinking about how the last journal didn't end so well. But I would not let history repeat itself, I couldn't. The word "witch" wasn't even in my vocabulary when I first started journaling. I had a lot more supernatural knowledge now. *I'm in control of my magic.* I pushed my hand back to the paper and continued.

I decided to start writing again in a normal, non-magical journal. It took three whole months for me to finally mend my head on how I could've been betrayed by my own therapist. Well, a posing therapist. Nonetheless, I actually

felt that when I was writing things down, it was helping with my anxiety. So, here we go again…

Life has been pretty normal lately. Other than practicing magic when and wherever is safe. Then, researching Anchor history in my spare time, trying to learn more about syphoning. Except there isn't much information to be found. So, maybe normal life is not the correct term. How about uneventful. Which I am very happy about. The last thing I want is more trauma from Immortals being assholes.

I check the dagger daily, and everything seems to be holding as it should. It is still dull and magicless. The strangest thing started last week, though. My Mark has started to fade. Haven's is completely fine, which makes me wonder if I did something to piss off the universe and am being punished for it. My eyes keep staring at it, willing it to darken again, but nothing changes. Day by day, it's fading and fast.

Jaxon is holding up pretty well. He hasn't said much about his parents, which could be a very bad thing. Grieving happens in stages, and he seems to be keeping himself busy working at Swig and Jig and attempting to build a foundation for a home at JFK. His mind seems to be elsewhere, though, even while his physical body is here with me. I'm worried about him but haven't figured out a way to bring it up to him without triggering anything.

Declan is also grieving. Only his dad is still around. Sort of. I guess, it's not even his real dad, but the only dad he's ever known, and that has to be tough. I remember what it was like losing my mom from abandonment, and it tore me apart. But it's Declan's silence that scares me. I'm worried about him, and I'm even more worried about who he might finally crumble in front of.

Aisling has been busy practicing the new magic that her aunt gave her. She and Aunt Lynn have been searching for her Anchor, but only coming up with dead ends. There were only so many babies born in October in Crystal Rock, though. It shouldn't be this hard. One of us will find them, eventually.

Aunt Lynn has been slowing down lately, and we're thinking it's the link she has with the Immortals making her deteriorate. She's tired all the time and has no energy. We have to unlink her before it's too late.

My parents have been playing honeymoon all over again. They seem to be making up for the lost time. Which I'm not even mad about it. I have not seen my dad smile this much in a long time, and for that, I am very thankful. My mom has been trying to help me with the syphoning research as much as possible. She

passed down our family's grimoire to me, in hopes that we could find something in there. It seems that the book has not been that well taken care of over the years, and a few pages are missing or barely holding onto the binding. My great grandmother was an Anchor too and had been the one to drop it in multiple batches of potions, rivers, and who knows what else. Now my grandmother seemed to take better care of it. I sure wish I could've met them and maybe get some answers. We will keep searching for now.

Speaking of syphoning, the magic that I have consumed, both good and evil, seems to be balancing out pretty evenly for now. That first month after I drained the Immortals of their magic, it took a pretty dreadful toll on my immune system. I laid in bed for a good two weeks just feeling nauseous and ill. Then, it started to subside on its own. Either way, this is still all pretty new to me. I'm learning, though. I think we all are.

I closed the journal and stared at the plain cover, smiling at the thought of this being nothing more than a journal for my thoughts and secrets, but this time it was only for me. I set it down and grabbed my new tourmaline and amethyst wire wrapped necklace that Jaxon had made for me and fidgeted with it before heading outside. The sun was already high at noon, but there was a chill in the air today. Fall weather here in Wisconsin sets in pretty quick. I loved the cool breeze, but was not ready for the season that followed the falling leaves and pumpkins. The holidays this year were going to be different. Great for me, with having my parents together again, and bad for Jaxon, without either parent. The thought made me sick and I needed a new thought.

I glared at my left forearm at the fading Mark and huffed in annoyance at the unknown. *Why would it be fading?* What good are grimoires if they don't have the information we actually need? I was just glad that I was taking a semester off of school to figure out my answers and work between the movie theater for a little while longer and help at the bar when needed. Now that I was old enough to serve the liquor and make some decent tips to add to my savings.

I walked down the road, unsure of where I was trying to end up. I just started walking without looking back. My brain felt like a whirlwind today, and I just needed to focus on one thing at a time. My legs were leading the way while I was in deep thought. I hadn't realized that I had made it to Jaxon's childhood home before freezing.

What was I going to do here? This place brought back so many memories, and I didn't know if I was ready for some of those to roll in. The guilt of his parents being gone still lingered with me, and seeing this house made me feel like Margo was screaming from inside for me to leave. She asked me to take care of Jaxon, but what if I couldn't protect him as she wanted? My heart felt heavy.

I walked slowly up to the front door and tried to jiggle

the handle. Locked. The house was empty, and the lights hadn't been on in a long time. The inside was abandoned. I decided to walk to the backyard and just look through the window, which would've been under Jaxon's old room. I reached the window and realized I was too short to even see inside. I needed something to stand on. I looked around the yard and found an empty bin that hopefully could hold my weight.

What am I even doing here? What am I looking for?

I stepped onto the bin, as my breathing quickened, and peered inside the room. My eyes needed a minute to focus through the dark.

Empty.

I laughed to myself at the stupidity of thinking anything was going to be there. My heart slowed, and my breathing became even again.

Stupid.

I jumped down from the bin and put it back before walking back to the front yard. My heart stopped as I realized the previously closed front door was now open. My heart pounded. *Wasn't it closed?* My stomach started to twist uncomfortably. Was someone here? I froze, just peering toward the open door. My feet wouldn't move. I had to choose whether to walk up and close the door or go inside or run away. I had to decide now, and my decision needed to be quick before losing courage. I walked toward the house and made it to the open doorway.

Chapter Two

Jaxon Oakes

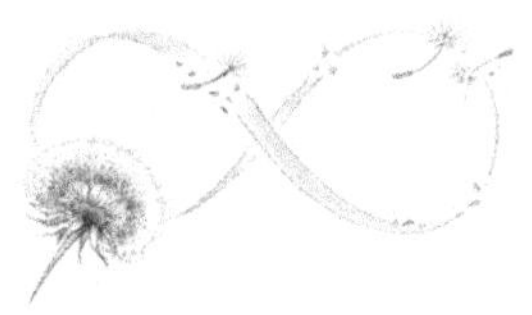

My brain felt heavy, like it was in a fog today. I couldn't sleep, yet I was not ready to wake up this morning. The dream kept coming back to me of my mom. She kept telling me to look harder, but I had no idea what I was even looking for.

Freya didn't know about this dream, and I didn't plan on telling her. She had enough on her plate with the syphoning, and even though she said she wasn't worried about her Mark, I saw her staring at it every day. Unfortunately, even I had never seen a Mark fade. Besides when it was on her back and being hidden by magic. Only this time, no one was hiding hers. And I had no idea what I was supposed to be looking for. I just had to keep busy. I needed to get out of bed. The dreams are not real.

WAKE UP, JAXON!

I knew they were gone. I wasn't trying to make up some dream scenario with them off on vacation and coming home soon. I was not a child. I knew what death was, and it was okay. I was dealing with it, just maybe in my own way.

I wanted to finish the house at JFK, not just for me to escape to, but for me to accomplish something after a tragedy, something to be proud of and hopefully help me overcome the loss. At least I had Freya and her parents to keep me occupied. They really have been great to me. Beyond great. I was just ready for some more space.

I kept debating on going back to my childhood home and staying there for a while, but the thought of asking Freya to come with me and be away from her parents seemed selfish. She just got her family back, and I wanted her to enjoy them all being together for a while before we started our own journey. I was trying not to be selfish with her, so maybe I should stay at my old home without her and give her space too. I doubted she would let me, but maybe it was worth a try. I loved that woman, and the thought of being too far away from her scared me, but maybe that was what I needed to trigger my emotions so I could finally grieve and then grow. I'd just go check out the old home and see how I felt around it.

I jumped in my car and left the mended JFK. Something was telling me to go there, but nothing physically. I just had a feeling that I needed to see it. I rolled down the windows and let the cool air clear my thinking. I had a good twenty-minute drive until I got there. Hopefully, that was enough time to clear my head.

I pulled up to the house and froze, as the door was wide open. I had the only key to the place so for that to be open was impossible. My heart raced with adrenaline at the thought of someone squatting in my family home. I threw my car in park and leaped out the door, running toward the front open door.

I heard the floorboards creak upstairs in my parents' old room and lost it.

"This house is not for sale! Get out!" I yelled in my most tough guy voice.

I heard a female scream come from up above and ran up faster than my feet could take me, tripping on the top stair and catching myself before smashing my face. I quickly looked up to see her standing there.

"You scared the hell out of me, Jax," Freya yelled.

"Me, scare you? You scared me! Why are you even in my home?"

She froze and started to fidget with her fingers and looked toward the floor in her shy, embarrassed manner before answering. "I don't really know. I just started walking and this is where I ended up." She shrugged nervously.

"I didn't mean to scare you, Frey. I thought you were a squatter or something," I said calmly while reaching for her and rubbing her shoulders.

"What are you doing here?" she questioned after collecting her embarrassment.

"I, uh, well... I." I paused, now I was the one stumbling. "I guess I don't really know, either. Just trying to grab a piece of my past, I guess." I shrugged, not really sure. My heart started pounding when I looked around the empty room.

"I miss them," I said accidentally.

Shit. Now she's going to worry again.

"I know." She reached for me to hug me tight. "Is there anything I can do for you?"

"Let's get out of here," I said quickly before my

emotions got the best of me. I needed to be strong in front of her.

"Okay." She smiled and grabbed my hand as we started to head toward the doorway of the room.

We froze and tensed together when a light started to beam through the closed closet door behind us, blinding the doorway with light. We both turned our heads slowly. I inched my way closer to it with Freya hiding behind me, fire in hand. Just in case. I smiled to myself at the preparedness. I opened the door slowly, ready for anything that may attack us, confused to find only a book lying on the ground with the pages bright as the sun, glowing as if the pages needed to be turned so the magic could release itself. I walked toward the book as the glowing disappeared, and it became an ordinary book again.

Huh? What the hell was that?

I went to pick it up, but Freya beat me to it and lifted it into the air to examine it closer. The book looked like an old ordinary book, but why would it have glowed? She looked up at me frowning and confused. The book was nothing. She turned the pages while I stared over her shoulder. There was literally nothing.

"You saw the glowing too, right?"

"Nope, just you." I laughed and nodded my head. "Yes, I saw it too."

She smirked at me and made my heart beat faster. This woman had me wrapped around her fingers for eternity. "Maybe we can run it past the others and see if they have any ideas?"

"Good idea. Let's get out of here." I smiled as I pulled her into my arms for a kiss.

Chapter Three

Aisling Meadows

"Can't we just stay in bed today? I really don't feel like doing more research," I begged as Declan shook his head across from me, pulling me closer to him, kissing my neck slowly, pulling me on top of him.

"We have to find your Anchor, Ais. Just in case those assholes wake up," Declan said stubbornly. Well, knowing that he still loved Eric, which pissed me off, but I got it. Declan had no idea who the man really was, but the way Eric hurt my aunt all those centuries ago mades me hate him even more.

We had no new information, and we checked every hospital birth record. No one shared my Mark. It was hopeless. Everyone that was born near my birthday never even left town, and I checked their arms personally. I was starting to think that maybe I wasn't an Anchor witch and just a witch with transferred magic. Not all witches got second chances, but thankfully for Aunt Lynn who gave my great, great, great, whatever, a life worth living. I smiled thinking how lucky I was to have her. Declan noticed my smile change from sexual intent to loving.

"What are you thinking about?" he asked between kisses.

"My aunt," I answered.

"Mmmm, I could think of her all day long too." He made a kissy face toward me as I jumped up, pushing him off the bed we were sharing.

"Ew! Stop it!"

"Hey, no blood relation!" He boomed with laughter as I tried to catch him as he leaped across the bed escaping my reach. He came up from behind me and lifted me up, laying me back on the bed. "I'm just kidding. It's you, babe. It's been you since day one," he whispered sweetly. It was always hard to resist his charm.

"Fine, you're forgiven. This time." I smirked and grabbed his face to kiss him hard again. We rolled around in the bed for another minute longer before I decided we should start researching something.

"Hey, speaking of my aunt..." I hesitated. "She's starting to decline faster. I noticed it the other day, she's trying to hide it from me, but I saw her hands and they are starting to marbleize, and she is freezing all the time."

"All the more reason to look for a way to unlink that sexy babe."

I rolled my eyes at him for the added inappropriate comment but nodded my head at the research part. Aunt Lynn said when she linked herself to them, it was an unbreakable bond that was supposed to end in death. The immortality was not part of the plan, and for centuries, she had tried to unlink herself with no luck. Her not being an

Anchor could make it easier to break her seal. It was all uncharted territory, so we weren't exactly sure what would work best. Aunt Lynn had been so quiet and accepting of her fate, but I would not.

"Just one more kiss," Declan demanded.

I smiled and kissed him quickly before turning around to get ready to head to the old archives at the library. There had to be something we were missing.

Chapter Four

Haven Vine

Dinner with Mom and Dad tonight sounded like the best plan I'd had all week. The last few months had been a lot of trial and error work of trying to unlink Lynn from Eric with no progress. She was aging rapidly, and it had to be because of her being linked to a decaying, hopefully soon to be a corpse, Immortal in a sealed cave. I promised Aisling that I would do everything I could to try and help her aunt, and now the pressure of it had a clock ticking. When I closed my eyes, the guilt of wasting time sleeping consumed me. My brain needed a break from research and potions all ending in literal puffs of smoke. Aunt Clara was helping as best as she knew too. But dinner would be a nice break.

On another note, getting to know Dad the last few months has been amazing. I was a little jealous that Freya had all the extra time with him, but I was thankful I had Aunt Clara too. It was crazy to think of another life, but amazing to have the opportunity to have it all now.

Freya had been a game-changer in my world of not

many girlfriends. I was a little nervous about the dream I'd been having lately with her betraying me, and I really hoped that wouldn't ever happen. I just kept repeating to myself that she would never.

"Earth to Haven?" Ezra asked while walking closer to me at the newly remodeled pottery shop. I jumped when I realized I was not paying attention to my surroundings again.

"Sorry babe, just thinking."

"When aren't you thinking? You're my genius woman." He smiled and kissed me on my forehead as he walked behind me to rub my shoulders. "What are you thinking about now?"

"Do you remember when I told you about my betrayal dream?"

"It was not real. She would never do that. That woman has a heart of gold and would put her life on the frontline to save any one of us. I've seen it with my own eyes." He smiled, trying to be reassuring.

"I know, it's just that—" I took a deep breath before continuing, "The dream keeps happening. It has to have some kind of meaning. Right?"

He shrugged his shoulders, which was not the response I was looking for. I exhaled, defeated. "Honestly, I think you could use some more sleep. Why don't you take a nap on the cot in the office? I've got today covered."

He didn't want to argue with me and maybe he was right. I feel like I hadn't had solid sleep in a while now. I should close my eyes for a little bit. I smiled and kissed him before agreeing to the deal.

"Oh, and, babe?" I turned to see what he wanted. "I'm

much more dreamy to dream about." He smiled and laughed as he winked at me. "Love you" he mouthed before turning to the front of the shop, leaving me to rest quietly.

"Love you," I yelled back loud enough, hoping it made him blush.

I grabbed the blanket and wheeled out the cot. I took my glasses off, rubbing my tired eyes, but knew that sleep would be hard. But I laid down anyway. My brain seemed to be in fast motion right now and sleep seemed to be the last thing that could happen for me. I rolled my eyes at the thought of a nap during the day and felt like I was wasting precious research time trying to find that unlinking spell so we could finish what we started. I just had this sick eerie feeling that something bad was about to happen if we didn't find something soon.

I could feel my eyes starting to get heavy. Maybe I was just tired after all. I yawned and before I knew it, I was closing my eyes.

"Freya! We need to talk about this! You can't just sacrifice yourself because *she* wants you to. Come on! Talk to me," I screamed at her, but she looked past me as if I were nonexistent. Only she was staring straight toward me. As if I wasn't standing in front of her, begging. "Stop being so stubborn and just listen to me! We can find another way!"

She looked up to me, finally with a stare that was haunting. "This is the only way," she said quietly while looking at her glowing Mark on her forearm and holding the stupid Viking dagger in her other arm facing it toward her Mark.

My eyes widened as I yelled for her to stop, but again she wasn't listening to me. Damnit, Freya. I grabbed the dagger and plunged it into my Mark before pushing her past the spiral of darkness that was trying to consume her and letting myself fall in it.

I woke in a sweat in the office right where I started. I sat up quickly and examined my surroundings. I looked at my Mark and froze when I noticed it was glowing. What was the universe trying to tell me? "I'm listening," I whispered softly, waiting for a sign of what to do next. When nothing happened, I threw the blanket off and grabbed my glasses to glance at my phone.

Unknown number missed phone call.

Weird.

Everyone I knew was saved on my phone. Oh well, I thought as I tossed it on the foot of the cot and sat myself up. My phone chimed again. I grabbed it, now annoyed from the lack of actual sleep that I really needed and glanced at it.

New voicemail.

I dialed in my passcode and listened carefully to panting breaths on the other end before a man's voice spoke quickly, who I did not recognize.

"Haven Vine, I have your answers for your research. Meet me at 1222 Rivershore in one hour. Come alone, or I'm gone." The line went dead.

Who the hell was that, and how did he know about the spell I'd been working on? I couldn't go alone without letting someone know, but the thought of having a problem solved sounded even better. I looked up the address on my phone and saw a house not far from Freya's home pop up. Worst case scenario, if I screamed loud enough, someone would hear me. I thought quickly about how to get to Crystal Rock without Ezra suspecting anything extra, knowing that he would not let me go alone. Probably for good reason, but everyone was counting on me to save Aisling's aunt. I had to go, to at least check it out.

> Haven: Hey, I might've found something. Call you later, K?
>
> Freya: YAY! Okay, call me when you can!

My heart pounded as I headed out the back door, leaving a note for Ezra to read later that said I went home to sleep. I took off quickly, feeling extra guilty for lying. There wasn't any more time to feel guilty now, though, as I started to drive out of Iowa back into Wisconsin over the bridge. The decision has been made, too late now.

Chapter Five

Freya Chamberlain

I couldn't bear to tell Jaxon that the book, even though visibly blank, had his mom's magic written all over it. I could feel Margo screaming through the pages to get a message out to him. My stomach felt sick as I sat in the passenger seat next to him holding the book on my lap. Fidgeting with my tourmaline to help distract me from saying more than I was ready to. There was something special about this book, and we needed to find out what it knew. I flipped through the pages again, but nothing was on them. Just old, rugged pages with coffee stains and ink splatter throughout, but no words and no pictures. But it had glowed, and that had to mean something more.

I smiled when my phone buzzed and I saw the promising words from Haven come through. I really hoped she found something. Even a glimmer of hope would make the next few weeks better. I just had this bad feeling that something bad was about to happen. Things had been "normal" for too long, and we all knew how the universe liked to jump in and play her games.

We drove down the road back to my home, where hopefully my mom had some insight on this book. I looked over to Jaxon to see him in deep thought. I could see the look of disappointment across his face, which made my heart sink. Disappointment that I was in his childhood home unexpectedly, or disappointment of not finding what he was looking for? That I wasn't sure of. What he was looking for at the exact time I was there too was still unknown.

We reached my home and walked quietly inside. My mom was sitting in the living room next to my dad looking through paint colors mindlessly. I didn't even know if they were actually looking or if they were just sitting close together for intimacy. They had the look in their eyes that I remembered as a kid, it was the look of love. My heart swelled with a happiness I had almost forgotten. It was a childhood heartfelt memory that I could get used to.

"Sorry to interrupt, but we might've found something," I said quietly.

"You two were at the library?" my dad questioned, eyebrows raised in suspicion. "That's not your normal routine for a weekend."

We had a routine? I smiled a little to myself at the idea of a life spent together, making routines and habits.

"No," I laughed. "This was glowing in Jaxon's old home." I handed it over to my mom who was sitting on the edge of the couch now with wide eyes. She knew something but was being quiet. I made a mental note that I would have to ask her privately later. She silently flipped through the book and looked up when she was done.

"It was glowing?" she questioned. "There's nothing in

it. Are you sure it wasn't the sun beaming down on it or something?"

I looked to Jaxon, who looked back to me, both of us in agreement that we were not crazy.

"Could it be spelled by magic?" I asked, hopeful.

"I mean, with magic, anything is possible. I just haven't seen one like this before. There's literally nothing," Mom said.

The hope I had deflated when she looked up to me in an honest know-nothing look. She stood up and went to the kitchen, and I followed her. Just to be sure that I wasn't missing something. Jaxon sat down defeated on the couch examining the book. Once we were alone in the kitchen and out of earshot, I whispered to her.

"I felt Margo trying to send me a message when I grabbed the book." I felt stupid saying it out loud.

"Margo?" Her eyes became wide. "Honey, you have to stop feeling guilty about what happened. It wasn't your fault."

"No, I'm not making this up. When I touched the book, I saw a vision of her. There's something more to that book. I just didn't want to tell Jax and disappoint him."

She looked at me curiously before asking, "You really think it was her?"

"Yes."

"You really want to take this further? I mean, life is pretty good right now."

"We're losing time."

"We need to get it to Aunt Clara then. Have you checked the dagger lately?"

"Every day."

"Good."

Hope grew that Aunt Clara would know something more, and that made me feel better. The dagger question triggered me to think she knew more than she was still telling me. I reached for the dagger and checked it quickly once she walked back to the living room to tell them of our road trip. The dagger was magic-less still. I let out a quick breath before sheathing it again. She told Jaxon he needed to stay and help my dad pick out paint colors for the bar and then go help bartend until got back. He nodded without hesitation. His and my dad's bond was unbreakable lately

Chapter Six

Haven Vine

Something was off as I pulled up to the address. I swore that was Jaxon and Freya that just pulled away a few seconds ago. Maybe I should text her to turn around and walk through this with me. No, I couldn't.

He said to come alone, and this might be our only lead. I couldn't let this one get away.

I looked at the two-story house and stared at the shutter that was broken on the second floor, waiting for one more windstorm to take it down, and thought of Aunt Lynn's life just hanging by a thread just as the shutter, which made me jump out of the car, determined to find the answers for her. I stood next to my car and gazed across the yard at the house, hesitating. The home was abandoned, but it didn't look rundown, besides the broken shutter. At least Freya lived up the block so if anything went wrong hopefully she could get to me quick. Why would he send me to an empty house?

I walked toward the front porch and peered into the windows.

Abandoned.

My heart skipped a beat when the front door opened by itself. I jumped back, eyes wide, and examined my surroundings while trying to manage my breathing and not let my heart leap out of my chest. For a brief moment, I debated on running back to my car, but I couldn't let fear get the best of me. I walked toward the front door with my palm igniting with electricity as a taser just to be on the safe side and walked through the front door.

"Hello?" I whispered as loudly as my dry, cracking voice could.

Silence.

My heart beating was the loudest sound in the whole house. That's it. Time to leave.

"No," I heard a man's voice boom from upstairs, and on instinct, I headed for the front door to leave as I heard footsteps catching up to me and fast. "Haven?" the man's voice asked from behind me.

I slowly turned with a sickening pit in my stomach. Who was this man? What did he know? Why did this man look familiar? Where did I know him from? I studied his face silently before nodding to his question.

"Yes, I'm Haven," I whispered, shakily.

"Good and not good." He shook his head. "The information I had for you is now missing. I can tell you what I remember, though."

"Missing?" I questioned.

"I left the book here for safekeeping, and it's gone. I will have my wife do a locator spell to find it again." He seemed frustrated.

"I'm sorry, but who are you?"

"I can't tell you that, just know that I'm on your side."

"And I'm supposed to just take your word?" I huffed and tried to steady my breathing to show him that trust needed to be earned. He stepped back, eyes sincere. He had a secret that he was holding back.

"Jaxon," he whispered and hesitated. "You can't tell him, just know that I am trying to save you all."

I looked at him, confused. Staring with furrowed brows at the mention of Jaxon. I didn't understand the meaning behind it. I stared at him longer before letting my mind go into shock.

He was Jaxon's father. That was why he looked so familiar. You could tell their features were similar, the only difference was age. My heart pounded faster than hoofs during a horse race, and my breathing sped up. My brain lacked the oxygen that it needed. I felt dizzy, and my legs wobbled. I tried to catch myself with the wall that should've been closer behind me than I thought and missed before stumbling toward the ground. Darkness consumed me as I just saw a ghost.

My eyes opened to a dark house, it was much later at night than I had planned on being away from the pottery shop, and I was alone. My head was hurting. I lifted myself to sit up and noticed a small cushion under my head and a note inches from my face. I reached too quickly for the note and unfolded it, tearing it in half.

Jaxon can't know yet. Please. I will call you when I find what we need.

-C.O.

. . .

My eyes scanned the note for any clues as to this being a setup or anything out of the ordinary. I read the note again and again. He was here looking for a book that was missing. What was it, and what did it have that we needed? I stood up and grabbed my phone. Ezra, missed calls. Shit, he's not going to be happy about this. He was home, and now he knew that I wasn't. I decided to keep it my little secret until we had more information.

I called him back and just said I was on my way to dinner with my parents. I told him I must've fallen asleep on the beach and lost track of time. He didn't question me, but I could feel the tone change on the phone. He knew I was lying.

Chapter Seven

Aisling Meadows

The cold air almost took my breath away as I stepped outside to try and clear my head. It was hard to believe that my birthday was in a few weeks, and I hadn't even started planning anything yet. *Who am I?* Walking down the street, I contemplated if I should go out of town with my small circle of friends or go big and celebrate with the town at the parade. So many decisions to make and so little time. I needed to call Freya and see what she thought. I knew I was the planner, but she always knew best. Ying and Yang kind of thing.

My mind felt like it had a million things running through it, and maybe I should start journaling like she did. Maybe it would help me clear my thoughts, or at least sort them out so I could conquer them one by one before sundown. I smiled, knowing that if I gave myself until sundown, I really would get everything done because that was just what I did. That's why finding my Anchor and unlinking my aunt had been getting under my skin lately. Two things that I couldn't figure out, and they had been sitting on my imaginary list for too long now. I was getting annoyed with myself.

Walking a few more houses away, I turned around to go home. It was always strange walking on this block, where Jaxon used to live. So many memories as a kid with him and Freya in the neighborhood. I shook my head, remembering that he was alive and his old home was just a house. I could see the broken shutter from two houses away and laughed, remembering the night I saw the two shithead kids from next door throwing rocks at the abandoned house, breaking the hinge for the shutter, and the look on their face when I came screaming up to them, chasing them back to their mommy and daddy. Pretty sure they wet themselves at the crazed woman with a bigger rock in her hand, defending my friend's home. Definitely was not going to use it, just a scare tactic to get them to flee. Freya would've been devastated if she had seen it back then.

I froze. Choked on my own breath.

Who the hell was walking out of Jaxon's home? Isadora? No, impossible! Who the hell was that? I squinted a little harder in the dark, trying to let my eyes focus before realizing the car parked across the street was recognizable.

Haven! Wait, Haven?

I walked up to the porch as she had her back turned to me, closing the door tight.

"No one is home!" I yelled, intentionally. Making her scream and jump out of her own skin, while turning around and gasping for breath. I sat back and cackled at the innocent little prank that I probably shouldn't have pulled, but the opportunity was there. I had to.

"What are you doing here? Jaxon doesn't live here

anymore, probably have more luck catching him at Freya's house. Honestly, though, I don't think she will be too happy seeing you trying to get after her man." I laughed again, and her eyes widened in terror. It was a joke. Geez.

"Jaxon's home?" Haven asked cautiously.

"Well, his old home, technically." I looked at her more serious now. What had her spooked?

"The door was open as I was on my way to my parents' house for dinner, so I went to close it, that's all," she said with a shrug.

"Oh, okay. The wind probably blew it open." I shrugged back with her. "You're heading to their house now?" She nodded. "Mind if I join you guys?" I asked.

"The more the merrier." She smiled, and we walked to her car. Something was up, she wasn't telling me something, but I wasn't going to push it.

Chapter Eight

Jaxon Oakes

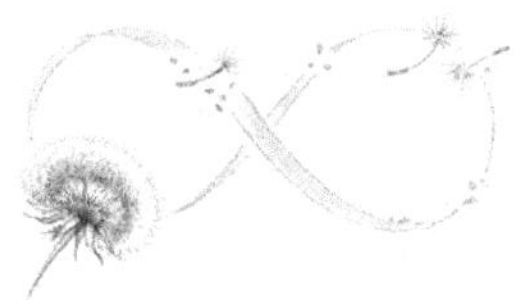

I didn't say anything when we drove back to Freya's home, but I knew that book. I remembered seeing it as a child. At least, I thought it was that book. Only I remembered my mom studying it with words or symbols on it. I didn't want to scare her into thinking I was losing it. So, I decided to keep my mouth shut and see what the others thought.

Jim and I waited for Haven to show up for the dinner that was supposed to happen tonight, but now with this new magic object, it would have to be postponed. We would have to bring her to the bar with a narrowed down palette of paint colors to choose from so that the color choosing wouldn't be put on me. I was going to pass this torch.

Aisling and Haven walked through the front door. I knew one was coming, not the other.

"Hey, Dad. Hey, Jaxon. I hope you don't mind that I brought a friend with me?" Haven smiled and hugged Jim.

"Aisling is always welcome, she's family." Jim smiled

and nodded at the girls. "Change of plans, though. We are heading to the bar for dinner and Mom will meet us there soon with Freya. Hope that's okay?"

The girls nodded. Aisling loved playing darts there mindlessly, beating everyone as she still held the champion place in town. So, she wouldn't mind passing the time and playing there.

"Where's Declan?" I asked her quietly. I hadn't seen them apart in a while. She was holding on to him so tightly to make sure he didn't crumble.

"He's looking into a lead with my aunt, and I just needed a break." Aisling smiled, but her smile was sad underneath the act.

"We will find a way to unlink her," I whispered back and rubbed her shoulder. Her smile grew brighter as she nodded.

We made it to the bar and only had a few locals there. Jim decided to run to the kitchen and start his famous egg burgers and seasoned fries so it was just Ais, Haven, and me sitting at the table opposite of the barstools. Haven seemed distracted, over the past few months I'd gotten to know her pretty well and her facial expressions were far too similar to Freya's. I could read her like a damn book. Old man Jack walked in. Aisling smirked and stood, walking toward him, ready to keep her name in first place on the chalkboard above the darts.

"Hey, you okay?" I asked Haven.

"Yeah...I, um...Yeah, I'm okay."

She looked away quickly, and I debated on prying and then I thought if it was that important, she would let her sister know. Maybe it was guy troubles with Ezra, and that I did not want to hear about.

I looked toward the kitchen and started to get up to leave when Haven reached for my arm gently to keep me in place. I sat back down and stared at her worriedly.

"I went to your childhood home earlier today."

My eyes grew wide and confused. "Wait, what? Why?" I asked, even more confused now.

"I just had a feeling I was supposed to go there, and when I pulled up, I think you and Freya had just left, is that right?" She was embarrassed, her face flushed.

"Yeah, we were there. That's why dinner plans were changed. We found a book, and it was glowing at first, but when she went to pick it up...Nothing." He shrugged. "Your mom and her are heading to Clara's now to see what she thinks."

"A book?"

"Yeah, it was about the only object left in the whole house."

She stood up quickly. I looked at her cautiously.

"I'm going to go meet up with them."

"Hey, wait—" She stood up, cutting me off. I sat back, crossing my arms as I watched her walk to the kitchen, letting Jim know that she was leaving. Okay then, just Ais and I now, but Ais was occupied with darts, so really it was just me and my thoughts surrounding that book.

Chapter Nine

Freya Chamberlain

The drive along the Mississippi always had my mind wandering with too many things at once. It could be peaceful and awful at the same time. I looked over to the running river and just focused on the calmness of it flowing while we made our way to the house. We no longer needed to stay in hiding, and the concoction spray was no longer necessary. Eric already knew where she lived. He destroyed half of her yard and doorway the last time he was breathing. Then Isadora destroyed JFK, but that also was being mended, slowly. But it was much better now than it was three months ago since we were mending everything. Aunt Clara was at the mended doorway when we pulled up and was waiting, eager for us to arrive.

I walked out to greet her, happy as she kissed my cheeks, pulling us into her home. My hands were heavy with a book that held too many secrets. Only they were secrets that we would need to dig deeper to find out. Or at least, I hoped that the secrets would be revealed if this was the universe helping us. I sure hoped so.

"Let's see, dear. What do we have?"

I handed over the book to her with hope. She glanced at it then skimmed through it. Her brows furrowed into what seemed like frustration, which made my hope start to deflate. She didn't know anything.

"Any ideas?" I questioned, breaking her silence.

"Looks like an ordinary book to me." She examined the cover and flipped the pages again. "You said it was glowing?"

I nodded quickly.

"I might have something." She took the book and headed to the kitchen, as we followed.

She started opening her cabinets and pulling out little bottles of herbs and concoctions, tossing the jars over her shoulders, discarding the ones that didn't matter today. As she threw them, they landed perfectly upright and floated in the air in order next to where I was standing.

Magic.

I smiled at the insane new life I was living, excited to see things that I never imagined possible. I glanced at the names of the floating bottles and shuddered at the one labeled Wolfsbane. I could handle witches, but something about other supernatural creatures existing terrified me. I think Immortals were enough to worry about for now.

Her body paused as she examined the jar of dark liquid she pulled from the back of the cabinet. Exhaling slowly, she handed it to my mom to read the label, who nodded in approval.

"Five hundred year old squid ink, only with a twist." She opened the lid, and the color went from dark blue to a bright green, then to a maroon and continued to shift to the colors of the galaxy. I looked up in confusion. "When the oxygen interacts with the liquid, it activates its magic. If we add a few drops to the pages, it should show whatever kind of magic may be hidden." She didn't look too confident about it.

"The bad news?"

"It could evaporate the entire book, depending on the spell." My eyes grew wide. *Shit.* What if this was our only lead and we lose it completely? She capped the multicolor liquid and handed me the bottle. "Whatever you do, do not get this on your skin. It is a magic stealer, trying to stay alive." I tried to swallow as I held the jar awkwardly out in front of me, safely. "Take it with you and decide what you want to do. Then, just bring it back when you are finished. You will figure it out." She smiled and hugged me tight.

So, that was it. No incantations or spells to try and unveil what this thing was. Just an evaporating liquid that could set us back even further. She could float jars and have visions, but trying to uncloak a spell on a book was out of her hands, literally.

Ugh.

Haven barged into the house as we were getting ready to say our goodbyes. I smiled wide when I saw her because it had been a few days and maybe with her here, then our magic could figure this book out.

"Hey, Haven, where did your lead take you?" I asked.

"Well, nowhere, yet. I hear you might have a lead, though?"

I handed her the book with hope that us both touching it at the same time might trigger the glowing again.

Nothing. Damnit.

She grabbed the book and looked it over just as I did and everyone else, clueless.

"Did you try to syphon it?" she asked.

"Only about a hundred times while in the car, home and here. Nothing happens." I shook my head, wishing it were that easy.

"Squid ink?" she asked Aunt Clara.

"I already gave her the bottle, but we know what can happen." Haven nodded her head and seemed wary of using the ink herself. That would have to be our last resort. We couldn't lose our only lead.

"Where did you find this?" she asked me.

"Jaxon's old home. It was glowing, or at least, I thought it was, but now I'm starting to think that I'm making this all up." I shrugged my shoulders and shook my head. Feeling defeated.

"Do you mind if I borrow it?" she asked cautiously.

"Honestly, I wouldn't mind at all, but it's from Jaxon's home, and I think he might want to run some tests himself first. Let me talk to him." We nodded in agreement, but she seemed irritated.

Alex chimed in to break the silence of defeat. "Hey, girls, how about this weekend we take a break, and we go to the fishing float with your dad and make up for this dinner night?" She paused and turned to Clara. "Do you want to go too?"

"How about you four just go, and I'll go next time," Aunt Clara promised, her mind already made up. We hugged and decided to meet up with Dad and Jaxon at the bar.

Chapter Ten

Haven Vine

I decided to call the number Mr. Oakes called from earlier. Of course, disconnected.

Ugh. How would I tell him that Freya and Jaxon had the book that I was assuming we needed? He would know how to reveal it. I would just have to wait and hope that Freya avoided the squid ink until then.

Ezra walked in the door and met my eyes as I slouched deeper into the couch trying to bury myself between the cushions. I waited for the disappointment to cross his face, instead he smiled and mouthed, "It's okay." I relaxed, knowing that I was not wanting to argue with him for my own reasons that I couldn't tell him.

He walked to the kitchen and grabbed the bottle of herbs that he always takes to clear his head. I didn't know what it was about today, but something told me to look at the bottle. I grabbed it once he set it down. Goldenrod elixir. I studied the label a bit longer, and my eyes widened when I realized what he had been taking for the last year.

"Ezra, why are you taking this?" I tried to ask innocently, but I already knew the answer.

"It keeps my head clear, otherwise I feel like I'm in a fog."

"Babe, this is going to suppress your magic. It fights infections, and magic isn't an infection. Do you know that?"

"I don't have magic," he whispered softly to what was meant to be to himself.

I stopped pushing the magic talk with him. I already knew how he felt with the guilt of not being able to save his parents, but suppressing his magic even more was not going to help. He was going to have a mental magic overload if he kept pushing against the universe. He needed to let her do her thing and take the gift of magic if that's what was supposed to be. I didn't push my opinions about the subject, but now I felt the need to dump that bottle of purple liquid. What if he was supposed to hold a part in this whole magic world that could save us all, and here he was, being too afraid to open himself to the magic?

"Did you get a lead?" he asked, changing the subject.

"How did you know?"

"I know you, babe. You are too determined to let sleep consume you for too long." He walked over to me, kissing me sweetly. "I love you and your witchy brains. You know the truth wouldn't hurt me, if that's why you're hiding it."

"I know that." But my heart melted at his touch, making me forget what we were talking about. *How did I get so lucky to be this loved?*

"Hey, not to change the subject, but did you decide on

what you want to do for your birthday? It's going to be here sooner than you think," I asked him.

"How about we just skip this year? We can restart next year." He smiled and walked to the living room with Aunt Clara and her books. Birthdays were another tough subject for him, and avoidance seemed to be his way of dealing with life lately too. It was going to build, and he was going to burst one day with too many emotions bottled up. Maybe he needed a therapist, not Isadora, but a real one.

Chapter Eleven

Aisling Meadows

"Hey, Jax, I'm going to head back home to meet up with Declan, you good?" I asked him while he was sitting at the table, picking at his now cold fries. Jim was behind the bar finishing washing the glasses from the night. I offered to help one too many times, and he yelled at me that he would have to start paying me with all the help I offer and the business I bring in with the dart competition. Undefeated, again. I laughed to myself at old man Jack thinking he was winning when I was just letting him catch up for a minute before ending the game as the winner once again.

"I'm good, do you need me to walk you home?" He offered, always the polite one.

"Nah, Declan will meet me."

"Alright, text me when you're home please."

I kissed him on the cheek and thanked him for always caring. He is like a protective older brother and was afraid to lose anyone else. That hurt was sticking with him, and I hoped that one day he could heal.

I walked toward the door to leave while waving back at Jim for letting me crash their family night. He winked back at me. I left and started walking when I saw a man at the end of the street under the streetlight, and for a brief moment, panic crossed my mind. Now regretting not taking Jaxon's offer to walk with me. Then, I realized it was Declan. He must've been walking toward the bar already when I told him I was leaving. I ran to him and jumped into his arms. Kissing his neck fiercely, missing him all day.

"Hey, babe," he said when our lips finally parted.

"Hi," I kissed him one more time before letting him set me back down. Hand in hand.

"Do you mind going for a drive with me?" he asked cautiously. I stared back at him suspiciously.

"I mean, sure?" I hesitated. "Everything okay?"

"Yeah, I think so. I just have this feeling that my dad, I mean... Eric is trying to send me a message, and I just want to check the cave to make sure the seal is good."

"Oh." I hesitated and studied his expression.

"You don't have to if you don't want to. I just want some peace of mind."

"No, that's fine. We can go check. Whatever makes you sleep better." I winked, assuring him that it wasn't a big deal even though my insides were twisting.

We drove up the bluffs, watching for falling rocks during the night. It was a little more terrifying than daytime driving. We made it to the curve in the road which would either bring us to JFK or the cave, and my heart started to beat rapidly. Three months ago, we sealed this place and then I came up here daily for a month with my own blade and palm ready with blood just in case the cave opened. Knowing fully that if I had to react that I would be the reason my aunt's life would end. A part of me still wondered if I should've just ended things back when I had the chance, but my aunt's image always came to mind, and I was happy with the extra time.

We reached the end of the road before having to hike the rest of the way to the cave. I grabbed his hand to walk with, hiding slightly behind him for protection, even though I would be able to protect him more than he could protect me. I brought my empty palm up and ignited a glowing flame to light the sketchy dirt path the rest of the way.

There it was, straight ahead. Looked normal. Well, normal as in the boulders that had collapsed with the glamour spell we used to cover the cave entrance were still standing. Behind the glamour was the entrance. We walked up, and the boulders glimmered in a way that only a witch would know it was spelled shut. I touched it and felt it tingle, the magic still holding strong. My heart relaxed as I could feel my unwanted ancestors inside. I looked at Declan and smiled in approval.

"Happy?" I asked him.

"I guess so. I just feel like something is off." He and everyone else that kept saying that. I hoped that we had more time.

"I mean, it's sealed. I don't know what else you are looking for." I shrugged.

He put his arm around my shoulders and turned us around back to the car. Then, I heard it. The haunting scream of pain that seared into my head forever. I dropped to my knees trying to catch my breath. The scream continued as I covered my ears to try and quiet the sound. I looked at Declan, who was kneeling next to me unaffected by the scream.

"Don't you hear that?" I battled to beat the scream with my voice.

"Ais, what are you talking about?" he yelled back, looking around our surroundings. "I don't hear anything." I lifted my hands off my ears and listened again. Nothing, but silence now.

"Somebody was screaming," I yelled, frustrated. "I know what I heard."

"Okay, I believe you. Let me call Freya and have her check the dagger."

He stood and grabbed his phone out of his pocket and speed dialed her. My head started to shiver as a whisper infiltrated my thoughts. My eyes started to quiver as I felt the world slipping away from me, and darkness took over.

"Do not listen to her. Keep us locked in here. She will kill everyone. Please, you have to block her out of your thoughts. She doesn't know your blood related to us, so she will kill you. Do not open the cave." His voice was screaming in my head. *"She's trying to syphon from me. She's fully awake!"*

My eyes opened with the bright light of the morning sunrise peeking through the blinds. I looked across at the light through a window that I didn't recognize. Where am

I? I looked in the other direction and saw Declan sleeping in a chair located in the corner of a hospital room. Freya at the foot of my bed in another chair, leaned up against Jaxon sleeping. A hospital room? What happened?

I tried to sit up and blood started to pool on the white hospital blanket that was trying to keep me warm. I grabbed for the tissue box on the table, but Declan beat me to it and grabbed a few out and wiped my nose. Holding them in place to help slow the nosebleed. My eyes wide with panic.

"What happened?" I asked worriedly.

"You passed out, near the cave. Yelling something about someone screaming," Declan explained calmly, but the look in his eyes was nothing but worry.

My head cleared as I remembered the night more clearly. There was a scream. A painful, haunting scream. It was Isadora. I froze as the conversation came back to me, and tears started to fill my eyes, clouding my vision. I shook my head trying to clear it. Reaching for more tissues. Jaxon and Freya were sitting in front of me, eyes wide with concern.

"She's awake," I said once my breath was caught. "Eric got in my head last night, he told me she's trying to syphon his magic to escape. He screamed to keep the cave sealed." I looked at all three of them and they stared back at me with more fear than I had processed in my own head. If she was awake then our time was running out. I needed to see my aunt.

Knock, knock.

Aunt Lynn walked in the hospital room, just as I was thinking of her. Only she was looking even more bright and glowing than usual. She wasn't desiccating anymore, which only meant that her connection to this earth was awake and getting stronger. As happy as I was to see her healthy again, this only meant that the Immortals were really awake, and we were screwed.

Chapter Twelve

Jaxon Oakes

I knew the minute her aunt walked in the room with a glow to her skin that something was wrong with our Immortals. I looked around the room and realized that Aisling and I were the only two that noticed the danger we were going to be in. I stood up and hugged Aisling, then her aunt and walked out of the room to think.

Eric connected with her somehow to warn her. *But why?* Didn't he want out just as bad? We needed to know more. I pulled my phone out and texted Freya letting her know I was going to check the cave out with Ezra. She had to have just opened the message and was in the hallway with me before I got to the exit.

"I'm coming with you."

I didn't argue with her, I just nodded, and we walked out together. She had Haven and Ezra on the phone as we reached her Jeep. She told me that they would meet us there ASAP. Freya checked the dagger as we sat in the Jeep and let out a heavy sigh as the dagger still had a dull look to it, meaning the magic was still syphoned out of it.

I looked at her, sitting quietly in the passenger seat, knowing that the weight of the world was growing on her shoulders again. I just wanted to take a little weight from her and let her get some rest. We drove up into the bluffs, which felt like a never-ending drive with my tense shoulders and clenched jaw. Haven and Ezra were parked on the path when we pulled up. I let my shoulders drop a little until I saw the concern on Haven's face which brought me back to the reality of our situation.

"How's Aisling?" she asked before reaching us.

"She's going to be okay," I said reassuringly, and I hoped that was true.

"Have her take half of this now, and the other half before bed. It should help with the magic hangover headache she's going to have." Ezra handed me a jar of purple liquid. "It'll help suppress her magic for a few hours to give her mind some rest." I didn't question how he figured that out, but I took the jar and set it in the cupholder carefully, trying not to break it.

"Let's head up to the cave," I said, eagerly. A part of me wanted them to be awake, to kill them myself. Instead of losing the chance I could've had while lying in a bed recovering from death. I knew we couldn't kill them yet, though, and the bitterness of them still on this earth while my parents were gone pissed me off even more.

We walked to the cave, and the glamoured boulders were holding strong. Haven grabbed her extra hagstone and looked through the hole at the cave and nodded.

"It's still strong." She smiled, and her shoulders relaxed.

I went up just to feel the magic for myself and agreed when I felt the tingling vibrate under my palms.

"We still have time," I said, quietly. Not much, but some.

We started walking back when I noticed Freya's bag was glowing. My eyes went wide with horror. The dagger. Damn, maybe the time I thought we had was even less. I quickly glanced back to look for any changes to the cave when suddenly my ears started to hear the piercing screams that Aisling had described. I dropped to my knees on the dirt gravel and covered my ears, which felt like they were bleeding at the high-pitched woman's screeching. I looked over, ears still covered to see Ezra matching my stance. Both of us had wide eyes, covering our ears. The twins, panicking, were unaffected.

They don't hear it?

I stood up, awkwardly with my ears still covered nodding to them to run, and darted toward the Jeep to try and escape.

We reached the cars, and the scream was still lingering, but much quieter now. I unplugged my ears and stared at the girls, who seemed completely unaffected, only scared at what was going on.

"You heard that too?" I asked Ezra. He nodded, but was silent. "Just screaming?" I asked, and he hesitated.

"A man's voice said to run," he said, catching his breath.

"Eric's?" Freya asked.

"Yes." He looked to Haven and pulled out another jar of purple liquid and sipped on it, shaking his head. She looked at him worriedly. What the hell was he doing drinking a magic suppressor? If he was an Anchor witch, then he needed to play his role too.

"Freya, the dagger is glowing," I said out loud. She inhaled sharply and grabbed it, full of magic again. She checked her Mark and hadn't let out an exhale yet, her Mark was still fading. She shook her head, ready to cry.

"Can you still feel the magic from the others inside you?"

She nodded, letting one tear fall before wiping away the others. So, only the dagger had magic again, but not all of it yet from the passed souls. When the syphon wears off, the magic doesn't fully leave her. I thought it would've just been a wear off and release of magic, not making her a ticking time bomb with the consumed magic and a fading mark.

"Why do you think only some of us can hear the voices?" Freya asked, distracting me from her magic future.

"Maybe because they killed our bloodlines," Ezra answered quickly.

"Not Aisling's," Freya answered defensively. I could see her head racing a mile a minute trying to figure out the magic world.

Ezra huffed and paced back and forth, shaking his head, stuck in his own world.

"We will figure it out," I said reassuringly, rubbing Freya's shoulders to try and help her relax, knowing that she did not need the whole weight of the world on her shoulders again. I had doubts, but wouldn't tell her that.

We could get through this.

We had to.

Chapter Thirteen

Freya Chamberlain

Journal: October

It's been a few days since we went up to the cave. I still can't shake the sight of Jaxon and Ezra terrified and covering their ears. There was no screaming that I could hear, and that worries me even more. Why can't I hear it? There has to be a connection with Aisling somehow, but how?

I haven't told Jaxon yet, but the book vibrated yesterday, as if it was trying to unlock itself, while Haven and I messed around with it. I think we may be getting closer to breaking the cloaking spell. I don't want to use the squid ink unless absolutely necessary. I am not ready to lose our only lead. Speaking of Haven, she's been acting weird lately. Seems like her head is elsewhere, and her phone is glued to her hands as if she's waiting for the world to call and solve all our problems.

I almost lost the hagstone she gave me yesterday. I had it in my pocket, and when I tried a spell on the book from my grandmother's grimoire, the book ended up throwing me back, and the stone flew out of my pocket, making me search for over an hour for it. Talk about bad luck. Whatever this book was hiding, it sure as hell was doing a good job at keeping secrets secret.

The dagger has kept a glow to it, which makes me think either something is coming for it or from it, and I haven't decided which would be worse yet. I tried to syphon from it, but nothing happened. My magic may just be too faulty.

Aisling's head throbbed for an entire day before the magic suppressor kicked in and let her get some better rest. She seems better now, though, and has had no more blackouts since. I'm worried about her. Eric was sending her a message to help us? Or was he setting up a trap? How can we trust anything that comes from those sociopaths? We need to come up with a plan and fast.

On a better note, we're going fishing this weekend. Just my family, and I'm excited to spend some quality family time together and maybe just forget about magic for one day and just enjoy ourselves.

I looked around the bedroom and just tried to tell my mind to shut off for a moment to let me think clearly. My mind was feeling like mush lately and too much anxiety was standing in my way. The weight of the world was coming back on my shoulders and I needed to break free. I planned on heading back up to the cave before we leave for the fishing float. My mind was made up, and I needed to do this for myself.

No one was home with me, so no one would try and stop me. Everyone was preoccupied today. I grabbed my jacket and keys and headed for the Jeep. A chill was definitely in the air, more so than it had been lately. Winter was definitely coming. I shivered as my Jeep warmed up. I looked over to the passenger seat with the book sitting there, screaming at me to figure it out. I shifted the gear and headed for the cave.

I didn't know what I expected, being back up here. I just wanted to have peace of mind that we had more time. But did we have more time? I walked to the cave, book in hand, and squid ink in my pocket, wrapped in bubble wrap, just in case. I reached the cave and saw the magic boulders hiding the entrance. I looked through the hagstone and realized everything was as it should be. Silence, eerily quiet. I think I was expecting the screaming to happen for me this time. *Nothing.* I sat down, the book on my lap, hagstone on top of it, and stared at the cave entrance.

"Eric, if you're helping us, then talk to me. Differences aside." I hesitated and looked around to be sure I was alone. "Say something, anything."

Silence. This was stupid. I grabbed the bottle of squid ink out and made the executive decision to use it. I unwrapped the bottle and lifted the lid, getting ready to put a single drop on the book. I glanced down at the book and panicked. Tossing the book off of me, juggling with the jar to not spill the ink. The book was revealing itself underneath the stone. I capped the liquid stealer and leaned forward to grab the book and laid the stone back on top of it and started scanning the front cover, seeing words from another time across the book. I opened the book, too quickly, ripping the first page and pushing it back together while running the stone over the rugged pages. Viking runes were written all over the pages.

I had to tell Jaxon! I grabbed my phone, book, and stone and headed back for the Jeep. This was the breakthrough we needed. *Come on, answer the phone!*

"Hello?"

"Babe, I figured out the book! Meet me at JFK," I said excitedly.

"I'm actually already there."

"Oh, well, great. I will be there in a few minutes then." What was he doing there late at night? I thought he was helping at Swig and Jig.

I needed to call Haven and let her know too.

I pulled up to JFK and hopped out of the Jeep with the book. Jaxon was standing under the tree. As I walked toward him, he met me halfway and pulled me into a kiss before reaching our spot.

"What did you figure out?" he asked excitedly.

"Here, look!" I handed him the book with the stone. "Look through the hole, and the runes appear."

"I don't see anything." He looked up, confused.

"Babe, look again. The symbols are all over the page," I yelled at him, frustrated.

"There's nothing." He handed the book back to me and shook his head.

I grabbed the stone and scanned through the pages again. Nothing.

What the hell was going on?

"I swear, I was just at the cave, and it was working."

"You went to the cave? Alone? Freya, that's not smart. What if they had broken out and went after you? What if they kille—"

"The seal is fine! They didn't. I'm fine," I said, irritated at the book, not at him.

"Promise me you won't go back there alone anymore. Please. I can't lose you too."

I looked up and saw tears forming at the corners of his eyes. Guilt building inside me. Knowing that going there alone was stupid. Even though something good came from it, but he was right, what if they would've been there. I would be dead right now. I nodded. "I promise, I'm sorry." I hugged him, hoping that forgiveness would happen sooner than later. "I swear there were markings all over these pages by the cave."

"Okay, I believe you. Let's head back there, tomorrow after the fishing float. Together. Deal?"

"Deal."

Chapter Fourteen

Jaxon Oakes

My mind raced through the night. If Freya cracked the book's magic, then hopefully we were one step closer to unlinking those Immortals and then I could kill Eric, for good. What he did to my parents could never be forgiven. He took too much from me, and with him still breathing on this earth, I would not rest until he was officially gone. He could not take anyone else's families away from them. I wouldn't let him.

Freya was sound asleep, with her head laying on my chest. I stroked her hair while looking up at the ceiling. *Damn, Mom, I miss you and Dad.* I knew grieving could take time, but damn, this feeling of emptiness was really taking a toll. When Freya said she figured out the book, a part of me was happy and then another part of me was sad that our research could be coming to an end and then what would I have to do to keep my mind busy? I would have to finally accept and grieve. I wasn't ready for that. Not yet.

I looked across the room to the book sitting on the dresser. I slipped my arm out from under her, trying not to wake her. I sat at her desk and examined the book again with the stone. I just want to see what she saw. Damnit! I flicked the book closed too fast and sliced my finger on the edge of the page, blood dripping onto it. *Shit.* I opened the book back up to wipe it off, shocked realizing that my blood was traveling along the page to the center of the binding. What the hell was going on? I sucked the dripping blood off my finger and rubbed my eyes with the opposite hand to make my vision readjust. My eyes grew wider when I realized I was not making this up.

The blood swirled into an infinity symbol in the center and started to glow. The page lit up with symbols, no, writing. I knew this language. I remembered this from my childhood. That symbol there meant Anchor. My eyes followed each symbol that lit up, and I grabbed Freya's journal and pen and started copying them down, one by one, before they disappeared again. Each symbol looked familiar, but I couldn't remember what some of them meant. I jotted them down to look them up later. I flipped through the pages to see what I could decode before the blood stopped swirling, and the pages went blank again.

That was insane. I looked at the journal and back to the now blank pages of the book and sat there in awe. I had no idea what just happened or why, but hopefully, these symbols amounted to something we could use.

Unfortunately, my study books were burnt in the house fire. This was going to take time.

"Hey, everything okay?" Freya asked groggily, while sitting up.

"Sorry, yeah. Great, actually."

She stood and walked over by me to see what I was doing.

"Is that my journal?" she asked, confused.

I laughed, "Yes, but I wasn't reading it. I swear... these symbols appeared in the book, I was just copying them down."

She grabbed the paper and studied them herself. "These are what I saw too. What do they mean?"

"I don't know all of them, but this one is Anchor, and this one is dagger. So, it looks like we are right where we started." I looked them over and realized another symbol stood for blood and sacrifice, but I wasn't going to tell her that right now until I knew what they meant.

"Well, can we go back to bed and save the world in the morning?" she asked while leaning down to my neck, kissing it softly. Then, more aggressively, pulling me toward the bed.

"Ugh... only if you let me make you pancakes in the morning." I smiled between kisses.

"Mmm, please."

I grabbed her and carried her to the bed, lifting my shirt over my head and tugging at hers. There wasn't going to be much sleep before the sun came up.

Chapter Fifteen

Freya Chamberlain

The sun was bright, coming through the blinds, sooner than I wanted it to. Ugh, just another hour of sleep would be nice. I looked over and realized that I was alone in bed. "Jaxon?" I whispered while scanning the empty room. Where the hell did he disappear to now?

I jumped up and pulled on my clothes to head downstairs and check the rest of the house. I heard movement in the kitchen and froze for a second, realizing that I felt a little on edge since the cave and was being cautious. I slowly turned the corner and saw Jaxon, standing in just his shorts in front of the stove, making pancakes, eggs, and bacon. Now that my fear was gone, I smelled the food. My stomach growled, realizing I had skipped dinner last night too. My parents stayed at the bar last night to lock up and would be home soon for our family fishing date. I smiled when I saw him flipping the pancakes and thought that this could be a forever thing that I could get used to.

I walked up behind him and whispered, "Morning," kissing his bare back. "Smells delicious."

"Morning, love." He turned and grabbed a mug from the cabinet, pouring me coffee. "Figured you're going to need this for today. Sorry for keeping you up all night." He winked at me and handed me the hot cup.

"What are you going to do today?" I asked, sitting down with the steaming mug.

"I told Jim that I would start painting the trim today while you guys are out. He didn't ask, but I figured it would give me something to do."

I laughed, knowing that once he had his mind set on something, that was it. "You can stop trying to suck up to my dad. He already loves you."

"Suck up?" He huffed and laughed. "Please, your dad is glad to have another man around the house."

I laughed and nodded. "True."

My parents pulled into the driveway and Jaxon turned and ran upstairs quickly, while yelling, "Watch the pancakes."

I jumped up and grabbed the spatula and watched them become golden before flipping them over. He came walking back down with his shirt on and grabbed the utensil back. I laughed when I realized he didn't want my dad to catch him half naked in his kitchen. "So much for how much my dad loves you, huh?"

"I mean, he definitely loves me, but he doesn't want me naked in his home with his daughter. Another reason we need our own place." He winked, and I smiled.

"Morning, kids." My dad walked in smiling, "Sleep well?"

"Um, excuse me. Did YOU sleep well?" I asked him,

laughing when I saw my mom walk in behind him with my dad's oversized shirt on her and he was still wearing his bartending shirt that smelled of burgers and beer. She blushed, knowing she had just been caught. "Ew, Mom, Dad, ew!"

"Do we even want to know what you guys did last night?" she said defensively, laughing. "Come on, we're all adults here."

"Ew!" I said again and threw a finished pancake toward her. She caught it and took an obnoxiously huge bite out of it before sitting at the table, laughing.

"Haven is on her way, is there enough for her too?" Dad asked Jaxon.

"Of course," Jaxon said while adding more batter to the pan.

We sat there eating and drinking coffee, talking about normal life. We didn't bring up the book symbols or anything magic. I think we all just wanted a normal day. Haven walked in and joined us for breakfast. I jumped up and grabbed her a mug of hot coffee too and had her sit next to me. She seemed to be in a good mood today. The sun was shining, the chill in the air was there, but today was supposed to be an unusually warm October day. Mid-seventies was perfect for a fishing day on the float.

Dad packed up the poles, Mom made the sandwiches, and I grabbed the dagger and got dressed before we headed out the door.

"Do you mind putting this in the drawer in my dad's office? It's Ais's birthday present. I just don't want her finding it here," I asked Jaxon.

He smiled, kissed me, and grabbed the small present before jumping in his car to head to the bar, paint can in his other hand. My dad hugged him for helping him start the job that Mom is pushing to get done. Jaxon is basically saving his ass from her wrath.

"What do you mean, you've never fished on a float before?" Dad asked Haven. "That is unacceptable for a daughter of mine!"

"Aunt Clara doesn't really fish."

"And why isn't she here with us too then?" he asked.

"She is busy today, leave her alone," Mom defended her. "Fishing isn't for everyone."

"Lies," my dad laughed. "If you live near the Mississippi, then you better earn your fish fry."

We laughed and agreed that she should've come with us. Maybe next time. Today was just a normal, simple, family day, and I was happy for my now grown family. We made it to the river. There was the raggedy flag that we needed to raise for Rick to know we were ready to be picked up by boat to take us to the Iowa side for the wooden float. Rick has owned the place for years, and it had been passed on through generations, slowly replacing each withering board as needed for safety. I hoped the place would always be around for others to enjoy. The float was secured onto the land and butted right next to the dam. So, we wouldn't float away today.

We made it to the float and picked a place to set our stuff up at. Dad got the lines in the water right away to not miss the prime fishing hours. He sent Haven to the inside of the float to show her how to jig for the bluegills to use to catch the bigger ones. I looked to them and smiled when I realized that Haven had not had this growing up. This was normal to me and all new to her, and I was happy she was getting a chance to know our old family traditions now.

"I love this. This moment is very..." She looked over to Haven and my dad then back to me. "It's serendipitous, I think is the best word for it. Such a pure chance that we even have this day together." My mom smiled as she walked over by me and pointed to the scenery. "All of this is everything that I have been wanting for so long."

"Well, I'm glad we're all here too." I leaned into her and hugged her tight.

"Nothing could ruin today." She smiled, and I nodded back at her.

Hours had passed, and the sun was at high noon now. I had reapplied sunblock twice already but could feel the sunburn starting on my neck. We still had a few more hours to fish before our time was up for the fee. I grabbed my hat out of my bag and dropped my hair down my back to block the sun as best as I could. It helped, a little. I took a break from fishing and sat on the ledge of the float with my feet dangling with the monster sturgeons that I'm sure were passing by my feet. I didn't tell Haven about them, otherwise she may have been spooked to come back out here. She came to sit next to me and did the same. We looked at each other at almost the same moment, it was kind of creepy. Definitely a twin thing. We laughed.

"This is really cool," she said. "So, we can do this again?"

"Absolutely! We can do this whenever, maybe next time we can bring our boys and Aunt Clara."

"This is a tradition?" she asked, surprised.

"I mean, yes. Most weekends during the summer's early mornings before Dad has to get to the bar by lunch time. Rick keeps trying to sell this place to Dad, but he's not ready to give up the bar yet."

She smiled and looked back out to the river to take it all in.

The owner of the float took his boat to cross the river for another pickup of a fisherman who had raised the flag. He said he would be right back. I looked across the river as the boat turned and was heading back with one person. Odd. He didn't have any poles with him or any gear at all. I squinted and stood quickly. No! Not him!

Eric...

"Mom, it's him!" I yelled. "What do we do?"

She ran to us, Dad next to her. We stood side by side and ran to the edge of the float to have as much distance as possible from him.

He hit the owner over the head, knocking him out on the boat and walked to us casually, as if we had not just put him down three months ago. What the heck did he want?

"Get back!" I yelled to him as he inched his way closer. "Ignis." My hands ignited with fire. "I said, get back." I lifted my fire and threatened to throw it at him.

"Didn't we already do this?" His voice made my spine shiver. I looked for our escape route.

How did he find us?

"How did you get out?" my mom asked.

"You can thank Isadora for that."

"What do you want?" Haven asked.

"Calm down." He adjusted his suit and looked down at his hands. "I'm just here to talk."

"We're not talking," I said with disgust and moved closer to him. He staggered back for a brief moment before walking closer to me.

"We're talking, one way or another." His face was angry, as if he was a child not getting his way.

"She's right, we're not talking." It was my dad's voice that spoke up and he walked in front of me, stopping me from advancing on him. "You need to leave."

"Funny, you're the one I came to see." He paused, annoyed. "Fine, let's do this the hard way." Eric announced and leaped in the air toward us. My dad pushed me hard out of the way as Haven started to charge her hands with electricity and my mom took water from the Mississippi. They tried to shock him midair. It was too late, though. Eric had my dad in his grip and jumped into the river with him, pulling him under the rushing water.

I jumped in after them, realizing that the current was stronger than I expected, and it started to pull me down faster. I panicked and started to swim toward the Iowa side where my mom and Haven were running on land to meet me. Eric, not far behind me, joined us with my dad dragging behind him. Not breathing.

"What have you done?" My mom screamed and started CPR on him. Haven quickly ran her hands over his chest. Her hands started to extend vines from her palms, wrapping his body with them, trying to heal him. I had never seen her healing powers do that before; she has been practicing and getting stronger. I stood in awe for a brief second before looking back at Haven and seeing tears rolling down her cheeks.

The situation became a reality when I focused back on

my dad, not moving. I crawled to shore and spat up the water before standing, facing Eric. Crashing into him with pure force. His hands reached for my neck and lifted me into the air, pushing away from him. This wasn't happening again. I reached for his arm to syphon, only to realize he was one step ahead of me. He grabbed my wrists, pinning them behind my back with his other arm around my neck. I thrashed, trying to free myself of his unimaginably strong grip.

"Just wait," he whispered in my ear.

Wait? Wait for what? Tears started to stream down my face while watching my mom and Haven fail at saving him. Please, not my dad. Eric would pay for this. My mind started to plot revenge as he held me against my will. He would be a dead man by sunset, no matter what it took. I pushed my body against his, kicking him in his stomach making his grip loosen. He became more aggressive and restrained me with a force that I couldn't break. Magic.

"I said, wait," he yelled.

My dad started to cough up the water as they leaned him to his side to spit up the river. My body collapsed with relief, slipping out of Eric's grip and running toward him. Lifting his face to verify he was breathing and hugging him tight. "Dad?" I bawled as he coughed up more water. "We're here, Dad."

He sat up quickly, trying to orient himself, soaked in river water and staring back at Eric.

"Time to wake up, brother," Eric said before walking back to the boat.

My head throbbed with confusion as I watched him walk away, leaving us all alive.

I looked back at my dad and saw his forearm glowing with his very own Mark.

Chapter Sixteen

Aisling Meadows

"Come on, Aunt Lynn, please." I pleaded with her to come with me to the store for a birthday outfit. "I hate shopping alone. Freya is out with her family, and Declan doesn't let me get any actual shopping done, plus he tries to go into every fitting room, and I will never get an outfit that way. Pretty please."

"Shouldn't you be resting?"

I rolled my eyes, annoyed that she's been so cautious since the cave incident. "I'm fine." Plus, with all her energy back lately, I needed to take advantage of the extra time I had with her.

"Okay, stop. I will go if you stop talking about him, please." She laughed, and I smiled in agreement, zipping my lips. "Do you really need another outfit?"

"You only turn nineteen once."

"You only turn every age once."

"You've had way more birthdays than I will ever have."

"Ha, not by choice, my dear," she said.

I winked and smiled. Mouthing the words, thank you.

"You know you could always glamour one."

My jaw dropped as I realized how much more I could do. "I'll keep that in mind."

We headed to the store, picking out outfits that would keep her distracted from the fact that Declan is rummaging through her home right now trying to find her grimoire or anything that would help unlink her. I just had this feeling that she was hiding something from me, and I didn't like that. After a thousand years, she never came up with a spell? Come on. She had to be at least working on something, and I wanted Declan to find out. The past few days, each time I tried to go over there, she would insist on meeting me elsewhere, which made me think she was hiding something, and I was about to find out what.

We browsed each rack multiple times, each time she would pick out something different and look for my approval. Declan just needed more time so I kept stalling.

My phone buzzed as I was in the changing room.

Declan: There's nothing here.

Aisling: Keep looking!

I walked out, hanging up the outfits, disappointed that none of them were what I wanted. I met Aunt Lynn in the store, and I begged her to grab something to eat with me until she agreed.

"Hey, I think I have the perfect dress for you. It's something I have in my closet. It's fit for a celebration." She smiled, and I agreed on checking it out after as long as we spent more time stalling while grabbing food.

Chapter Seventeen

Jaxon Oakes

This paint was going to take way longer than I was thinking. I stopped and looked around the bar, realizing that I only had half of the trim done. I walked behind the bar and grabbed a soda and sat down for a minute.

"What did I sign myself up for?" I asked myself.

"Oh, pretty boy, Oakes."

The voice sent a shiver down my spine. I jumped up and moved toward her defensively, ready to kill.

Isadora.

"Not even a hello? Come on, didn't daddy teach you better manners?" She said with a smile. "Oops, I forgot, he's dead." She brought her hand up to her lips into a shocked expression.

"Shut the hell up," I said, pushing her back against the wall, ringing my hands around her throat. She choked on her breath, gasping for air. I could feel my hold on her tighten as fear set in.

Am I going to kill her?

I have to kill her.

Now.

I have to.

She stopped gasping and smiled, grabbing my hands from her throat. "Did you really just hesitate? You couldn't even kill me while I gave you the chance? Pathetic." She pushed me back and threw me to the ground with unnatural strength. "Need me to show you how it's done?" She walked behind the bar and grabbed a steak knife and pretended to plunge it into her heart. "You can't hesitate. Now, where is she?"

I stood up and had a split second to either run out of the door or push back. "Who?"

"Your lover girl. I want her, and I always get what I want."

"Stay away from her," I said with adrenaline coursing through my veins.

"Mmm... I love how defensive you get with her. A love like that is dangerous."

"What do you want?" I asked, my voice starting to shake.

"I told you, I want her," she said while pouring herself a shot of whiskey. Licking her lips seductively after taking it, she leaned over my book that I left on the counter, away from the paint splatter, and started reading it outloud. "Huh. This book looks familiar." She paged through the book as I stayed silent, not wanting her to take it. "Glamour and memory spells." She turned the page. "Anchor separation." She laughed. "Now who in their right mind would make themselves that vulnerable?"

I was frozen in place. Realizing she could see the invisible markings and she was reading exactly what we needed.

My heart pounded silently. I didn't want her to think the book was of any use to her, so I quickly changed the subject.

"Well, she's not here. So, leave."

She set the book down and walked toward me, knife in hand. *No.* Not again.

"Fine, I'll leave." She reached me and went to plunge the knife into my torso, but I grabbed her wrist and twisted it around, piercing her own abdomen. She winced for a moment before pulling it out and forcing it into my side, twisting it hard. Hot liquid came running down my side, and a sharp pain shot through my body, making me fall to the ground. "Don't ever tell me what to do," she whispered in my ear, then walked out of the bar.

I put pressure on the wound and leaned against the bar, trying to get it to stop bleeding. I wished I wouldn't have put the closed sign on now. Any person could help at this point. I reached for my phone in my back pocket and dialed Freya. The room started to become blurry. Shit.

"Hello?" her voice quivered. I could tell she had been crying. What the hell happened? Who hurt her? My senses told me to go to her, but I could feel my body becoming weaker. I was losing too much blood. The bar around me was fading. I tried to put more pressure on the wound and realized that my fingers were becoming weak, and the rag was soaked in blood already.

"Freya, help me," I whispered, as I dropped the phone and closed my eyes to rest.

. . .

"Oh, honey, what are you doing here?" My mom's voice whispered. I opened my eyes, shocked to see her sitting next to me at the bar. I looked around, and we were sitting in a booth across from one another with the book laying open between us. I stared in shock at the runes and spells all over the pages.

"Mom, how can I see this?"

She looked back at me, confused. "Honey, you could always see this. What are you talking about? What's going on?"

I rubbed my fingers over the letters and watched as they lit up as they were grazed. I looked back up to my mom and froze.

"How are you here? Eric killed you and Dad."

She smiled and pointed to the book. "Stay on track. This has everything you need. Don't let Isadora take it back. It is meant for us."

"I didn't," I said defensively.

"Good. Love you, son." She smiled as she started to vanish.

The pressure on my side became heavier, and it felt like a tickling sensation moving back and forth where the knife had been. I tried to open my eyes, but the lights were too bright. How long had I been out for? Did I die? Again? How many times could that happen before I stopped returning?

"Jax?"

I opened my eyes and saw her staring back at me. Beautiful. She was here.

"Sit still, I'm trying to heal you." It wasn't Freya at all. It was Haven. I opened my eyes again and refocused them on her.

"Freya?" I whispered.

"She's behind you." She pointed above my head as her hands wavered over my injury again. "Now keep him still. Geez, he's lost a lot of blood."

Freya kissed my forehead, as my head was laying in her lap. Her eyes were full of tears. This woman had cried one too many tears for me, and I was getting tired of being the reason for them. This woman deserved the world and only happy tears. *I'm so sorry.*

I laid still, listening to Haven. Alex and Jim were pacing by the door.

"What do you remember?" Alex was asking Jim. He shook his head, as if in disbelief. What were they talking about? "Is it true?"

"I don't know, I mean—," He slid his sleeve up, and a Mark was glowing on his forearm. I gasped at the sight.

"Yeah, that happened," Freya said, shaking her head and bringing her attention back to me. "Who did this to you? Eric?"

"Isadora," I whispered with a raspy voice.

Her eyes filled with horror. "What did she want?"

I hesitated at the answer, knowing that she would think this was her fault, even though Isadora was just a psycho. She would've done this even if Freya had been here. "I hesitated to kill her. It was my fault."

"Jaxon, why was she even here?"

I exhaled, trying to think of another reason and came up short. "You, she was looking for you." Freya gasped and closed her eyes while holding onto me. My wound began to itch as it was healing. I looked down at it and watched as Haven's hands worked their magic. Only this time, vines were extending from her palms, which explained the tickling part. I looked past the magic at the new scar forming. I was beginning to get too many battle scars at a young age. How many more before I died for good?

My eyes went back to Jim, his Mark's glow was starting to subside and his symbol was appearing. A Viking compass? Wait... What? Why did he have a Mark at all? Let alone that ancient one? I pushed myself up to get a closer look as Haven pushed me back down.

"I said, don't move."

I huffed and laid back down and waited patiently to get a closer look.

Chapter Eighteen

Haven Vine

I stepped back and caught my breath. Thankfully, no one died on my watch today. I loved being a healer, but man, being in charge of a death watch was not fun, either. Syphoning sounded like more fun. I looked over at everyone in the bar, and my heart sank at the thought of losing any of them now that I just got them in my life. My dad noticed me inching closer to the wall, away from everyone, and reached me quickly.

"Hey, it's okay. We're all okay." He grabbed me and pulled me closer to him. "I've got you, honey."

I leaned into his hug and let out the sobs that I had been holding in since the river. I took a deep breath and let my mind focus on what was next.

"Isadora could read that book," Jaxon interrupted and pointed to the bar behind him. The word "book" caught my attention. It was the book from his father, and if Isadora could read it, then that meant either that the magic was breaking through or that we were missing something. I gave my dad one more big squeeze and walked over to the book, expecting words to appear. When I reached it, I froze in disappointment.

Again. Nothing.

I slammed my fists down on the bar, irritated that the Immortals were free and we had no leads. Now we were back to running and hiding all because I failed at finding the unlinking spell before time was up. Time was never on our side, and I was starting to get pissed off. I took the book and threw it across the bar, screaming in frustration. "Screw this book."

Freya, Jaxon, and my parents looked up at me in shock. They did not expect me to be the one to break. My dad leaned over and picked up the book, wiping off the cover.

"Why is a book of runes upsetting you? Have I missed something?" my dad asked, innocently.

"What did you just say?" I asked, shocked.

"These symbols, they're ancient and I haven't seen them in centuries—" He froze, as did everyone else. We all looked up at him as he flipped through the pages. Each page, he flipped faster and faster. "How do I know this?"

My mom reached him and rubbed his shoulders. She seemed to still be a little standoffish as to who this man really was.

"Dad?" Freya questioned and walked closer to him, but was careful to get too close. "Do you know who we are?"

"Of course I do. You guys are my family. Well, and of course Jaxon better be my son in law someday." He smiled and looked around at everyone.

Okay, it was him, but how could he read those symbols? How could he even see them? I ran across the room to him and looked over his shoulder at the pages.

Empty. "Dad, what do they say? Because I don't see anything."

Jaxon pulled himself up and checked his injury, now healed, and walked over to us. "Yeah, Jim, I don't see anything, either. I only could see some symbols after I dripped some of my own blood on it yesterday." He walked over and picked the knife up off the ground and walked back, slicing his hand enough to draw blood from his palm and holding it over the pages, which absorbed the blood in a twirling matter as symbols started to appear. I gasped, as I realized it was a blood sealed book. Probably passed down in his bloodline. Which was why Mr. Oakes was looking for it. No wonder it appeared blank to everyone else. Now the other question was, how was my dad able to see it? I froze, looking at Freya, who mimicked my worry.

"What does it mean?" Freya asked me. "Please tell me Jaxon isn't... related. Right?" She stood and wavered back toward the bar. Jaxon looked at her and shook his head.

"There's no way." He looked at her, then back at me. "Haven, tell her that's impossible."

I looked at Freya again and let every scenario run through my head. Of course, I haven't told them about meeting Mr. Oakes and that he's alive yet. So, of course, all of this information was only with me. I needed to see Mr. Oakes again. I needed answers, but how?

"Can you read the symbols? Is there anything about unlinking in there?" I asked my dad, avoiding the questions that I didn't have answers for.

He glanced up after reading a few pages and looked straight to Jaxon. "This is your mother's book. This is her handwriting. I remember her."

"Well, of course you remember her. She was your friend." My mom chimed in. "She was in love with you." She gasped, realizing she had said too much. She looked at Jaxon and shook her head, "I'm sorry, Jax. I didn't mean that."

"Yes, you did." He shrugged. "She's dead. So, nothing to worry about now." His eyes were sad. I had the feeling that I should've healed his heart instead of his stab wound.

"What I meant was, in highschool, she and I had a fallout because we fought over Jim. Callum wasn't in the picture yet. There was nothing more, once your father came into the picture. I promise."

"No," Dad interrupted. "I knew Margo long before highschool." We all froze. "She was my friend as a child. Her and," he paused, "Isadora. They were twins."

"Dad, they look nothing alike. I don't know, you must've hit your head or something," I said, stepping back to look him over. "I think that water did a number on you."

"No, I remember her. They were fraternal twins. I just... everything is kind of a blur. I can see glimpses of my past. I see the symbols, but I can't remember what they mean. I just can't fully put it in order. Eric, we need to find him. He's my brother."

I busted out a laugh, more in shock that this was most likely true, but my brain needed time to process this. If Eric and my dad were brothers then that makes Aisling his long-lost niece from generations later. And if Margo is Isadora's sister, then Jaxon is only a descendant of an Immortal, but not related, right? My head was trying to make sense of everything.

Then, my mind went back to the book. Jaxon could

read it, and so could Isadora and my dad. It was Margo's book, so she could read it. What if being near the cave with a blood relative of Margo activated the book with the hagstone? What if this really was true? Or what if with them being twins, they share the same DNA and that's why the book was activated?

"Anyone talk to Aislynn or I mean, Lynn lately? I have a feeling that's where we can find Eric." My dad spoke, and I felt as if shock was still consuming us all, because no one responded.

Chapter Nineteen

Aisling Meadows

I drove Aunt Lynn back to her place so she could grab the dress. Declan called me to let me know he was going to leave the house and meet me at home. I couldn't believe that we were investigating my aunt, but something inside me said that something was being hidden.

We turned onto her road, and I froze when I saw Declan's car still parked outside of the house. *Damn.* I needed to stall. Why hadn't he left yet? My heart was beating a mile a minute. I drove past her house, trying to act as if nothing had happened.

"Forget where I live or something?" Aunt Lynn asked me, confused, pointing behind us.

"Ope, I'm so sorry. My mind was wandering," I lied and drove a little further before turning around in a driveway and heading back to her home. Damnit, Declan, get out. I willed his actions to be fulfilled as we approached her home. He was still in the house, but Aunt Lynn must not recognize his car. I parked the car, and she said to hold on, and she will go grab it. I nodded and waited for her to get to her door and enter before running out of my car and running up her porch stairs, two at a time, reaching the door and whispering Declan's name.

I looked around the doorway and into the dining room when a hand came around my throat and pushed me up against the wall. I froze when I saw who it was.

Eric.

His gaze met mine, and his eyes softened when he realized who I was. His grip loosened and he set me down. Aunt Lynn came running down the stairs as I choked on my own air. I looked to her and back to Eric, raising my hands with fire, ready to kill this bastard for good knowing I would destroy her home in the process. I threw my hands up, facing toward Eric and froze when Declan stepped into the room behind him.

"Ais, stop," Declan said.

My palms stayed lit as my head felt like it was in fight or flight mode.

What the hell is going on?

"Explain," I yelled to anyone who was going to answer.

Eric looked toward Declan then back to Aunt Lynn, who nodded in approval.

"I'm here to help," Eric said.

"Shut the fuck up," I yelled and threw my fire against him, throwing him into the wall.

Lifting my other palm to hit him again, Aunt Lynn grabbed my wrist and pleaded for me to stop.

"Let me go," I screamed. "He took too much from us, let me go." I struggled to release both hands and go after him. Declan jumped behind me and restrained my arms from hurting Eric more. "Let go of me." I thrashed in his grip. He took me and turned me around to face him, body up against the wall and his face inches from mine.

"Listen to me. He's here to help us." He looked back to Eric and faced me again. "Trust me, I know him, enough to know when he's lying." He loosened his grip on my wrists. "I'm going to let you loose, but you have to promise me that you won't kill him."

I huffed and looked toward Eric, who had my aunt babying him, as if nothing had happened three months ago. "Get away from him," I demanded. "Then I'll listen." I looked to my aunt, and she nodded and backed away with her arms up in surrender. She walked back toward Declan and me while Eric stood and straightened his suit before taking a seat at the table across from us, pretending like he owned the place. Declan released me and took a step back to watch my next move. He reached for a chair and motioned for me to sit.

"I'll stand."

He and my aunt sat down as I stood. My arms crossed, my patience thinning, waiting for an explanation.

"Izzy broke out. She syphoned my magic that had finally started to come back and was able to break through the seal. I tried to stop her, but she's strong. She has never been stronger than me in the thousand years we have lived. I have no idea how her syphoning came back, but now that makes her more powerful than me. We need to unlink her from us and kill her, otherwise we have no chance."

My head spun as he talked. I grabbed the seat between Declan and Aunt Lynn and sat down. My head felt heavy. "I don't understand." I looked around the room, trying to catch my breath. "A syphon? Like Freya? But how?"

Eric adjusted his posture and rubbed his hands through his hair. "It's kind of a long story. So, the short story is she was a syphon as a child, and a twin. She killed her twin who was also her Anchor, which pissed off the universe and took away her syphoning powers. So, for a thousand years, she has been trying to get it back by collecting Anchor witches' souls and consuming their magic. Somehow the fight with Freya must've triggered her magic. We need to get rid of her. She's very unstable."

My attention broke when someone pounded on the front door. Declan looked at Eric with a panicked look. Eric nodded to him. Declan jumped up and walked toward the door. I stood with him and followed, fists ready with magic. He peeked through the curtain and relief crossed his face. "It's Freya and her family." I jumped in front of him and grabbed the doorknob, flinging it open. If Eric was lying then we could all go up against him.

"Where is he?" Jim asked, walking into the home. I stepped back, confused. "Where is Eric?"

My eyes grew at the words coming out of the mundane. What was he going to do? I pointed to the dining room as we all followed him into the small room, which kept getting smaller with everyone that was in it. My body froze when I saw Jim's Mark on his forearm. *Okay, for real, what the hell did I miss?*

"You," he pointed to Eric and advanced on him.

Chapter Twenty

Freya Chamberlain

When I saw Eric sitting across the room, my heart pounded hard and my body struggled to contain the magic and hate that I wanted to use against him. I wanted him dead, no matter what information he had for us. He couldn't be trusted. My dad must've felt the same way because he flew across the table after him, pinning him against the wall, bashing his fists into Eric's head. Blood spurted from Eric's mouth as he blocked the next blow, grabbing my dad's fists and pushing him back.

"Are you done?" he asked my dad, wiping the blood from his lower lip. Aunt Lynn jumped up to run to his aid. "Sit down, let's see what you remember." My dad stepped toward him, ready to continue the blows when Declan stepped between them.

"Sit, everyone, sit," Declan said, frustrated with his hands in the air in a surrender stance. Since when did he start trusting Eric again? I thought Declan was on our side?

My dad stood and shook his head at the request of sitting and crossed his arms.

Eric looked annoyed. "I guess, no one wants to listen today." He glanced toward me and Jaxon and then his eyes squinted at the book Jaxon had. "Where did you find that?" Eric asked. Jaxon took the book and held it tighter against his chest, ready to die for it. "That is Margo's, where is she?"

"Is that some kind of sick joke? You killed her, remember?" Jaxon spat back at him, furious.

"She's still in hiding then," Eric said. "Where did you find that book?"

"What the hell do you mean she's in hiding? You killed her and my dad. You sick bastard." Jaxon pushed the book into my arms and lunged toward Eric, ready to kill him. I fumbled with the book and grabbed his arm, pulling him back while Declan pushed him against the wall.

"Explain what the hell is going on, otherwise we will let him go and he will kill you," I said, helping to restrain Jaxon as best as possible.

Eric stood up and paced behind the table, which was the only object distancing us from each other.

"That's your mother's book. We had a plan. She was supposed to come find you when Izzy became contained. Obviously, something got messed up with our plan, if Izzy is still breathing." He looked around the room and stopped when he reached my stare. Jaxon had let his shoulders relax as he listened. "Margo is still very much alive. She's Immortal. Margo and Izzy were the first set of natural born Anchor twins. Long before Izzy and I became anchored together. That book is Margo's. Only she can access it."

"My dad can read it," I interrupted.

"Interesting. He's not even blood related. I can't even read it."

"He's not blood related?" Jaxon questioned and looked at me with relief.

Eric shook his head. "Margo's spell must've somehow linked you to her book, otherwise that book would only be blank pages to you as it is to all of us, except maybe for Jaxon," Eric announced, looking at Jaxon, who silently nodded.

"It only worked with my blood, though, but Isadora can read it too."

"You've seen her recently?"

Jaxon nodded and touched the side of his newly formed scar.

Eric nodded. "Hm, must be a twin thing. They share the same DNA. Best to keep it away from her."

Jaxon flinched, then became still.

"I could see it with my hagstone when I was near the cave."

"Huh. Anyone else?" When no one else answered, he pondered. "Maybe being close to Izzy there triggered it to reveal itself with the stone. Those are helpful in our world, you are lucky to have found one."

Lucky to have found Haven, I thought, as I smiled at her.

He made me think of the screams coming from the cave before they escaped, and I realized that only Aisling, Jaxon, and Ezra could hear her. Which made me wonder if Ezra was somehow related in their bloodline too. I tried to place where he could have fit in the timeline with Margo and came up with nothing. Unless he came from a branch of

Isadora's son somehow through the generations like Aisling, but Aunt Lynn would've known of him. Wouldn't she have? Protected him?

"Margo hasn't come to find you yet?" Eric interrupted my thoughts.

Jaxon just stared blankly back at him. "My mother is dead and my father."

"Your mother is immortal. As long as she had her Labradorite stone necklace on and stayed hidden. We need to find them before Izzy figures out she's alive. Then, everything we have worked toward for a thousand years will backfire. I have been protecting your mother for centuries. We need her to unlink us." Eric ignored his sneer. Then he looked at my dad.

"Burning them alive doesn't seem very protective."

Eric slammed his fists down on the table. "Damn it, they're alive," he yelled, and now I couldn't tell if he was convincing himself or Jaxon.

"Jim, come on you had to back me up on this. You have to remember who you are. You are the first original Immortal. Mother tried to replicate the spell for immortality on me. The universe became angry when she succeeded. The natural world became unbalanced. The storms brewed in the mountains, and the ships sank at sea. You have to remember, it was more than just a fairytale." When he didn't respond, Eric continued. "No one is supposed to live forever. We became cursed. Mother and every witch after her who tried the spell. Hence how the Anchors came about from certain bloodlines. We were never supposed to live longer than a century, if even that. Back in those days, sickness and war spread through the villages, and we were going into every battle that we could. Mother was being maternal and tried to protect us from death. Only she was playing God with time, and the universe played back. Immortality spells started to link Anchors so no one would live more than a hundred years, but were given a second chance at a wrongful supernatural death if the other was alive. Brother, you are the only true Immortal without an Anchor on this earth, and it was only by default. Izzy and I have only sustained this long because of the dagger, because the souls have helped stop us from aging."

My dad paced the doorway between rooms, head shaking.

"But I have aged."

"Conception I assume." Eric pointed to me and Haven. "Somehow mother nature played her role when you guys conceived magical Anchor twins, and they were able to start your aging process. Seems about eighteen years or so. Children have a way of messing with the magical world, a loophole when done right."

"We hid the girls' Marks when they were born. Could that have been stealing his immortality to keep them hidden?" My mom spoke for the first time since the river.

Eric debated on it before nodding. "With magic comes many loopholes. As long as he has his Mark, he cannot be killed. Aging or not, at this point."

My dad looked like he needed some of Aunt Clara's overload tea. His brain was firing with new information, and he was trying to connect the dots. Haven was awfully quiet during this whole scene. I glanced over to her, and she was staring back at me with a haunted look. I mouthed the words, "You okay?" She nodded and looked away, grabbing her pendant necklace and twirling it. She knew something but was being silent. I made a mental note to pull her aside in a little bit to see what was on her mind.

"How is Isadora linked to you if she was linked to Margo?" I asked, trying to get as much information as I could gather to decide what was true and what was bullshit.

"The universe linked me to her after she killed Margo. Izzy was stripped of her magic for years. If one tries to consume their Anchor's powers, that severs the bond. And ultimately it pisses off the magic world and our ancestors. After my mother cast the immortality spell on Jim, she then attempted to cast it on me, but instead I was gifted with lovely Anchor, Isadora. I had not known at the time that I would have a run in with another who shared my Mark. Our ancestors interfered with my mother's spell because why should we get second chances and no one else?" He inhaled sharply. "Izzy's Mark reappeared that day along with her magic. Only she never got her syphoning back. She began by searching for her sister whom she had believed was dead until one day she saw me coming off a ship that was coming back from battle, and she noticed my Mark glowing the closer she got, which is what started our thousand year journey. Well, then the affair happened, of course, and well, you know the lies that were told and rearranged over the years. But believe what you want with that story."

He looked over to Aunt Lynn and his face became saddened as he watched her flinch with his words. As if she was reliving her shattering heart caused by him and his betrayal.

"My brother is the only one with the Immortality Compass. He is one of a kind. Indestructible, hence why I never had to worry about him over the years." He pointed to my dad.

"But who was Margo linked to then? I'm trying to understand, but I feel like every word you spit out is full of shit," I said.

Eric rolled his eyes and smirked. "Her own mother became suspicious of Izzy's childhood intentions with dark magic alongside her father. She gave her a Labradorite stone necklace spelled with unbelievable amounts of magic and never ending life itself as long as it was held close or worn. So, Margo didn't die that day that Izzy attempted. Her Mark did disappear, but she was very much alive thanks to her mother's close eye. Margo ran to Greystone land for protection and started her personal revenge task to get her healing magic back. It's taken Margo much longer than expected, as she needed to find her strength and courage to face her sister's betrayal. Over the centuries, she has always seemed to have an excuse or an obstacle to our plan. Then she met Callum and started a family and became even more preoccupied." He cleared his throat as he looked around the room and studied everyone's expressions.

"Unfortunately, Izzy became obsessed with getting her syphoning back. One night, she killed a pair of Anchors and realized she could become more powerful and live longer by consuming witches' magic with the dagger. It felt like syphoning again, but instead with a dagger. She was ready to live forever to spite the ancestors who stripped her of her magic. Eventually, our aging stopped, and she became a power hungry witch, who loved the idea of staying ageless and beautiful. She claimed to be a goddess and would kill anyone that got in her way. The world thought us to be a pair, when ultimately, I have been plotting against her since the day I thought my son had died. She became obsessed with that dagger and its power. While for me, that dagger was my daily reminder of how she tricked me into believing that Anchors were destined to be together. I did not know the truth until it was too late. I blamed her then, and I still blame her now. She has taken everything from me, and I want it all back."

He looked over to Aunt Lynn, and she looked at him with sorrow filled eyes. She was falling for this bullshit too, everyone was. He was lying. He had to be. My mind was racing from everything that happened today. It was supposed to be a normal family day. He continued to talk, which brought my attention back to the story.

"The hatred I felt toward Izzy that day, I knew it could not be love, so instead, I plotted my revenge. Time is nothing when you are immortal. A thousand years has felt like a short while to make this plan work. It took decades to come up with a plan that would rid her for good. Margo found me and begged for me to work with her. She had Jim with her, and they were willing to team up with me. Unfortunately, after all this time, I believe she is realizing... "

"Stop, just stop," my dad said. "How do I get these images in my head to stop spiraling? I can't think straight. I see what I believe are my childhood memories, I think I see you and them, but then there's moments of darkness and nothing. I don't understand why everything is so jumbled." My dad walked over and sat down at the table with his head in his hands in defeat. He looked up at Eric."Brother, you have to help clear my head."

The word 'brother' made the entire room silent. Eric was the only one with a smile on his face. He stood and walked toward him. I quickly jumped in front of him, blocking his way to my dad in a defensive stance. "Back off."

"I can help him."

"You're not doing anything to or with him. Back off," I said again, only this time I pulled my magic through my palms and felt fire ignite.

He stepped back with his hands up. "Okay, then you do it."

I sucked in a deep breath and let my magic settle, looking down at my fading Mark, wincing at the sight. His eyes followed mine, and he grimaced at my forearm.

"Or better yet, maybe Haven should do it." He nodded toward my arm, and I quickly covered my Mark.

"I can do it."

"Fine, whatever you say." He shook his head in annoyance. "I guess stubbornness is in our blood." He smirked and stepped back.

"Shut up, you are not family, you are nothing. I don't trust you, and I won't until I see the Oakes are alive and well, and even then, I won't trust you," I said, looking at Jaxon, who nodded.

"Fair enough. Haven, you will need to help your sister. Healing and syphoning go hand in hand if you want to be at your best. Help balance their health as she syphons the blocks of magic to unlock his memories."

"How do I do that?" Haven asked.

"How do you heal? It's the same thing," Eric answered.

"I think we should try what he says." It was my mom who spoke up. She had been so quiet this entire time that I almost forgot she was with us. "With Izzy free, we don't know how much time we have. Any help would be better than none at this point. Plus, three months of being free has made me realize I won't go back to running." She looked at me with an almost pleading expression. She walked over to me and put her hands on my shoulders, "You know I would never do anything that could hurt your father. I would rather run than put him in harm, remember? I just have a mother's instinct." She smiled.

I nodded and agreed with her blue doe eyes, and for a brief moment, I felt that she was using her power of persuasion on me, but then I realized that if this worked, then we would have another Immortal on our side, and that had to be a good thing.

"Haven, go stand across from Freya on each side of your dad. Interlock your arms around his head," Eric said. "Freya, you need to start syphoning the magic blocks, and, Haven, when you start to feel the pull of magic, then you need to start healing. That should, hopefully, balance out the magic. Freya, start small. We don't want to lose his Mark too."

I looked at Eric and glared at him one last time before I took my position next to my father.

Everyone stood back and braced themselves.

"If something feels off, then you make us stop. Do you understand?" I locked eyes with my dad, and he nodded, terrified, but agreed. "Alright, here goes nothing."

Chapter Twenty-One

Jaxon Oakes

I stood across the room, Eric was on the opposite side from me, thankfully. I wanted to strangle the man, but if he really had information on my parents' whereabouts, then I would need him alive. Or he could be full of bullshit and then I would get to kill him soon enough. This time I was not lying in a bed, defenseless, healing from my own death. I looked back at Jim and watched carefully for anything that seemed to be a trick. Jim's face seemed aged overnight, he seemed to be fighting a true battle internally, only this one was with his own memories.

The girls stared at each other, hesitating. I was sure they were afraid to hurt him. I knew I would be. Freya closed her eyes, and Haven followed suit. I felt like I should close mine and wait for things to be over, but I knew I had to keep my eyes on Eric, just in case. Both of the girls were breathing anxiously, then simultaneously, their breathing became even and matched one another. The room became silent. I braced myself for the magic impact that was going to explode through the room if this went wrong.

I kept my eyes shifting between them and Eric, waiting for anything to feel off. Alex mimicked my behavior. She had her whole family in the middle of all of this, and it could very well be a set up. Then, the connection matched, and all three of their Marks started to glow. I could see the magic being pulled from him to Freya, blue waves of static transferred from one Mark to the other. Then, Haven's Mark lit up with green static as her healing powers did their job. Each symbol glowed brighter when the magic transferred. I had never seen anything like it. It was incredible to witness such a thing. I made a mental note to add this to the family grimoire for future reference.

The room's energy began to feel like it was spinning. I grabbed the table edge for balance, but leaned in closer to watch them carefully. Something started to feel off, something wasn't right. The energy in the room began to shift. I looked at Freya just in time to see her nose start to bleed. I quickly turned my attention to Haven, who had her eyes closed still, but seemed unaffected. I turned to Alex who was already looking back at me with worry, "Something's wrong, we have to stop this," I yelled.

Alex nodded, and she exhaled as she realized she wasn't alone in her decision. We rushed to the duo, pulling the twins apart. Freya fell back into my arms on the floor, panting heavily, trying to catch a breath. She was choking on the air she was trying to consume. I glanced at her glowing forearm that was fading faster now. "Hey, hey, Freya, look at me." I grabbed her face and forced her to look at mine. "Breathe. It's done." She gasped for a breath and slowly let the oxygen expand her lungs, nodding her head as she closed her eyes and exhaustion took over her.

"I remember." Jim's eyes flew open as he stood up. "Margo and I spent years together after her incident with her sister. She came to our family, asking for hiding and a safe space, knowing that she could never go back home. Her necklace saved her life. She stayed with us until she and I decided to leave and start fresh. Away from all things tainted. We made a pact that we would go after Izzy and get her magic back. Unfortunately, Izzy got too close to us, and we needed to change our plans. That damn map from Lynn started to track me on the map the closer we got to her. My immortality was a huge marker of power that started to show up. We had too many close calls before we were ready. Together, we decided to use an immobilizing spell on me and laid me to rest in that same damn cave. It was only meant to suppress my magic and keep me in hiding until she was gone. Margo was supposed to come back for me, but—" He looked at us and froze. He realized that the memory syphon took a toll on Freya, and his rambling turned to fear as he dropped to his knees, joining me.

"She's okay," I said quickly. And he looked to Haven, who nodded too. "But my mom didn't get to wake you up because Eric and Izzy stayed here in town instead. If she would have woken you, then your magic would've shown up on the map, leading Izzy right back to you," I finished his story, realizing this was real.

Jim nodded as he grabbed his head. His head must be pounding to have a magic block just ripped apart at the seams, flooding years of memories right back in.

He stood and walked over to Eric. Grabbing him,

pulling him into his chest, embracing in a long, overdue hug. "It's been so long, little brother."

"Longer for me." Eric said.

"Don't let me sleep that long again," Jim said, and they both laughed.

"Where is Margo now?" Alex interrupted their reunion.

"She should still be at the safe house in Iowa," Eric answered. "If I had known they were still in hiding, then I would've gone there first. Been a long damn day."

"They are alive. Well, at least, I know Mr. Oakes is." It was Haven who finally spoke. "He called me. I didn't know it was him at first. He was looking for that book at your old house."

My eyes grew wide, and my body weight shifted to not disrupt Freya resting. "And you're just telling me this now? Knowing that he was alive? What the hell, Haven?" I could feel my blood boiling, and my breathing quickened. But Freya was in my arms, keeping me grounded.

"I'm so sorry, Jax, I didn't know for sure or why or how. I was just looking for answers before I could say anything. I needed to be sure." She pulled a piece of paper from her pocket and handed it to me. It was my dad's handwriting. "He asked me not to say anything, but now there's too much going on to not give you the proof."

I read the paper over and over, letting the fact that my parents were still alive sink in. It'd been three months. Had I missed any signs or clues from them? My brain went into overdrive, replaying everything in the last three months. I couldn't focus. I looked down at Freya and took a deep breath. Freya's eyes opened, and she sat up quickly. My thoughts slowed as I watched her intently. She would be the one to keep me whole. I took a deep breath and let my emotions subside as I changed my focus onto her. Her body shifted back into me, leaning for support. She was exhausted. Whatever magic she just performed took a toll on her, and her damn Mark was getting worse. *Fuck.* If anyone could help Freya, then it would be my parents. They knew more about magic, and now it made even more sense. My mom had had a thousand years to practice.

"Take me to them." I looked up at Eric and calmly said again, "Please, take me to my parents."

Chapter Twenty-Two

Aisling Meadows

The house was finally quiet. Aunt Lynn went to her room, and Declan and I had the living room to ourselves. With my parents still out of town, we decided that staying at a home unknown by Isadora was best for all of us. The others left to go to the safehouse for Jaxon's parents. I couldn't believe that they were alive, I mean, thankfully. And Jim was an Immortal, not just any Immortal, but the first Immortal, and he was my great great great whatever uncle. I guess that meant that Freya and I really were related.

"Hello, Ais?" Declan interrupted my thoughts.

"Sorry, babe," I looked up at him. "What did you say?"

"I said, should we have gone with them?"

"No, I think they need to do that alone. My head is pounding from all of this shit."

He jumped up and walked into the kitchen, rummaging through the cabinets and bringing me back a glass of water and a medication to stop the pounding. I threw my head back and swallowed the pills quickly. This was not going to work. I needed a distraction to help clear my head.

"Can we go for a walk?" I asked him.

"I thought your head was hurting?"

"It is, but I think a walk and fresh air is what I need."

"Okay, just let your aunt know, so she doesn't worry."

Aunt Lynn gave Declan a tracking bracelet that was similar to mine, and we left. He twirled it around his wrist, annoyed at the piece of jewelry he would have to wear from now on with a psycho Immortal on the loose. We started walking down the road and headed for the river, which wasn't too far. The chill in the air was coming back on this October night. I shivered, wishing that I would've brought a hoodie with me. He noticed the movement and wrapped his arm around my shoulder, pulling me in close to him, feeling his body warmth was helping to balance mine.

"How are you doing?" I asked him, not daring to look at his expression. "You know, the return of the dad and all."

"Honestly?" he asked while looking down at me. I nodded as I braced myself for the answer I was sure I didn't want to hear. "I feel like... I feel... I don't know. I keep trying to wrap my head around this." He inhaled sharply. "Why would he take me to begin with? Did he kill my parents, or did Isadora and then he felt guilty leaving a crying toddler, ya know? I want to trust him because he's the only person I've known my whole life. He has been tough on me, but he's never left me, and he's always had a purpose or lesson for each situation that has happened. As screwed up as that seems. I don't hate him." He vented in one single breath before brushing his hands through his dark curling hair and tried to collect himself.

I stopped walking and gazed up at him, examining his facial expressions, and the hurt that was in his eyes talking about Eric made my stomach churn. As much as I hated the man, Declan still loved him in his own way. I guess he was the only father he could remember. A whole life living with a killer, how sad for Declan to know nothing different. He should have been raised in a house full of love and laughter. He deserved better. Instead, he had a strict father who stole him from his biological parents.

"Do you trust him?" I asked.

"Before I knew who he really was, the man had never lied to me."

"That you know of."

"I think he's being honest. I'm a pretty good judge of character. I mean, I got you, didn't I?" he said, smiling and looking to the upcoming river. He laughed and shrugged his shoulders as we pushed on to the sound of the water flowing.

I would have to believe his judgment on this one. I let it go as we continued to walk. The river was rushing. We made it to the small beach after crossing the railroad tracks. We sat down on the beach, and I leaned back, letting my hands bury themselves into the cold sand. Not helping my body temperature, but the energy I felt from the earth was very needed in this moment. I never knew the connection to the earth until my Mark appeared. Now, if only my Anchor could be found.

Declan sat next to me and was leaning forward, picking at a piece of driftwood that had made its way to shore. His dark curls falling into his eyes and his arms flexing with each rip of the wood. Whoever his parents were, he looked as if he was made from a pair of Greek gods. He was beautifully handsome, and I could feel my heart skip a beat as I stared.

"I love you." The words escaped my lips before I meant them to. He looked back at me, studying my face. His smile formed, and his entire body shifted into mine, his arm on my back, laying me back into the sand gently. His hand came out from behind my back as he used his arms to balance himself over me, and he started to kiss my neck, shoulders, torso. I moaned at the warmth of his lips on this cold fall night. All of a sudden, my body was no longer cold. His lips touched mine, and his eyes met my gaze, smiling as he leaned against my body.

"I love you too."

I smiled and tugged at the button on his jeans, as his kisses continued. My body temperature was rising. His lips made it to my throat, making my neck crane to the side, as his beard stubble tickled me. I unfastened his jeans and tugged on them. He stopped and looked me in the eyes with a serious look.

"Not here, babe," he said, pulling at his jeans.

"I said I needed a distraction. Will you help me?" I smiled, innocently.

"A distraction, huh? That's what I am to you?" He huffed in a sarcastic way and laughed.

"Fine, I can be whatever you want me to be." His lips crushed mine, and we were no longer cold.

* * *

I had no idea how much time had passed, but the distraction definitely helped clear my head. I could finally catch my breath and relax. We laid there in the sand, losing track of time when footsteps approaching made me jump up and stare behind us.

"Aisling? Declan?" A man's voice questioned.

Declan jumped up and stood defensively, pushing me behind him.

I squinted past him, trying to let my eyes adjust at the face in the dark. "Ezra?" I asked and smiled when I realized we weren't in any danger. "What are you doing out here?"

He let out a sigh of relief. "I've been trying to get a hold of Haven for the last few hours, and she hasn't responded. I'm really starting to worry."

"Oh, man, you have no idea," Declan exclaimed. "The fishing trip turned into a family reunion to say the least."

"What's that supposed to mean?" he asked. "Is she okay?"

"Long story short, she's okay. Jim and Eric are brothers. Jaxon's parents are alive, and Isadora and Eric broke out of the cave. Oh, and Isadora is a psychopath, which we already knew." I answered his worried look. His face went from relief that we had seen her to confusion at the short story that would need a longer explanation, but my head was finally starting to feel better, and I did not want to get into it again. It was bad enough that I came from Eric's bloodline.

"So, where is she now?" he asked, worried.

"On their way to Jaxon's parents at a safehouse across the river."

"For fuck's sake, couldn't anyone have called me and let

me know what the hell was going on? Instead of them taking off and you two rolling around in the damn sand."

"Hey, man, chill. Haven seemed overwhelmed earlier, just give her some credit. There's a lot going on," Declan yelled back, pushing his way closer to Ezra.

"I should be with her! Protecting her. She's more fragile than you two know." Ezra inched closer, then stared at me before stopping himself. He shook his head and turned, starting to walk away.

Damn, he's pissed. I ran toward him, pushing past Declan's reach. Feeling pulled toward him to help.

"Hey, Ezra, look at me. It's okay. She's okay. It's been a crazy day, I swear she isn't ignoring you." I rubbed his arms in hopes that he could calm down. "Seriously, try calling one more time, I'm sure she's on edge with everything that just happened." He looked at me, eyes glazing over with tears as he huffed. What was going on with him? He was so angry. In the past few months I'd never seen this side of him.

"Yeah, you're probably right. I'm sorry." He sniffed and wiped the tear that started to roll down his cheek. "I just... It's just been a long day, and she's been wandering off lately in search of unlinking cures and everything, and I'm just afraid that she is taking on too much. I don't want her to get hurt."

"No, I get it. I promise, she's okay. We will all keep her safe." I winked at him, and he seemed to calm down. "Besides, we have magic on our side." He winced at the word magic. "Sorry, Ezra." He should have magic too, but he was too stubborn to let it in. "Just call her again or try

Freya's phone. Maybe her phone got water damage from the Mississippi."

He nodded and smiled. "Yeah, you're right. Sorry, Ais." He hugged me and started walking away. I watched as he disappeared into the dark.

"What the hell was all that about?" Declan asked.

"I don't know. He seemed so angry, that wasn't like him."

"No, I mean... why were you so worried about him? He's a big boy, he can take care of himself."

"Babe, what the hell? He's our friend. We need to stick together."

"Seems to me that he would only listen to you, maybe I'm being jealous, but damn, man, he's a big brute, and that hug was a little unnecessary."

"Stop it," I yelled, putting my hand up. "We are not doing this. That is Haven's boyfriend. He and I have never been alone together, there is nothing there besides friend-ship." I grabbed his arms and pulled him closer to me. "You are the only man in my life, please don't mistake my kind-ness for anything else."

He grabbed my face and tilted my chin up to reach his eyes. "Okay, I'm sorry. He just watches you sometimes, and it makes me mad as hell. Lately, I've noticed he seems... I don't know. Like protective around you."

"Protectiveness isn't a bad thing." I laughed.

He huffed.

What the hell was he talking about? Were we talking about the same guy? Ezra? Geez, first Jaxon was jealous of him and now Declan? He barely talked to me. He'd been around more while Haven and I have been looking for an unlinking spell, but never alone with me. What the hell, there was nothing going on. He was just a nice guy, a little tempered tonight for the first time, but he was usually unbothered.

"We're done talking about this." I put my arms behind his neck and pulled him down to me to kiss me. I rolled my eyes as he pouted. Then, as our lips lingered together with his height, they were barely touching, he finally gave in and kissed me back. Letting our world be semi normal again. What was in the air today or maybe in the water? It'd been strange, to say the least.

Chapter Twenty-Three

Haven Vine

We drove across the bridge to get to Iowa. We passed the casino on the way with its parking lot full and I laughed to myself at how so many people were there gambling their life's earnings away while we had bigger life problems on our hands. I took a few deep breaths while my anxiety was starting to get the best of me. I looked down at my hands, and they were shaking. I tried to steady them by sitting on them. My mom noticed my movement and put her arm around me in the backseat, pulling me into her.

"It's going to be okay." she whispered.

I nodded and just let my head lay against her shoulder. Freya was exhausted and leaned on her other shoulder. Both of us were just physically and mentally drained by what was supposed to be a family day. Well, I guess, it turned out to be an even bigger family day. Freya intertwined my hand into hers our across our mom's lap, and we just sat there, silently, but together.

Thinking of family, I thought of Aunt Clara and Ezra

waiting at home for me and how wrong I had been for not even sending a text to either of them. There just hadn't been a spare second. I grabbed my phone and realized it was dead. My mom, one step ahead of me, handed me her phone.

"I already let Clara know what is going on," she answered my own thoughts. I smiled at the relief. I decided to text Ezra, just in case he was not by her to know what was going on. Feeling stupid that my own mom had time to let Clara know, yet I had been silent. I sent a quick text, letting him know that I would charge my phone and call him in a little while, but that I was okay.

Ezra: Glad you're okay. Love you.

Haven: Love you too. Thank you for putting up with me lately.

Ezra: Wouldn't have it any other way.

I smiled as I reread the words. I wished I would've given him a heads-up sooner. He was probably so worried, and it was my fault. I handed back the phone and closed my eyes for a few minutes. The ride was silent, everyone seemed speechless, or maybe we were all holding our breaths waiting to see Jaxon's parents. We followed behind Eric, with my dad driving. Jaxon was sitting up front, so I couldn't see his expressions to make sure he wasn't mentally and physically breaking.

We turned on a dirt road that was leading into a group of overflowing branches. I sat up, anxious at the unknown. We drove slowly through them and up the winding path, which seemed to take a lifetime to get there. The moonlight shone just enough to show a small cottage at the end of the path. Eric flashed his lights three times before pulling up to the place and turning off his engine. Dad pulled up behind him, engine still running. Eric jumped out of the car and looked back at us, not waiting for us to walk with him to the porch stairs as he knocked on the door.

Jaxon leaned forward in the passenger seat and waited. His chest wasn't rising. He was holding his breath. We all were. I knew his dad was alive, Mr. Oakes made that apparent a few days ago, but I hoped his mom was too now that we knew they were not Anchors like we had recently thought. The door opened, and a woman greeted Eric with a hug. Jaxon opened the door and ran toward the cottage. It was her. Eric stepped aside to let them have their moment. Mr. Oakes appeared behind her and pulled Margo and Jaxon in, hugging them tightly. We waited a moment in the car before we all got out and walked toward the house. Margo froze when she saw my dad.

"Does he know?" she asked Eric.

"Hello, Mags, it's been a long time. We have much to talk about." My dad walked up and hugged her tight. Flicking her Labradorite stone necklace and smiling. My mom walked behind him shyly. None of us knew the depth of their relationship in the past, and I could tell it made all of us feel a little awkward. We walked into the house, and Mr. Oakes pointed us to the living area for seating.

Margo stopped me and stared, mistaking me for Freya. "Sorry, you must be the twin? The resemblance is unbelievable." I nodded and kept walking but turned to watch her next interaction.

She grabbed Freya and pulled her in for a hug. Jaxon standing next to her.

"Freya... I... I am so sorry. I was just trying to protect my boy. Please, you have to understand."

Freya stepped back and tears rolled down her cheeks. "I understand." She pulled her back in for another embrace. The guilt she was living with would finally be able to rest. I hoped for Freya's sake.

My mom watched them carefully while standing in the hallway. Protective. Margo saw her gaze and walked over to her while the rest of us followed Mr. Oakes. Margo and my mom were talking in the hallway, and I tried to listen to their conversation, but was interrupted by Mr. Oakes. "Haven, glad to finally meet you, officially. Sorry about our first encounter. I was trying to be careful, and when the book was gone, well... it threw me for a loop."

"It's okay. Jaxon has the book now. They had beat us there by five minutes." I smiled and shrugged.

"I had to contact you, you were the only one who wasn't around my boy every day." He smiled, and I understood why now. "Callum." He pointed to himself.

"Nice to officially meet you," I said, shaking his hand.

"Son, you have the book?" He turned and asked Jaxon.

He nodded and ran out to the car to grab it, running back in with it securely in his arms.

"Please say the unlinking spell is in here so we can end this?" Jaxon asked his dad.

"Unlinking spell? That's not—"

"That's not what's in that book." Eric interrupted. "That book has the only spell in there to kill an Immortal. Right, Margo? Or was that a threat to keep me around?"

"Well, it has both," she answered and grabbed the book from Jaxon. "We're unlinking Isadora from you first, then you can do what you want with her. But first I want my magic back. We will have to Anchor you to Jim to keep the world balanced. We can not unlink an Anchor without linking you to someone else, or you will start to desiccate yourself. It's all about balance, and the magic world craves it."

"Wait, what about Lynn? Who will she link to?" I asked.

"Who is her Anchor?" Margo asked.

"No, she's linked herself to Eric and Isadora for the last thousand years."

She huffed. "Well that makes more sense now. I always wondered what kind of magic she was using to stay alive." She inhaled slowly. "Well, honey, we can only do so much. She was not part of my equation." She shrugged, and I looked at Freya and Jaxon, who were just as shocked as I was. Even Eric flinched at the words. Who knew what his feelings really were, though.

"No, we will unlink Aunt Lynn too. She deserves to live her life," Freya said.

"She has lived her life, plus extra centuries of it. I can only unlink someone if they have an Anchor to reattach to. Eric will use Jim, and there is no one else. Lynn will be unlinked, but I cannot pair her to anyone else. My hands are tied. That is the way the magic world works, it must have balance, my dear."

I watched as Eric stayed silent, seeming as if he was plotting his own plan for her. Was he going to sacrifice his link for Lynn? No, he's no hero to anyone.

"This is bullshit, there has to be another way. I'm not doing this again," Freya yelled and walked out of the house, Jaxon chasing after her. I followed them and met them in the driveway.

"We're not letting her die. We already went through this three months ago. She lives. It's that simple," Freya screamed while pacing back and forth angrily. She was fuming.

"Hey, hey... Look at me." Jaxon was trying to calm her down. "She will live, we will find a loophole."

"So now we're back to square one," I said out loud and covered my mouth, not meaning to say those words. Jaxon's eyes darted toward me with a 'shut the hell up' look. "I mean, I have an idea. I don't know if it will work, but we can try it. With Lynn not being an Anchor, she may not need someone to link to." Freya looked up at me with hopeful eyes and was all ears. "I'll explain later, let's go back inside and listen to the rest." She nodded and wiped her tears. She kissed Jaxon and turned, walking back into the cottage.

"I know you don't believe that, I know that look," Jaxon said to me. "I just didn't want her to break more right now. Something is going on with her magic. Her Mark is almost completely faded, and her energy is low. It's like the magic inside her is consuming her mortal life." His eyes welled with tears that he quickly pushed back. Taking a deep breath and shaking his head, he continued, "I think we're running out of time and I don't know if it's just her magic or her life."

"I didn't realize it had gotten so bad. I've been so focused on researching lately that I haven't really been here mentally for her or Ezra, or anyone really." I sighed heavily and could feel tears forming in the corner of my eyes now. I was trying to please everyone and take on the world, but now the world was taking on me. Jaxon walked over to me and sat me down next to him. He put his arm around my shoulders and pulled me closer to him.

"You are a people pleaser. I get it. You need to take care of yourself first, though. The world can wait." He kissed the top of my head and rubbed my shoulder. "The world will not burn while you get some rest, or at least, I hope not. You are pretty special." We laughed, and he let me rest my head on his shoulder for a little while longer in silence as I inhaled the fresh air.

Chapter Twenty-Four

Freya Chamberlain

I walked back into the house, breathing more evenly, knowing that Haven would think of something. I would have to trust her confidence. The others were discussing what had happened in the cave and how Isadora had her syphoning back. Margo sounded shocked. I stayed behind the wall and just listened, feeling as if I was walking into a conversation that wasn't meant for me.

"Freya's fight with her must've somehow triggered it to come back. That is going to be a little more tricky than I was hoping for. If only I had my healing powers back, then I would have a better chance against her." Margo stood up and paced behind the couch. "Damnit, we should've done this before the kids' car accident, when she started setting up her therapy office. We waited and now look." She paced back and forth. "If she's syphoning again, then my mission is over. There is no winning against that. My immortality has been for not—"

"We weren't ready then." Eric interrupted. "She would've seen it coming. I had to get her back to believing I loved her still. She thought I was in love with Alexandra, you know that."

"Everyone was in love with her, Alex has always been the center of every man's attention. Her damn persuasion could get anyone to follow her. I would be worried if I were Isadora too. You stalked her and then chased her for almost two years. I thought you were sleeping with her too."

"Excuse me?" My mom interrupted, fuming. "I never used that on any man or anyone close to me in my life and I was running for my life! I thought he was going to kill me! I chased him away from my family and yours to keep everyone safe, and the only thing you were supposed to do was keep my family safe and look where that led us."

"I kept my family safe."

"Of course you did, because your family is all that matters to you."

"Damn right it is. Then, Freya had to walk back into my son's life, and now we're back to square one."

"You could've told me that you were working with Eric. Could've saved a lot of heartache for everyone, but now I get it. You wanted the split. You wanted Jim all to yourself."

"You shut your mouth, you worthless witch. You should've stayed the abandoned mother and ex-wife that you were. I liked you better that way," Margo muttered, and I started to turn to defend my mother, but paused when she said my name. "Freya was never supposed to find my boy again."

"Jaxon would've made his way back to Freya, one way or another. They are destined to be together, and you know that."

"According to Clara's visions, but she's been wrong before."

"Not about this, have you seen those two together? Oh, that's right, they stay away from you because you're a nuisance to them. They will marry and have grandchildren, and they will never be around you."

Shock crossed my face at the fantasy of my future. I hoped that whatever vision Clara saw was real because a future of any kind at this point would be amazing.

"Enough!" my dad yelled and stood between the two of them. "Alex, Margo, stop. This has nothing to do with them. It's about me, and we know it. We've each had different lives together in different times, different centuries."

Margo huffed as my mom sighed.

Callum spoke, "I'm going to grab some tea for everyone." His footsteps walked toward the hallway that I was standing in. Shit, he's going to catch me listening in. I stepped back toward the doorway, but I was too late, he turned to see me, surprised. He winked and shook his head, mouthing, "It's okay." His face, looking like an older Jaxon, made me smile.

I thought about their words and wondered about Aunt Clara's vision. My heart leaped at the thought of forever with Jaxon, but then the way life had been since the Immortals came around, I hoped that life would have a forever or even just another ten years. Jaxon and Haven walked in behind me, which made me jump. Jaxon grabbed my hand, and we all three walked into the living room together. Breaking the tension that was rising.

"Margo, what do you need for the unlinking spell

then?" Eric asked, changing the subject.

She opened her book, and Jaxon walked over to look at it with her.

"How can I see the symbols now? Before I needed to use my blood."

"My smart boy, using your blood. This book is sealed for our family, however, it's still in my possession, I haven't passed it down to the next generation yet. Eventually you will be able to see it naturally without me near."

"Well, Isadora and Jim can read it too," Jaxon said, and Margo looked up from the weathered pages at Jim.

"Izzy, yes, she is my sister. But, Jim, you can read this?" She pointed to the pages and turned it toward my dad. He nodded. "Hm. Well, that is a new one. Let me see your Mark."

She walked over to him and lifted his arm up and examined his forearm, then his pupils and pulse. "Strange," she said. "You must've consumed my magic somehow while sleeping, which could be why you woke up. I always thought the old man from the bar was some kind warlock himself and woke you, then took you under his wing." She rubbed his Mark. "Unless..."

She closed her eyes and started to chant incantations that I did not recognize, as if it were an entirely different language. She opened her eyes, shocked.

"Jim, you must be a syphon too. I can feel my own magic within you, only little bits of it, but it's definitely there." She stepped back and examined him from head to toe. "But how? I don't recall this being in the past. Unless, being sedated for so long, your body went into fight or flight and started to consume the spell itself." She let his arm go and paced back and forth. "But when you woke up, you didn't remember anything from the past. I saw you. You walked into the classroom with Alexandra giving you the tour of the high school. I was shocked to see you, but your Mark was nowhere to be seen. I grabbed a seat closer to the two of you and listened to your conversation with Alex about the bar owner giving you a job and a place to stay. Lord knows, the old man needed the extra help. He was on his last days and had no family to pass the bar along to. So, I listened, and you seemed so normal, knowing nothing about your past. So, I made a decision to let you go, knowing that I wouldn't be too far to check in on you from time to time. I wanted you to start over, and I was with Callum then, and I knew I had a choice to make."

"And you chose me, of course. I mean, have you seen the way my eyes sparkle." Callum walked back into the room with a pitcher and glasses. Breaking the tension, we all laughed. It was no wonder where Jaxon inherited his sense of humor.

Margo stopped pacing. "Jim, you produced twin Anchors," she looked into his eyes with hope. "What if you are both a syphon and a healer yourself? Only someone very powerful can create them."

The theory actually made sense.

"That might be why I felt so drained during the memory unblocking, and Haven wasn't affected. You might have been syphoning from me while healing Haven. I mean, either way, it worked," I said and shrugged. This magic world would never be normal to me.

"There's only one way to find out." My mom stood up and walked between my dad and me. "Freya, syphon from me, and honey, I need you to try to heal me as she does it. Otherwise, it's going to hurt like hell." My dad's eyes widened, and he stood up quickly, stepping away from us.

"No way, I might remember my past, but I don't remember a thing about how to use magic. I don't even remember using it. I might just be immortal. I don't think I even have magic."

"Only one way to find out." She walked closer to him and grabbed his hands. "I trust you."

"I don't trust myself," he said, shaking his head, "What if I hurt you?"

"I won't let you hurt her." Haven walked up next to her and smiled. "We're a family, we protect each other at all costs."

"Oh, what the hell did I get myself into?" He scoffed before walking toward us.

The four of us met in the middle of the room. A salt circle poured for us to step into, just in case something didn't go right, then theory was the salt would keep it concealed to one area. Our mom walked to the center and the three of us formed a triangle around her. Haven's hands were ready to work their healing.

"Dad, get ready. I'm going to start pulling her magic."

His hands were shaking as he put them on her shoulders, mirroring my stance.

Haven said, "Just breathe and try to focus on giving instead of receiving. Imagine a wound that will only heal if you willed it to."

He understood, or he seemed to. "Here goes nothing."

Before I knew it, the room started to spin as I syphoned my mom's magic, only I didn't feel any magic coming toward me, instead I felt my dad pulling my magic from me. My hands began to shake as my magic felt like it was being ripped from me completely along with the souls.

"Oh, no…"

My legs wobbled, and I used the last of my strength to disconnect my arms from his as my body went down faster than I could even try to catch myself. Instead of hitting the hard ground, someone slid underneath me and broke my fall. But it was too late. The room had gone dark, and I was slipping away. My breathing was slowing, and I could feel emptiness inside me. The souls from the dagger were no longer within, my own magic was walking on a thin line to stay with me. I felt my Mark on my arm tingle, and I knew it was fully disappearing. I would be either magic-less or dead in a minute, or maybe both. I let the heaviness take over my chest.

The room was dark, but I could see small orbs floating above me. I squinted and tried to make out the pretty little glimmering that was above me. Unknown, I examined my surroundings and realized I was alone aside from the sea of orbs overhead. I stood up and reached my arm up to try and see if the glowing orbs were a mirage or real. One swam closer to me, giggling like a child as it neared my hand. The light brightened as it touched my fingertip and a small tingle of electricity extended to me, tickling my hand. I smiled when I realized what the orbs were. They were all souls. My borrowed souls.

"Are you coming for me?" A high-pitched girl's voice asked from the orb.

"Coming where?"

"He said he would come for me. Tell him he's late." She *giggled and floated back to the ceiling.*

"Wait, who are you?"

But it was too late, she was gone in the sea of souls again and the room around me started to get brighter.

The tingling began to course through the rest of my body that originated from my Mark. The room started to come back to me, the light burning my eyes as if I had just been let out of the dark. Haven was in front of me, healing my body from the death of magic. I looked behind me as my body was saved from falling by... Eric? He was underneath me, cradling my body carefully while Haven worked her magic. I blinked heavily. Was I seeing this right? Three months ago, he tried to kill me. For two years, he chased my mom away from us. He stabbed Jaxon, killing him, and burned his parents alive, well, sort of. Why help me now?

I sat up, awkwardly, trying to balance my body but feeling very woozy still.

"Whoa, no. You need to sit still," Eric's voice said quietly.

"Get off me," my voice cracked.

"Freya, sit still. Your Mark is in a worse condition than what I had first thought. Any more syphoning done by you, and you will lose your magic altogether. Something isn't right. It should be recharging itself after each encounter."

"Yeah, well, it's not," I said, pushing myself off him. "And unless you know how to fix it, get the hell away from me."

Chapter Twenty-Five

Jaxon Oakes

I'd never seen Freya so angry before. Today was the first in my whole life that I saw her react in a way that scared me. Even after her destructive years, she was never this cold. She will never forgive this man, nor should she. He's a pyscho, but knowing that he's from her bloodline now and is related to her was kind of even more terrifying.

Three months ago, she tried to kill him and had every intention to without even knowing the truth. What would Jim have thought, if by some chance his magic was triggered after the fact and his own daughter had killed his brother? The brother who knew his past and how to save his future. What a twisted scenario. How did you change your whole manner toward someone just because they were blood? How did we team up with a man who had so much hatred and killing in his past?

Freya walked past me and grabbed some loose paper by the desk and a pen and stormed up the stairs into the unknown. I wanted to chase after her, but knowing her, she would need some time to cool off and clear her head. I made a mental note to go and check on her in a few minutes and just let her have her space.

I saw my mom walk past me in the opposite direction toward the kitchen, and I jumped up to follow her. I was still in shock that she was here, but it was a good shock. Death was never really final when it came to her, and right now, I was truly thankful.

"You really think we can trust him?" I asked, nodding my head back toward the other room with Eric lingering in there. Unwanted by everyone, except maybe Jim.

"There is no other way. I've spent a thousand years trying to get rid of him, only to have to keep him closer. His intentions are good, just his temper is a little unstable. I prefer him over my sister any day, though."

I stood next to her, trying to wrap my head around the fact that she was standing in front of me. I stared at the Labradorite stone and was mesmerized by the iridescent colors. Hatred grew inside me from her not coming to find me for three months, then shame for me doing the same to Freya, but only for longer and unintentionally.

"Three months, Mom." I shook my head, looking at the ground, focusing my attention on anything other than anger. I looked up at her only to find tear filled eyes.

"If there was any other way, I would've come to you. My book was at our old home, and I was here. I couldn't even get a message to you without giving away our location."

"A text or call would've been nice, this isn't a thousand years ago. You wouldn't have to send a damn bird or a dragon or whatever the hell you guys did back then." Scoffing at the irritation building, I knew that it was true, she could've found a way. Dad found Haven, but not me. I was out of the loop.

"Jaxon, please... Just understand that I was trying to—"

"Let me guess... keep me safe. Well for fuck's sake, Mom, it didn't work. The trauma of trying to cope with losing you both has not been easy, and let alone to find out who you really are is kind of something that should've been brought up at some point during my childhood. Like, hey, you're an Anchor witch, I'm an Immortal with revenge on my very own twin sister and Dad is just an earth witch and only has one chance against supernaturals. Like, some sort of knowledge would've been nice. I feel like I just found out I'm adopted." I froze and looked back at her. "Am I adopted?"

She laughed, "Absolutely not, I have stretch marks to prove it."

I shook my head and laughed softly, but frustration consumed me. "So many damn secrets and I'm supposed to just let everything go back to being one big happy family with you guys? Living with the Chamberlains for three months felt more like family than my entire life with you guys feeling like a lie now."

She gasped, tears over spilling onto her cheeks. She wiped them away and more followed. She had nothing to say, and I knew that the words were just out of anger, and I didn't mean them all.

Now what happened from here? Did she expect me to just move back in with them and go back to as if nothing has changed? We surely could not go back to Genoa and pull off another amnesia story with them too. Too many people knew about the house fire with them in it. There was no explaining that on the news. My mind raced with options of the future.

"Please, baby, please just..." She stopped and looked toward the doorway. Jim was walking toward us. "Forgive me, please," she said out loud. I wasn't sure if she was talking to me or him now. Damn, what kind of twisted love story did she have with him? That's probably why she hated Freya, the daughter of a man she loved but with another woman. Something finally made sense.

"We can talk later." I walked over to her, closing the space between us, and pulled her in for a hug. "I love you, Mom. Words can't express how happy I am that you're alive. Next time, just send a damn bird. Okay?" I kissed her head and walked away, leaving Jim and her alone.

Chapter Twenty-Six

Freya Chamberlain

This world was fucking unbelievable. *Eric, my blood? Come on! Could today get any worse?* I just needed a minute to either accept this or end this. He couldn't be on our team. There's no way we could trust him. My mind raced, and I could feel the rage growing inside me. My magic started to tingle through my fingertips, and I was ready to let it out. Why should Eric get to see another day? He was a thousand years old and had killed too many. He didn't deserve anymore sun rises. I ran to the window and opened it letting my rage flow through my fingertips and rush out of me, releasing energy into the open sky. I caught my breath and closed the window.

So many things started running through my mind as I slowed my breathing to a normal pace. How would we safely unlink Aunt Lynn? Does she need an Anchor? How am I supposed to fix my Mark? Was my syphoning going to kill me? Would I be me without my magic? What was that vision all about? Who was that soul? Why come to me now? What the hell was going on today?

My body felt exhausted, and honestly, I knew that I couldn't take him on right now, my magic felt weak. I glanced at my faded Mark and grimaced. How did I get this back? Eric knew something, but I didn't want information from him. I could figure this out on my own. At least I hoped so. I set the paper on the floor of the room and started writing, knowing I would have to glue this page in my journal later.

Journal Entry:

Well, technically, not my journal at all, but a sheet of paper that Margo had laying around. That's right, I said Margo. I know, I'm still trying to wrap my head around this ghost too. We're all staying the night at the safe house tonight. Aunt Clara and Ezra are to meet us here so we can come up with a plan.

Another plan. And then what? Another plan and another one? I mean, come on. These plans are starting to suck.

Where do I even begin?

My dad is not mundane at all. He's immortal, and not just any immortal, but THE original Immortal. How does that even happen? Well, my grandmother was a witch who decided that life was too fragile and wanted a failsafe when it came to her kids. I am not a mother, but I can see where that selfishness may be wanted. So, having an immortal father actually

makes the psychopath Eric my uncle, by blood, not by choice.

UGH!

We spent weeks planning against him, and my mom spent nearly two years running from him, tearing my family apart. Or maybe it made us a stronger family in the long run, but come on, how can I work with him now?

I can't!

On a better note (or at least I hope so):

Jaxon's parents are alive, and for that, I will forever be grateful. Now I can stop living with the guilt of getting them killed that has been looming over me for the last three months. I just hope they are on our side. I guess, anyone who is against Isadora is with us. But how can sisters become so torn apart? Now that Haven is in my life, I can't imagine life without her. To kill your own sister for her magic is very sadistic. Let's just hope we can take her down for good this time. Unlink Eric, still debatable. Then save Aunt Lynn from her dying fate again. My Mark, unfortunately, will just continue to fade.

I looked over the paper and winced as the words "Eric my uncle, and Dad is immortal." I read it a thousand times before finally folding the paper and shoving it deep down into my pocket, as if the lower it went, the less truth it held in ink. I walked back to the window in the upstairs room and peered outside. Pitch black, nothingness for miles. Surrounded by trees and darkness. No one would ever find this place unless you were looking for it. Aunt Clara and Ezra should be here soon, and I was going to wait up here until they showed up. Hopefully, she would bring some of her magic tea. I sat down on the floor and grabbed a cushion from the chair across the room and laid my head back on it while looking up at the eggshell ceiling waiting for the headlights to luminate it.

I heard a slight knock on the door before it creaked open. I looked up expecting Jaxon, but instead, it was Jaxon's dad. He had a shy smile and seemed to be cautious to enter. "Do you mind if I come in?"

I nodded and sat up quickly. He walked toward me and sat on the ground next to me.

"I'm sorry that today has been so overwhelming." He inched closer cautiously. "I noticed your Mark today, do you mind if I see it up close?" Callum asked genuinely.

I hesitated for a moment, holding my arm cautiously, knowing that I didn't need another supernatural person to tell me what I already knew. I was a fading witch and would probably lose my magic. I lifted my arm up slowly and laid it out toward him. He grabbed my arm gently and turned it, examining every inch of it.

"Hmm," he said. "When did this start to fade?"

"About three months ago, after syphoning from Isadora and Eric in the cave."

"I see," he said, rubbing the Mark. "Do you mind if I try something?"

I questioned him with an odd look. "What do you have in mind?"

"Well, Jaxon told you I'm an Earth witch, right? That he and I are, anyway. Magic is all about balance and the Earth. So, when magic starts to fade, it's usually because it's becoming unbalanced, and we can't just take without giving back, if that makes sense?"

I thought about it for a minute and looked at him, smiling for the first time since earlier this morning on the river. He was right. Giving and taking needed to be even. "Any idea on how to do that? I'm supposed to be a special syphon and can't seem to figure out how to release the souls that have been borrowed."

"I knew it, that's exactly what is going on." He stood up and walked to the window, gazing out at the headlights that started approaching. "We just have to release them back to the magic world. We can do that. Simple."

I looked at him dumbfounded and waited for more of an explanation. He stood there as if I knew what he knew.

"Callum! How do I do that?" I yelled, only realizing that he was sifting through his own head to figure out the sequence, then laughed. "I mean, Mr. Oakes, please help me figure that out."

He looked back at me and smiled. "We can do that. But first, my dear. You need sleep, and maybe some food. It will tire you out even more than you already are," he hesitated. "The only way I will do this is if you promise to not judge Margo after everything and give her another undeserved chance. Please?"

My eyes grew big at the sound of her name. I laughed at that being his only request. "I'm pretty sure she needs to give me the chance and not the other way around." We both laughed and for the first time tonight, I felt relief and a weight come off my shoulders.

"We will have to have your sister help with it, so she will need rest too. She seems almost as tired as you. You two need to keep your strengths up and spend more time together. Your magic will grow the closer you are to one another."

"I thought you were an Earth witch?" I questioned. "So, how do you know so much about, I don't know, everything?"

"Big brain and too much time on my hands researching the magic world. Plus, it doesn't hurt to have the oldest grimoires and be married to a know-it-all thousand-year-old witch." He smiled and winked at me. "Two doors down, there's a guest room that hasn't been slept in. I'll let Jaxon know you're in there. Please get some rest. You are safe here. We are completely off the map. I'll bring you something to eat when you wake." If his cooking was anything like Jaxon's, then I could sleep easy knowing that my belly would be filled with something delicious soon.

"Thank you." I smiled back at him. "And, Callum, I'm really glad that you two are alive." The guilt I had been feeling was definitely going to be some of the weight lifting from my shoulders.

He smiled as he reached the doorway, "Me too, kid."

Chapter Twenty-Seven

Haven Vine

As soon as I saw the headlights shining through the curtains, I jumped off the couch, knowing that it had to be Ezra and Aunt Clara, otherwise we were in for it. I ran to the door and peeked through the window, realizing it was her car coming down the long driveway. Relief washed over me as I went outside to meet them. I laughed when I saw Ezra get out of the still moving car that she was driving. I ran to him and jumped in his arms. He didn't move an inch with my weight crashing into him.

"I'm so sorry, babe, about the secrets, it's just that... " He held his hand over my mouth.

"Shush, it's fine. I know you were trying to take on the world, per usual." He grabbed me and pulled me up and closer to him, letting his lips crush into mine.

"Thank you," I whispered to him between kisses.

Aunt Clara walked out of the car as Ezra set me down, and she pulled me to her and squeezed me tight. "Are you okay, sweetie?" She looked me up and down and turned me around. "Are you hurt at all?"

"I'm okay, just tired. It's been a crazy day with the family," I said in annoyance, "Next time, you are coming with us, no excuses."

She nodded and agreed with a smile. We walked toward the house, and she handed me a bag. I opened it, realizing it was full of salves, herbs, concocted treats filled with every magic ingredient you could use. Upset stomach, migraine, anxiety, sleep, or my favorite one, the everything magic granola bar. One bite of this, and it literally was the overload tea in granola form. letting your body just relax and give you the protein needed. It truly should be on the shelves of every store, but the ingredient list would scare non magical customers away.

I pulled it out and took a bite without hesitation. "Thank you." She rubbed my back as she pushed me through the doorway.

I handed out the snacks to everyone, insisting on them all having one, skipping past Eric, because screw him. Uncle or not, I still hated him. My dad noticed the gesture and grabbed one for him and tossed it at him. Eric caught it and scowled at the bar, setting it aside.

"See, he doesn't even want it. So, don't waste it on him," I said to my dad.

Eric cleared his throat, pulling my attention back to him, who grabbed the bar and opened it, taking the most obnoxious bite he could and swallowing hard.

"That one was poison," I said to him, and the look on his face was priceless. Fear in the face of an Immortal. I smirked and walked past him into the kitchen with Callum, going to offer help with cooking whatever it was he had started to create out that had the whole safe house smelling of aromas that made my stomach grumble. We hadn't eaten since early this morning, and my stomach was not being quiet about it. Ezra followed me to the kitchen. Surely, he would not leave my side from this point on, which I was grateful for.

"Whatever that is," I pointed to the stovetop, "smells absolutely delicious. Can we help you with it?"

Callum turned to us and smiled. "Actually, you are just the person I needed to see." He walked to the back counter and grabbed two bowls, filling them with soup. Cutting pieces of the freshly made bread from the counter and laying them on top, he handed them to us. "You eat, then get upstairs, first door on the right, and get some rest. Your big guy can go with you. I need you to help me with Freya's Mark and those souls at sunrise, so I need you well rested and fed. Deal?"

I smiled at the thought of fixing her magic. The thought alone was weight lifted from my shoulders as one more thing I could check off my to do list. I nodded and walked over to him, a man that I had only met one time, but I could feel his soul, and I knew he was a good one. "Thank you."

He winked and smiled, "Hey, that poison joke... best one I've heard yet. Wish I could've seen his face."

I smiled back at him, and Ezra shook his hand, thanking him as he followed me upstairs.

Chapter Twenty-Eight

Aisling Meadows

The moon shone bright over the river onto the sand, the chill was in the air, but the moon lit up the beach as if it were day. I leaned closer to Declan to feel his warmth against me. He must've fallen asleep because his breathing sounded like a slight snore and it was adorable. I was sure if we were still together when we were older, the snoring would drive me nuts, but for now, the light rumble was beautiful and being close to him made me happy.

My mind wandered at the thought of Aunt Lynn being healthy and alive right now but at what price? Was it selfish of me to want her to live forever, or at least forever in my lifetime? She had been a mother figure to me my entire life. Not replacing my mother, but damn, she came close. With my parents traveling so much for work, she had always been my constant. I just couldn't imagine life without her. At least not yet. How did we unlink her from them?

Declan started to stir next to me, and a part of me wasn't ready for the snuggling to end, but the chill in the air was starting to get to my bones. I could always start a little fire next to us, but that would draw unwanted attention. I just wanted to be left alone with him. His body turned closer into me as he tugged me closer.

"What are you thinking about?" he whispered.

"Just silence. My mind is peaceful right now, I'm afraid of leaving this spot and letting the chaos back in," I said honestly. He looked down toward me, letting his eyes meet mine and shook his head.

"We will get through this. I know it."

The word 'we' made me smile, feeling shy all of a sudden at the togetherness. I nodded and inhaled sharply, hoping that he was correct. The thought of the world burning in Hellfire because of a psychopath Immortal made my stomach turn. Who knew what she was capable of now that she has her syphoning powers back? She was experienced and dangerous, and Freya's syphoning had been tricky the last three months. She didn't like to admit it, but I knew her too well to let that get passed me.

"We should get going," I said to him with a frown.

"Okay, do me a favor first."

I stared at him with my eyebrows raised.

"Take a deep breath in."

I listened and inhaled obnoxiously, letting my cheeks fill with air and holding my breath. He grabbed my face and pushed the air back out, making my exhale unexpected and letting out a funny sound, which made us both laugh out loud and sit back in the sand, giggling like children.

"Thank you," I said, happy for the distraction.

"That's what I'm here for." He stood and reached out his hand to me as he lifted me to my feet. I brushed off the sand and wiped his back clear as we started to walk back to

Aunt Lynn's home. He wrapped his arm around me, and I felt protected. Even though, magic-wise, I was probably the stronger one between the two of us.

We reached the home, and everything was as we left it, one light illuminating through the closed blinds. We reached the door, and I froze when I reached for the doorknob, as it turned on its own, and the door flung open, making me jump back into Declan's arms. A scream escaped the back of my throat, and I inhaled sharply.

"Aunt Lynn! What the hell? You scared me."

She laughed and held onto the door, waving at us to come in. "Sorry, I was tracking you with your bracelet and knew you were close. Easy spell for this non-witch to manage." She smiled.

"What are you still doing up?"

"I was waiting..." she hesitated and looked me in the eyes. "Nevermind, it's silly of me."

"For Eric," I answered for her and huffed like a child. "Why him? He tried to kill us all. Come on, you deserve so much better."

"Oh, honey, Eric and I have a history from long ago. I was not waiting for him to swoop me up and take me on a date. I was waiting for him to call me and let me know what ingredients I needed to round up for the unlinking spell and if he had found Isadora yet. She is still MIA since her encounter with Jaxon."

I flinched at the thought of Isadora hurting Jaxon again and realized my breathing was on hold. I let out an exhale and nodded.

"Should I be out looking for her or something?" Declan asked.

"Absolutely not," I chimed in, turning to face him. "You will not go anywhere near her again. That bitch is nuts, and she already tried to kill you once."

"Aisling is right. She is probably on a vengeful rage, and if she saw you, then it might trigger her hate for Eric right now, and who knows what she will do."

I wondered what her reaction would be to seeing any of us at this point. Would she try to kill us all at the next encounter?

"Do you think that if she knew I was blood related, that it might trigger something inside her to be... I don't know... kind?" I asked, doubtfully.

My aunt shrugged her shoulders and shook her head. "Honey, I have no idea. She is not stable and never has been. I have kept my distance for a thousand years from them and watched her crumble from afar. I listened to stories from towns that she destroyed. She is as evil as they come. Her motive has always been power and trying to find an heir. The sooner we can get rid of her, the better."

"What if she knows me to be her heir?"

"We are not using you as bait to her. She's unpredictable."

"What if the unlinking doesn't work and killing her hurts you too?" I asked.

"Then, so be it. I accepted my fate three months ago. Every minute has been on borrowed time, and I have been so lucky to have this time with you."

I could feel tears coming back with the realization that we needed to unlink her, like yesterday. I frowned at the thought of a world without her. Declan's arms came around my shoulders as he pulled me tight to him.

"It will work," he whispered.

I nodded, wanting to believe him.

We headed upstairs to the guest bedroom, which had been my room since I was young, and the house seemed so silent that we could hear a pin drop. I mentally was preparing myself for my aunt's phone to ring to hear what Eric had to say. I sat on my bed, and Declan stood by the window, peering down the street, assumingly waiting for his adoptive father to show up at any moment. We were both on edge, and I would give anything to get back to the beach and let reality be forgotten about for a little while longer.

I laid my head on the pillow, and before I knew it, I could feel my eyelids closing and a dreamless sleep consumed me, letting my mind finally rest.

Chapter Twenty-Nine

Freya Chamberlain

"It's time to let us go, little witch. We are ready to be set free," a voice whispered to me. I looked around the room and realized I was at the beach along the Mississippi. I tried to figure out how I got here and who was talking to me. I glanced down each side of the beach, and each way came up empty.

"Hello? Who's there?" I asked. Feeling afraid of who might answer back.

Silence.

"Please, talk to me." I jumped when my request was answered.

"It's time. Do the spell, it will work." The woman's voice whispered to me, and a cold shiver ran up my spine. She was here. Behind me. I expected a little tiny soul to be floating in the air. I could feel her soft voice close to my ear. I turned to look at her and was shocked when instead of a floating soul, it was a woman. Older but familiar, standing a foot away from me. I stared back at her and tried to place where I knew her from. Her glasses sliding down the brim of her nose and *her smile was brilliant. I reached my hand out to touch her, and something jolted through my hand making me jump back.*

"Who are you?" I demanded.

"You know who I am," she said sweetly.

I studied her features and gasped when I realized who she was. She was my future self. No, she was future Haven.

"Haven?" I asked.

She smiled and winked back at me. "Everything will be okay. I'm not far away." She nodded before she put her hands up, and I saw her Mark, carved out of her arm as she shoved me further away with her magic still intact as a jolt of electricity came through her fingers and pushed me back to reality.

My eyes flew open. I didn't know what time it was, but the sky was still dark out, and I could hear people talking downstairs. I reached for my phone and glanced at the time. Two o'clock. I had been dreaming. Talk about a guilty conscience. I knew I had to let the souls go, no matter how much extra power they have gave me, they were not mine. But why would Haven appear, and why was she so aged? I made a mental note to ask if she had the same dream too. I pushed the dream aside for now, knowing that we were Anchors, and as long as one of us were alive, then the other would be too.

All in all, the nap wasn't long, but my body and mind felt rested enough. I felt like I could take on the day. I glanced down at my Mark in hopes that maybe, just maybe it was normal again and whatever demons or souls were fighting inside me had subsided on their own. The Mark was still faded. *Damnit.* I sat up and rubbed my eyes to make sure I was seeing clearly and checked the Mark again. I shook my head and huffed like a child. I leaned back against the wall counting my breaths, letting my anxiety relax and told myself that Callum had a plan.

The door creaked open, and Jaxon came walking in. I was half expecting to wake up with him next to me, but realized that we had a lot going on and that he probably was catching up with his parents. I smiled at him when he walked in with a tray of steaming food that smelled delicious. My stomach growled, reminding me of my hunger.

"Good morning, or actually night still, but glad to see you're awake. Did you get enough sleep?" he asked, sweetly.

I nodded, and he walked over to me with the tray. Whatever concoction his dad made smelled amazing, and the fresh bread smelled delicious, but was no longer warm. I must've slept through anyone walking in here earlier with the food. I gladly took the tray and started to eat. My body felt rested, but my stomach growled for energy.

My mouth watered at the aromas of the stew, and I never looked up once to talk. I just concentrated on filling my belly with warmth. Jaxon's laugh pulled my attention back to him and made me realize I was not alone in the bedroom.

"Sorry, I was hungrier than I realized." I laughed.

"Don't apologize, I ate like three bowls already. It's been a long day. Comfort food." He smiled and patted his stomach before sitting down next to me. He grabbed my hand and pulled me closer to him. I leaned into him while chugging the water he brought up for me.

"That's moon water. Clara brought it for you."

I choked on the last guzzle. Hesitating, what the heck was moon water?

"Was I not supposed to chug that?" I asked.

"Sipping is usually better, but you must've needed that. Fully charged by the moon from last night per your aunt. Sip all day to make the good intentions stay. Or she said something like that. Or maybe it was sip all day and the goblins come out to play." He smirked.

I gasped and realized he was joking when he busted out laughing, making me laugh too. "Okay, stop it. Goblins are not real, are they?"

"Freya, you are so gullible. Of course they are not real." He laughed. "I mean, I have never met another supernatural being outside of our witching world, but there are legends of werewolves, fae, shapeshifters, and even vampires. So, if we exist, they must too, somewhere. Hopefully, not here in Crystal Rock, though. I think our world is complicated enough without anything more."

"Agreed." I glanced over at the window and saw the sky getting lighter, the sun would peek through soon and the ritual would begin. I really hoped that Callum knew what the hell he was doing. I rubbed my Mark and willed it to darken. Still nothing. "Do you think your dad can really fix this?"

"I've been talking to him while you were sleeping, and the plan sounds legit."

I looked into his eyes, and they were honest. If Jaxon trusted the plan, then I would go along with it too.

"Okay, well, the sun will be up soon. Let's get going," I said, standing up.

"Woah, hold on. I think you're forgetting something?"

I smiled as I leaned in and gave him a kiss. "Good morning or night to you too." I blushed as I saw his cheeks fill with warmth and a smile upon his lips. He nodded in agreement that I had read his mind.

We walked downstairs, and everyone was still there, only now Aunt Clara was in the living room too. I scanned the entire living space and glanced into the kitchen, but Haven was nowhere to be seen.

"Where's Haven?" I whispered to Jaxon, now worried that my dream meant something more.

"She's resting upstairs, Ezra is with her."

My shoulders relaxed. I smiled at the thought of her safety and that she wasn't alone. I walked over to the table where Aunt Clara was writing in a book. I glanced over her shoulder at a formula she had written down. Mugwort, chicory root, and elderberry? I had never heard of any of these. Were they even from around here? She looked up at me and smiled.

"Don't worry, child. We will get you fixed up. Your Mark will be fine. Callum knows what he is doing. Trust the process." I nodded back to her, glad to have the reassurance. "Margo thinks we should do the spell in her old home instead of out here. Her home is very old, and the walls themselves hold magic that can help contain the souls until we know we are not releasing anyone we shouldn't. There is a man in there named Ragnar, who must not be released."

My heart started to race, thinking of the power leaving

me but also a power that didn't belong to me. I did not want any bad ones roaming the earth, either, and I didn't want to know what Ragnar had done to make him have to stay. We had an hour before sunrise, so if we needed to move, then we needed to do it now.

Eric, reading my mind, jumped up. "Do we have everything we need?"

"Lynn has the ingredients and will meet us at Margo's home with Aisling and Declan. I think we are ready," Aunt Clara said confidently, which started to make me feel much better. I didn't like that Eric would be there for it, but as long as he stayed in the background, then I could tolerate him.

"Does anyone know where Isadora is?" I asked everyone. No one reacted. Meaning, no one had any idea where she had wandered off to. Which meant no one knew if she was waiting for us at the end of this road or if she had others helping her. Basically, no one knew anything, which made my anxiety rise. We didn't know what we were truly up against and then there was me, a faulty magic witch who was about to give up the only extra power that had helped defeat her in the first place. Then, Eric, who was not fully back to his immortal strength yet since she drained him. My dad had no idea how to even use his magic or hadn't even had any basic training. Margo and Callum were supposed to be dead and had been hiding because they were scared of her and her capabilities. Ezra and Aunt Lynn, both magic-less, were now a liability being with us. Haven exhausted herself. Mom and Aunt Clara were clever, but their magic was nothing against a syphon Immortal who had been harnessing power for a thousand years. Jaxon and Declan's earth and water magic wouldn't hold her down, either. Aisling could stand a chance if she had her Anchor with her. I shook my head, thinking of our chances to myself, and at this point, we were fucking useless against her.

"It's okay, we will be okay," Jaxon said next to me, rubbing my arm. I nodded, knowing that he was full of shit and that we were all going to die one of these days sooner than I had hoped.

We drove back into Wisconsin and made it to Jaxon's home. It was exactly as we had left it. Quiet and hopefully empty. Eric walked in first with Margo and Callum trailing behind him. I inhaled and waited. Callum walked back out and waved for us to come in. It was clear. I let out a sigh of relief.

We all gathered inside the living room, now being in close quarters forced us to be side by side without much elbow space. The safe house was much more spacious and also had seating. This abandoned home was basically empty. Aisling, Declan, and Aunt Lynn knocked, and Margo let them in before spelling the door shut behind them. I smiled when I saw Ais. She ran up and hugged me.

"You good?" she asked, and I nodded. "You sure?"

"I'm okay. Just ready to get this figured out." I raised my arm, and she rubbed the Mark.

My mom directed the women to get to the four corners of the house to put a protection spell on the home. It should help seal the souls in and keep out an unwanted Immortal for the time being. Aisling and her aunt walked to each corner. Her aunt was explaining the spell and what she would have to do. Her aunt handed her something small and closed her palm around the object. She was handing her coins from the noise of them clanging, then I saw the copper. Pennies. What the hell were those for?

Eric walked up next to me, making me step back from him as if his body was on fire and I didn't want to get burned. "Pennies will be used to perform the spell and then left in each corner stacked to maintain the seal until we are ready to release the souls. The copper helps keep them here. Simple, but very effective." I stared in doubt. "Not all magic needs to be complicated."

My eyes widened at the thought of a stack of pennies holding in hundreds to thousands of souls. Magic was wild sometimes. Simple things were hard, and hard things were simple. Magic didn't always make sense.

Callum poured the salt circle and directed only me to get in the center. Haven was to stand in front of me outside of the circle, my dad behind me behind the salt. Some witches would wake up feeling a little more powerful today once the souls find their way to their heirs. I would feel less powerful, but more myself. I hoped.

I stood calmly in the center and glanced around at everyone watching me carefully.

"Is this going to hurt?" I asked out loud to anyone that knew the answer.

"It shouldn't, if it becomes too much, then tell us to stop," Callum answered.

"And what if I can't speak?"

"Then, shoot off some purple electricity from your fingers, and we will stop the ritual. I will have Margo looking out for that signal. Here, drink this." He handed me the concoction that was written down on paper. Mugwort, chicory root, and elderberry. Great, that didn't sound good at all, and the smell was not pleasant. "Plug your nose, it'll go down easier."

I nodded and slung it back. I placed the dagger down across the floor in front of me. "Okay, let's do this." Jaxon stood behind Haven staring straight into my soul, or the souls of the others. I wasn't quite sure which.

Haven raised her palms, ready for anything. Callum stood behind me, next to my dad with a book open. I was ready. Eric slung back a shot of the concoction and walked into the salt circle next to me, and I jumped back, scattering the salt by my dad.

"What the hell? Get back," I yelled.

"Hush," he said sternly. "I'm here to help you control the transfer. So, you don't get killed, niece."

"Shut it, I am no family of yours."

"But you are, whether you like it or not."

"Get out, or I'm not doing this."

"Do it with me, or die by being consumed by the evil soul that is trying to eat you alive." He gave me a hard look, and it was a look that made me dare not to argue with him. I looked back to Callum and then to Jaxon, and both of them nodded as if they knew this was the plan all along but had kept it secret from me. Haven looked to him and then back to me and smirked.

"If he does anything, I will obliterate him in the salt circle with the black magic we've been practicing." She lied but had everyone convinced that she knew more than she did. I smiled and played along with her and nodded back. I could feel Eric's eyes burning into me. He shook his head and pulled out a necklace from his pocket and pulled it over his head, straightening my old tourmaline and amethyst necklace around his chest. I flinched as I realized he had a part of me with him, and now that pissed me off. He must've noticed my staring.

"It will keep me connected to you during this transfer. It has your blood in it. Things may get a little dark, so I need you to stay close to me and trust me, neither of us want these souls consuming us."

I huffed at the word trust. How could I trust the man that tried to kill me and my family three months ago? Only that he didn't kill my dad when he had the chance at the bar or my mom while chasing her or even Jaxon's parents. He could've killed me many times and didn't. Maybe he really was living a double life to please Isadora but had another plan all along. My brain ticked away at the seconds. I shook my head and brought myself back to reality.

"Whatever, let's get this over with."

Eric's hand touched my shoulder as I grimaced, wanting to break free of him. *Just focus on getting my Mark back and not on his murderous hands on me.* I closed my eyes as the chanting started.

Chapter Thirty

Freya Chamberlain

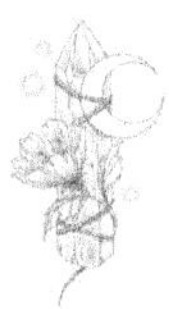

My heart raced as the room started to fade, and the chanting of the surrounding witches became quiet. I could still feel Eric's heavy hand on my shoulder, but I was trying to keep him at arm's length in the small circle. *Just focus.* I slowed my breathing and let the magic do its job. Time to heal my wounds, and be a semi-normal witch again. Breathe.

With my eyes closed, the room became silent, and I could no longer hear voices. My shoulder began to feel lighter. I opened my eyes slowly to see where I was. Shocked. Standing alone in an empty house in a salt circle. What the hell? Where was Eric? So much for helping me. I hesitated before stepping out of the circle and figuring out what I was supposed to do next. I closed my eyes as my foot stepped down on the other side, and I waited for a jolt of lightning to kill me.

Nothing.

I closed my eyes as I stepped completely out. I exhaled

with relief as I opened my eyes and noticed that I was still breathing.

"Thank you to whoever kept me alive, no thanks to Eric, the abandoning asshole," I yelled to the empty house.

The house was quiet. I half expected it to talk back to me. I walked to the kitchen first, then upstairs to Jaxon's old room, I opened each door, and every room was empty. Maybe the spell didn't work, and now I was forever trapped in this purgatory alone. I reached the front door and stepped outside. The world seemed normal, just empty. I literally was alone. Panic started to course through my veins, and I could feel my hope depleting fast.

I looked up and down the eerily empty road and shuddered, ready to be woken back up. I hated being alone. The feeling of being in Crystal Rock alone for who knows how long was terrifying. I grabbed my phone from my back pocket, and of course there was no signal, no power at all. Duh. That was it. I wanted out of here. I raised my hands to the sky and got ready to release some purple electricity to get the hell out of here, but my eyes caught a glimpse of my Mark, and I froze. It was healed. I stared in disbelief and rubbed my skin to make sure it wasn't a mirage. Something was working in here, and for my magic, I was thankful.

A scream broke my stare and brought my attention in the direction of the river where it came from. Deep down I knew I shouldn't run toward the danger, but something inside me told me that was where I was supposed to go. Plus, if that was the only sign of life in this place, then I would need to find it. I ran toward the Mississippi and felt my feet move faster than they would in real life, which was probably some magic trick. I was running as if my supernatural speed was normal. I made it to the river much too quickly. I slowed and steadied my head from overload.

The beach was crowded with people. All walking toward a man, shouting and pushing him into the river where the current was moving, ridiculously fast. He would be washed away for sure, and that would be the end of him. *Eric.* That would be the end of Eric. I smiled at the thought. Then realized, he might be my only chance at making it out of this alive.

"Stop," I yelled, as I reached the front of the crowd, standing in front of Eric, forcing them to go through me to get to him. The witches froze at my sight. An angry scar faced man in front led the rest of them. These were the souls, I honestly had expected floating bubbles not actual faces. I could feel a connection to them all still.

"Let us have him! He was supposed to set us free! He forgot about us!" the man leading the crowd yelled, and everyone started to nod and agree with the man. "He lied to us. All of us."

The scarred man waved toward the crowd, encouraging them to push forward. They started to merge against us again. They were going to push us both in the raging river with whatever monsters lurked in there now. I looked down at a glow that caught my eye, it was my Mark, fully charged and ready to take on the world.

I lifted my arms and said, "Ventus," as I threw them out toward the angry crowd, forcing the wind to push through my fingertips and push back against the crowd. I smiled as I felt my magic returning inside me. Whatever this spell was doing, it was working. Eric held onto my shoulder lending his magic to me. It flowed through me, giving me an extra push against these angry souls.

The crowd stopped yelling, and I stopped the wind gusts and waited for retaliation. When no one moved an inch, Eric finally spoke.

"I have been trying to release you all for a long time. Izzy is still in the mortal world, and she has become more powerful than I ever imagined." Eric spoke cautiously as he walked closer toward the crowd, and I followed. He could need my help again, or maybe I let them eat him alive and I run for the bluffs to send a signal to Callum to get me out of here. I smiled to myself at the thought of it and then shook my head back to this reality that we were in. I needed him. Damnit, I hated saying that, but it was true.

The scarred man stood, now smirking in front of us, his face looked as if he had been through literal hell before being transported here. The closer he got, the better I could see the brutal scar as if it was made by a claw of a dragon itself, jagged and wide. He definitely needed stitches when it was done, but who knew how old he was. The scar went across his face from his eyebrow to his upper lip. Someone did some damage to him. I shuttered at whatever battle he had been in to get here.

"The sacrifice you all have made has not been made in vain. Freya is a syphon, and she was able to take on all of you without killing herself. She is by far the strongest witch I know. We are here to release you to your rightful homes."

The scarred man now glared back at me as if ready to kill me.

The crowd began to whisper to one another, and the hope started to fill my thoughts.

"Prove it," a woman in the back yelled.

I stepped forward to show them my syphoning trick and then the lady said, "Prove how she can release us."

Shit. I didn't know how to do that.

Eric turned toward me and whispered, "We need to show them something."

I shook my head. What the hell did he want from me? He was supposed to be the mastermind.

"Just follow in my steps, confidently, please," he whispered, and something inside me said to trust him.

He looked out to the crowd and pointed at a tanned skin female with long black hair, a little older than myself, and called to her. "Ember, come here." The beautiful woman smiled and walked toward us. Beautiful hair, high cheekbones, bright blue eyes that could make any human melt, and a positive energy radiating from her. This woman had to be part goddess, there was no way two humans produced her. She reached us, and Eric leaned into her, kissing her cheeks. "Hello, my dear. I'm sorry I took so long."

She smiled and shook her head. "I knew you would come back for me." Her childish voice was familiar. I tried to place where I recognized it from. My mind was swimming with too much information still, and I was having a hard time placing reality, dreams, visions right now. "Hi, Freya."

Who was this woman, and what did he plan on doing to her? I smiled at her before a sickness consumed me as I realized he wanted me to release her soul. I had no idea what I was doing. Plus, I couldn't even release the souls when Isadora needed me to save lives back at JFK. So, how would I do it now?

"Hold her hand," he said quietly. He grabbed her other one. "Freya, send our beautiful friend here back to her rightful place among the living." He yelled loud enough for the crowd.

I looked at him and my eyes felt like they were going to leave their sockets, and anger filled my face making me turn red. I was too warm now, dizziness from my blood pressure rising. He stared at me and gave me a look to do it now. I took a deep breath in and tried to calm my nerves while I closed my eyes and pretended to know what I was doing. I was clueless. I felt her hand fade and then the crowd murmured frantically. I opened my eyes and peered down at my empty hand and then to Eric, who was smiling.

"See, I told you. She is who we have been waiting for," he said to the crowd of souls, who all cheered loudly. He just made me out to be something that I was not, or at least I had zero clue what I just did. "Now she needs to rest until the red moon rises. This is a big crowd for her to take on." He grabbed my arm gently, and we walked off the beach as the souls were thanking me while walking past and smiling. Except for the scar faced man. He was glaring at us as we walked past, making the pit in my stomach grow.

Eric and I walked silently back to Jaxon's home, and I just kept staring at my visible Mark and wondering how the heck I did any of that. Where did she go? Is she safe? Did I kill that poor girl?

We reached the door and walked inside, only we were not alone this time. I gasped as I saw Ember sitting across the room on the couch, smiling. I looked back at Eric who pushed me through the door toward her.

"What the hell, Eric?" I screamed.

"Quiet down, we are not out of this yet."

I looked around the home and outside the windows to the road. It was just us.

"Start talking," I threatened with my flames coming out of my palms effortlessly.

Ember laughed and waved for me to come sit next to her on the couch. I hesitated before walking toward her. She had very inviting eyes, and something told me she was good. I sat down next to her and stared.

"How are you still here?" I asked her.

"Oh, it's a simple magic trick, I'm a teleporter. Only problem was once I jumped into the dagger two years ago, Eric was supposed to get me back out, and I haven't heard from him until today. I knew he would come for me. I trust him with my life. So, I waited here."

My mind froze as I realized two years ago, my mother and Aunt Clara took the dagger from him and ran to hide it. *Shit.* They were the reason she was stuck here.

"So, wait, you're not dead?"

"Oh gosh, no. I mean, I hope not. My body should still be back home with my mom, Oxana." She glanced at Eric and questioned him with her stare.

"Yes, of course it is. Your mother would never give up on you."

"What took you so long anyway?" she asked him, slapping his arm. As if her tiny frame could hurt him.

Eric ignored the slaps as if he was used to her playfulness. "Izzy. Then, a pair of Anchors stole the dagger, and we have only just recently got it back."

She frowned at his words. "Those bastards," she said, and I sunk lower into the seat, not wanting to admit it was my own family. "Took you long enough. I was almost ready to give up on you and end it myself. That one soul here is feisty, as evil as they come. Worse than Izzy."

"That's why we're here. The souls. Freya syphoned them from the dagger, and they are consuming her. Her Mark is fading in the real world. I don't think she has long. It has to be him, he must be getting stronger."

"Who?" I interrupted.

They both ignored me as Ember nodded, then looked toward me and held out her hand for my arm. She examined my Mark, and nodded again. "Yes, the evil one is holding tight to her. We can release the souls from her, but we will have to make sure he does not get out of here. He will burn the world down, both magic and none." She paused. "We need to go see my mother."

Eric inhaled slowly. "I was hoping we could do this without her. She's not very fond of me, and once she realizes that Izzy is no longer on my team, she may not help us. Plus, she hates men, not just me."

"She is my mother, she will help me, and since I trust you, she will have to too." She giggled like a child before walking over to kiss Eric on the lips. I wanted to vomit. Who could love such an evil man, a murderer? Bile grew in the back of my throat as I stood up and walked to the kitchen.

Who the hell was Oxana and why did we need her?

Eric walked into the kitchen and scared me as he creeped up behind me.

"Let me guess, another lover that you will screw over?" I pointed back to the living room.

"Ember?" He laughed. "She is young but brilliant. She knows my heart lies with Aislynn, or Lynn to you. She is merely a business partner who loves to be loved."

"You can't honestly love Aunt Lynn after all these years, so why drag her along?"

"She has been the only woman I have ever loved."

"Bullshit." I turned furious with the lies and pushed him back into the wall with my flame igniting an inch from his face. "You left her for another woman and made a child. You disgust me."

He grimaced and slowly grabbed my wrist, extinguishing my fire with ice. Seemed like his magic was recharging in here too.

"You don't know shit," Eric said and pushed me backwards against the opposite wall. "Lynn was my world, Izzy took her from me. She used a glamour spell one night and mirrored my Aislynn in every way. It wasn't until the next morning when we woke that I realized it was Izzy. It was too late. I knew we had conceived. I could feel it in my bones. I couldn't believe that my childhood friend could do something so cruel to me. I then knew that I had to tell the woman I loved that I would not abandon my unborn child. Just took me a long time to let her go. Aislynn discovered my secret and found out for herself as the only true part of the story goes." He stepped back and straightened his suit. "I have spent a thousand years with her broken hearted face in my mind, knowing that I shattered her. Three months ago, seeing her alive was the best day of my life. Of course, that was short lived when you sealed me in that cave, but I had her sweet face to see while I slept. Three months, waiting to talk to her again, while Izzy screamed and went crazy next to me. Like I said, you don't know shit." He let go of my wrists and backed away.

I stood silently. Trying to understand his pain, but there had been too much between us. I couldn't feel sorry for him now. I couldn't hear another word, so I needed to change the subject.

"Do you actually know how to set the souls free?"

He cleared his throat and slicked his hair back.

"Callum is working on that on the outside. We just need to keep the charades going in here until he shows us the sign. The moon will be blood red, and that will help you release them. They are speeding up time for us here, so we can harness that power from the moon to help you with the release. The red moon will be here by the end of the month. If we do not stop Izzy now, then she will use that to her advantage to get what she wants." He hesitated. "If Izzy gets to Oxana first or gets the dagger back, then she will consume the souls, and she will be unstoppable, even by me."

"Well, let's not let that happen."

"Easier said than done, you can't underestimate her."

"She's one person against an army," I said annoyed.

"She is her own army."

His words shook me. I thought he was the powerful one. But then I remembered that Isadora did syphon from him in the cave so maybe he was right. Maybe she was a hundred to one. *Shit.*

"What does Oxana have to do with any of this?" I asked, trying not to think about our winning odds.

Ember walked into the kitchen as if she was listening and waiting for her cue to shine.

"My mom has the amulet that we need to contain Izzy with. Kind of like this prison world. We were supposed to use it on her two years ago once I was safe in here, but of course, the dagger went missing. My mom felt betrayed by Eric thinking he took me, so she banished him from the reservation. So... long story short, once I'm home, she will give him the amulet to trap Izzy in it for good, and I can finally live a life outside of the reservation and be free."

My jaw dropped. Eric had a plan all along, and he was planning on going against Isadora, only my mom and Aunt Clara ruined his plan. And no wonder why he wanted the dagger so badly. It was never to kill Anchors, it was to get Ember out of this realm. My family was the reason we were in this mess to begin with.

"Your voice, where do I know—"

She laughed, "Your dream was weird. I was just trying to get in your head and nudge that stubborn brain of yours to get here. I knew you were strong, but your stubbornness is almost as bad as Eric's." She giggled, and Eric laughed with her.

I glared at him.

"Told you," he said.

"Wait, why were you in this realm to begin with?"

"Two reasons. One, to check on the souls, mainly the good ones. Two, to make sure our amulet was identical to hold her in hers once she was contained I needed to make sure both worlds held them. My mom was friends with her as a child, but even she has become irritated with Izzy's actions over the centuries. So, two years ago, she believed it was time to lock her away."

"Why not just put her in this dagger?"

"This place was created by Ragnar's wife, for him and him alone," Ember announced.

"He's the evil one?" I asked.

"Yes, unfortunately, this world is starting to collapse. Ragnar has started to regain power from all the extra souls in here. He is not one you want to cross paths with. This dagger was meant to hold one soul and one soul only. So, you can see why we are bursting at the seams here." She paused, realizing this was all new to me. "We must release these souls before Ragnar consumes more of them and then we will need to have Izzy locked away in her own prison world. The amulet. It was forged of fire and dragon's blood about a thousand years ago just for her. My mother has stayed alive a few centuries by wearing the amulet. She stays ageless and beautiful with it on. She would like to pass the immortality on to me, but only once Izzy is contained."

"Dragon's what? Wait, she's immortal too? How many Immortals are there?" I thought of Margo's necklace and realized that there was more magic in this world than I could ever imagine.

"Well, my mom is immortal because of the amulet, and without it, she will start aging naturally again. Eric and Isadora are because of that magic dagger and these souls. Those are the only ones I know of. Unless you know of more?" She looked to me, then to Eric, who was giving me a look to shut the hell up. "I mean, I'm not immortal, I was made out of both of my mother's blood and a piece of a Jasper fossil that was split in half. The witching world blessed my mothers with me as a thank you for protecting the amulet for this long and probably wanted an extra person to pass it on to when they are ready. My mother is getting tired, and she wants to live the rest of her life with her wife this time. My other mother is just a normal witch, with a short hundred-year life if she's lucky."

Holy shit. So, she didn't know about Margo or my dad, which by the look Eric had given me, made me realize that he intended on keeping that our secret. I stared at Ember, trying to find her flaw, but she looked so human, so real. I reached my hand out to touch her for confirmation that she wasn't a mirage. She giggled when my fingers brushed her skin.

"I'm real enough, just wasn't born naturally. Basically, I was a test tube baby with a little bit of magic." She smiled and played with her long black hair, twirling it.

"How do we know that Isadora hasn't gone after your mom already? Now that she has her syphoning back."

Eric interrupted, "We don't. That's why we should've done this last night, but you needed your rest, or this world would be crumbling from the inside out even more."

As soon as he said it, the entire Crystal Rock shook. An earthquake shivered through the ground. I grabbed the side of the counter and balanced myself. *Shit.*

"What the hell was that?" I yelled.

"The dagger is crumbling. They need to hurry up out there. I don't know how much time we have."

"How long until the red moon is ready?"

"Hopefully soon. Time works differently here. We just

have to keep a low profile until then. Once we get Ember, me, and you out of here then we can get to Oxana."

"What about the other souls here?" I asked, confused by the plan.

"I'm not worried about them right now. I just need to get Ember out of here. The rest we can work on later. They won't be consuming you anymore."

Anger rushed across my face, and I could feel my blood boiling. He had no intentions on saving them, he was saving Ember as a bargaining chip.

"The souls can stay here for the time being. Once we have Izzy locked away, then we can worry about separating them from Ragnar to their rightful places. But they are not my priority right now, so if it comes down to saving you and Ember, then so be it. They've waited this long. They can wait another week."

The entire world shook as soon as he said the words. This place was collapsing. We needed to get everyone out, except Ragnar. My adrenaline pulsed with anger, and I made it a personal choice to make sure each soul would be saved either with or without him tonight. "Can the souls survive in our world?"

He froze at my question.

"Can they?" I screamed at him now. "Answer me!" I now felt like it was my duty to save these souls from this crumbling prison world and hoped that it would keep holding together for Ragnar to stay.

"Yes, I think so. But we don't have time or energy for that kind of transfer right now. And what if Izzy realizes the house has souls there, she will have a whole new power source. They need to stay in the dagger world for now."

"You mean the collapsing world."

The ground shook again, "It's only collapsing more because you are here with so much power, and Ragnar can sense that. The sooner we get Ember out of here, the better."

My hands trembled, realizing there were too many unknowns and too many risks and the thought of the souls being consumed by Isadora would make her unstoppable, pissed me off even more. I needed to do everything I could to make sure that woman would get no more power, but I also needed to save these souls from collapsing into blackness. "What happens if she consumes the souls?"

He shrugged, "Then, it's all over for everyone."

I walked to the sink and turned the cold water on to splash my face with, trying to let the water cool me down before I did anything I would regret. My mind spun at the thought of Eric trying to take her down years ago. If my mom and aunt would've never taken the dagger, then my mom never would've had to leave. None of this would've happened. Maybe 1 wouldn't be a witch, or maybe I wouldn't know Haven. I guess, you had to take the good with the bad.

"Why didn't you just tell my mom about this? Why chase her away from her home? From her family," I asked Eric, feeling unsure of what would've been the right thing to do.

"I wasn't chasing her." He hesitated, inhaling deeply and letting it out slowly. "I had to get her away from my brother. Izzy was getting too close to town, and I was afraid that she might trigger his Mark. Her obsession with power was consuming her, I couldn't take a chance with Jim. He was the only good part of me I had left from my past. He's the only one who knew the good in me, and I needed him to remind me of that once Izzy was gone. So, I grabbed Clara to get Alexandra's attention. Only she caught me off guard and took the dagger. The plan crumbled from then on. I had to be careful around Izzy, or she would've suspected the betrayal. I had to play along and keep her away from your dad, and it actually played out well."

"Besides the fact that you nearly destroyed my family and nearly killed Jaxon and me."

"That truck driver wasn't me," he spat out, defensively. "You think I would kill the only niece I thought I had? Had I known you were a twin, then we could've done so much more. But even so, why would I kill my own family?" His jaw clenched, and his eyes were filled with anger. "I tried to save everyone from Izzy. Only everyone kept getting in the way. When you had her at the cottage, I was angry. I thought you all just ruined the only hope I had to get everyone out alive. I never would've killed you, I just needed you to calm down with your magic. You were a killing machine that day, and I'm glad you let me live because I knew you could've ended me the minute I saw you walk out of the cottage doorway. You had the look of your ancestors in your eyes, and we were warriors. You could've killed me then and probably even still right now."

I smiled when I realized I had the strength to scare him or kill him or at least, I did then. That power will be gone soon once I lose these souls' borrowed magic. The power was not mine to keep, though, and I knew that. It never belonged to me.

"You could've killed me without magic that day." He smirked as if reading my mind.

"I had the help of all these souls. That will be gone soon."

"No, Freya. You have more power than you even know. So does your sister. That's why Izzy is so powerful. She stole her sister's magic, and now with her syphoning back, she is stronger than all of us. So maybe together, you and Haven could do some viable damage, but apart... our chances are slim. Unless you consume Haven's magic too, then that would be a fair fight between you and Izzy."

"Absolutely not!"

"Well, of course not."

Ember was sitting quietly on the countertop, looking back and forth between us as we spoke. She was pretending to throw air popcorn in her mouth. She cleared her throat and my eyes focused on her little frame. She was smiling and looking back at me. Giggling.

"She doesn't know, does she?" she asked Eric while never taking her eyes off of me.

"Know what?" I asked.

"The Anchor twins are the most powerful together. It's been a thousand years since we have seen a pair like you with a Mark. And you have like the brightest aura surrounding you that I have ever seen. I can't wait to see your sister's." She giggled and walked away.

I laughed out loud and looked at Eric. "What is she talking about?"

"Ember is different. She can teleport through dimensions, she can see auras, and she has visions, only her visions are more like prophecies. She can see the future.

Only the future continues to change. She saw Alexandra pregnant, which brought me back to town. My brother had produced an heir. I had to see for myself. Alexandra thought I wanted to keep the child for myself, when reality was I wanted to protect you. Had I known there were two of you, then we could've saved the world from Izzy eighteen years ago. The universe took long enough to help us out."

"Well, had I known that I was a witch and that you weren't trying to kill us, maybe we could've worked together." I looked back toward the direction Ember had walked off in, after giving Eric my very own hate stare. Ember was something, that was for sure. Maybe she was the most powerful one, and she didn't even know it yet herself. She seemed to be the whole package. "I'm going to get some air."

I walked out the back door and went to the edge of the yard where the metal picket fence met with the empty neighbors' home behind them. I looked up to the sky and realized that time did move differently here. The sky should've been early morning or so, but instead, it was already past noon. Hopefully, the red moon would be up soon, and we would have a short window to succeed in the soul transferring and Ember freeing plan. I inhaled and let the cool air make my lungs shudder while expanding wider than a normal breath would handle. I closed my eyes and sat down on the grass leaning against the fence, letting the earth lend me some energy to feel connected to myself again.

"Haven?" a voice whispered from behind me, making me jump up and walk backwards toward the house. "Wait," she said, a little louder. "Please." Her eyes were pleading for me to stay. I just didn't know who was in here, or if I could trust anyone, including Eric. I studied her face and realized she looked familiar.

"Freya," I answered and pointed to myself, still leaning toward the house. "Do I know you?"

"Of course, you are the twin. My boy is dating Haven. I see your face, or hers, in his mind when he tries to connect with his magic. He is so afraid of it, though. I feel him fading further away. Do you know why?"

"Ezra?" I asked, trying to put the pieces together. "You're his mother." I answered my own question. "He doesn't have his Mark yet."

Questioning eyes looked at me as she shook her head. "Impossible. He had his Mark as a child, he was born with it. I had to glamour it to disappear to keep us in hiding, which should be long gone by now." She pointed to her own forearm and traced a symbol "His magic has always been with him, we just didn't know who his Anchor was. It was as if they were being hidden from us too." She stepped closer to the fence, and I realized I was mimicking her, meeting her in the middle. Her eyes were kind, but her face was sad. She was taken from our world and away from her child and for what? For Eric and Isadora to gain power.

"I'm so sorry that you are here." I shook my head, angered that she too had lost time with her child too.

"Oh, honey, no. I came here willingly."

My eyes grew wider with shock. Who in their right mind would do that?

"Eric gave me the option, he didn't want to do it, but Izzy wasn't giving him a chance. She would've killed me in cold blood like my husband, but instead, Eric told her he wanted to do the honors, and when she walked away, he told me about the dagger and this world. He promised to try and find a way to bring me back, or at least save my magic and soul from being wasted."

"Why not fight him off?" I blurted out without thinking.

Her eyes became full of tears. "There was no fighting them off. Izzy was killing for fun, and she was unbelievably strong. She was on the hunt for the child who could give her the sections of the Jasper fossil, so she could make her own child. When she found out Oxana did it, then she went crazy. Killing frenzy to get the one thing she desired. Her own child."

So, these people here had no idea about Aisling and her being a descendant, either. I inhaled sharply and let her words sink in. I watched her lips closely as she talked because every word reminded me of Ezra. He was a spitting image of her. I would have to tell him all about this when we get back.

"Did Clara come for him?" Her question brought me back to focus.

"Yes, she did. She made sure to help raise him right along with his foster parents."

She nodded and smiled wide. "Please, do me a favor and tell him that I am always with him, and his magic should come out to play. He will remember me saying that to him as a child. Hopefully that makes him want to be who he was meant to be."

I agreed and smiled back at her. Guilt started to brew inside me, knowing that Eric's plan wasn't fully intended on saving the souls, but to keep them in this prison world. We needed to set them free. This was beyond me, though, I didn't know the first thing about souls.

"I should've known it was you and not Haven. I remember when we pushed Izzy into the exploding wall, and I laughed inside here, happy that I was finally able to help with the revenge for my husband's death." She laughed, and I smiled back at her.

"Yeah, the strength you all gave me was a little intense. Thank you, otherwise I would've been dead that day." I shivered at the thought.

"You are stronger than you think. I don't think you needed us at all." Her hand touched my arm, and warmth radiated from her. I could feel her intentions were pure, and everything about her was pure innocence. She did not belong here. She belonged in the normal world with Ezra. My heart felt ready to shatter. I needed to bring her back.

"There has to be a way to bring you back. Magic has limits, but there can always be a loophole, right?"

"Oh, darling. I appreciate your intentions. My body has been dead for too long. I know it is just my soul left, and I am ready to be freed at this point. I want to pass my magic on to my boy and be free. But Ragnar can escape this place in full form since it was intended for his actual body."

I felt tears starting to build in the corner of my eyes and shook my head, not ready to give up. "There has to be another way."

"Just keep my boy safe and make him brave enough to use his magic again. You will be amazed at what he can do. My magic will not transfer to him without his Mark visible and then all of this time spent here will be for nothing."

The door to the house opened and Eric stood in the doorway. "Freya, you should get inside. We have work to do." I waved him off, annoyed at his interruption.

"She can come in too." He nodded toward Ezra's mom. She smiled and waved to Eric.

I had her walk to the gate and open it for her, letting her inside the house to join us. If she was here, then were Declan's parents here too? I made a mental note to ask Eric when we were alone. To meet Ezra's mom, though, was already a bonus on coming here today. I hoped that I could help heal his heart with her words, and I really hoped that I could save her and bring her home with us.

Chapter Thirty-One

Jaxon Oakes

They had been in that trance for too long, this shit was starting to piss me off. At least she looked peaceful, as if she were sleeping, but for fuck's sake, why were we trusting Eric to help her in there? Uncle or not, he couldn't be trusted. He tried to kill all of us and had been the nightmare of stories for centuries.

I paced back and forth in my old home and decided I needed some space. I walked up the creaking steps to my old room and sat down in the middle of the floor. I looked around at the empty walls and smiled at how many good memories were made in this room and this home. This house would always be a good memory.

I sat quietly and enjoyed the silence, looking around the empty room. I remembered when Freya and Aisling would sneak out and meet me in the backyard, tossing twigs and pebbles at the window, waiting for me to realize they were waiting. We would go down by the river and stay up until sunrise just bullshitting while Freya sat with me, and her warmth would make my heart feel whole. Ais would always end up skipping rocks across the river, complaining about boys that couldn't plan a date to her standards or that didn't have any style. I used to feel bad for any man that would end up dating her, until she met Declan. He was perfect for her. She needed someone who would let her do all the planning and just go along with it. She liked being in control. Her heart was always happier when she was making others happy, and Declan loved not having to plan anything, he liked the guidance as to what to do. They were polar opposites, but somehow, they worked. Thankfully, I liked Declan, because if I had to spend time with another couple and the man was a douchebag, then I would have a problem. At least he was friends with me first, and I knew what type of guy he was for Aisling.

Geez.

How much longer? I could only keep my mind distracted for so long. I stood up and walked to the window and stared out toward the river. A knock on the door pulled my attention back to reality, and I looked up to see Ezra walking in.

"Do you mind if I join you?"

I nodded and waved him in, annoyed that I was interrupted from enjoying the peace and quiet but secretly thankful for the company to help distract my thoughts.

"Haven has been in that trance for what feels like forever." He shook his head. "I feel useless."

"Same here, bro. Both the girls are basically in a coma until that red moon is ready in there."

The room became silent, and I waited for him to say

something. I looked back to him and saw that he was struggling with something.

"What's up, man? You've got something on your mind?" I asked.

"With everything going on, I feel like I'm failing Haven." His words were not what I expected.

I shook my head, "Failing how?"

"If I let my magic back in, then I can protect her more. But if I let my magic back in, then my Anchor is going to get between us."

"What the hell are you talking about? It doesn't work like that."

"I know who my Anchor is, and if I let my Mark come back, then I'm afraid the connection will ruin my relationship with Haven. There is a bond with your Anchor, like how Eric and Izzy are drawn to each other. For a thousand years, no matter how psycho she may have become, he had to save her back at Clara's house. He had every urge to protect her when she was in danger, and I'm afraid that the bond I have with my Anchor may ruin what I have with Haven."

"So, don't let it. Ezra. You love Haven. No one will get in the way of that."

"She will."

She?

"Who?" I asked.

He shook his head. "I can't bring my magic back." He pulled out his elixir and slung it back like a shot of bourbon, exhaling after he swallowed.

"Ezra, man. We are going to need your help to win this

fight. I'm pretty sure that suppressing your magic might get yourself killed, or even worse, Haven killed." I hoped that my words would at least sink into him and let him ponder that. "I can't force you to do that, but I'm pretty sure that your magic didn't kill your parents. Don't let yourself get killed over something you had no control over."

He stayed silent.

"Ezra, who is it?"

He stepped back and hesitated before walking out of the room.

I shook my head, not understanding why anyone would want to hide their magic in the world we lived in. He could do so much good if he just let it in.

I let myself soak in the quiet a little longer before heading back downstairs. My mom was sitting in the empty kitchen on the only wicker chair that was left since we moved, sifting through herbs and bottles of elixirs that she brought from the safehouse. She looked up at me when the damn floorboard creaked in the usual spot. I always swore that was the board I tried to avoid when sneaking back into the house. It could wake up the whole town. She laughed.

"You could never avoid that plank."

"You guys never fixed it." I laughed back.

"It was my way of knowing when your hands were in the cookie jar as a child and then when you would sneak back in when you got older. It was my personal alarm for you." She smiled and waved for me to come over by her, hugging me tight when I reached arm's length. It felt nice. Three months ago, I thought I would never have this comfort again. It made me realize what Freya had gone through with losing her mother and then me. I felt like I could finally relate to her. Here I was, thinking that Freya knew everything that was happening, and instead, she thought I was dead. I let the thought bury itself again and just embraced the hug.

"I missed you, Mom," I said quietly, afraid that if I said the words too loud that I would wake up from this dream and she would be gone again.

"Oh, honey, I am so sorry for not letting you in on this. We had to stay away. My sister has a brilliant mind, and I could not let her know differently. I have avoided her for a thousand years, and I couldn't run into her now."

"You wanted us to kill her?"

"No, I wanted Eric to bring her back to me. The unlinking spell was ready. We just needed Jim to wake up his Mark, that was the final step. But Eric never came back for us with him and the herbs for the spell lost their potency. We didn't know who had won, and if Izzy saw me alive, then everything would have gone to shit. All the years of planning and being careful would've been for nothing. Once that link is broken and I get my healing powers back, then I can take this necklace off and start aging again. It's time to live a semi-normal life alongside your father. The timing is finally perfect." She grabbed the Labradorite stone and tucked it under her shirt.

I smiled sadly. I didn't want to think about a life without my parents again. Living three months without them was enough. But I knew that in life most parents did not outlive their children. "Let's just make it through this week first, okay?" I put my arm around her and pulled her closer to me.

"I'm sorry about everything with Freya. I'll admit it was

my own jealousy of her mother that made me so protective of you. I just was afraid that she would hurt you. Especially when Alexandra walked away from Jim so quickly. I tried to find her for the first few months to explain our plan, but she was one good hiding witch. Then, after the accident, I knew Izzy was getting closer. I couldn't risk any more exposure with our family. We had to leave."

"Mom, can we just not think about the past right now? I'm more concerned about our future. Freya is in my life, and I'm not going to lose her again. And maybe Alex deserves an apology."

"Maybe you're right." She smiled. "You sound so much like Jim does with Alexandra." She sighed. "I get it. Love is love. The connection is undeniable. You two have that bond, and I know I should be happy. I just worry, and I have a hard time letting you go. I've spent a thousand years without a child and then when I met your father, my whole world changed. I will do anything to protect you, at whatever cost. One day, when you have children, you will understand."

"Let's just hope we get to that one day, Mom." My eyes were met through the kitchen window at a set of eyes glaring back at me. "Shit, she's here." I stood up and braced myself, blocking my mother.

Isadora was standing on the other side of the house and raised her palms toward the windows. A screech escaped her throat, and a flash of blinding light came toward us, shattering the windows, throwing me back against the counter. I coughed up blood, gasping for air. "No," I choked out, as I ran to the doorway to check on Freya and the circle. We couldn't let her get in here.

The circle was still intact, the girls still in a trance with Eric. My dad ran to the corners of the house, whispering gibberish that I couldn't understand. The pennies were all still stacked. He looked up for the first time in my life with fear in his eyes.

"Jax, where's your mother?"

I looked around the room and realized that I left her there alone. *Shit.*

"Mom?" I yelled and ran back into the kitchen with glass shards everywhere. Isadora was not inside the home, but she had my mother levitating against the kitchen wall by pure force. My mom's hands were being held against her chest, and she was unable to get loose.

"Mom!" I yelled and ran toward her, trying to release the hold on her.

"Mom?" Isadora said with a shocked expression. "Oh, no, you don't. Back up now, or she dies."

"You would kill your own sister?" I questioned, hoping that some form of humanity would trigger something good inside her. The darkness that reached her face told me otherwise.

"I killed her once, why not again? Makes sense why my syphoning was taken from me so long ago. She defeated death. She's the whole reason why my powers were weakened. Time to finish what I started," she said from the doorway and tried to break the barrier spell that was surrounding the house. Frustrated, she pulled my mom toward the doorway, a shimmering blade in hand.

Fuck that!

I jumped in between them and pushed my mom back further away from her grasp, getting one of her hands loose from the magic hold. My mom twisted her wrist behind me and aimed it toward Isadora, sending pure energy into her.

Isadora stumbled back and then pushed her body back against the barrier and started to pound on the invisible shield. The whole house vibrated from her strength. Damn, if she kept this up, the entire house would collapse and the souls would fly in all directions once they were released. She has taken so much. My hand grazed my scar where she had stabbed me the other day. Anger coursed through my veins, and I could feel a side of magic coming out of me that I didn't know I had. I lifted my palms and felt the earth listening to my request to borrow from it, and I lifted the ground she stood on, including the entire house. I stayed focused and levitated the home a football field off the ground. If our neighbors thought we were weird before, they would most definitely know something was up now. Fear shot across Isadora's face for the first time, and finally, I felt strong enough.

"Leave now!" I yelled.

Her expression changed back to hard bitch. "Oh, sweet nephew of mine that my sister has kept hidden from me. Selfish, really. What are you going to do? Earth me to death like your pathetic father?" She wickedly laughed, her fear now being masked.

No words were needed. I was just pissed. I took the house and its foundation she stood on and spun it into a sickening tornado, giving her no other option, except to hold onto the side of the broken shutter that was left hanging by one nail. One more gust of wind would let her fly like the witch she was all the way across Wisconsin. I felt my magic inside me start to poison my veins, I was no longer borrowing from the earth, but I was tapping into something much darker. I started to not feel like myself. *To hell with her and Eric's link. I'm going to kill her now. Eric with her.*

My mom grabbed my shoulder, and the dark thoughts started to subside as I looked toward my mom. I inhaled sharply as a flash of light flew from my chest straight into Isadora, sending her swirling through the sky as the house slowed and leveled back down onto the ground. I looked to my mom, questioning her own magic.

What the hell just happened?

My chest burned with too much oxygen as my mom shared her magic with me. I felt like I was going to hyperventilate. I steadied my breathing and stood back up.

"What was that?"

She shifted her body back toward me and inhaled sharply. "I just lent you some strength. Simple, really."

My own mom knew how to release magic? Why hadn't she said anything sooner to help Freya? Did she know an easier way to release the souls? Did she know more than she was telling everyone? What were her true intentions? Frustration consumed me.

"Why didn't you help Freya?"

"I can't."

"Why?" I yelled. My guard was up, feeling betrayed. "We have been trying to find a way to release those souls from her since she consumed them over three months ago. And here, all along, you knew how to transfer magic? What else do you know how to do?"

"It doesn't work that way, I can only lend to my own blood. You and her." She pointed toward the now broken wall, shaking her head. "My magic has been faulty without my healing powers." Tears rolled down her cheeks, and I realized how mean I was being to her after her sister had just tried to kill her, again. I grabbed her and pulled her in close. Protective of her broken heart. Isadora had no good left inside of her. Her soul was dark, and she needed to be gone from our world.

My dad ran into the kitchen, staring at the shattered windows. "Are you guys okay?"

"Yes, we're fine," my mom answered.

"The circle?" I asked, worriedly.

"Fine, yes. All good."

I nodded with relief.

"Was it her?" he asked.

"Unfortunately," I said while nodding.

"I could use some help in the circle. That tornado kind of sped up my watch, and now I don't know if we are ready for the transfer in the next few minutes. But if Izzy is coming back, then we don't have much of a choice."

We gathered ourselves and walked into the room with him. Everyone seemed to be recovering from the spin.

"Sorry," I said to everyone, as they collected themselves.

Aisling laughed, "I guess you are stronger than you thought."

"Yeah, bro. What the hell was that?" Declan asked, smirking.

"I was angry." I shrugged.

They laughed as Aisling took her place back at the

corner for penny patrol and Declan stood beside her, protectively.

"Stay angry," Aisling said, before turning her head back around, focusing on her job until the transfer was over.

I smiled and wished the strength would stay.

Chapter Thirty-Two

Freya Chamberlain

There was a shift in this dimension we were in. I felt like I was going to puke. My head was spinning, something was off. I looked to Eric who was leaning over the railing of the steps, looking just as green as I felt.

"What's with you two?" Ember questioned.

"Something must be happening in the real world, my bets are on Izzy. How about you?" Eric said, standing back up, running his hands through his hair and straightening his suit.

"My bets match," I whispered, letting fear wash over me. What if she hurt someone I loved while I was stuck in this place with her ex-mate? *Ugh.* "Let's just get this over with."

"I have one more stop to make before the red moon starts." He walked toward the door, opening it. I followed him, out of curiosity. "No, you stay here."

"No, I come with you, or you don't go." I flicked my hand in the air, slamming the door shut and letting electricity trickle through my fingertips. It felt good to have my magic back, I just had to let my emotions help control the power.

He smirked and exhaled heavily. "You are your father's daughter." He laughed. "Alright, but no sidetracking. Time isn't our friend today." He pointed to the sky as the sun was setting at an unnatural speed.

I nodded and opened the door with the flick of my wrist again. I had to admit that my magic was back and felt amazing again. I thought without the power of the souls I would feel weak, but instead, each minute I felt my body getting stronger. As if the souls were consuming me like a parasite and now my body was healing. I could kill him if I wanted to. I smiled at the idea of what I thought was to myself as we walked down the stairs.

"What are you smiling for?" Eric asked me.

My smile disappeared, and the hard look came back. I rolled my eyes and kept walking silently.

He laughed. "Okay, little Jimmy. I have to admit, I'm jealous my brother got to raise a child and I didn't."

I huffed at his arrogance. "You have Declan."

"I meant, my own child."

"He is your child. Parents don't have to be blood. Parents are who raise you and do it right." I walked further ahead of him, not wanting to have a conversation with him about something he obviously had no idea about.

"Declan was not meant to be with me. He was an accident."

I stopped walking and turned to face him. Furious. "Declan is a great man, and he has a heart of gold, and if you think for a second that he is a waste of space in your life, then you are the exact piece of shit that I thought you were." My finger was now pointing into his face, shaking with anger. He pushed it aside and smiled.

"I'm glad you think so highly of him. As do I. Are you sure he's not the one that sparks your heart?" he asked, making me grimace at the thought. "Accident, meaning his parents weren't supposed to be there that night."

I stepped back and looked into his eyes. They looked sincere, so I gave him a minute. "Explain."

"There was a fire at their home. I had happened to be taking a night walk, pondering on what my next plan with my brother would be. Knowing that he was now a father and to wake him up would turn his whole life upside down, and with his Mark back, he would show up on the map again. Making him go on the run, along with Alex this time. I couldn't let Izzy find him. So, I had to wait, let him live a mundane life for a little while until things were closer to being set in place. Only life started to distract us all from our missions." He cleared his throat and exhaled slowly. "Declan's parents were stuck in their home that had caught fire, and it was collapsing. Izzy was walking away from the scene, she had started it. I knew what she had been looking for, and it wasn't there. Another family already had the other fossil half, protecting it from her. So, I ran in. I heard the screams of a woman and a child crying. When I reached the woman, she pleaded for me to help get the wooden beam off her already dead husband. I knew it was a waste of time, but I did it anyway at her request. When I leaned over to help lift the beam another portion of the house started to collapse onto us. She screamed and pointed toward the closet, where the cries were coming from. I ran to the door and saw a dark-haired, blue-eyed toddler sitting there, crying while holding his blanket. I reached for him, and a part of me went soft. A part of me remembered the little boy I lost centuries ago. His mother—"

A woman walked up behind us and made me jump. Eric blocked me, protectively.

"Pleaded for him to save the child, just take him and save him. Eric tried to be a hero and lifted both my son and me to carry us out of the house, but the ceiling collapsed, and a beam tragically pierced into me. Making my escape impossible. Instead of Eric leaving me to die a lonely and painful death, he used the dagger and brought me to this place instantly. No pain, just peace. So, here I have been, able to watch over my sweet boy grow up in his dreams. Eric saved my soul that night and raised my boy for me." She smiled as she reached us. "I'm Grace, Declan's mom."

I took a step toward her and examined her features. I could definitely see a resemblance, but Declan must look a lot like his dad too. I smiled back at her.

"Declan is sweet. He dates my best friend."

"Aisling, yes, she is going to keep him on the right track. Strong woman, maybe a little bossy." We both laughed, and I nodded.

"Dreams, huh?" I questioned, nervous that my ancestors were spying on me too.

"More like glimpses. I can only see what he lets me see. His subconscious does the rest."

"Hm, kind of weird, but I like that he has his own guardian with him." I grabbed her arm and pulled her ahead of Eric and whispered, "So, Eric really saved you?"

She nodded and smiled. "So, I shouldn't kill him?" Her eyes widened in horror.

"He's legally my son's father now. So, please don't. Although, I have seen your magic, and I know you could do it, but I'd prefer you to let him live." She patted my back, and Eric joined us, as we walked back toward the house.

"Glad you finally made it back here," she said to Eric.

"Sorry it took so long. The world has been a little crazy."

"Time works differently here." She smiled.

Eric smirked and leaned into her, hugging her tightly. "I hope I haven't been too tough on him. I'm still learning to be a father figure."

"He loves you. He was so young when we passed that you swooped in and gave him the love he needed."

Love? *Ew.* This man couldn't be capable of love. Could he? He practically killed Declan to trigger his Mark. Who does that?

"Okay, stop. Just for a second." I stood between the two of them, pushing them further apart. "Eric, I swear if this is some kind of sick illusion to make me not hate you, then you are really going to piss me off."

"Why would I want you to like me? I like your hatred toward me, it reminds me of me. The revenge Freya is who I pictured my own daughter being like."

I gasped and became silent. I was not vengeful or hateful toward anyone, except him. Oh my god. I was giving him exactly what he wanted. A hateful witch ready to tap into darkness to rid him and Izzy. That was it. I gritted my teeth. It was time to be nice to him.

"I'm sorry. Maybe you're a hero after all. First Ezra's

mom, and now Declan's. Or you have a soft spot for beautiful women and children."

"No, I've saved men too. This place is crawling with them."

Grace nodded and laughed. "Too many men, in my opinion. Is the spell ready to get out of here?"

"That's the plan. You can transfer your magic and be at peace."

"Do you know if I will be able to see Declan for a minute, before..."

She couldn't say the words, and I didn't want to think about them, either. No witch was coming out alive here, their souls would be at peace and their magic would transfer to their rightful heirs. I wished I had more time to work on a loophole.

"I truly don't know," he said.

"I believe if you dream it, you can make it happen," I chimed in, not really sure how true it was but sometimes a little hope could go a long way. She nodded and hugged me tight.

"Do you mind if I get a letter together for him? Just in case?"

"Of course," Eric answered.

We walked into the house to join Ember and Ezra's mom.

The house felt warm. There was no evil here. There was no Isadora trying to kill everyone. This place was not a prison, it really was a peaceful place for souls. I hoped that the amulet for Isadora was more of a prison than this. She had taken too much from too many. It was time to put her away. She split up enough families in her lifetime. Including her own.

The sky was getting darker. The red moon had to be rising soon. Hopefully we had everything in place, and yet I still had zero idea what I was supposed to be doing. Whatever it was, I was going to try and pull Grace and Ezra's mom back with me.

"I never asked, what is your name?" I glanced at Ezra's mom and waited.

"Eleanora, but most people call me Nora." She smiled, and again, I saw Ezra's smile.

"It's nice to meet you, Nora, officially. I'm pretty sure no one is going to believe me when I tell them any of this."

"Grace told me she is giving you a letter, do you mind if I do too?"

"Of course."

Eric walked into the kitchen, seeming distant. I followed him with curiosity.

"What's wrong with you?" I asked when we were alone.

"Nothing," he lied. Now I could tell he was related because his face matched my dad's when he was in deep thought.

"Okay," I said and walked away, knowing that he needed to get something off his chest and by me walking away it would spark his desperation to get it out.

"Do you really think I am so evil?"

I stopped walking and smirked to myself before turning around to face him.

"I think that you have spent a thousand years doing wrong, where the world is afraid of you."

He swallowed hard and nodded his head. "You know, when you live this long, time is nothing. The problem is I have spent a thousand years cleaning up Izzy's messes and not actually living a life." He walked toward the door to the backyard where the sun had set and the red moon was rising in the same direction as if this prison world didn't have any sense of direction. I followed him to see where his thoughts were taking him.

"You really want to get rid of Isadora?"

He nodded and looked up at the moon rising.

"What if we can't unlink you?"

"Then, lock us both up or kill us. I am getting tired. I am ready."

"But what about Aunt Lynn? You've only just got her back."

"That woman has survived this long without me, she will be better off. I have hurt her so much that the love she still has for me is undeserving. I came here with you to make peace with the three women in that living room and also with you. Anything that happens from here is okay by me. Just promise me that you finish this. I want my brother to live a long normal life without looking over his shoulder." He inhaled sharply, then released it. "Promise me, that if there's no way to get her in the amulet, then you kill her, even if we're still linked. Lynn already agrees with me."

I stared at him. Looking at him for the first time without letting my hatred fill me first. His face was not hard, but strong. As if he has lived a long life full of dark, deep secrets. He had ageless skin, which would be from the souls he consumed to keep himself alive. His dark hair was slicked back, and a piece in the front was falling just perfectly across his emerald eyes. Three months ago, I remembered seeing him through the phone and being terrified and then fighting him in the bluffs. It wasn't until I started syphoning from him that the softness in his eyes started to come through. As if I consumed the darkness that had been consuming him all along.

I reached over and hovered my hand over his shoulder while he was looking down. I debated on the closeness and then gave in and let my hand fall onto his suit. The closeness shocked even myself and had a scent of a peaceful woodsy night air and cedar. Which did not match his temper at all.

"It's not going to come to that, and if you really help us, then maybe you can join us for Thanksgiving dinner this year." I smiled my first genuine smile since we'd been here. He looked up at me and studied my face. I nodded. "I'm serious. Family is forever."

Chapter Thirty-Three

Freya Chamberlain

The moon was starting to rise, and the fiery orange tone was changing to red. It was almost time. I just hoped that Callum was ready and that Eric knew what the hell he was doing. The furniture had been moved out of the living room while Eric and I were talking. The room was almost empty, besides the salt circle that was created. It matched the one back in the real realm.

"Why a circle anyway?" I asked anyone who knew the answer.

"Circle of life, of course," Ember answered. "Everything in the world revolves in a circle, the earth, baby to elder, animals eating others to survive. All circles of life. The most stable form in a pile of chaos." She smiled. I nodded, taking it all in.

"I really hope you know what you are doing," I whispered to Eric.

He walked behind me and rubbed my shoulders. "Syphon from me." Shocked at the request, I hesitated for a moment before realizing that whatever we were about to do was going to take a lot of energy. I closed my eyes and pulled on his magic, feeling my body strengthen, making myself feel immortal. I could feel his magic coming through his fingertips and started to feel drunk with too much magic now. I stopped the transfer and put my hand on his, lifting his grip, forcing him to release me. He stepped back for a brief moment and examined his palms, rubbing the tingling out.

"You're ready." He smiled back at me and patted my back. "Let's get these women out of here. We will come back for the rest."

I could feel my brows scrunch at the disappointment in the plan, but no one else fought the idea. So, maybe he was right, maybe I could only do so much right now. I hoped that he was right. Ember instructed me to get into the circle. I obliged. Grace and Nora took their place opposite of each other at the salt line. Eric walked up next to Ezra's mom and kissed her cheek as she handed him her letter. He whispered something into her ear, but I couldn't hear his words. She smiled and nodded. Eric took his hands and placed them gently along her face, and they both closed their eyes while a glow illuminated from his palms. A minute passed, and she opened her eyes, now full of tears, but with a smile and thanked him for everything.

Then, he walked to Declan's mom and kissed her cheek as she handed him her letter. Only, she pulled him in tighter and kissed his lips, making me turn away, not wanting to take her moment away from her. I looked back just in time for him to embrace her, pulling her tight against his body, leaving no space between them and letting the glow get brighter between them. The glowing stopped as he let their foreheads linger while she whispered, "Thank you for the borrowed time to watch my boy grow up." He stepped back and quickly wiped a tear rolling down his cheek.

My mind raced with a way to bring them back, but I didn't even know what I was doing so how would I bring back the dead without causing some kind of added problem? Eric grabbed Ember's hand, "Are you ready to go home?" She smiled and jumped up and down in a childish cheer.

"Freya, please remember to tell Ezra what I said," Nora said, and I smiled as I remembered her words.

"I will."

Eric stepped into the circle and grabbed my hand. "Repeat after me."

He began to speak when the door flew open, and a crowd of witches marched in.

"You promised us," a woman yelled.

"You liar," the instigating man with the scar chimed in.

"Never should've trusted you," another man sneered.

"You bastard," a woman said, as she spat.

"Just going to leave us here? This place won't hold."

"Ember, it's time," Eric yelled, as the room filled with more souls.

How could I leave them all here now? The looks on their faces were too much to bear. They needed to be free from here just as much as anyone. The ground beneath us rumbled again. What if this place collapsed before we made it back, or what if I didn't live through the week to make it back? I had to get them all out today.

She began to whisper words I did not understand.

Then, Eric followed with Latin, I listened to his words carefully and tried to repeat them, feeling the pressure with the angry souls circling us but unable to touch us in the circle. The yelling was becoming louder, and my head started to panic. There was too much noise, and I couldn't concentrate anymore. Damn, I couldn't even hear Eric. I threw my hands up to my ears as the world became too loud, and my head was ready to explode. It felt like the souls were screaming inside my head. Maybe they were still connected to me. I screamed, trying to make my own silence in my head.

Losing my connection with this world, I sent the salt flying in the air. The scarred man from the crowd started advancing on us, pushing Ember out of the way. He grabbed me and pulled me against him, knife to my throat. Eric's eyes were a warning for me not to move. I froze along with everyone else and then the noise finally settled. Eric looked toward the window at the moon, and I saw the time was now or never. The red moon was completely full, and at this rate, soon it would be phasing into the third phase of fiery orange. I looked at him, now more angry than ever that another plan was about to fail.

"That's it!" I screamed, as I pushed back against the man threatening me, using my electricity to zap him like a taser. This was the evil man that needed to stay. His skin touching mine made my entire body shiver. He was evil. "Ragnar," I whispered, and the scarred man looked up and smirked with an evil agenda on his mind.

"Back up, now!" I yelled. "I am trying to set you all free."

The crowd murmured and seemed divided. Nora,

Grace, and Ember exchanged worried glances between one another. I nodded to them with reassurance that they would make it out of here. They were breathing heavily as the crowd finally backed up.

"Stay still for this to work," I said. "Ventus," I whispered, as the wind came through, lifting the salt and placing it back down into place. "If anyone crosses this barrier before I say so then I will send you to another dimension," I yelled, letting the power of being in charge consume me.

Everyone obliged and squeezed back in the now full house. Eric stepped back into place only this time he had the dagger in hand, ready for a fight. He stared at me cautiously before restarting the Latin, and I repeated his words while holding his free hand.

"Evincere, statera, pax, requiem, translatio." I carefully repeated each word and stared at the souls in front of me. With that, one by one, each soul glowed bright and then vanished as it charged toward me. I could feel each one hit the barrier of the chaos circle of life and then disappear through me, each one whispering a surname as it traveled through. With each soul passing through, my magic was starting to deplete, it was becoming exhausting. I could feel my nose begin to bleed, and I tried to wipe it with my free hand, but the blood started to gush. *Shit.* How many more were there to pass through?

I looked around the room and realized we were only halfway done. I looked at Eric who was staring back at me, his chanting stopped as he saw my face.

"That's enough," he said, pulling our hands apart. Only this time the souls kept transferring as I kept chanting louder. I grabbed Eric's shoulder and started to syphon his magic to keep going. His body fought back against me with force, but I was controlling him now. He was trying to stop me, but I was in charge, and I wasn't going to stop until every last one of them were free.

"It's not over," I yelled and continued to chant in Latin.

He fell to his knees as I drained him, struggling to release my grip. I shoved him with his own borrowed strength into the ground, then away from me and continued.

He slowly gained his balance and stood, trying to push toward me. I held up a shield of force to keep him back. He was making me use more of my magic than necessary right now, because I would not stop until this was complete. He pushed hard past my invisible wall and grabbed me from behind to cover my mouth. I gripped onto his arm and syphoned his last drop, and this time I threw him out of the circle, throwing the shield back up, only to keep him out. Now that I knew the words that were needed, I kept going. Ember looked to Eric cautiously, debating on who she was supposed to be helping. "Keep going," I yelled. "We have to save these souls."

I continued, each one getting harder to focus. Ember looked at me horrified as I could feel my eyes pour with wetness. I wiped the tears and realized it was blood. I pushed my fear back down and kept going. We made a promise to these souls and I intended on keeping it. Grace and Nora came next to me, supporting me in my decision. Then, Ember willingly grabbed my shoulders letting me syphon from her to finish this. There were only a few more left. I pushed myself harder as each one soared through me. Eric was trying to break the magic wall to stop me, pounding hard against the wall.

"Freya, stop! You will kill yourself!" he screamed, but I drowned out his voice and chanted louder.

I could feel Ember begin to tremble as her magic was depleting. I let her go and kept going on my own. I was so close to undoing this mess. I pushed Eric harder back against the wall and pulled the last of the souls through the circle, one by one.

All that were left standing were the boys' mothers, Ember, Eric and myself. *I can do this.* I lowered my hand in Eric's direction, putting the shield down and grabbed Nora and Grace's hands. Eric ran back into the circle, trying to pull my hands from theirs.

"Freya, you will kill yourself!" he yelled again.

I ignored his warning. I had no other choice. I pulled the last of my strength to push them through to our real world. Their light was so bright, and their souls were so full of good that they actually made my body feel bandaged from the damage that had been done. They had a light to them that was good.

I sent them through. I smiled when I felt the weight of them leave this place, knowing that I did something right. My body started to tremble now as I could feel myself becoming weak. I was at the end of my magic for today, or maybe for forever. I started to feel lightheaded, and the room was becoming dark. We were going to be stuck here. The thought terrified me, but at least I saved all those souls today.

I felt pressure on my neck as a sharp blade pushed

against my throat. There was something off about his soul, something evil. I could *feel* his sickness and damaged soul. *Ragnar.* I could not let him through. I was so worried about keeping Eric back that this man snuck up behind me. He couldn't leave this place. He was the evil one they had been talking about. My stomach turned, and bile grew in the back of my throat. He would not pass this barrier.

"Keep going," Ragnar demanded.

I stopped the chanting as he pushed the blade tighter against my throat. Eric ran to me with force, knocking the man down and wrestling with him against the wall out of the circle. The man grabbed Eric and pierced the blade through his ribcage, just missing his heart. Eric winced but took the man and pushed him further away from me. I tried to force magic through my palms in his direction to help him break free of the evil man's grip, but failed.

"Get Ember and you out of here," Eric yelled between blows.

"I'm not leaving you."

"I said, go!" Eric demanded, as my bloody tears rolled down my face. I watched Ragnar lunge with the knife again for a clear shot to Eric's life.

A blood curdling scream escaped my throat as a white light emerged from inside me and across the room, throwing the last of my magic out toward Eric, trying to give him the briefest moment to take advantage of the situation. He jumped up and pulled the knife from Ragnar's hand and twisted it around to kill him.

Ember, unaffected by the burst of magic, ran into the circle to help keep me standing and reached out toward Eric, pulling him and the man closer with her own magic.

Reaching for Eric's hand to bring him back into the circle, she left the man just at the edge, outside of the circle. She whispered in her unknown language as the red moon passed and the strongest power depleted faster. I willed the last of my magic to come through while the room became pitch black as my body felt like it was being ripped through dimensions. Either this was death, or we were being teleported out of the chaos. I hoped it was the second one.

Chapter Thirty-Four

Jaxon Oakes

The room shone bright from the quarter moon as I waited for this stupid trance circle to end so I knew Freya would be okay. The circle started to shake, the salt shifting as shimmering orbs started to shoot through Freya's body and circled above her head, maintained in the salt circle. I stood up and walked as close as I could get to her without disrupting the trance. I watched as each one came through and her nose started to bleed, then gushed, then her eyes started to pour blood. She whimpered as each one transferred.

"Stop this, you're killing her!" I yelled, as my parents tried to hold me back from pulling her out. I pushed through them. Whatever was going on in that dimension was killing her. I would be damned if I let her die today. Declan ran over to me and threw me against the back wall, pinning me with force that could only be magic. I pushed back toward him, trying to harness my mom's magic. "Get off me. She's dying."

Alex ran in front of me, "You need to calm down." Her

hand touched my chest, power of persuasion trying to take over my emotions. I took her hand and pushed it off me.

"Don't ever fucking do that again," I sneered.

Alex held her hands up and forced me back against the wall, helping Declan, sure not to touch me again as she looked away from me. She was trying to save me from jumping in that circle where I could easily get myself obliterated.

Freya started to scream in pain with each soul forcing through her tiny body. How many more souls? I used as much strength as I had in me, pushing Declan off and moving Alex over before jumping into the salt circle. Being electrocuted by the force that was meant to keep the souls contained, I grabbed Freya and released her hand from Eric's and pulled her close against me as the jolts continued to shock me and souls kept coming through. Then, I felt my body get torn from hers and I was being held against Eric's body with a knife to my throat. Freya's eyes opened, panicked.

"Stop!" she yelled. As Eric dropped the knife and pushed me back away from him, he looked up and stared at the souls hovering. He looked back to Freya and laughed.

"You did it. I can't fucking believe it, but you did it," Eric said.

Freya wiped her face. I kneeled down next to her, wiping her face with my shirt. She was breathing heavily, but she would be okay.

"Do we have any of that healing tea?" she said with a hoarse voice, and Clara marched quickly toward the kitchen.

Alex joined us in the circle. Jim and Haven opened

their eyes and kneeled down next to us, smiling. The souls were swimming above us with an ominous glow, which honestly was kind of freaky.

"Did he make it through?" she asked Eric, shaking in fear.

Did who make it through? What happened in there? Why was she so scared?

Eric shook his head. "No, luckily, you stopped him. Ragnar is Isadora's father. I didn't want to scare you with that knowledge. He was the evil soul I was trying to prevent coming through." Eric hunched over, trying to catch his breath. "He wasn't supposed to find us there. That dagger was created as a prison world for him. Seems that world is broken and starting to crumble from the inside. We can't let him out. There, his power is weakened. Here, he will destroy the world." His chest dripped with blood as I realized he had been injured.

"Hey, get him some tea too. He's been injured," I yelled, as Eric sat down in the center of the circle, pulling his jacket off and ripping his shirt off. Lynn ran to him now, panicking. Haven eyed me and waited for my response.

"Do it," I answered her silent question.

She put her hands over Eric and started to heal him quickly. The open wound sealed as his wincing slowed. He looked up to Haven and sat, astonished.

"Thank you," he whispered to Haven, rubbing his newly formed scar on his chest to add to the many others. It was no wonder why he always wore suits to hide them all.

"I'm guessing you thought I was Ragnar, that's why you were trying to kill me?" I asked.

Eric nodded, still trying to catch his breath. "He had

Freya by the throat. I'm sorry. I thought you were him. Dimension swapping and all."

I nodded, understanding that keeping Freya safe was my goal too. At least we had one thing in common.

Haven pulled herself over by Freya and hugged her tight.

"Are you hurt?" she asked her. Freya shook her head and smiled at her, pulling her in tighter.

"Well, I hate to cut this reunion short, but Izzy knows we are here. It's time to move," Lynn announced.

I looked up at the souls and pointed. "What about all of them?"

"They will have to wait. They will be safe here with the protection spell up. Izzy cannot get in here."

"I will stay with them," Callum chimed in. "They could use some company." He smiled and looked up. "Izzy only came here because Eric is here. The sooner he leaves, the better. You are always drawn to your Anchor."

My dad was right. We needed to go, lead her away from here. If she consumed these souls, that would be the end for our world. We all agreed.

"We need to get to the casino," Eric announced.

"Ember?" Freya asked, and Eric nodded.

What the hell had happened in that place, and who the hell was Ember? Clara walked over with the healing tea and handed one to each of them. Freya gulped it quickly as I helped her stand up. Eric did the same and then walked over to her as I stepped in front of him, out of instinct, closing the space between them. I felt Freya's hand on my shoulder.

"It's okay," she said.

Eric walked up to her and hugged her tight. "You did good."

She smiled. "You saved my life, he was going to kill me."

"You saved mine first," he said, as he let her go and wiped the rest of the blood from her face.

"What was the light between you and them?" she asked Eric quietly in his ear, not meaning for anyone else to hear her as he handed her envelopes.

"I shared all the memories I had of their boys, from little on up. One was a little more involved in my life than the other one, but I kept my tabs on Ezra too," he whispered and stepped back, winking.

Clara handed them both mugs filled with more steaming healing tea.

She was going to have to fill me in on this little family reunion. How much time had she spent in that place? And now they were friends? It was only a couple of hours here. My mind raced with worry. I should've gone with her. I stared at her, waiting for any sign of destruction or emotional breakdown. *Nothing.* I relaxed and let myself stop worrying. She could protect herself. She was stronger than I had been giving her credit for. She didn't need me to keep her safe. She could do that herself.

She finished drinking her second cup of tea, and within minutes, she was already seeming back to her normal self. She hugged her parents and then walked back to me and kissed me hard. Not seeming to care that the room was full of too many eyes. I could feel my cheeks flush at the unexpected PDA, but didn't care. She was alive, and she was back in my arms. I glanced down at her Mark and noticed it was healed. I smiled and kissed her harder. Jim cleared his throat, reminding us that we were not alone. She laughed as she stepped back and looked me in the eyes, kissing my cheek.

She walked over to Aisling and handed her an envelope while whispering into her ear. Aisling's eyes grew wider as she studied the paper in her hand before putting it in her pocket. Freya then walked over to Ezra and asked to talk to him privately. Haven looked up, confused at the gesture. Haven looked back to me, and I shrugged. Ezra nodded and followed her to the kitchen. Haven and I followed and stood behind the wall by the kitchen, just within earshot of what was about to be said.

"Your mother was in there," Freya's voice whispered gently.

"Are you sure it was her?" Ezra asked, his voice choked with emotion.

"She said," Freya hesitated, "your magic should come out to play, and Nora wrote this for you."

I heard an envelope ripping and paper being unfolded, then Ezra started to sob, like a child. Haven reacted and tried to turn into the kitchen for comfort, but I grabbed her arm and stopped her, shaking my head and pulling her back.

"Give him a minute," I whispered to her. She nodded and leaned back against the wall.

The room became silent as I heard Ezra sniffle one time, clearing his throat and collecting himself. She must've seen Declan's parents too and gave Ais a letter from them.

"Ezra, your mother is beautiful. Inside and out and she has some strong magic she wants to give to you. She said that if you don't start accepting your magic, then hers will go to waste."

"I'm not ready for it," he replied. "My magic is what killed her in the first place."

"No, it wasn't. Eric can tell you that."

"Eric is a liar. My magic is what triggered my family on the map. If I hadn't been playing with my toys and levitating them, then they never would've found us."

"Ezra, no, you were just a child. That wasn't your fault."

"I was old enough to know better. My family had the stupid fossil half she was looking for. We were in hiding, but I couldn't resist pulling my action figure from under the couch with my magic, and the next thing I knew, the door was blown in by the Immortals. My mom made me hide in the closet until the woman with the glasses showed up. So, I never saw their faces, but I remembered their voices and my mom begging for them to leave. When my mom didn't give up the location of the Jasper fossil, she killed them."

All of this killing over an object. Maybe this world was crazier than I thought. I looked to Haven who now shrugged. I decided it was time. Their little reunion was about to get bigger. I pulled Haven with me, and we joined them in the kitchen.

"What's so special about a fossil?" I asked.

Ezra turned toward me suddenly, seeming annoyed at the extra ears listening in. "It's very powerful. That's all I know."

"Ez, do you have it with you?" Haven asked him.

He walked over to her and grabbed her, pulling her tight against him. "I don't remember where it is right now.

The elixir is not letting me locate it. It's hidden in my memories. I will get it back."

For a bulky man, he seemed to be so fragile in that moment. I actually felt sorry for him. I looked to Freya as she walked toward me, pulling me out of the kitchen away from everyone and upstairs. We walked up the creaky old wooden stairs, and she pulled me into my old room. She closed the door and pushed me against one of the empty walls and started to kiss me.

She caught me off guard. I stopped her and looked into her eyes. "Freya, what the hell happened in there?"

She shook her head and kept kissing me hard. I gave in, ready to escape from reality too. My lips crashed down onto hers. Lifting her into my arms and turning us, I pinned her body against the wall, forgetting about the shit we were in outside of this old room. Her breath became panting, and her hands started to flicker with magic. I looked down, distracted by the bright light coming from her. Still holding her tight in my arms, I glanced at her Mark, glowing brighter than ever.

My eyes were met by her smile. "I'm okay," she whispered. "Better than ever. Just kiss me." She pulled my face back to hers and let our lips linger as the glow started to fade, but her Mark remained whole. Taking the small win for the moment, I kissed her with everything I had.

Chapter Thirty-Five

Aisling Meadows

What a night.

I looked around the room and stared at everyone talking in multiple conversations. I tried to listen to them all, but honestly, my head was swimming with the recent events. I think I needed to get out of this house for a bit. I looked to Declan, who seemed to be feeling the same way. He nodded, reading my mind. Exhaustion was getting the best of me.

I walked to the closest corner of the house to double check that the pennies were holding strong. I glanced up at the floating souls and smiled. We did something right so far. A hand touched my shoulder, making me jump. I turned quickly to Aunt Lynn standing behind me.

"You ready to leave?" she asked.

I nodded. "Are we going to your house?"

"Yes, they want us to take the dagger and cloak it. Freya, her parents, and Jaxon are heading to that casino with Eric. Callum and Ezra are going to watch over the souls here. Clara, Haven, and Margo are heading to Clara's garden. We all have a role to play."

I walked over to Alex, and she handed me the dagger. The Hildisvinian handle zapped me when I touched it, and the obsidian blade glimmered with a strange shimmer. It didn't look like the same dagger that I remembered from three months ago before Freya syphoned it. Of course, that was before my Mark had been triggered. So maybe my eyes weren't open to the magic of it now.

"Ais," Eric said, and I turned around automatically when hearing my name being called. But he wasn't talking to me at all. My aunt smiled and walked toward him. I turned away to not intrude on their moment, but to also not vomit at the idea of them having a past together. Curiosity got the best of me, so I listened intently, pretending to stare at my phone. Everyone had scattered, and it was only them in the middle of the room. I walked slowly toward the doorway, getting ready to leave.

"Please be safe out there." He reached up and brushed her hair back, caressing her face. If I didn't hate the guy so much, then I would think it was a sweet gesture. "You gave up your magic. Give me your hand," he demanded.

"Eric, no. I don't need your magic. I am okay."

"If Izzy sees you, she won't hesitate. She believes you took everything from her."

"So be it."

"I will not let her take anymore away from me then. Call me selfish. So, either you borrow it for you or do it for me. It's borrowed magic from Declan's mom, she demanded that you borrow it until this is over. She knows I will do what I can to keep you safe. She gave it to me in case the soul transfer didn't work. Plus, Izzy may go after me first. So, it'd be safer with you." He handed her Freya's tourmaline pendant, now shimmering with a galaxy of colors. She closed his hand and pushed it gently back toward him, refusing the magic.

"I am still linked to you two. So, even though I don't have magic, I still am anchored to you. I will live to see another day."

"If she and I die, you will die, and that is blood I cannot have on my hands. I already thought I killed you a thousand years ago. I just can't do it again. Please. I need you safe. Don't make me burn this world down to keep you alive again. I will do what it takes to give you the life you deserve. So, for everyone's sake, please hold on to it."

She leaned up toward him and kissed his lips sweetly, taking the pendant from him. I hadn't noticed that I had turned back toward them and was watching every private moment. Eric grabbed her face and pushed his lips harder against hers. I could feel my cheeks flush at intruding on this private moment.

I turned quickly and walked out of the room. I leaned against the wall and thought of his words. He would burn down the world for her? What kind of toxic love was that? Ruining the lives of others for his own personal gain? *Narcissistic ass.* But I had to admit that deep down the weight those words held was something that I would want Declan to do for me too. The amount of love behind those words was nothing, but the intent of actually doing it was something else entirely, and Eric was that type. Maybe Declan was more like Eric than he thought.

The dagger in my hand brought my attention back to

the moment. The obsidian blade was shimmering and almost seemed to intensify as I gazed into it. Someone was still in this thing, weren't they? I could feel a pull to the dagger, and not in a good way. Who was Eric hiding in here? The canine of the handle pierced my palm as Declan walked up next to me, scaring me and breaking my gaze.

"Ouch," I yelled, annoyed that I felt so jumpy lately, dropping the dagger. Declan reached out, quickly, catching it. He grabbed my bleeding palm with his free one and examined it.

"Are you okay?" He took his shirt and ripped a piece from the bottom, applying pressure to the now pierced hole.

"You just scared me, sorry. I'm fine," I said, pulling my hand away from him. "Can we just get out of here? I need a distraction."

"Or maybe some sleep." He laughed as he handed me the dagger. "No offense, but you look exhausted. Beautiful, but exhausted."

I laughed. My eyes did feel heavy, and my head felt overstimulated. "Fine, distraction first, then sleep. Only for a little bit, though. We can sleep once Isadora is gone."

He smiled, "Will I ever be more than a distraction to you?"

"You are much more than that," I said, grabbing his head and pulling him to me, letting his lips crush mine. "I love you, Declan."

He smiled between our kisses.

Aunt Lynn walked into the hallway. Declan stepped back quickly. She blushed for a moment and pretended to not see anything. A shimmer on her chest caught my attention to her small frame. She was wearing Freya's necklace. Now that I knew that it had Declan's mom's magic in it, I would have to make sure that not only was my aunt safe but so was my boyfriend's mother's magic. Now realizing that the envelope goes with the magic, did I tell him now or wait in case Aunt Lynn needed it? She would not let anything happen to it. I trusted her.

We walked down the road to her house, which was not far from Jaxon's old home. Declan had his arm around me, keeping me warm as we walked, and my aunt walked next to me, away from the road to keep her protected.

"Do you think this Oxana chick will still help us? The story Freya told us doesn't seem like she's in good standing with my dad. I mean, Eric."

"He's your dad. You don't have to do that to yourself," I said.

"Well, I know, but—"

My hand flew up to his mouth and closed his lips from coming up with any excuse. If he considered him his father, then that was it. I would not let him fight his inner demons on what was right and wrong with the only man he'd known to raise him. Declan nodded, and I removed my hand.

Aunt Lynn spoke while we continued to walk. "I personally don't know Oxana, but I hope so."

We walked silently up the stairs of the front porch as Aunt Lynn grabbed her house keys.

"Aislynn, the pagan witch. What a blast from the past. Aren't you supposed to be, I don't know, dead?" A voice laughed from behind us. I turned around to see her standing there.

Isadora. Standing tall and fierce. Ready to cause trouble.

Fuck.

I fumbled for my magic infused pendant, hoping that it was still charged from three months ago, trying to ready myself to protect my aunt, Declan's mother's magic, and the dagger all at once.

"I'll take that dagger now."

"Fuck off." I yelled, shielding Aunt Lynn and forcing her to get behind me.

"Oh, how cute, hiding behind your niece. What, are you powerless now?" She chuckled.

My palms lit up with green crackling energy, ready to burn her alive. I grabbed the dagger and steadied it in my hand with the pendant in the other. Screw Eric's plan. I was taking this chance now. If I could knock her down with the pendant, then we could unlink them sooner than later. I hoped.

Isadora glared back at me, and confusion clung to her face.

"Oh my god, she really is magicless." She laughed demonically. "What a coward. Giving her magic up to a newbie. Not smart, old friend."

"Shut it," I said, as Declan threw his arm across my chest to keep me from advancing. I looked at him, and he shook his head.

"Yes, listen to your little boy." Each word she said was making my blood boil even more. My palms started to burn with anger. The magic needed more skin to linger on before I could release it, so I rolled up my sleeves and let my forearms ignite, making my Mark glow even brighter. I was no longer cold, but my adrenaline had me on fire.

"Impossible,"she yelled, as she glared at my Mark. "What kind of magic is this?" She advanced on me with inhuman speed and pulled my arm in front of her to examine it. Syphoning my magic as she held it to keep me frozen in place. Making my fire extinguish and me powerless against her. Declan tried to push between us but was thrown into the fence, being held down by her forceful magic. I gripped the pendant with my free arm and forced it down into her arm, letting the elixir rush through her veins. Giving me a brief moment of an advantage. Her syphoning stopped, and she backed away. Declan stood up and ran back to me, standing in front of me.

"Stupid girl. Her magic couldn't hurt me then, and it sure as hell won't hurt me now." She laughed and pulled the pendant out, flicking it into the yard.

Her magic should be weakening as the elixir ran through her veins. I watched the black magic course through her arm, traveling up her neck. Without thinking, I gripped the dagger. I had a theory, and I hoped it would work. If I succeeded, then Eric would thank me later. I would need to leave the dagger in her heart until we could unlink them. Keeping her reviving with an instant kill. Again, it was just a theory.

Isadora stared back at my Mark, trying to put the pieces together that she would now never know. "Who are you, girl?"

I smiled when I looked back at her, hoping this would work.

"Remember your baby boy that you carried? Well, he lived," I said as I ran toward her, piercing the blade through the air, aiming for her heart.

Chapter Thirty-Six

Freya Chamberlain

It was time to meet with Oxana. She had the amulet that we needed to lock Isadora away. Killing her wouldn't be an option until we could unlink her and Eric first. She was going to see that coming now. We figured it was best to split up the Anchor pairs as best as possible. That way if something didn't go our way, then at least our advantage would be a second lifeline in a separate location.

So, Haven had to stay back with Aunt Clara and Margo at her cottage in the bluffs, gathering the herbs in the mended garden and working on the unlinking spell. Callum and Ezra were going to stay with the souls. Ezra seemed to want to be close to his mother. Aisling, Declan, and Aunt Lynn were heading back to her house to keep the dagger separated from the house filled with the souls. If Isadora got that dagger, then she would try and syphon the souls that were no longer there and figure out what we had done. If she got to the souls, then she would be unstoppable. The rest of us headed across the river to the casino. Jaxon and I drove in my Jeep to have another vehicle ready in case anything happened. Jaxon was not going to leave my side for a while after all of this, and honestly, I wasn't complaining.

He held my hand as we drove across the river, and we could see the massive casino in the distance. I really hoped that this Oxana lady would listen to us. I also hoped that Ember made her way back to her body. I looked down at my Mark and smiled when it was whole again. Jaxon caught me staring and let go of my hand and rubbed my Mark while holding onto the steering wheel with his free hand.

"I'm glad it's whole again," he said, "but, you've never broken to me." He kissed my hand and made me blush.

"Why are you so good to me?" I genuinely was curious.

"Making up for lost time still, remember? The asshole part of me will come out eventually."

I laughed at the change of mood. "Doubt that. You are pure goodness. You are not from a tainted bloodline like I am." I grimaced at the thought.

"Isadora is my psycho aunt." Jaxon looked back at me and smirked. "I haven't decided who's worse yet."

I laughed.

"Plus, you are nothing like Eric," he reminded me.

"I am more like him than you know, and I'm starting to realize that power runs in my blood, and that terrifies me. I'm afraid if I have to kill Isadora that my blood will run cold and evil will consume me like it has with others."

He laughed, "You will never be evil. Angry? Sure. But evil? Never." He smiled.

I smiled back, hoping that he was right.

The casino parking lot was full. Eric better keep his

temper and not cause a scene in front of all these mundanes. We parked and walked in, following behind Eric and my parents. My mom kept turning around to check on me. "I'm fine," I mouthed to her. Jaxon looked toward me to see who I was talking to. I nodded toward my mom, and he smiled. He grabbed my hand as we walked toward our next plan.

The automatic door opened as we reached it, and we stepped inside. My nose burned with an odd sensation. We followed Eric to the blackjack tables where a tall, skinny woman stood dealing the cards. I looked at her wrist where her Mark was visible. Three circles connected. It looked similar to my mom's, only hers was without the spirals. She looked up and instantly threw her hand in the air, waving magic through the casino. The people disappeared, and only she and us remained.

A glamour spell.

"Get out!" she yelled and jumped over the table heading toward us with fire in her eyes. "Get off the reservation."

Shit.

I threw my hands up with electricity, pulling energy from the slot machines surrounding us. There was so much energy running in this place that my magic felt strong. I pushed my sleeves up, revealing my glowing Mark to her. Then, I realized I was pulling more than just from the slot machines, the entire place was filled with magic. She had the oxygen infused with magic. These people were under a spell, and that could be why this place was so packed during the weekday, losing money.

She stepped back and let her fire extinguish as a tanned

skinned woman ran up next to Oxana. Her features resembled an aged Ember. *Her other mother.*

"You stay. He goes." She pointed to Eric. "Or I kill him now." She disappeared from in front of me and reappeared behind Eric, knife to his throat and the amulet glowing around her neck. "You choose."

I froze for a minute, trying to find my voice for the right words. "You're a teleporter, just like Ember."

"What did you just say?" Oxana looked to her wife, then back to me as confusion set in.

"Let him go," a female voice yelled from the back room. I turned to see Ember in real life walking toward us, smiling.

Oxana dropped the blade and stood frozen as if time itself had just stopped. She dropped to her knees and started to cry as her wife joined her. A reunion that was much needed in their hearts. Ember teleported to them and embraced her mothers.

Oxana brushed Ember's hair out of her face and felt it to make sure this was reality. "How are you here? Are you really here?"

"Eric and Freya came for me." She smiled. "They saved me." She winked at me. "We need to talk. It's about Izzy."

Oxana froze at the name and glanced back at Eric. "Ragnar?"

"He's still there. He's getting stronger, though," Ember answered her.

"What ideas did he plant in your head this time?" She spit out toward Eric.

"He didn't plant anything. He brought Freya to me.

She's the key." She nodded toward me. Oxana eyed me up and down and looked back at Ember.

"How sure are you?" she asked Ember.

"Positive, she's the Anchor. She can set things right with the Immortals, her and her sister."

I had no idea what Haven and I were supposed to do. A few months ago, I was an ordinary girl trying to gain my father's trust back and graduate highschool. Today, I was some powerful witch who held the key to balancing magic. I still couldn't find my voice and just listened to their exchange.

"If she is the key, then who is her Anchor?"

"Her Anchor is her sister. Identical twins, Mom. They are the new ones. They are here to destroy the original red moon born witches. Things can go back to normal, and Izzy's father will stay trapped for eternity."

My heart stopped as I replayed her conversation in my head.

"Destroy the original twins? As in Isadora and Margo?" Jaxon was already staring at me before I had put two and two together. He stepped back from me and was shaking his head.

"They're not supposed to be here. The magic world is crumbling because of them. Izzy has been destroying our world for too long, and the universe is starting to push back. If you don't destroy their magic before the next solar eclipse, then every witch will lose theirs. It's already begun to happen. The dagger world is crumbling inside, isn't it?" Oxana asked.

I nodded. "We can't kill Margo," I said quietly, shaking my head. "I can't."

Ember stood and walked toward me. "You and your sister were born for this reason. Either the original twins are destroyed, or they destroy all of us. I am fully made of magic, I will disappear if they stay. Izzy has overstayed her welcome, and now we will all suffer."

I looked her up and down and just stood, shaking my head. "There has to be another way."

"Their magic is what shook the world a thousand years ago. When Izzy stole her sister's magic and tried to kill her, the entire witching world started to fall apart. Each witch that was born after became elemental. We used to be born with full power, mind control, teleportation, telekinetic, we were so much more, not just elemental. Pretty soon, we will have no magic at all, and I will be nothing."

Oxana stood. "She's right. I hate to even say it. I have known those two girls since they were born. I don't want them to leave anymore than you do. But the magic of two sets of Anchor twins is too much for one world to hold."

Jaxon spoke from behind me. "Why wouldn't my mom tell me this?"

"Who is your mother?" Oxana asked him.

"Margo. Isadora's twin."

Oxana gasped at the connection. "Your mother knew. She's always known. Margo was the one who told us of the prophecy nearly a century ago."

I stepped back by Jaxon and rubbed his shoulders. "Babe, don't worry, there is a loophole. I could never kill her. Ever."

"You will if it's your destiny. You won't have a choice. You don't understand, Freya. Prophecies are made to be fulfilled, and if you don't do it, then there will be consequences."

My mom walked over to us. "She's right, we will find another way."

My dad had been silent for too long. I looked back at him, hoping that he had something to add. He seemed deep in thought. "Dad, do you remember any of this?"

"I guess I have been sleeping for a long time. I had no idea that I had even fathered twins until recently."

"Izzy's father started all of this. He was a wretched man. He had no heart or soul once they were born. He couldn't even look at those poor girls. He pitted them against one another. He wanted their power for himself. He was willing to sacrifice his own children to gain their power and take over the lands. That's when their mother and I created both the dagger and this amulet." Oxana reached for her necklace and rubbed the glowing crystal. "I kept this one, and once their father had been captured in the dagger, it was given to a dear old friend who practiced magic but wasn't an Anchor. She was to pass the dagger onto her daughter Aislynn for protecting. She was to pass it on for generations to come, but we all saw how that turned out. We were supposed to be the keepers of these worlds to make sure that they didn't get in the wrong hands. There's too much power in the two objects for any one person to consume." She glared at Eric.

"Woah, I never consumed the magic. Izzy did. I am her Anchor. She lives, I live," Eric chimed in. "Ais gave me that dagger centuries ago, how was I supposed to know who it contained back then? If you guys would have trapped Izzy in that amulet years ago, then none of this would be happening. I only found out Ragnar was in it two years ago. Izzy kept that secret for nearly a thousand years."

"We couldn't unlink you from her," Ember interrupted.

"Since when had anyone cared about my wellbeing?" Eric yelled. "Izzy had drained me of any life that should've been lived for far too long. Back then I wouldn't have cared to die."

"But you care now?" Oxana asked.

Eric froze and looked toward my dad and then me. "I would prefer to live a little longer now that I have my family back."

Oxana laughed. "Since when did you care about anyone but yourself?"

"Since I found out my son lived on, and I have an actual blood heir."

All he has ever wanted was to pass on his legacy to an heir. He finally had that. This conversation was becoming too much, and it needed to get back on track.

"Will you help us?" I asked Oxana.

She looked to Ember, who nodded happily, and then glanced at the rest of us. With a heavy exhale, she nodded.

"Fine, but if Izzy figures out that I'm helping you, then I'm out. She will not take my family away again."

"Fair enough," Eric said.

I nodded an agreement, understanding that family is everything.

My phone buzzed. I grabbed it and saw Aisling's name flashing across the screen.

"Let's head to the office. I need to get these people back to giving me their money." She waved her hand, and everyone reappeared. The laughter and clamoring continued with a new dealer at Oxana's table. Had people really not noticed us here? I could definitely feel the tinge of magic in my nose now. Magic was weird.

I answered my phone and heard an unexpected voice.

"She took her, she took them. I'm going to kill her. Freya, she took Ais and Lynn. I'm going after them. I'm going to burn this damn town down until I find her!" Declan was screaming into the phone, not making sense.

Ais had the dagger; they were supposed to be keeping it safe. If he says her name, I was going to lose it.

"Isadora, that bitch," he yelled.

"Fuck!" I yelled, and the others stopped walking and turned back toward me.

So much for time being on our side, yet again. This hourglass kept running out of sand, and every plan I wanted to work kept getting ruined. These immortals were really pissing me off.

I grabbed Eric's head from behind and slammed it into the wall, pinning him against it, pulling the worthless pocketknife from my jacket out as I raised it to his throat. "Where did she take them? You bastard. You played us."

Everyone was frozen, staring at my knife millimeters away from Eric's throat. Of course, he would come back shortly, but having this moment of power was what I needed to remind myself that I could kill him without my magic.

His hands came up in a defenseless gesture. "What happened?"

"Don't act like you didn't split us all up so Isadora could get the dagger from Ais and Aunt Lynn. You brought us as far away from them as possible and let her get away with the one thing we needed to keep. What are you planning?" I pushed the blade harder against his soft skin, forcing my hand closer to piercing him.

"Freya, I'm not with her."

"Shut the fuck up. After a thousand years with her and then trying to play me in the dagger world with all those white knight stories, it was bullshit. You set us up." Tears started to roll down my cheeks as anger and betrayal consumed me. I wiped the tears quick and clenched my free hand tighter, so my nails dug hard into my skin, letting the pain remind me of what he put us through. *Pain. Kill him.* But then I could smell his calm woodsy scent again. I tried to hold my breath and focus on the hate, but something behind his eyes said this wasn't his doing.

My thoughts raced as I hesitated at what the truth was. I jumped as my dad's hand curled over mine, and he grabbed my other hand with the blade and pulled it away from Eric's neck.

"Freya, look at me. Hey, kiddo, look at me." I tried to see my dad, but instead, I saw an immortal man that had lived longer than he was meant to. Was he even my father? So much had happened that I started to shake, and my nerves became uncontrollable as I sank to the floor in the middle of the hallway outside of the office, where people in the casino could see me have my mental breakdown.

Jaxon rushed to my side. He had my phone up to his ear, listening to Declan. Oxana was staring at me and smiling.

My dad leaned down by me. "Hey, breathe." He inhaled sharply and tried to bring me back to reality. "He's on our side. You might not trust him, but trust me." I was sobbing when I looked up at him. There were no other emotions that I could've felt in that moment. I calmed my breathing down and looked to Jaxon who was deep in Declan's story.

Jaxon hung up the phone and picked me up, carrying me into the office, following Oxana. The room was filled with everyone now. I sat quietly, trying not to crumble. Isadora had my best friend as leverage. She would kill her, and we still didn't even know if Ais had an Anchor to come back. She could actually die tonight, and it's all because I didn't just go to her and let her syphon my magic and the souls. Now my best friend was in danger because of my selfishness for wanting to keep my powers.

Eric walked toward me as Ember jumped in front of him, stopping him from advancing.

"I wouldn't," I could hear her whisper. "Her aura is all over the place right now, she will kill you." Ember kissed his cheek and walked behind her mother, standing behind the big desk, separating my group from them.

"Declan said she had help, a man in a car pulled up and took them with her. Any idea who it might've been?" Jaxon questioned.

"She only knows one man that would bow to her bidding and neither of you are going to like it," Eric looked to Jaxon then to me, daring to see my glare.

"I don't think we like any of this already," Jaxon said.

"Hired help from a truck driver, willing to crash into kids to bring a dagger back to town."

No. The driver from the accident, not just any wreck, but ours. My breathing started to speed up, finally hearing that it was all a set up from the ones that had planned it. Two years I lived with PTSD from the entire situation that was still very real. I would wake up with night sweats with that man's face stuck in my head. I had always pictured a demon behind the wheel before the impact. My hands started to shake as I remembered the night all too well. I tried to catch my breath, but instead, my body went into a full-on panic mode, becoming unstable. My eyes rolled back, and a vision started.

The cold dark room was making me uncomfortable. I looked around and realized that this was not the casino. A vision had not happened in awhile since completing my Mark. Only this one was different from the others. This vision felt new. I could sense myself being in this moment; it just hadn't happened yet. This was a future prediction. I studied every moment to try and take it all in, I walked through the dark hall and whispered, "Ignis," to light up the darkness. It wasn't a house. I studied the walls and realized I knew these walls. I knew exactly where I was.

The cave. The cold, wet cave. It was silent. There was nobody in here but me. I walked faster to the center. If my vision brought me here, then it brought me for a reason. I ran to the middle and huffed as I reached the entrance to the opening of the space where Isadora and Eric had laid to decay for those three months.

I gasped when I saw bodies lying on the cement stones that had been empty recently. I walked up to them slowly, realizing a woman was lying still, then another woman laid next to her. I saw no chest risings from either woman. These ladies were long dead, becoming stone. I shook my head as I reached the center. Gasping for a breath, I looked into the beautiful marbelizing face that I knew all too well. Aisling and her aunt lay dead on the rock. "No!" I yelled, "Wake me up, wake me up! Please, someone wake me up." I screamed in the echoing walls of the cave. "I hate these visions. I hate my magic. I just want my life to be normal again. I hate all of this. Wake me up."

"Stupid child." Isadora walked up behind me. "All of this pain over your magic? Why not just give it to me then?"

I wiped the tears from my face and turned quickly, yelling, "Ignis." Raising my hands with fire, I threw it at her. "You. Did. This!" I screamed.

She dodged the flames and chuckled as if this were all a game. A game that I was losing.

"Not yet, but I will. I just wanted the dagger unlocked. My father was trapped inside, and I just needed a little bit of your unwanted magic to get him out," she said quickly before I let my hands recharge with a fireball. "But instead, I found another way."

"They had nothing to do with this!" I yelled, pointing to the women. Then, letting my hands fall to my sides, weakness from being heartbroken crashed over me, and I bawled like a coward in front of her. "She was of your own blood, and now you killed her. You killed my best friend." I shook my head, trying to remind myself this was only a vision. Wake up, Freya. This hasn't happened yet, and I won't let it.

"My own child was taken from me because of her." She looked at Aunt Lynn's body with disgust and spit at her. "Centuries I have looked for a way to bear another child. A key to unlock that dagger and get my father out, only Aisling let me in on her little family lineage secret. With her, I can pull him out myself." She smiled. "I need him back, as he has something that belongs to me."

"We could've found a way. Anything, but this." I pointed to the women. "There is always a loophole," I whispered.

"You had your chance to help me. But you chose to be a selfish little syphon girl," Isadora said sternly, as the scarred faced man from the dagger walked up behind her, whispering in her ear. She smiled and rushed toward me, grabbing my arm and syphoning my magic from me until the cave went dark. Ragnar laughed loudly, sounding closer and closer to me.

Chapter Thirty-Seven

Haven Vine

We made it to the bluffs. Immediately after parking, I walked to the garden, but froze.

"Woah, something is happening." I tried to balance myself as a flash of a scarred face man laughing demonically in my face crossed my mind.

Aunt Clara grabbed my arm and helped steady myself from the dizziness. Then, as soon as the face appeared, it disappeared. I looked up to Aunt Clara as her face was filled with concern.

"I'm okay. I don't know what that was all about," I said honestly.

"Let's get you inside, maybe you're dehydrated or hungry. It's been a long day."

I shook my head, "I'll just sit out here for a bit. I'm okay. I promise."

She nodded and helped me sit on the front porch while I looked out at the garden. I smiled when I realized that one of the perks of being a witch with a garden was that magic would keep everything alive year-round, no matter how brutal the Wisconsin winters. No wonder why Aunt Clara always had everything we needed on hand. I stared down the rows at the names listed, hoping that the names would trigger the neurons in my brain to come up with another back up plan. There had to be something that we missed or anything that could give us an advantage. I just wished we had more time.

*Time...*Time was the one thing that has been screwing us over. How could we slow down time, or at least slow down her time?

Thyme!

Of course. I jumped up and ran to the opposite row, grabbing the purple creeping thyme that was making its way through to the next row already. Why didn't I think of this earlier? Thyme could be used for so many things. So many healing properties. It can help deflect negative energy, or hopefully negative people. Then, my favorite use, slow down time itself. I used to use it for studying the night before exams, and I swore by it. Of course, it was a tricky spell that we would need to use. But we could definitely use it somehow. I ran inside to see what they thought.

"Aunt Clara, can we use this?" I held up clumps of the purple flower and dangled it out in front of me. She grabbed a handful of it and examined it.

"You are my genius. Why didn't I think of that?" Aunt Clara spoke.

"I think we are all a little on edge lately." She smiled back at me. "You think we can slow her down with this, or maybe change the course of time somehow?"

Margo looked up from her book and hesitated.

"Changing the course of time is dangerous, it comes with a huge price. Our magic comes from the earth, and borrowing time like that is not natural. That is tapping into a darker magic that we shouldn't. We really don't need any more darkness coming our way. But I do think we can use it to help our situation." Margo reached her hand out to examine the thyme herself. "Are you thinking what I'm thinking?"

"Lure her into a location with this stuff to keep her trapped in slow motion until we have that amulet?"

Margo nodded. "We need that amulet now. Especially if she is in the cave right next door to us. I'm sure Oxana won't give it to Eric. I should've gone with them."

I jumped when my phone vibrated in my back pocket. I reached for it quickly.

Freya.

"Hello?"

"Are you at Aunt Clara's already?" she asked, frantically. Her breathing was uneven. Something was bothering her.

"Yes, we're here. Why, what happened?" I quickly pressed the speaker button to share the information.

"Isadora took Aisling and her aunt. Declan called and then I had a vision. I think she's going to kill them. She's trying to free her dad from the dagger, and now, unfortunately, she has the that too."

My brain froze for a moment while I put all the pieces together. If she had the dagger and Aisling, then we had an issue. With her syphoning powers back, we were even more screwed. I grabbed a pen and paper and started to write up my ideas.

. . .

Thyme - Slow down Isadora
Leverage - Give up Eric for Aisling and Lynn
Unlink them - Then kill her
Last resort - Release Ragnar from the dagger
and kill him

We didn't have many options. I stared at the paper and realized none of them were ideal and none of them really were winners.

"Can you guys check the cave?" Freya's voice came back. Her voice quivered. "Please, we're across the river still at the casino, and sometimes my visions are wrong. I just... I just don't want to fail."

"We will check it out. Does she still wear her locator bracelet from her aunt?" Aunt Clara asked.

"I believe so."

"Good. We will see where she's at."

"Call me back as soon as you can, please."

"Don't worry, child, we won't let anything happen to them," Aunt Clara spoke.

I could hear the doubt in Freya's voice as she hung up. None of us could be making promises right now on things out of our control. One good thing, Freya had her magic back thanks to the soul extraction. Bad part was she was not nearly as strong as she was with the souls.

"Luckily, we have blood samples from each of you since those pendants were made," Aunt Clara stated.

She grabbed a map of Crystal Rock and reached for the

vials of blood in the top cabinet, clicking through the tubes to find the right one. She lit a candle and poured a few drops on the map as she waved her hands over it and started to whisper.

"Invenire."

To find someone it was easy enough. I could've tried this spell. I watched as the blood droplets gathered and formed a trail to JFK and then to exactly where Freya thought they may be. I froze, realizing that my breathing had stopped before the locator spell even started. They were at the cave. My heart raced, knowing that either Freya's vision had already happened, or it was about to.

I closed my eyes trying to start my own vision. I had been practicing them since we completed our Marks, trying to master controlling them. I could feel my hands shake as nothing came up, finally exhaling the breath I had held in. I was under too much stress to let my mind focus.

I grabbed the thyme and a knife from the kitchen and walked out the door, Aunt Clara trailing fast behind me.

"Where do you think you're going?"

"I'm going after Aisling. She needs my help."

"Haven Alexandra Vine, you will do no such thing. We need to be prepared, otherwise a dead witch is not a helpful witch."

I stopped in my tracks and turned quickly. "We never should've given her the dagger. You hid it for two years here safely, and now it's out of our hands in less than four hours. For all we know, Aisling may be dead. I cannot sit around here and wait to find out." I turned back around and took a step away from her, knowing that her eyes would be sad that I was disobeying her wishes.

"Somnum," Aunt Clara whispered from behind me. Immediately, I regretted not taking Latin in school, but I knew this word. It was used a lot during my childhood. A damn sleeping spell. Damn her. My body became weak, and I slowly started to crumble into her arms, catching me and bringing me to the cold ground as my eyes slammed shut on me. The sleep came on quickly. The only thing was that my mind didn't rest, instead I knew what was happening, I was getting sucked into the vision I had called upon minutes before.

There she was, in a cave. Aisling and her aunt tied up. They were sitting at the back, away from the opening. I ran toward them, trying to reach them before anything bad happened to them. I did not want Freya's vision to be fulfilled.

"Hey, please listen to me. I'm coming for you guys. Hang in there. Do not let Isadora have your blood."

Aisling perked up at the sight of me and smiled with relief. "She just left. Please help us. She has these ropes spellbound."

I reached for the ropes, and they burned as I touched them. They were soaked in some kind of toxin. Their wrists were raw from the poison. I grabbed Aisling's hand and saw dark veins crawling up her wrist from a puncture wound that was at the thumbpad of her palm.

"What happened here?" I pointed to the infection.

"I got poked by the dagger and then this started to spread across my hand." She shrugged. "It must be infected."

"I think it's something else entirely," I said and exam-

ined it further. "Do me a favor and hold on. I will come to you."

They started to fade as the sleeping curse was lifting, and I could feel the vision disappearing. I looked at Aisling and her aunt once more. "Please hold on." She smiled and nodded before my eyes opened.

I opened my eyes to an empty house. It was too quiet. I jumped up and checked each room. They had left me. Probably went to the cave without me. I grabbed my phone and called Aunt Clara, nothing. Then, Freya, nothing. Geez, would someone let me know what was going on?

I walked out of the house, grabbing my winter coat. The temperature was dropping fast for October, and I wasn't ready for the snow yet. But there was a chill in the air, and I needed to keep myself warm to keep my fears from making me shake even more.

I had a handful of creeping thyme in my pocket and hoped that if anything, shoving it down her throat would do something.

I called Ezra, who finally answered.

"Please tell me that the souls are safe?" I asked, while holding my breath.

"Yes, why? What's happened?"

I quickly filled him in on the night's events and my vision that was brought on because Aunt Clara didn't trust me to go with them.

"I'm heading to the cave. Ais and her aunt are there. I think they need my help."

"The hell you are, you are not going alone. Stay home, I will come meet you. We can go together."

I knew I shouldn't have told him, but he was right. If Isadora was there and I went alone, then tonight wouldn't end well for one of us and we all knew it was me. I sat down on the porch and looked out toward the garden.

"Haven, please wait for me. I'm already in the car."

"Okay, I'll wait," I said, as a chill crept through my entire being. Something was off and sitting here wasn't getting us anywhere.

"Promise?" I heard the ignition start and the worry in his voice. I realized that I had caused him a lot of worry lately and distance and nodded my head before realizing that he couldn't see me.

"Babe, I promise, I'll wait," I said, making myself promise to sit still until he got here. Like Jaxon said to me, the world wouldn't burn without me, it could wait. At least, I hoped so.

I hung up the phone and sat quietly. It was so dark out, and the chill was not inviting. I waited ten minutes before I stood up to walk back into the house to wait, but then a bright green flash illuminated the sky above where the cave was located, high above the trees.

What the hell is that?

Chapter Thirty-Eight

Aisling Meadows

My head was throbbing as I looked around at my surroundings and panicked, as the room was so dark I could barely see in front of me. But something deep inside of me was telling me to just hold on. I wrenched my body to realize that my hands were tied. I whispered, "Ignis," and let my hand ignite from behind me. The freezing room lit up, and I recognized the area. I was in the cave. I turned quickly to check around me. I was alone. *Where was my aunt?*

I pushed myself up and walked toward the wall of the cave and listened. Nothing.

"Aunt Lynn?" I whispered, afraid that if I spoke too loudly, then the cave would crumble and I would lose her forever. "Declan? Please, anyone." My eyes became wet and made me even more frustrated that I couldn't wipe the tears away. I tugged hard on the ropes, letting the friction burn my wrists as I tried to rip them apart. I turned my palm upward toward the rope and tried to burn them free.

Nothing happened. Ugh, a magic seal had to be on the rope. I hated her. Isadora was going to pay for this. I reached for my phone that was supposed to be in my back pocket and froze as I realized it was gone. I was alone in a cave with magic bound ropes containing me.

I ran toward the entrance of the cave. I needed to get out of here and find my aunt and Declan. I could see the moonlight shining at the end of the cave. I ran faster, harder, to get out of this place. I needed to know that my boyfriend and aunt were safe. I made it to the edge and bolted through the entrance before I was thrown back into the air with a zapping electricity that sent me back into the deep, dark cave. My head hit the ground, making it throb. Another magic trick. Having enough of the quiet, I screamed in frustration, hoping that someone, anyone could hear me. "Someone help me!"

When no one answered, I stood up and paced back and forth along the entrance, praying that someone would come for me. I rubbed my tracking bracelet and willed it to show my location to anyone who was a friend of ours. My hand was starting to throb, so I turned quickly to try and see where the pain was radiating from then I saw the dark hole at the pad of my palm, the fire illuminating the wound.

"Damn, that dagger," I whispered. "Great, now I'm going to die of sepsis, not even something supernatural, and without my Anchor, I'm a goner."

I tried to rub the injured palm and got even more frustrated that my tears were falling, my hand was hurting, and I was alone in a damn cave that was supposed to have the Immortals sealed in it still. I screamed louder this time and let my body drop to the floor.

"Oh, shut up, child."

I looked up at the entrance, Isadora stood in front of me, dragging my aunt back to the cave.

"Let her go!" I screamed.

She laughed. "Don't boss me around. Plans have changed."

"Where's Declan?" I asked, frantically.

She smiled and shrugged her shoulders. I wasn't sure if she truly didn't know or if that I didn't want to know what she did to him already.

Anger flowed through my veins, and my heart raced. I stood up and pushed against the seal again, willing it to break. "Let me go."

She grabbed the dagger and turned my aunt around, facing me now. She was unconscious. Whatever she had done to her, she was going to pay for it. Isadora grabbed the dagger and held it tight against Aunt Lynn's neck.

"Listen to me, little love, or I'll kill her now. Never liked her anyway."

Now I laughed, letting my emotions settle and bring out my inner bitch. "She's linked to you and Eric. You can't kill her." I leaned against the side wall of the cave and waited for her response.

She looked down at my aunt and shook her head in disgust. "So, that's how she's made it this far. Clever." She dropped my aunt and walked to the seal of the cave.

"Sit," she said calmly.

"I'll stand," I spat back.

Her magic took over my body, and Isadora forced me down. "I said, sit."

I glared at her as my body unwillingly sat. I didn't think

she had that kind of ability. I waited for her next words while I brainstormed mine.

"I need your help."

I laughed. "Go to hell."

"Oh, honey, I'm already there. I just don't want to drag you and your fake aunt down with me." She exhaled slowly. "See, I have an issue. My father is locked in this dagger, and I can't seem to get him out. He has something that I want back. According to your infected hand, you can break the seal. Blood of my blood." She smirked.

I looked up to her and kept my mouth shut. I needed to stall her. Someone would track my bracelet and find me. Right?

"What did you do to Declan?" I asked, wincing at the thought of anything bad happening to him. I held my breath as I waited for her answer.

"Do you really care that much? You could be so much more powerful. You don't need a man in your life. Let alone that one." She huffed in annoyance. "You could control the world with a twist of your wrist, and yet you are breaking over a man and that woman." She pointed back at Aunt Lynn and shook her head.

"It's called caring. They mean something to me."

"Right, that love shit, that's a lie. Biggest lie taught in life. Everyone knows that love is a man-made emotion just to make people feel better who need the attention. Love is not real. Power, now power is real, and you, little love, deserve more power than you let yourself have."

"Stop calling me that."

She smirked, "Suit yourself, little brat." She flicked her

wrists and lit up the entire cave in an illuminating glow with a starry night taking over the ceiling. I looked up in awe at the beauty in the sky. "Power is everything." She smirked and waved the starry night away.

I knew I needed to change the subject. I needed as much information as I could get from her while she was willing to talk. "What is it that your father has for you? Destruction of mankind?"

She laughed. "He stole something from me. I want it back."

"How am I supposed to do that?"

"Your blood. A descendant's blood is the only way to set him free from the dagger." She studied my expression.

I froze as I thought about the souls already released, something was not correct about her theory. If Freya could syphon them out with a little bit of harnessing of the moon's power, then what was stopping her?

"Why don't you just syphon him out?" I asked, still trying to buy time.

"I already tried that. My mother locked him in there, and she made it part of her spell that neither Margo nor I could release him, only a descendant's blood would break the seal." She inhaled sharply. "Stupid, really." She shook her head and started to change the subject. "Your 'aunt' filled me in on the rest of your little secret. You see, I had no idea my child lived. Would have been nice to know a thousand years ago. Believing that your child is dead for that long really takes a toll. Some say, one would go crazy. Then, to lose the man I loved, knowing he didn't return the same feelings because of her." She waved her hand back to Aunt

Lynn and spat at her. "Everything was going as planned before she came around and ruined everything. My child was the key to freeing my father from that treacherous prison world." She inhaled sharply, "Once my child was killed, it became my immortal mission to produce another heir, but your lovely pagan ruined that for me too. Cursed me to be sterile, unfair, really. I would've been a wonderful mother."

I laughed even louder now. "You would've destroyed your own child."

Isadora glared back at me before waving her hand and sealing my mouth shut. My eyes widened as my lips were stuck. I could feel the burn of magic inside my mouth as I tried to pry it open. I had never wanted to use so many threats at that very moment.

She ignored my attempts and continued to talk, "All I did was lure your aunt's lover to me and made him give me my child. We used to be old friends, long before she came along. Eric needed an heir too. So, it was a win-win. I could have picked any man but, really, who better than my very own reborn Anchor and childhood friend." She smiled. "You can blame my sister for all of this. The universe never would've given me another Anchor had she just died when she was supposed to."

I sat silently as my lips were still glued shut, but my glare could say a million words for me.

"So, now you're going to free my father from this thing." She tossed the obsidian blade into the cave, breaking the barrier that was holding me in, which gave me a theory. I could feel the magic seal loosen on my wrists and then my lips unsealed. Only this time I would be careful with my words.

"How am I supposed to do anything?" I leaned forward and showed my tied hands behind my back.

She smirked and waved her hand in the air, my hands freed from the ropes. I pulled them out in front of me and rubbed them gently. They were burned from trying to get out of the hold. She waved her hand again, and the rope burn disappeared.

"Anything else?" she asked. "You really are whiny for a descendant of mine, little love. Aislynn really ruined you."

I stared at my healed wrists a little longer, at first in awe and then to control my tongue before I regretted saying anything more to her. Once my nerves calmed, I looked back up at her.

"Wake her," I demanded, pointing to Aunt Lynn.

"You release him, then I will wake her. You have my word."

I laughed again. "Your word is worthless."

"Her life is worthless." She pointed to my aunt. "Unlinking her would take me seconds. I'm a syphon, remember?"

I froze. "Wait, you can do that?"

"Stupid child, I am a thousand years old. I can do everything. If you would have picked better friends, I could've trained you to your true potential, little love."

I ignored her stupid nickname again. "Wait, can Eric do that stuff too?" I needed more time to stall. I couldn't release her father, let alone I didn't know how.

"Eric is worthless too, just a pawn in my game."

"This isn't a game," I yelled, frustrated.

"Oh, but to me it is." She walked closer to the entrance and leaned against the outside wall. "Hurry up and decide. I just need your blood. I don't need you alive for it."

Shit. So much for stalling. She was going to make me release him first. My mind raced as I thought of any other way. If she really knew how to unlink my aunt, then leaving her here while I got help would be out of the question. Unless she was lying. Freya couldn't unlink them, and none of the elders said anything about her being able to. My gut was telling me to run. But if it was wrong...

My stomach turned at the idea of being wrong. *Do I take the chance?* I had the dagger now. *What would Aunt Lynn want me to do?* If I ran from here, slid down the bluffs, then I would be on the right path to Haven's house. Someone should still be there. I hesitated for a brief moment, weighing out my options. But I already knew the answer.

I held the dagger out in front of me and went with my new theory. I pulled the dagger tight to my chest and ran toward the cave entrance, praying that the barrier was down. Relief washed over me as I pushed my way past her. Pulling my energy to my palms and throwing every fierce piece of magic I had toward her, my Mark glowed a strange green glow, illuminating the entire sky. I had never seen anyone's Mark do that before. Isadora flew back from the entrance onto the ground a football field away, and I took off running for my life.

I could hear her screams echoing in my head as I jumped over the bluff and slid down, ungracefully, to the bottom. Bruised and cut from every damn branch and boulder getting into the way. My body felt like I had just been hit by a bus, I would need some healing tea and fast. But first, I needed to run and run as fast as I could. She had superhuman speed, so there was no stopping at this point. *Keep going. Run!*

The air in my lungs was crushing cold, but my chest was burning with too much forced oxygen. My lungs were aching beyond belief. I reached the road and kept pushing myself faster to civilization. Headlights came into view ahead of me, and I froze for only a moment and then jumped over the rail and watched carefully as the car slowed. My breathing uneven, and my head feeling light-headed from the sudden pause in motion. I vomited, then became silent while the car stopped. I held my breath and waited.

"Aisling?" a man's voice yelled as his car door opened. "Ais?"

I peeked above the rail, recognizing that voice. "Ezra?" I asked cautiously while trying to catch my breath.

He ran toward me, pulling me up and over the rail. He gave me a once over. "Ais, are you okay? Are you hurt?" He pulled me closer to him. I leaned into his hug and embraced it. Something about him made me feel safe. I started to sob as I realized I wasn't alone. Even though he was magicless, I wasn't alone.

"What are you doing here?" I asked, still catching my breath.

"Long story. Here, get in." He put my arm over his shoulders to help get me to the car. "Woah, your Mark is glowing green. You better fill me in."

I nodded as I jumped in the passenger seat, laying my

head between my legs, trying to catch my breath still. For a brief moment, my stomach turned on me again, but settled. Wait, how did he find me? Why wasn't he with the souls? Where was Haven? Was he working with Isadora? Anxiety got the best of me, and I grabbed the dagger and held it up against him.

"Why are you on this road and not with the souls?" He had missed Haven's turn back there so if he said Haven I would jump out of this car and run.

He put the car back into park and put his hands up in front of the steering wheel.

"Woah, Aisling. I'm heading up by Haven, she called. Clara and Margo left her there alone. Please, believe me."

"The turn was back that way." I didn't halter as I kept my hand against him.

"Ais, I..." He took a deep breath. "I just had a feeling that I was supposed to keep driving this way, I swear. Something was pulling me here. I was just getting ready to turn around when I saw you. I don't know how else to explain it."

A part of me wanted to believe him, but right now, my trust for anyone was on a thin wire.

"Here, check my phone. Haven called me a few minutes ago, and I left right away to get to her." I grabbed his phone from his jacket pocket and quickly scanned the information. The dagger held in place.

He wasn't lying. Her number popped up on the screen.

I dialed her number back on speaker and waited for her to answer.

"Hello?"

"Haven, was Ezra on his way to you?"

"Ais? What's happened? Are you okay? Wait, why do you have his phone?"

"I'm here too, babe," Ezra said.

"Yes, he should've been here like five minutes ago." She inhaled sharply, "Ais, are you okay?" she asked, nervously.

"Now I am, sorry, Haven. I just had to be sure that he was on our side," I said.

She laughed in the background. "Of course he's on our side, but no worries. It's been a wild night. How did you two meet up anyway?"

"Wrong turn, I guess. We will see you soon," I answered.

He slowly put his hands on my arm that was holding the dagger and lowered it. "See, you can trust me, I promise. I'm more than on your side."

I let him lower the dagger all the way and pulled it in close to me, hanging up the phone and letting the tears fall again.

"I'm so sorry, Ezra." I sobbed. "I just..."

"Don't apologize. You were scared, and honestly, you are brave for being out here alone."

Alone.

"My aunt, I left her at the cave with that psycho." I choked out as I wiped my tears. "I had to, she wanted me to release her father from this stupid dagger," I said, as I dropped it to the floor of the car, shakily. "My aunt would've made me run too. Right?"

"A thousand percent, yes." His arm came over as he

rubbed my shoulders, instantly feeling more relaxed. "You did the right thing," he said, as he put the car into drive and turned it around, heading back up the bluffs toward Haven. For a brief moment, I thought I saw a glimmer of a Mark shining through his skin, but my tears were glistening in my eyes so it was hard to tell what I saw.

Chapter Thirty-Nine

Jaxon Oakes

I looked over at Freya, sitting in the passenger seat with the window down, letting the cold air come through, making the car much colder than it needed to be in October. I turned the heat on the highest setting in her Jeep to try and keep her warm. She looked like she was shaking, but most likely from all the adrenaline and anger, not the cold. She hadn't said much since leaving the casino. Ember decided to join us, but rode in the car with Freya's parents and Eric instead. Oxana gave her the amulet before we left. She made her promise to keep it in her hands only, but Ember left me with a secret before we left.

I grabbed Freya's hand, and the chill of her fingers made me shiver.

"Hey, we will get to them." In time, I hoped, but I kept that to myself. I would make damn sure that we did everything possible to save them. Isadora should've died a thousand years ago.

Freya looked up to me and half smiled. I rubbed her hand with my thumb and tried to take on her pain.

"You need a clear head going into this, babe," I reminded her.

"Trust me, my head is clear. I'm going to kill her." The words did not sound like her, and they made me do a double take at her expression. I wanted to feel her heart and make sure she had not changed since the dagger adventure. "She doesn't deserve a prison world. She doesn't deserve to live any longer."

"What about Eric and Lynn?"

"I'm working on it."

She faced back toward the river as we drove.

"Freya, you know that I would do anything to protect you, but if you don't let me in, then I don't know how to help you."

"Don't get in my way. That's how you can help. I can't save everyone, and I don't want to live without you again," she said shakily. I could see she was trying to hold her emotions in, but on the surface, she was ready to break. I hated that she was trying so hard to hide her fear.

Damn.

Her phone chimed as we were coming to the curve to reach JFK and the cave.

"It's Ezra."

A pang of jealousy loomed over me.

"He has Ais, they are heading to Haven's."

I slammed on the brakes. "How?"

She exhaled heavily for the first time, as if she had been holding her breath the entire car ride. She turned and looked toward me, smiling. "He saved her."

"And Lynn?"

She shook her head. "Not yet."

"Call Declan and let him know before he does something stupid." I squeezed her hand and smiled back at her. "New plan, Haven's, here we come. Let's just hope that it doesn't start with another fight at her place."

She nodded, but kept smiling.

We drove on the gravel driveway where Ezra's car was parked and before I could even put the car in park, Freya ran out and toward the house.

Ais came running out, crashing into Freya's arms. "You're okay?"

Relief washed over me.

"Is Declan on his way?" Aisling asked.

"Sounds like it."

"Good, I know what Isadora's true intentions are. We have the upper hand, and I'm the only one that can give it to her. I'm the descendant."

Haven walked outside by us as Ezra stood in the doorway. We walked into the home as Haven mimicked Clara by sealing the doorway as we walked through. An extra precaution wasn't a bad thing right now.

"You're a lifesaver, Ezra," I said, as I walked past him into the kitchen.

He shrugged, "Right place at the right time, I guess. Her aunt is still up there, though. We need to get her back."

"We will." Haven walked over by us. "Hey, I hear that Clara and my mom ditched you. Any idea why?" I asked her.

She shook her head, "I have a guess, but I still would've been better off with them."

"Keeping the Anchor pairs separated and safe?"

She nodded.

I agreed that it was probably the safest move so far. Safely sealed in this cottage that Isadora did not know about. It was about the only house that she had not been to while awake, which gave me an idea.

"Hey, what if we lure her into JFK? It would, for one, keep her away from the souls. Two, she won't come looking for us here, keeping this place safe. Three, we can have her bring Lynn with her."

"What about the part where she kills us?" Ezra chimed in.

"Well, she won't kill her." I pointed to Aisling, knowing that she was the key to her plan now. "I'm pretty sure that we have the upper hand on demands right now."

"She said she didn't need me alive." Aisling answered.

"She also didn't kill you when she had the chance." I answered.

Aisling shrugged. "She said she knows the unlinking spell," she answered, nervously while looking around the room.

I froze, "She read the symbols in the book at the bar, but it doesn't mean she knows how to do it, or even is able to."

"How sure are you about that?" Freya asked.

"I mean, it's a theory."

"A theory we will have to trust at this point," Haven said, agreeing with me.

"Any idea where your mom and Clara took off to?" Ezra asked.

I pondered on the thought for a second and then realized I already knew the answer. They went after the amulet. It was the only piece that could hold Isadora with her syphoning back. "Give me a second." I grabbed my phone and dialed my mom's new burner phone. "Please tell me you are not on your way to Eric?"

The phone became silent. I could hear her exhale heavily before answering. "Son, we need that."

"Damnit, mom! I already have it!" I yelled into the phone, knowing that separating again was how I lost her three months ago. Separating was the last thing we needed right now. Ember caught me at the casino before leaving, and she handed it to me. She whispered that I would know what to do with it, and she would meet us when it was time. I gave her Freya's tracking bracelet before we left. If only my mom would have stayed here, then we could have had the extra help on containing Isadora. Now we would have to do this without her. There was no time to waste. She might know the spell. She would surely head to the house with the souls, thinking that we are back there.

"Don't go anywhere near Eric right now. I don't trust him," I said before hanging up the phone. I looked up, and everyone was staring back at me confused. I pulled the amulet from under my shirt and showed it to everyone.

"We need to get Isadora in here. Ember is going to help us."

Freya looked up at me and smiled. "Do you have a plan?" She walked toward me and kissed me.

Chapter Forty

Freya Chamberlain

Standing in Aunt Clara's living room with the others made me smile, even in a world of chaos. We were the next generation of this witching world, and we were going to make it. I stood up and paced by the window to make things more clear on how we were going to lure her to JFK. I tried to wrap my coat tighter against me to warm me and hold my anxiety from making me visibly shake. When my hand brushed the bulge in the pocket, my body froze. I reached into my pocket and pulled out the jar of squid ink that I had forgotten I had. An idea came to mind as I held the liquid in my hand, examining it. I pulled the lid off and watched as the purple galaxy became activated. I quickly sealed it and looked up.

"Hey, Haven, how much do you know about this stuff?" I showed her the bottle.

"The ink. Hm, are you thinking what I'm thinking?"

"Magic eraser for an Immortal?"

She nodded, and I smiled back at her.

"Do you think it would work?"

"Only one way to find out. Let's keep it as a last resort." She winked.

I nodded and placed it back in my pocket. I looked at Haven and studied her face. I couldn't get over the fact that her mannerisms were so close to mine. Her glasses and slightly shorter hair were the only things that separated us now that she dyed her hair. I watched her turn and sit next to Jaxon and Ezra, and a thought came to mind.

"She wants Ais to unlock her father from the prison world, right?" I pointed to Ais, who nodded. "And she wants to take my syphoning powers for security, right?" Jaxon nodded. "So, how about we give her what she wants?" I looked up, and everyone looked back at me like I was crazy. "Hear me out." I paced the window again and tried to put my thoughts in order. "Haven, you take your glasses off and wear some contacts. Then, I'll shorten my hair enough to make us visibly identical. You, Ais, and Jaxon go to JFK. We will have her meet you in the field with Aunt Lynn, alive. Aisling, you will go with them and bring the dagger. We will tell her that we will trade relatives. Once we have Aunt Lynn, we will have Ember teleport you all out of there. Isadora will be standing in the field alone and fatherless."

"She will be watching from afar before entering the field. She will know she's being played," Ezra said.

"No, she won't. She doesn't know Ember is here, and this way if she goes after Haven, she won't get my magic, and I will be alive to be Haven's lifeline. She wouldn't dare kill her only hope of releasing her father, so Ais will be fine too."

"Why not trap her in the amulet then?"

"We can try. I'm just not exactly sure how to do that."

"Your mom left her book on the table. You think you can find out how to contain her?" Haven asked Jaxon.

He nodded and walked to the couch by the book, opening it and slicing his hand, letting the book glow.

Ezra stood up and walked to the kitchen. Haven watched him walk away and followed him to the kitchen, while I stood here, waiting for any reply.

"It could work. The amulet is used like the dagger. We need to mark an 'X' across her heart with this piece." Jaxon looked up from the book, examining the amulet. Then, he pondered the scenarios. "We can try it. If she thought she was getting a two for one special at once, then it could definitely lure her in."

I nodded and looked toward the kitchen. Jaxon shook his head as if I should leave them alone for now. Something was going on with Ezra, and I didn't like it. I ignored Jaxon's request and walked into the kitchen.

Haven was standing behind Ezra who was sifting through the cabinet.

"I'm coming with you," Ezra said to Haven.

"No, you have to stay here, without your magic you are a liability. I can't focus and keep you safe."

I knew I had walked in on something that I wasn't meant to hear, but I needed to ask.

"Hey, did I offend you?" I asked.

"No, I just..." He turned toward me, and Haven watched carefully. "Freya, I messed up. I've been taking this elixir, and my magic has been suppressed for a long time."

"So, stop taking it."

"See that's the thing. After what you told me about my mom, I dumped it. The problem is my magic isn't just going to reappear like that. I need something to help bring it back faster."

Haven watched me carefully. "Could you maybe syphon the elixir from him without stealing his magic?"

I looked at each of them and debated on my strengths. It wasn't like I was going to syphon souls again. I could syphon a poison, couldn't I?

"Do you think it would hurt my magic by consuming it? Now isn't really the best time for me to be magicless." I saw him flinch at my words, "Sorry, Ezra, I didn't mean—"

"No, I know exactly what you meant. I know. It was stupid to ruin my magic. I just was scared of what my Mark might do to my future."

"Ezra, it's just a Mark, it doesn't define you as a witch. Only you can decide what kind of magic you have. You make decisions in life, and you have to deal with the consequences. So, be a good person, and life will treat you back the way you deserve. Give me your hand," I said, as I reached for him.

"Not now, you're right. We need you strong right now. My body just needs time to reset itself." He pulled his arm tight against his body.

"Time is the one thing that hasn't been on our side," I said, as I walked back into the living room by Jaxon.

Chapter Forty-One

Haven Vine

Freya had a good idea, we could pull this off. Plus, if she was safe, then I would feel better about my recent dreams. I didn't need her trying to sacrifice herself in the middle of all of this. I just found out that my family was bigger than I expected, and I needed her to stay in my life. Having her around lately made my life feel complete. I looked back at Ezra and smiled.

"Babe, your magic will be back before you know it." I grabbed his arm and looked for a hopeful Mark.

Nothing.

"Can I try something?" I asked, and he nodded.

I put my hand over his forearm and wrapped vines around his arm. I knew it was probably pointless, but I had to try. Freya needed to keep her strength up right now, and her magic took a toll on her much faster than mine. I thought for a brief moment that his arm glimmered and then nothing. My eyes widened. The elixir had to be wearing off.

"Did you see that?" I asked excitedly.

He took my face into his hands and laughed. "Babe, you will believe anything that is good." He kissed me sweetly. "Keep your strength up. We're going to need it."

I let his lips fall against mine and just embraced the normal moment for once. Although nothing surrounding us was normal. I still took it all in and let love win.

"Freya and I are going to be nearby. If anything seems off, then you need to get out of there. Promise me?" He pulled my face back from his lips and gave me a look that made me lose the love moment and crash back to reality.

"I promise."

"I love you, Haven. You are everything to me. You are the only reason for keeping me in Prairie du Chien." He kissed me again, pulling me into his arms and lifting me onto the kitchen counter, embracing my body into his arms and squeezing tight.

I laughed, "Babe, I love you too. I'm not going anywhere." I kissed his forehead and smiled.

"You better not."

We walked back into the living room. Freya and Aisling were in the bathroom, sheering her hair shorter to match my length. We both had a black long sleeve shirt on, and without our jackets, we already matched perfectly. I walked in by them and took my glasses off, grabbing my contacts. Freya handed me her moonstone earrings and tourmaline pendant to borrow. We stood next to each other in the mirror and just stared in disbelief at the resemblance.

"Kind of creepy, ladies." Aisling laughed. "I'd swear, if I didn't spend my whole life with you, then I would be fooled too." She smiled as she grabbed my hair and played with it.

I laughed, "I'm Haven." The three of us looked at one another and laughed even louder.

"I guess it will work if we can fool the lifelong best friend," I said.

I pulled them into me and hugged them tight. We giggled like children on a play date, only this was not for play. This was life or death.

"I guess I should make the phone call." Freya grabbed her phone and dialed Isadora's phone number, hoping that she kept her number after she had been discovered. She hit the speaker button as it rang.

"Miss Chamberlain," Isadora's voice answered and mockingly laughed. "Need another appointment scheduled? Finally going crazy?"

I watched as Freya tensed and her lip quivered. I grabbed her arm and encouraged her to talk.

"You have my aunt. I want her back."

She huffed, "She's not actually your aunt. I don't see why you care so much. She's just a magicless woman."

"I want her back, alive."

"What do I get out of this?"

I nodded to Freya to offer the deal.

"You can have my magic. I just want her alive."

"I want the dagger too. Get your little witchy friend to bring it back to me. Her blood is from a pure line, and I want it."

"She's pure, you're not," Freya snapped.

"That's just your opinion." She laughed. "Eric surely thought I was pure enough to leave your precious aunt for me."

"You tricked him," Freya yelled.

"Oh, honey, he's got you wrapped around his finger now too, doesn't he?" I could hear her voice rising. She was getting angry. "He will betray you too. Just wait."

Freya had to get back on track. I could see her adrenaline starting to pulse through her veins. I muted the phone for a second, "Hey, just get her there." She nodded, and I unmuted the phone.

"The field, bring Aunt Lynn, now."

"The dagger, don't forget. Or your aunt will have a new trick to show you." The line went dead.

What did she mean by that?

We stood, silently looking at one another.

"It's just a game to her," I said.

Aisling nodded, "Agreed."

I looked down at her hand and saw the veins darkening further up her wrist now, nearly reaching her ancient Mark. "Hey, does that hurt you?"

She looked down at her palm and then to Freya. "No, it happened after I got poked by the dagger. I think it's infected."

"Isadora's father is more evil than she is, and he's trapped in that dagger. I'm assuming that by you getting punctured it started the cycle already to release him. She needs your blood, and we don't know how much she needs," Freya answered.

"Well, then let's heal that up and get it to stop spreading through her veins," I said. Aisling smiled as I waved my hand over her injury, and the dark veins started to disappear, and the wound started to close.

"Thank you," she said, pulling me in for a hug.

"That was probably the easiest job I'm going to have all

day," I said and laughed, even though I knew it was me being honest.

There was a knock on the door, and Declan's voice boomed through the whole house "Where is she?"

Aisling grinned and ran out to him.

"You think the amulet will hold her when we get the chance?" I asked.

"I don't know." Freya looked up and grimaced. "A year ago, I was studying my ass off to graduate high school. Now we're trying to take down a crazy witch."

Freya and I stood in the bathroom, and I knew she felt the same as me. "She's never going to stop, is she? Unless we kill her."

"I don't think so." She hesitated, "I've never killed anybody before. I know she deserves it, but I'm scared that killing her will change me. I don't want to become like her."

"Oh, Freya, you are nothing like her. She killed her own sister. There is no amount of good left in her, and if we don't do it soon, then who will she go after next? It's either her or another innocent family."

"I just..." A tear rolled down her cheek. "I know it needs to be done, if we can't lock her away, then killing her is a must. It's just that, what if she's consumed by darkness, and what if that darkness transfers to me somehow? I was dying from the inside out with her father's soul sucking the life out of me. I can't imagine taking on her darkness too."

I saw the fear she was remembering, and I knew I needed to be the one to either lock her away or kill her. Whichever came first. I could not let Freya take this on too.

She had already done too much for all of us, and I knew she would do anything to keep us all alive.

I reached for her arm and pulled her into me. "Hey, don't think about that right now. One thing at a time. You are not taking on anything alone anymore." I linked my hand into hers and raised it in front of her. "You and I are meant for this, together. The universe made us for this exact purpose, that has to mean something." I smiled, and she wiped her tears with her free hand and squeezed mine back. "We will get Lynn back one way or another."

"Promise me that you aren't going anywhere," she demanded.

"I promise."

Chapter Forty-Two

Jaxon Oakes

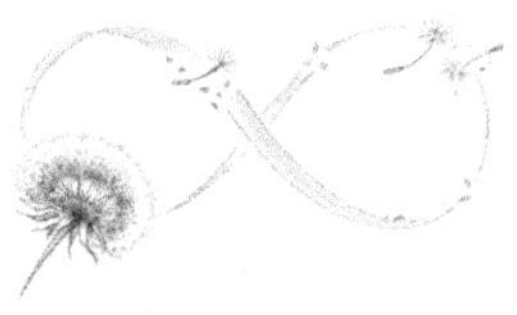

My mom and Clara were on their way back, but we didn't have time to wait. They never should've left to begin with. I told them the plan, and they agreed that it was a good plan. If Isadora could unlink Lynn, then she would surely kill her. Mom didn't like the idea, but she trusted my judgment.

"If anything seems off, then get out of there." She made me promise. "We will meet you there shortly." Which made my mind more at ease.

"Love you, Mom."

"I love you more."

The line disconnected and a pit in my stomach lingered. I couldn't lose her again. I wanted this over before they even arrived at the field.

"Hey, you guys, super off topic right now, but my birthday is next week. Promise me that we at least live to see another year?" Aisling asked nervously.

"Let's sure hope so because the Halloween parade is one of my favorite traditions for your birthday," Freya said.

"Your birthday is on Halloween?" Haven asked.

"The one and only witch that was born on a holiday that suits me." Aisling twirled around and laughed. "Witchy witch here, only this year I actually know it now. So, I'd like it to be epic."

Haven glanced at Ezra and stared as if she was communicating with him telepathically. I looked between the two of them and realized what Ezra had said to me earlier finally clicked. He didn't want to ruin his future with Haven because he was Aisling's Anchor. With Freya in a prison world, my mind was too distracted to connect the dots earlier. How else would he have found her wandering while running from danger? He was Anchored to her, and now he was afraid of losing Haven because of it.

I quickly looked away and stayed quiet. Without his Mark, it didn't mean anything yet. Ais better be right about not being killed because her Anchor wasn't going to bring her back to life right now until that shit was glowing again. *Fucker*. A part of me hated him. He was so afraid of losing his love that he could be sacrificing both his and Ais's life because of it. I clenched my jaw and stayed quiet.

We drove toward JFK and pulled over at the bottom of the road from the field.

"She will be watching, so we need to make this convincing," Freya said before unbuckling and leaning into me. "Please, be careful. If anything seems off, then get out of there. Ember said to rip the bracelet off, and that will be her signal that you're ready." She kissed me and pulled away.

I nodded and pulled her face back to mine, kissing her longer. Haven and Ezra jumped out of the car. I ignored them. I didn't care about their love life right now, only mine. "Hey." I lifted her chin up and looked her deep in the eyes. "I love you, Freya."

She smiled, and her cheeks flushed with warmth. I rubbed her cheek and kissed her one more time.

"Yeah, well, I love you, infinity." She smiled and rubbed my Mark on my shoulder before she stepped out and walked over by Ezra.

Haven jumped in the front seat, and we made the rest of our way to the field and parked. I stared out at the mended field with a foundation for our house waiting to be finished. We needed to get through this, I had way too many future plans with her for anything to fall apart now. I grabbed Haven's hand and squeezed it hard. "Well, here goes everything...babe." She laughed, and I jumped out and opened the door for her, holding her hand all the way to the tree.

I hoped that this would just go smoothly. I twisted the bracelet once more before sitting under the tree and waiting. Haven sat next to me but with distance. It felt unnatural. I leaned closer to her to close the distance. If Isadora was watching us, then we needed to make sure she believed her to be Freya.

I leaned in toward her and started to whisper, "Ezra is Aisling's Anchor, isn't he?" She froze for a moment before mimicking my closeness. She leaned into my chest, laying her head against me. She seemed truly exhausted, and her tense shoulders started to relax while next to me.

"Seems so." She inhaled sharply. "I swear I didn't know. I don't think he realized either until the other day either."

"I think that's why Ezra could hear Isadora's screams

from the cave that day, he is connected to Aisling in a magical way."

She nodded, realizing how true this all was.

"Does anyone else know?" I asked.

"I think it's just us now."

"Good, let's keep it that way for right now. I don't want him to be a target while being magicless, and I don't want anyone knowing that Ais isn't fully protected yet."

She looked up at me and studied my face, making me fidget. "You really are just pure good, aren't you?"

"The white knight, I guess." I laughed. "I just want to save everyone."

"Just like Freya. You two really are perfect for each other."

"*We* are perfect for each other, Freya." I winked at her, and she smiled.

"She's here, isn't she?"

I nodded. I could see Isadora off in the distance. She was hesitating. I looked away quickly and pretended to not have seen her. I pulled Haven in closer to me and glanced out of the corner of my eye. I watched as Isadora started to turn around.

"Shit, she's leaving. Play along."

I grabbed her face and pulled her lips closer to mine and let mine brush into hers. It was an awkward moment in my head, but my body had muscle memory to Freya's lips, and I let my body take over. She kissed me back, and the moment became natural. I slowly stepped back and held her face as she stared back at me, shocked. I saw movement out of the corner of my eye as Isadora walked toward us with Lynn floating behind her. "Let's not talk about it," I said, as I helped Haven up, and we steadied ourselves under the tree waiting for her to close the gap between us.

"Miss Chamberlain," she acknowledged Haven as Freya. "Where is my dagger?" she yelled when she was closer to us.

"It's here, once Aunt Lynn is safe then Ais will bring it out," Haven spoke.

Isadora studied her face and seemed convinced at the switch.

"Fine," she huffed and waved her hand back toward Lynn. The spell she had on her vanished, and Lynn's eyes opened as she stood up behind her.

"Are you hurt?" Haven asked her.

Lynn examined her body and shook her head. "I'm fine, where is Aisling?" She had pure concern in her shaking voice.

Aisling started to walk out of the wooded area with Declan and came into the clearing. "I'm here, Aunt Lynn," she spoke confidently.

"Of course the mini Eric is with you." She rolled her eyes. "And the dagger?" Isadora asked.

Aisling pulled the dagger from her back pocket and waved it around in the air.

"Give it back to me," she demanded.

"Not until she's next to me."

"Two choices: Either you release my father from that wretched prison world or Freya willingly lets me syphon her magic. I wasn't born yesterday. Trust doesn't come easy, and I trust no one."

"Same time," Aisling bargained with the dagger in the

air. Declan stood protectively next to Aisling and watched every movement carefully.

"Better idea. Jaxon, since you have an Anchor, how about you hand me the dagger? I will release this worthless woman and then you will be free once Miss Meadows breaks the prison world down."

Damn, she really did have trust issues.

"Deal," I said too quickly at Lynn's safety being my priority.

Haven tugged on my hand harder than I had expected. "No, you're not going anywhere near her again."

"I'll be fine, babe."

She hesitated to release my hand. Something began to feel off. The earth beneath me felt like it was ready to shatter. I looked back at Haven who had pleading eyes not to move any closer. She knew something that I wasn't processing. She shook her head frantically, never losing eye contact.

"Oh, come on, I'm not going to kill him again. Been there, done that."

I pulled Haven's hand from mine as Aisling handed me the dagger. I studied the obsidian blade as I took a step closer to Isadora. I froze as I realized what Haven had been thinking and looked back at Haven. *I am her nephew.* And she knows it. As everything started to click, I retracted my step and tried to put more distance between Isadora and I, but I was too late.

The blade was pulled from my hand, and I felt the poison of the prisoner releasing inside me. *Fuck.* A writhing pain piercing into my chest made my lungs struggle to expand. Realization hit me as my heart raced too quickly and my breathing slowed.

I looked over and saw Aisling's horrified eyes as she was staring back at me. I tried to turn and find the real Freya, but she was nowhere in sight. I needed her right now. Something was wrong, and my body didn't feel like it was healing. I felt like I was dissolving. I could feel my magic fading. The worst of the pain was radiating from my infinity Mark and not even from the new scar that would form when I woke up. If I wake up. I looked down to see the dark veins expanding from my chest.

Something is wrong.

My mind raced. I looked up and watched as Aisling's palms raised up as she aimed her magic toward me, throwing a black smoking fireball right at me. She was trying to kill me. *What is happening to me?* I closed my eyes and accepted my fate, knowing that her judgment was usually right.

I waited for the impact, but nothing hit me. Her force pushed past me and knocked Isadora off me with the dagger flying into the air and falling back to the earth. I tried to dive for it, but I had no strength left in me. The dagger came crashing toward the earth, exploding into a million little pieces across the field.

No!

Haven ran to me and ripped the bracelet off me as the shock started to disappear and the actual pain caused by the wound started to set in. The wind picked up around us, and the sky grew dark far quicker than it was supposed to. An unnatural storm was brewing in seconds. The universe was mad at us. We had failed. I just released her father.

I couldn't move as my knees buckled from underneath me. *Shit.* My own blood just betrayed me. Haven leaned over me and flashed her healing hands over my chest, letting the vines wrap around my body, trying to hold me together.

"Jaxon, hold on," she yelled, but her voice was fading.

"Freya," I whispered and waited for her hand to hold mine. I just wasn't ready to be alone in whatever darkness was consuming me.

"It's not healing! Jaxon, please, hold on." Haven's hands waved over my chest again, only this time I could see the struggle in her eyes. "Freya!" she screamed.

Isadora stared at the shattered dagger and then charged toward Haven. Rage consuming her. Aisling jumped in front of her and tried to push her back but was thrown back.

"I'll take my chances with the worthless twin. Thanks, nephew. See you soon, Daddy." Isadora yelled, as she ripped Haven away and blew a kiss toward me before disappearing. I laid there, worthless.

Ember appeared and froze as she realized she was too late. "No, the bracelet just came off. No." She disappeared and reappeared with Eric at her side. "Eric, help him. The dagger is shattered. Her father is—"

Ember's words became faint, and I started to drown out her words, knowing that whatever fate was to come was because of me. Freya and Ezra came running into the field as Declan attempted to stop Isadora with a wall of water, but failed. Everything happened so fast. I then watched as Ezra kept running in the direction that Haven had disappeared, screaming empty threats into the air. I looked down at my chest and saw dark veins growing across the wound and my body. It wasn't healing. That was why it hurt so bad. I rested my head down onto the ground and watched the rolling black clouds winding above us as the un-forecasted sleet started to impale us. Freya shoved the ink back in her pocket and grabbed my head and rolled it onto her lap, it was pointless. I could feel her trying to syphon whatever poison was consuming me, but it wasn't working. Whatever Isadora had injected me with wasn't something we had medicine for. I tried not to give up, but my eyes were becoming so heavy. I could see my mom running toward me, but I just needed to rest my eyes, just for a minute.

I woke up with the wrong Chamberlain in front of me.

"Hey, kid, geez, I'm sure happy to see those pretty eyes again. Damn, you really had me worried."

I sat up and looked down at my chest immediately, feeling a little lighter. My chest was scarred but healed. The dark veins were gone. "What happened?" I shook my head trying to remember anything, reaching for my shoulder to check my Mark. It was still there.

"An ancient Viking salve was able to do the trick. Plus, these magic hands were able to syphon the prison world from ya, kid." Jim winked at me and smiled.

"Ragnar?"

"We don't know. He's out but hasn't shown his face yet."

"Damnit, it's all my fault."

"Stop," Jim raised his hands above his head and inhaled sharply. Then, I saw the dark veins growing up his arms. He had consumed the prison world, but at what cost?

"Jim—"

"I'm okay, son. The dagger's been destroyed. So, just heal up, and we can figure things out."

I processed what he had said and realized that the dagger had really shattered. I quickly reached my pocket and felt the amulet still in there. Relief washed over me.

"It's still there too. I don't think it can hold both worlds. I think we need to make another dagger for him."

I nodded, agreeing that we couldn't take any chances on pairing them together. "Where's Freya?" I scanned the room and realized we were at a hospital, not someone's kitchen table.

"She's out there trying to track Haven down. Eric is with her. We had her location with her phone apps and then she just disappeared. Cloaked, we're thinking."

I nodded. "A hospital?"

"Your wound was a little more complicated without our healer and the dagger. I was able to syphon the prison world, but your wound was causing some internal bleeding, and your Mark was fading so we didn't want to take any chances. The salve was just something extra to help with the scarring."

"So, how am I still here?"

"Ask your mother," Jim said.

"Is Lynn safe?"

"Yeah, she's here too. A little more complicated, but she's here. Izzy linked her body to her own before trading her over. Any pain inflicted on Izzy, Lynn feels it too. So, we're working on that still. Haven must've done a number on her because Lynn is pretty beat up. She's in the next room over just in case things get worse. Don't worry, we will get her back."

I heard Ais's voice echoing in the hallway, bossing the nurses around and demanding more warm blankets and chocolate pudding. "Is she okay?" I asked, as I pointed toward the doorway.

"Aisling?" Jim huffed and smiled. "That woman can survive anything. She's already plotting her revenge."

"Jim," I reached for my phone. I just needed to hear Freya's voice, to know she was okay. "I'm going after her." He waved his hand in the air, and my phone flew from the table, into his hand. Great, he had been practicing his own magic. Good for him, bad for me right now.

"I can't let you do that."

"Give me my fucking phone." I added, "Please." Irritation was starting to ignite in me.

"Listen to me for a second. We need you fully healed. We need all the Anchors healed if we're going to fix this." He hesitated. "And I mean *all* the Anchors. I need both of my daughters together. If you call her right now, then you distract her. She needs to focus on one thing at a time. I told her you are sleeping and comfortable. She was content with that answer for now."

I thought about it for a minute and just glared at him. "I'm wasting my time laying here."

"Your Mark was almost gone and you just had a nine-inch blade pierce through your chest, you should be dead. Heal so we can keep you alive." He mimicked me, "Please." He stood and walked towards the door.

"Jim," I yelled, "I'm sorry, she will be alright." When I said 'she,' I really didn't know which twin I meant, but he understood anyway. I knew now that he was more worried about his daughters getting back safely. So, I decided to heal in silence.

"Your mom could use your help next door with the spell book of hers." He nodded before exiting.

At least I could make myself useful that way. I sat up, let the dizziness subside, and grabbed the drink that was sitting next to me. I sniffed it and realized it was Clara's healing tea by the smell of Verbena and herbs. I gulped it down quickly and glanced down at yet another scar formed on my chest. I was starting to look like Eric. I grimaced at the site and was thankful for my second, third, and fourth chances at this supernatural world. I seemed to be the target of bad business lately. I jumped up and walked to the room next door.

My mom was flipping through pages of the family book with a pocketknife and bloodied bandages. She glanced up when I walked in.

"Hey, you're up. How are you feeling, sweetie?"

"I'm fine. Can I help you?"

She smiled and pulled up a chair next to her. "Sit."

I sat next to her and grabbed the book from her hands. I blinked, trying to focus my eyes on the pages filled with runes. "Hey, I can see this."

She looked at me, saddened eyes. "That dagger did a number on you. I transferred my magic I had left in me to you. I needed to keep you alive."

"But I thought you had a revenge plan?"

She shook her head, "Not anymore."

"But what about Freya having to destroy you and your sister? Now she will have to destroy me." My eyes grew wide at even the thought.

"There's the loophole. Freya needed to destroy my magic, not me. Same for Izzy." She half smiled. "How do you feel?"

I examined my hands and tried to think of my greatest desire. "Well, the revenge must've come through the transfer, because I still want to kill your sister." I laughed.

I looked down to see her Labradorite necklace still intact and was grateful for her immortality while she had it.

"Good," she smiled. "Now get over here, there should be a spell in here about repairing the dagger. Or maybe it's on the next page." She flipped the page again and waited for me to read it. I realized that she could no longer see the words. She no longer had any magic.

I looked down at my hands again, still trying to process.

"One day, you would've received my magic anyway, so what better time than now. We need to mend that prison world and get my father back in it. Jim can only hold that world for a little while before it starts to pull him into it. Jim thinks he's invincible, but that world was created for an eternal prisoner, and it's very strong. How he's holding it this long is unbelievable."

"How do we fix it?"

"You," she said and smiled. "All you, baby."

I looked up at her confused. She pulled out a bag with the shattered obsidian pieces and the intact Hildisvinian mandible handle. She handed the bag to me and turned the page of the book, pointing to a page with a spell that I could read and translate for the first time. I looked at the rune symbols and realized I knew an ancient language.

"This book is yours now. I have written down everything I know. Every spell in here needs a drop of your blood to work. Now, no one else can use these spells until you pass this book down to your children and so forth. Not even Izzy. Think of it as a lock and key, and you are the key." She smiled and rubbed my hand. "I should've given it to you when your Mark appeared. I just wasn't ready to give you up. I knew you would've found a way to fix things with Freya, and I couldn't let you do that. I needed Freya and you to grow without influencing one another."

I didn't fully understand, but I trusted her judgment on this subject because, as of right now, it seemed that she knew much more than she had mentioned to begin with. I skimmed through the spells and looked up, realizing Aisling and Lynn were sitting there quietly watching us. Lynn pulled a necklace off and handed it to Aisling while smiling back at me.

"Looks like you are more important than you thought." Aisling winked as she placed the necklace over her head and stood up, leaving the hospital.

I grabbed the bedside table and pulled it closer to me, laying the dagger pieces on it and lifting my hands over it to mend it.

"Here goes nothing."

Chapter Forty-Three

Freya Chamberlain

It was all such bullshit. Everything went wrong today, and if I would've just been next to Jaxon, then Haven never would've been taken. *She will be okay,* or at least that was what I kept telling myself. The plan was stupid. We never should've gone there without the elders. *Ugh.*

I kicked the bucket that was sitting next to Jaxon's old home, now filled with souls. Eric said he needed to see Ezra, who had barged into the house after Haven was taken. He pleaded to the floating souls to help him. Callum quickly placed him under a sleeping spell to calm him down before he shook the pennies too much and moved the magic hold.

I walked inside the house just in time to hear Eric talking to Callum.

"Wake him up," Eric demanded.

"He tried to break down the barriers that were holding the souls in here, he is unstable right now. He needs to sleep it off."

"His mother is one of those souls up there, and I'm sure

with Haven gone and his Anchor missing in action that he just had a nervous breakdown. Give him a second chance. I have something for him that will help make him ready. We need all the help we can get right now."

Aisling and Declan walked inside the home and joined the conversation. Declan needed to be far away from Jaxon right now. For one, he was his best friend and would help him out of the hospital when he needed to be resting, and two, he was his Anchor, and we needed them both alive. Separation was better for them right now since Jaxon seemed to be the target for Isadora and her killing frenzy.

Callum ignored them walking in and looked at Eric in confusion. "He doesn't have magic."

"We're going to trigger his Mark," Eric announced.

Aisling assessed the situation and gasped when she heard his words. "The hell you are. You can't attempt to kill him. He's been drinking an elixir to suppress his magic. If you come close to killing him, he actually might die." She pushed Eric further back from Ezra and stood protectively over him.

"Get out of the way, we are going to need him."

"Take one more step, and I'll add your soul to the ceiling," Aisling yelled.

Eric turned toward me and pleaded, "Freya, a little help here."

I laughed and watched Aisling manage to light up her palms with green orbs. "I mean, it looks like she is handling things just fine."

Eric growled, "Damnit, I'm not triggering his Mark that way." Aisling let the orbs dissolve, and her eyebrows scrunched together. "But now I have a hunch who his

Anchor is." His voice had become calm again. In his centuries alive, he wasn't used to being talked back to.

Aisling straightened herself and crossed her arms. Her Mark was glowing. "And who would that be?" she asked, annoyed.

"Well, who's standing in between us right now." Eric laughed and relaxed. Aisling gasped and turned around to Ezra and just stared at him. Her eyes wide with shock. "Damn, if we would've known that sooner, we could've planned things accordingly." Eric exhaled and leaned against the wall. "So, now can we wake him? I have something for him that will trigger his Mark."

Aisling hesitated and looked between me and Declan. Her eyes froze on Declan's.

"I mean, if he's your Anchor, then it would be good if he had his magic back as your lifeline and all." Declan huffed. "I mean, damnit, it could've been anyone. Why him?"

"We don't pick our Anchor, look who I got." Eric laughed. "The killer queen."

"Yeah, to match the king," Declan snapped back.

Eric crossed his arms and waited silently.

Ezra's mom had transferred her magic to him before I transported them here. They must've been afraid of it not working and wanted a failsafe... meaning Eric had Declan's too.

I cleared my throat and waited for Eric to look at me. "Do you have a gift for someone else too?" I asked, annoyed that I even had to bring it up.

He glared at me from exposing his secret. Had he

planned on keeping the magic for his own gain? "I do, but not yet."

Aisling looked to me and then back to Eric. "If you kill him, I will kill you. Understood?" Eric lifted his hands up in a white flag surrender and nodded.

"Step back, he's going to be angry," Callum warned.

Eric stood across from his sleeping body, and Callum stood behind Ezra's head while the rest of us stood to the side.

"Excito," Callum whispered, and Ezra's eyes flew open.

He stood quickly and became aggressive, trying to orient himself. He pushed toward Eric and paused when Aisling jumped in front of him.

"Ezra, stop." She put her hand up to his chest, and he paused. "Back up, and calm down." He did just that. No, he obeyed her.

I watched closely as I realized their Anchor bond was strong, only that Ais was controlling him. Whether that was due to her being a controlling person in real life or because of their link, I couldn't tell.

"You need to stay calm," she said, and his breathing became even.

"Wow, why can't you do that with Isadora? I sure can't do that with Jaxon," Declan sneered. He got pissed and stormed out of the room but kept himself in earshot.

I stood my ground and held my impulse from going after him. I needed to focus and not have any other distractions right now. I needed my sister back, and Ezra would help us.

"Must be because he was suppressing his magic for so

long that you became the stronger one," Eric answered, unsure if it was reassuring himself or he was answering Declan who was no longer in the room. "I have a theory."

"She's been holding his magic, hasn't she?" I asked, a theory that came to mind. Magic just didn't disappear, and Aisling had been very quick to learn everything once her Mark appeared, even her getting away from Isadora was not luck. She had extra magic on her side.

Eric nodded.

"Ezra, look at me," Aisling said, and he obeyed. "Listen, you love Haven, and I love Declan. We might be Anchors, but that is all we are. We will protect each other, but that is all. Do you understand?"

Ezra nodded and then exhaled with relief.

Aisling looked at Eric and smirked, "See, it wasn't that hard to not break my aunt's heart."

Eric winced as her words cut deep. A part of me felt sorry for him, but then again, he made choices, and he had to live with them. Unless he was under Isadora's spell too? No, he was just a typical man when another woman lured them into their chambers. Viking asshole.

"Don't worry, we are not Eric and Isadora. We will not become evil lovers too." She smirked, and Ezra laughed for the first time. "How long have you known?"

"Since the day you got your Mark. It matched mine. I'm sorry. I just—"

"I get it," Aisling nodded. "Haven."

Ezra nodded and looked down, trying to hide his emotions.

"Hey, promise me something," Aisling said, as Ezra

looked back up. "You protect me like a brother should, and I will do the same in return." She smiled.

Ezra lifted Aisling into a big bear hug. She looked so small in his arms. I smiled, knowing that he meant his pact with her.

"Ezra, I've got something for you. Your mother told me I had to wait until you accepted your magic, but we don't have time to wait," Eric announced.

"My Mark isn't visible yet. I don't want to waste it."

"Freya, syphon that elixir from him."

My eyes bulged. "Wait, what if it weakens my Mark again?"

"It won't. Trust me."

"That's a big trust to give you."

"Fine, then let's just transfer the magic and hope for the best," Eric said and grabbed Ezra's arm, pulling him closer to him.

"Wait!" I yelled, "Okay, I'll do it. But if anything happens, and we don't get my sister back because of it, then you're a dead man. Uncle or not. Understood?"

"Geez, you twenty-first century women are very bossy." Eric smirked. "Must be in our blood." Eric winked, and I glared back at him. "Alright, alright, I understand."

I grabbed Ezra's hand and looked him in the eyes. "This might hurt."

He braced himself.

I started to pull from him. I could feel a barrier trying to push me away, so I pulled harder, trying to break through the shield. I could feel the elixir in him, pure poison. The suppressor was hiding underneath the barrier shield. I closed my eyes and envisioned myself tearing it down piece by piece. I took a mental sledge-hammer and tore it down. Ezra grunted and inhaled sharply.

"Oh shit," he growled, as his breathing became more rapid.

There it is, push Freya. It's right there. I gave it another big pull and forced the poison to exit his body. *Got it!* The elixir was flowing through his veins in reverse and heading for me. The taste of bile rose in the back of my throat. It was an awful mixture, and I hoped that I would never have to taste it again.

"Just a little more," I grimaced, as I could feel my nose begin to bleed. Only as I wiped it, it was not blood, but black liquid, exiting me. I looked down, panicked as I realized the elixir was being extracted from him and then from me. I smiled as I saw the puddle of poison on the floor in front of me. Syphoning from him was not hurting me at all, but it was healing him. It just wasn't pleasant, but it was working.

I syphoned the last drop and looked up at Ezra. He wasn't making eye contact with me. He was distracted. He was looking down at his forearm. It was glowing with his Mark. Two triangles interlocking just like Aisling's, and it matched Eric's and Isadora's.

"It worked!" I squealed and jumped into his arms. "It actually worked. I healed you!"

I couldn't help but feel ecstatic. I was a syphon, but somehow, I was a healer for a brief moment too, and giving his magic a chance to come back felt better than taking it. *Haven.* She was just so pure as a giver. We needed to get her back now.

"Thank you, Freya! I feel more like me again." He lifted and hugged me.

Without hesitation, I said, "Now never use that shit again." He agreed.

Aisling joined us in a group hug and cheered. "Ezra, now go jump off the roof."

My eyes widened as Ezra set me down and walked toward the stairs for the roof.

"Aisling, what the hell?" I asked, horrified.

"I'm just kidding." Ezra laughed and walked back toward us. "Looks like the obeying is over, meaning my magic is mine again." He winked and smiled.

Eric walked over to him. "Alright, it's time. Welcome back to the witching world." He shook his hand and held it longer. "Now, this might be a lot to take in. It's your mother's magic and something else, just stay still." Ezra became serious and stood tall, closing his eyes.

A bright light glowed between their interlocked hands as Eric used his free hand to grip their hands tighter together. The light grew brighter and blinded us in the room. It only lasted under a minute before the light disappeared, and a soul above them flickered bright before it faded away into thin air. Ezra opened his eyes and embraced Eric in a hug.

"Woah, thank you for that." Ezra swallowed hard and then smiled.

I watched intently at the unexpected moment, wondering what the something else was now.

Eric nodded and cleared his throat. "We should get going."

Declan was sitting on the stairs in the hallway, peering

over and watching the entire scene. Whatever Eric gave to Ezra, I hoped he had the same for Declan. Aisling walked out by Declan and Ezra followed her.

"What did you do for him?" I asked.

"I transferred his mother's magic to him."

"What was the something else?"

He exhaled and started to walk past me, I grabbed his arm and pulled him back. "What else did you give him?"

"Time. Extra time together with his mother."

I stepped back and gave him a confused look.

"I let him have his closure with her. I will do the same for Declan, just not here, not now. Declan doesn't need that yet, he's not broken."

Broken. That was exactly what Ezra was. He had lost everything, and now he gained so much back, now we needed to get Haven back.

I grabbed him and pulled him in for a hug, "Thank you."

He stiffened for a moment and then relaxed and put his arms around me.

"I'm not as bad as you think."

"Well, let's not go that far." I smirked as we walked out to join the others.

Chapter Forty-Four

Haven Vine

It was so cold here; wherever we were there was no heat on or even insulation in the home. I looked around trying to figure out where we were. There were tools and ladder through the doorway of the room that I was sealed shut in. The house must be under renovations, but where it was located was impossible to tell.

I sat quietly, trying to listen for any sounds of rushing water or civilization. Silence at first, but then I heard it. The river was rushing nearby, which didn't give me much of a location, but at least it made me feel closer to home. I had no idea what she had planned or if I was getting out of here alive. But I was on my knees now praying that someone would come for me.

I heard the door creak open, and a man's voice was muttering to himself, getting closer to me. I grabbed the object closest to me, ready to defend myself. A razorblade. I braced myself as he approached the doorway.

"I have food for you, but if you try to kill me, then I

have permission to let you starve," he announced, as he stopped right outside the spelled room.

I held my breath as I debated on my options, "Okay, fine," tucking the blade in my back pocket for safe keeping.

He stepped closer to the doorway and set down a tray of food. Fruit, bread, and some kind of steaming soup. My stomach grumbled as I looked at the food, realizing that I was hungrier than I realized and also that the soup would help me from shivering in this cold room.

"Woah, she didn't tell me it was you." He stepped back after looking at me.

"Excuse me?" I asked, confused.

"Hey, now I didn't mean any trouble with the accident. She told me what to do, and I did it. I didn't have a choice. I meant no harm."

What the hell was he talking about? My mind raced as I tried to place him. *Nothing.*

"I have no idea who you are," I said honestly.

"The semi collision? No? I mean, okay. Nevermind then."

Then, it clicked. He thought I was Freya. Wow, we fooled him too. I laughed as he started to fidget with his hands.

"I know you. I'm not Freya, though. I'm her twin."

He gasped as he stepped forward, closer to the room. He was careful not to enter the barrier. I walked closer to him and examined his face.

"You said you had no control? Do you mean like you were spelled? Possibly?"

He shook his head, "I have no idea. She threatens my family if I don't do what she says. I just don't feel like myself while I'm doing it. It's almost as if I am being controlled, if that makes any sense."

"She's compelling you with magic. I can help protect you if you release me."

The man stepped closer, and I thought for a brief moment that I had won him over.

"I can't, she will kill them." I could see the strain in his expression, that he wanted help but didn't know who to trust. Isadora was threatening him, and he was scared to disobey her. His expression said it all. "Eat your food while it's still hot." He pointed to the tray and turned quickly to leave, leaving me alone with the food in the cold house unfinished.

I ate quickly, letting the soup burn my throat, to get some energy for whatever was to come. I just needed a little bit of hope to keep me going at this point. Once I finished the surprisingly good meal, I sat quietly. With nothing but time to overthink every scenario that had passed and anything to come. The room was starting to feel smaller and darker. My anxiety started to kick in that I may never see my loved ones again.

I thought of Aunt Clara and how lonely she would be if I wasn't there and who would tend to the garden with her. I thought of Ezra and how broken he would be, since I had held him together like glue since he was a child. My heart throbbed at the thought of him being alone again. He would most definitely take off and leave Prairie du Chien. I thought of Freya and our parents. I just got them back into my life. It just wasn't fair to have to leave them now. I needed to help them one last time. But how could I do anything while trapped here?

I looked down at my Mark that was finally whole after all these years. I traced my finger around the Unalome symbol and followed the endless knot. Who would've thought that after all these years that this symbol would be the end of me and my family? I guess we were no longer endless. Isadora was going to kill me. She had no use for me now. She would consume my healing powers and ruin the only chance we had at going up against her and Ragnar. Freya and I will no longer be a stronger together duo, and Freya couldn't take her on alone.

What if I took the Mark out before she could syphon my healing powers? I was sure she was just trying to keep me to lure Freya here to take both of our magic. What if I could beat her at her own game? I stared at the symbol and tried to think of any scenario that would benefit the others. I could do it. I could sacrifice myself. I just needed to get a letter to the others first as a goodbye because she would surely kill me once I did this. I looked around the room and saw a pad of graph paper and sketch pencils sitting across the way. I jumped up, and a small amount of hope came back to me. If anything, they would be able to find me with a letter explaining why.

I grabbed the paper and started to write but froze when I realized I had zero idea what to say. The door opened, and I quickly pushed the paper away and sat back down in the middle of the room and waited.

"Good, you're awake," Isadora said, as she walked into the sealed room.

I gasped as she made her way inches away from me. "What do you want from me?" I spat back at her.

"I want your and your sister's magic. It was meant to be

mine all along. I am the syphon twin. I am the strongest. You two should not have been born. Abominations. With you two here, you are just ruining my fun."

"The world is not yours."

She laughed and mocked me, "*The world is not yours,* shut it. The world is mine, and it spins because of me. I get what I want. No matter what the cost."

"Why are you so... evil?" I asked, baffled at her bluntness as a spoiled brat.

"You don't know a damn thing about me. Everything I have done has its reasons, and as of lately, you and your friends have been getting in the way. Now I'm just annoyed."

"What possible reason could you have to murder innocents?"

She huffed, "Are you kidding me? You really think I did all of that on my own? Eric had a huge role in everything. He forced me to kill or be killed long ago. Eric is the reason for all of the souls being trapped. He became sick with power and immortality and dragged me along with him."

"Funny, he says the same thing about you." I studied her expression, and something in her eyes made me question our alliance.

"Doesn't surprise me. He's always been one step ahead of me." She shook her head and looked out into the distance. "Listen, I know I messed things up when I went after my sister's magic. It was my father's idea. He tricked me. You would think he would be happy to have two witches, but instead, he resented us for taking his magic the day we were born." She clicked her tongue. "My mother banished him with that dagger. She thought we were spending too much time together. Only she didn't understand that I was practicing my darkness, and I was able to control it unlike many others before me. I was not evil, just powerful. My father gave me a mission to help get his magic back. So, I started my quest for him. Then, my mother locked him away without warning, and he decided to take something of mine with him, and I wanted it back."

"He's out, so get it," I said with annoyance.

"It's not that simple."

I sat there quietly, trying to process what she was saying. Her father was like a poison to her, seeping under her skin. Whatever he had, she was obsessed with getting it back. She would kill for it. Maybe the real question was what he stole from her. Maybe she really did have some good in her at one point, and he dragged her down into the darkness. I had to hope that there was still some good in her because, otherwise, my time was running short. She would kill me soon.

"What could he possibly have of value to you? You have all the power in the world." I carefully picked my words.

She looked at me and answered unexpectedly. "He's all I have left in this world. He's the only one that cares about me. When he left, he took my mother's soul with him, making me lose everything. I've lost my child, my lover, my friends, and all my family. He had her with him in that prison, and I want her back."

"I don't think 'care' is the right word. He seems to have been using you for his own gain." I swallowed quickly as I realized I said too much. My words flipped a switch inside her, and she became the Isadora that we knew.

"Stupid girl, I knew taking you was pointless. Your own father abandoned you and then your mother didn't even want you, so she sent you away. You are the most worthless being on this planet. No one will come for you because no one loves you." She laughed and stood up. "I don't need you to heal me. I will just take your magic for myself." She continued to laugh and started to walk away. "Stupid girl."

"Wait," I said, as she paused. "Will he give it to you? Her soul, I mean?"

I wondered if her soul was flying high in Jaxon's home, and she just had no idea.

She froze, facing away from me. "Can you heal the dagger?" She turned around and waited for my answer.

I stood speechless, unsure of how I was supposed to heal a magical prison world. That was not something I had practiced. When I didn't respond, her irritation grew.

"See, you are the worthless twin. This is why I need your sister." She turned and took a step away. "He left her in the prison to rot." She walked away silently.

I sat there, shocked that her one desire for a thousand years was to have her mother's soul and now it was lost as the dagger, shattered across JFK. My stomach turned as I realized her mission for the last thousand years had just been ripped away from her. If her father was out, then he would know the souls were out too, all but her mother's. My head spun as I realized I needed to get out of here to warn them and quick.

I almost felt sorry for her for a brief minute, as I knew that her words were meant to hurt me because she was hurting. I tried my damnedest to not let them get under my skin, but she was right. I have always been second. Our mother would come to me, but only after she had spent time with Freya first. Aunt Clara only raised me because she had no other choice. My mind started to make scenarios in my head. *Stop. She is getting into your head. Ignore her. Don't give her the satisfaction.*

I went back to the paper pad and started to write the letter that I was ready for. I grabbed the razorblade and set it next to me, ready to carve out my Mark after the letter was finished so no matter what, Isadora would not gain anything from me. No more power, and especially not from a set of Anchor twins. Dead or alive. I prayed I would still be alive after all of this.

My eyes widened as the paper before me started to burn. Ashes floating down under it. I tried to pat out the flames, but they continued to grow, but no heat was coming from them. A letter was coming through.

Haven

My name was written on the tiny, folded piece of paper with blood smeared across it. I quickly grabbed it and unraveled it, scanning the letter to see who the sender was.

Freya.

My heart raced as my body relaxed with relief. I read the letter multiple times to make sure it was real.

Stay alive. I'm coming for you.

The only way for them to have an advantage toward her would be to harness from the red moon. She would for sure syphon my healing magic from me before then, giving her more power than she deserves, yet again. Why she hadn't already done it made me wonder if she was afraid to lose her syphoning again, or was she just using me to lure Freya to her? I couldn't wait any longer to find out. I folded the letter up and placed it into my pocket. I took a deep breath in as I grabbed the razorblade and quickly whispered a numbing spell, hoping that it wouldn't hurt as bad.

"Isadora," I yelled, waiting to have her attention back.

She walked back to the doorway with her arms crossed. "What now, you whiny little witch?"

"I won't let you have me or my sister." I lifted the razorblade into the air and forced it down into my Mark, carving around the symbol until the Mark turned black and then vanished. Isadora attempted to stop me, but failed. Blood trickled down my arm, and the pain was there, but not horrible. The spell helped, thanks to Aunt Clara teaching me a numbing spell as a child until I could figure out my healing powers for myself. "Now you get nothing from me."

She lifted me up with inhuman strength, screaming into my face, but my magicless body was numb to everything she was saying and doing as she threw me away from her against the wall, making the room fade, matching my symbol before it disappeared. Now it was time for me to do the same.

Chapter Forty-Five

Freya Chamberlain

I knew I needed to give Haven some hope, even if it was just a small note. I knew if I was in her shoes that I would be panicking and feel alone and start to lose hope after the first twenty-four hours. I would plan on my next move, and if she was anything like me, then sacrificing herself would be my plan so Isadora couldn't gain anymore power.

I folded the paper enough times to make sure it could fit in my palm, so it was a small piece to try to transfer. Ember stood next to me and tried to explain her teleporting trick. She could not get to her because we had no idea where she was, wherever they were keeping her. She had to be cloaked. But I knew she was still alive because I could feel her, and my heart just knew it.

"Okay, focus, Freya. You need to imagine the object becoming weightless so you can push it through to her. You two share the same DNA as twins, so we can use your blood to try and send it through to her."

I nodded, poked my finger and let the blood pool into one small bubble at the tip before smudging it on the letter. I closed my eyes and concentrated.

I could feel the paper still in my hand and then nothing. I tried to close my palm on the empty air but was stopped by the paper still there. It had become weightless. Time to push it through. I pictured Haven and imagined her receiving the letter. I pushed all of my energy through to her and hoped she would get my letter. I had a plan to get her back, and I just needed her to be ready to escape. The letter went through, and I knew that she had it now. I could feel a weight lift from my shoulders.

Margo was teaching Jaxon how to unlink Eric and Aunt Lynn, starting with Aunt Lynn now. The hope was for her to not need an Anchor. Only time would tell. We had no other option at this point. Jaxon was also attempting to mend the dagger at the hospital while we located Haven. We all had a mission today, and they all are supposed to end with us staying alive. We needed to get Haven back and safely. We needed to harness the power from the red moon to lock Ragnar and Isadora up, but that was still two days away. I wished we could manipulate time here in this world and speed things up like the dagger world and get this over with today. I just needed Haven to hold on until we could locate her. I could feel us getting closer.

Something started to course through my body, something was happening. Something felt wrong. I looked down at my Mark, which started to burn. I tried to stop the pain radiating, but nothing was slowing it. My body started to shake as I felt power building inside of me. Not just my power, something else. What was happening? "Somebody help me," I yelled, not caring who came to me at this point. I felt off. My body started to tingle. I stared down at my Mark while trying to keep myself from falling over. My head started to pound like a splitting migraine taking over my body. I lost my balance and fell to the ground, trying to catch myself, screaming to try and release the burn.

Haven. An image of her popped into my head, and I saw her, laying on the ground, and her Mark was gone. She was alone and damaged.

"Hold on, Haven." The pain started to subside as fast as it set on, and I lifted myself back up.

Ember appeared in front of me, helping sit me up. "What's wrong?"

"I don't know yet. Something happened to her. I can feel it."

"Hold on. I've found her. She's moving." Ember closed her eyes to concentrate. "I don't know what changed, but she's traveling too fast to be running. They must be driving, and they're getting closer."

Eric and Ezra walked back into the house as Ember started to talk.

"Where is she?" Ezra asked frantically.

Ember closed her eyes, "I can see her. She's not alone, a man. I can try and grab her? But she's getting closer."

"No, let her come to us. Is it Ragnar?" Eric asked.

Ember continued to scan her vision and shook her head. "I don't recognize him." Her eyes remained closed. "They just turned on this street," Ember announced.

Ezra and I ran outside and peered down the street. The

others joined us, and we all waited with our magic ready in our palms. Whoever had Haven was either helping her or trapping us, but we couldn't take any chances.

The car was flying down the road, no wonder she was hard to teleport to. I turned my palms facing them and let my electricity charge into my hands, aiming them toward the car forcing it to slow down. Eric watched me carefully as I contained my magic and was able to safely bring the car to us.

A man jumped out of the car and ran to the trunk, pulling Haven from it. "Please, help her," he yelled, as he got closer to us.

I froze when I saw his face and recognized him. The semi driver.

"Get back!" I screamed at him, fire igniting in my hands. "Put her down and get back."

"I can't do that, Freya." He walked closer. "This is my second chance. Help her."

Ezra pushed past me and ran to her, grabbing her from the man's arms. "Haven? Baby, please open your eyes." He scanned her body and froze when he reached her carved out Mark. She did it. *Shit*.

Ezra laid her down and jumped up, pushing the man back against his car. "What the fuck did you do to her?" He grabbed the man and lifted him into the air, crashing him down against the hood of the car. The man yelped and gasped for air.

"Please. I'm. Trying. To. Help," the man pleaded, as Ezra pounded him into the car again. His Mark glowing as his fist broke through the hood. Eric grabbed the man from underneath him and pulled him to safety.

"Ezra, stop," Eric warned.

Aisling ran in front of him, pinning herself between him and Eric. "Hey, you need to calm down."

Everything happened so quickly. I ran to Haven and assessed her. I exhaled as I realized she would be okay. My note falling out of her pocket. I nodded to myself. "Ezra, she will be fine. Call Clara and get that tea recipe." I whipped my head around and stared at the semi driver. "And you," I sneered. "You have some nerve coming back here."

I grabbed the man by the ear and dragged him into the house, forcing him to obey otherwise my ignited palm would burn him alive.

"Izzy, she did this to her. Not me." He started to talk as I threw him against the wall, Eric trailing behind me.

"What did she do to her?" Eric asked calmly.

How could he be calm at a time like this? Everything was falling to shit.

"I was coming back on my supply run for her, and I saw Izzy throwing her around in the room. Her forearm was all bloody and gouged out," he said shakily. "I jumped between the two and begged her to stop. Izzy was furious. I thought she was going to kill me too, but she didn't. She walked away, and as soon as she left, I grabbed her and drove here. Izzy had mentioned this home a few days ago, and I just prayed that someone was home who could help."

"Liar." I brought the flame to his face and started to burn him alive. He did this. The man screamed in pain as his flesh boiled.

"Please!" the man pleaded, as he screamed.

Eric grabbed my hand and pinned them to my side,

away from his face. "Freya, what the hell are you doing? He told you what happened." I huffed and reignited my palm again as he extinguished it. "Damnit, Freya. If you can't control your anger, then you are worthless to us today."

I glared at Eric and tried to catch my breath. I looked at the man, and my eyes couldn't believe what I saw in front of me. The man was terrified and burnt. I did this. I hurt him out of anger. Oh my God. What had I done?

I pulled myself back and stared at my hands. "I, uh, I'm so sorry. I don't know what happened."

Eric pulled me back and grabbed my hands, staring at them.

"Who cut out Haven's Mark?" Eric asked the man while not letting go of my arms. The man was now gripping his face and writhing in pain. "Who? Was it Ragnar?" he yelled again when the man didn't answer. Dropping my arms and walking toward the man, he pinned him back against the wall.

"I don't know, I was too late to see." He cried, "Please, I was just trying to help. She said she could help me with Izzy's compulsion." He continued to cry, sliding his body against the wall to sit down on the ground.

"Freya, give me your hand," Eric said and pulled my hand toward him without consent. He examined my Mark before pulling a knife from his back pocket and slicing his hand. "Heal me."

I looked at him, confused that he had the wrong twin. "I can't do that."

His jawline clenched as he pulled my hand tighter towards him. "Heal me now, or I will kill Jaxon's father."

Callum had been standing to the side of us, staying quiet and watching carefully. I looked to Callum, who swallowed hard and gave me a pleading look to do what I was told.

I turned to Eric and pushed him back into the wall. "Do not threaten me," I screamed into his face.

He pushed me aside with unnatural human speed and grabbed Callum, holding his neck awkwardly in his hands. "Heal me, or he dies."

Shock took over me. He was serious. "Okay, stop! Let him go. I can't heal you, but give me your damn hand so I can prove it."

Eric slowly released Callum and walked back over to me, holding his hand out in front of me. "Heal me."

I hovered my hand over his and glared at the man that I thought was on our side. To my surprise, my hand started to grow its own vines from the center of my palm and wrapped around Eric's wound, wrapping the healing leaves around the cut. I stared in awe at the sight. *What the hell? I Iuven, what happened to you?*

"Mhm, just as I thought. She willingly cut her Mark out. Her magic found you as a safe zone." He laughed and looked up to me. "She will be okay."

I shoved him back. "Stay away from my family."

"You needed motivation. It worked." He smirked.

I looked down at my hands and just stared in wonder. What had happened to her? I ran toward the door as Ezra was carrying her into the house. I let him lay her down before I ran to her and waved my hands over her injured body. I willed her body to heal, and glowing vines came from my hands again and wrapped around Haven's body. I sat, staring in disbelief. Her whole body was glowing until the vines released her, and she lay completely healed. Only her Mark was now just a scarred area of flesh.

She opened her eyes and sat up quickly.

"Haven?" I whispered, tears ready to spill over.

"Hey," she said shakily, looking around her surroundings. "How did I get here?"

I laughed as I embraced her tightly. Ezra stooped behind us, pulling us together into a group hug.

The burned-faced man stared at us with his hand covering his fresh wound. "She's okay." He exhaled heavily and sat back. "Thankfully."

I released myself from the group hug and walked over to him and lifted my palm up to his face and let the healing magic do its job to undo the damage I had done. "I'm so—"

"It's fine." He rubbed his healed face and smiled with relief. "I'm the one that should be sorry. I have caused so much damage in your life, and I never forgave myself for what I had to do to you and your boyfriend. Your sister was my second chance of redeeming myself."

Haven stood up and walked over to the man. "You got me out of there?"

"Sorry I wasn't there sooner. I had no idea how far she would take things."

"Any idea what her next plan is?" Eric interrupted.

He shook his head, "She just tells me what to do and when to do it."

Haven shook her head. "You and your family are safe, you have my word." She turned toward Eric. "Cloak him and his family from her please. Because I actually keep my word when I say I'm going to do something."

"As do I," Eric said and walked with the man into the kitchen with a map in hand.

Ezra grabbed Haven and lifted her into his arms, kissing her hard.

Chapter Forty-Six

Aisling Meadows

I went out on the front porch to call Jaxon to see how the unlinking spell was going with my aunt. We could not do anything with Isadora until she was unlinked permanently. I still didn't give a shit about Eric, but we would have to unlink him too, otherwise she would continue to have a second chance at surviving whichever plan we went with. Hopefully, Jim loved his brother enough to be his Immortal Anchor for the next thousand years. I shook my head, thinking about living forever and how truly selfish it was or really how sad it was. To live and lose everyone you love, then start over. It just seemed sad.

"Just tell me that you are almost done with her?" I asked, annoyed at how long it was taking. Margo and Clara brought all the herbs they needed to the hospital, and it shouldn't take long now.

"Almost there, half an hour. I just needed to practice the spell a few times on a plant before I tried it on a living human. My mom is finishing the batch of sage and mugwort that she has to drink before I can start the spell to break the bond." He exhaled slowly. "Hey, just remember that once I do this, she will no longer be linked to either Immortal. She won't have a second chance anymore."

I thought about it for a moment and realized what he was saying. *She will be fragile.* Then, the more I thought about it, everyone was fragile. Aside from Anchors, mundanes only got one chance, and if they were lucky, they got a second one.

"I know. She will be normal, and that's what she wants. So, that's what she can have. Thank you, Jax."

"Yes, ma'am." We were both silent for a minute and then he added, "Hey, Ais. I think tonight might be a good idea for Declan to have his mother's magic back. Just in case anything happens to us tomorrow. I think he could use the peace."

"Already on it. After him finding out that Ezra is my Anchor, I feel that he could use a confidence boost." We both laughed.

"Who could use a boost?" Declan walked out beside me, making me jump.

"Hey, Jax, I've gotta go. Thank you again. Love you."

"Always, love you too."

I hung up, feeling a weight lifted that my aunt wouldn't be in harm's way for much longer. I knew that it was the right thing to do. I just had to give Declan the letter and give him the magic inside this pendant now.

I looked inside the doorway as I was playing with the magic filled necklace, and Eric watched me closely as Declan sat down next to me on the porch. I stared at Eric for assurance, and once I saw him nod, I knew that this was the right time.

"Hey, babe," I said, pulling him in and kissing him. Grabbing the back of his head and playing with his dark hair, I twirled my fingers in his loose waves as his lips found my neck. "I have something that belongs to you."

He pulled his lips away from my neck and looked back at me confused.

I pulled the envelope from my pocket and unfolded it for him, handing him the letter. "Your mother gave Freya a letter for you. I can give you a minute alone if you want?"

His eyes were filled with shock as he studied the writing. He didn't respond, so I quietly stood up and turned to head into the house to give him a minute alone.

"Stay. Please."

I turned back around to see him staring at me with his hand extended for me to come back to him. I smiled and sat with him. He smiled, but I could see the nerves growing inside him. I put my hand on his leg and steadied it from bouncing anxiously.

His eyes never left the envelope. I touched his hand holding the letter. "Only when you are ready."

He nodded, "I'm ready." He opened the envelope carefully and started to scan the letter. I watched his face and never looked at the letter, not wanting to invade his personal moment with his mother. I could see his eyes fill with tears, ready to spill over onto the delicate paper. His lips turned up into a smile, and he laughed, then continued to read. I waited patiently for him to finish.

He folded the paper and then looked out toward the sky while wiping his tears. He sniffled, then his eyes met mine.

"She wants to meet you." He smiled and chuckled at

the thought. "She said Eric can help."

I smiled back at him, trying to figure out how the heck we were supposed to do that. He turned his head toward the house to call Eric, but he was already standing nearby, waiting for his request.

"You read the letter?" Eric asked.

Declan nodded and smiled. He stood up. "I never knew."

"It wasn't anything you needed to live with, son."

Now I wished I would've read the letter. I was watching a very personal moment of growth and felt a little uncomfortable and was thankful that my parents were traveling so often for work that I didn't have to have these kind of awkward moments with them, even though I missed them terribly.

"You saved her soul, and you even tried to save my dad. I wish I would've known at a younger age. I wouldn't have been such an ass trying to find them."

"You were just a child, and I was learning to be a father figure." Eric shrugged, and I could see he felt uncomfortable too.

"Not just a figure. You are my father. Thank you for giving me the opportunity to grow up. Isadora would've let me burn." Declan grabbed Eric and pulled him in for his first official hug in probably years, if not his first one. Eric stood shocked for a minute before his shoulders relaxed, and he hugged him back.

"Are you ready to see her?" Eric asked.

Declan nodded. "She wants Aisling to come with. Can you do that?"

Eric smiled, "For your mother, I would do anything."

Eric pointed to the pendant, and I quickly grabbed it and pulled it off over my head, handing it to him gently.

"Well, let's get this over with. Join hands."

We interlocked our hands as Eric placed his hands on our shoulders. The porch around us became distant as our surroundings became bright and shimmered with a whimsical layer of magic, bringing us to a dimension that was peaceful.

I opened my eyes and waited for the bright lights to fade, and my eyes focused. There she was. His mother was standing in front of us. Her smile matched Declan's. I could see the resemblance, but he must look more like his father. She was so beautiful. I could instantly feel my eyes become wet with tears at this private moment. Declan opened his eyes, and without hesitation, he let go of my hand and reached for his mother. Pulling her physical body in for a hug, she leaned into his chest with him being so much taller than her. He leaned down and kissed her forehead as she just held onto him.

"Hi, Mom."

"Oh, boy, have I missed you. My sweetest Declan." She sniffled and pushed him back to look at him from head to toe. "You look so much like your father. Wow. This is the best day of my life." She looked over to Eric and winked, making him smile back at her. He turned around and stood quietly, letting the moment be theirs.

"Okay, let me meet this woman of yours. We don't have too much time here, and I want to soak it all in," Grace said and put her arms out for me to join them. I did just that.

Her hug was so warm and welcoming. She just had this sweet energy about her, and I wished we had longer together to get to know each other. I wished she would be at our wedding one day. Then, I froze, even thinking about that when we didn't even know if we would live through tomorrow's red moon. *Stop, enjoy this moment.*

"It's so nice to meet you," I said.

"Oh, sweetheart, the pleasure is mine. Anyone that can handle my boy has all my blessings." We all laughed.

Eric cleared his throat and turned around, handing the pendant to Grace. "Why don't you do the honors."

She nodded and took the magical necklace, breaking it in half and containing an orb of magic between her palms. The orb shimmered with blue waves crashing against its walls. It looked as if an entire ocean was contained in one little sphere. I stood and stared in awe at the beautiful moment. Eric grabbed Declan's hands and placed them palms up in front of Grace and stepped back.

Grace took her orb and whispered, "Magic of mine, flow to the next. My time is done, his time is more. Let his life be long and filled with oceans of love." She placed the orb over his open hands and slowly turned her palms over to lay parallel with his, pushing the orb into his hands and letting it absorb into his skin.

He closed his eyes as the power ignited inside of him. When he opened his blue eyes, they were a brighter shade of blue than I had ever seen. They shimmered like the ocean themselves. I looked at Grace and realized she shared the same blue. He had his mother's eyes and now her magic. It was such a beautiful moment that I could stay here forever.

The glow between their hands dimmed, and it was done. I looked between them and just stared in disbelief that this was my life right now. Declan pulled his mother into another hug and just held her.

"I hate to do this, but we have to get going," Eric said.

Grace nodded. "Thank you for bringing him to me. Please stick together," she said to Eric. Then, she grabbed me and whispered, "Please keep him on his feet, you are the best thing in his life, and I hope you stay." I smiled and agreed. Then, she turned to Declan, "I love you forever, and I will always be with you."

"I love you, Mom. Forever." They embraced and held onto each other as the bright light came back and the porch came back into view. The dimension was closing as Declan came into view, I swear I could almost see Grace in his arms still while standing on the porch before the light faded and we were back.

Callum walked to the doorway, "Hey did you—" He stopped himself when he realized where the soul had faded to. Grace was at peace now, and her magic was safe with her son. He nodded and walked back into the soul room.

"That was amazing. Eric, we need to do that for each soul up there. I mean, if we make it through tomorrow," I said, and he laughed.

"That might take awhile," he said.

"Well, as an Immortal, you have forever. Make that your next life's mission." I smirked and grabbed Declan, kissing him on his cheek.

"Love you, babe," he said.

"Love you, forever," I said back to him.

He winked, and his bright blue eyes shimmered in a way that made me believe that his mother would always be with him. I was happy about that.

Chapter Forty-Seven

Freya Chamberlain

The souls were swimming above us, and I couldn't take my eyes off them. So much power up there that belonged to descendants, to be freed. I watched as one of the souls flickered and disappeared, and I knew exactly who it was. I smiled, knowing that Declan was able to have his moment, and now he had his magic enhanced too, which would help us.

"Goodbye, Grace," I whispered to the ceiling. "Rest easy."

Aisling walked back into the house with them, and she smiled when she met my eyes. Haven was sitting next to me with Ezra on her other side. We finally had a minute to breathe, and I was thankful to have Haven back. Everything in this moment started to feel right. Tomorrow, we would have to fight. With harnessing the moon's power, we had no other choice but to finish this. But tonight, I just wanted to be with the ones I loved. I stood and grabbed my phone, knowing that I needed to be by Jaxon right now. I needed to have him near me, especially if this was our last night together.

I dialed his number and waited for him to pick up.

"Freya? Everything okay?"

"Everything is great. We have Haven back, Ezra has his Mark, and Declan received his mom's magic. Right now, I'm taking this as a win." I smiled, thinking of the good things that had worked for us and forgetting the bad.

"And I mended the dagger. Not the prison world part, but it's a start. Working on unlinking Lynn right now. A few more minutes."

"Promise me that if she needs an Anchor, then you will link her to my dad. We will figure out another one for Eric later if need be."

"Absolutely."

"Good. Seems like we are getting back on track. The only thing that's missing from me right now is you."

He laughed, and I knew that if we were together, he would be blushing.

"Well, that can be arranged. Just say the word, and I'll come over."

I looked up from the phone, and in the distance, I saw a lady and man standing at the end of the road. I squinted as I realized something was flying toward me. Not just something, but a ball of fire was heading straight for my face.

"No," I yelled and dropped the phone, trying to dodge the heat.

I could hear Jaxon, confused, unsure of what was going on. "I mean, I could keep resting at the hospital, but I'd rather be with you."

"Jax, they're here. Help!"

I pushed myself up and ran into the house, quickly sealing the doorway.

"They're here! Everyone get ready. We need to keep these souls away from them."

Eric got up from the stairs quickly and walked toward the window, peering down the street. "Shit. Ember, can you get us all out of here?" He looked to Ember as she nodded.

"No, we can't leave these souls alone," I yelled.

"She doesn't know they're here," Eric said.

"She will in a second," Ezra said, as the door flew off the hinges and went shooting down the hallway.

"I knew it," Isadora yelled, as she stood in the doorway, trying to break through the seal. "All this time, I was chasing you when I should've come to the direct power-source," she said to me.

"Get back," Eric threatened. "You don't want to do this, Izzy."

"Oh, but I do," she said, as she put her hands up to the seal and started to syphon the seal away. "Too easy." She smirked at her father behind her, as he watched her intently while she gained more power.

He met my gaze and smirked. "You should've set me free when you had the chance. That could've been me swimming up there."

"No," was the only word I could get out.

Aisling stepped forward with her green smoking palms of magic. I quickly jumped in front of her, facing her. "Stop, your aunt is still connected."

Aisling's eyes bulged. "So, we just let them take these?"

She was right. Aunt Lynn would be furious if we just gave up. Eric looked over to us while we debated.

"Girls." His voice was stern. "It's now or never."

Isadora looked up and smiled. "Yes, girls. Hurt me, hurt Lynn. Decide. Quickly," she sneered, and she already knew that we wouldn't risk it.

"Freya, Ember, go heal her now," Eric demanded, deciding for us as he rushed out of the house and charged his former lover and her father. I stood in shock as he plunged them fifty feet down the road, and the cement broke into the air and demolished the entire street. I ran out to the porch and watched as Eric and Isadora were fighting at an unnatural speed as they whipped each other back and forth through the neighborhood. Ragnar was making his way back to the sealed house.

"Keep him out of here," I yelled to the others. "Ember, get me to the hospital. Lynn is going to need more help than the nurses can give. Hurry."

She didn't hesitate as she grabbed my arm, and Jaxon's old home disappeared and screams from the familiar hospital room surrounded me. It was her. I pushed the door open and ran next to Aunt Lynn, who was writhing in pain, spitting up blood and bruising too fast. Jaxon was hovering over her, working on the unlinking spell. I stood on the opposite side, pushing my parents and Margo out of the way.

I hovered my hands over her body as the others in the room stared at me, confused. Vines extended from my palms and wrapped themselves around her thrashing body. The minute the leaves touched her skin, her body started to relax and the pain began subsiding. Jaxon's hands were hovering over her as he whispered incantations from a language I did not recognize. The book was laid out next to him, and he was reading off the invisible pages.

Aunt Lynn looked up to me with thankful eyes.

"We've got you," I said and looked back at Jaxon as he was focused on the book and his spell.

Ember was waiting behind me, tapping her foot. She was ready to send us back as soon as this was over, telling the others that Izzy was at the soul house and Eric was fighting against her with the seal still partially up.

"Should I syphon the souls to me until we can get them safely home?" my dad asked Margo.

"I don't think you should take on anything else right now. Your body is already struggling to hold a prison world together."

I looked up to my dad and agreed. "Once she's unlinked, Ember can bring us back to the house, and we can all protect the souls. Jaxon, how much longer?"

He broke his trance and looked up to me. "It's done." He stared down at her as her skin was glowing and healed. I waited for her to combust or disappear without having an Anchor. When nothing happened and she looked up and smiled, I knew we were okay. Jaxon smiled as he watched the shimmering of two triangles rise up above Aunt Lynn and disintegrate in front of us. "She is free from them and mortal."

I held the vines around her body an extra minute just to make sure that she was fully healed before leaving.

Jaxon walked over to me, breaking my concentration and lifting me up, hugging me tight. "Let's go."

Margo asked, "Ember, how many of us can you take back?"

"Whoever is willing."

"No, Mom, you stay here with Lynn. I can't risk losing you again. I will get Dad back. I promise. Alex and Jim protect that dagger at all costs."

Margo didn't argue. You could see that, deep down, she didn't want to fight her own sister and father. "Then, go." She kissed him quickly as Ember grabbed our hands. I watched my dad pull the dagger in tighter against his chest, my mom leaning into him protectively. Both of them watched us intently as we teleported.

Jaxon's home should've come into view as soon as we were back, but there was nothing there. I looked around the area and became breathless as I realized the house had been obliterated. We were gone for less than five minutes. *Impossible.* Ember grabbed my arm and pulled me hard away from the road as Isadora tried to grab me.

She was bloodied and bruised, but still standing.

"Well, that was fun. Hi, Ember. Tell your mom I say hello." She winked, then disappeared with her father trailing behind her.

I looked up and down at the street and tried to figure out what had happened in the small amount of time, shock coursing through my body. I could feel tremors starting as my stomach churned. She consumed the souls. We were all in danger now. The entire witching world was going to be on the run to stay alive.

"Hey, look." Jaxon pointed to the house as a shimmering dome appeared where the house should've been. I just stared, waiting to see what we were up against now. I lifted my palms, letting them ignite and braced myself.

Ember smiled with relief as she looked back at me. "It's them. I didn't know you had a protector on your side."

I stared back at her, confused as my palms kept the flames burning.

"One of those witches is a protector, they can throw a shield up to protect or hide others." She shook her head. "Geez, doesn't school teach you anything about our world?"

Jaxon ran over to the dome and yelled. "Dad?" He slammed hard against the dome, trying to break it but was thrown back a foot by electricity. My eyes grew wider as I watched from afar. My brain was still trying to process what the hell just happened.

The dome disappeared, and there was Ezra, with his arms lowering to his sides and his Mark glowing bright. He had done this. Haven stood up, looking up around the open skies. Aisling, Declan, Callum, and the semi driver stood too, checking their own bodies for injuries.

"Damn it, she syphoned the souls," Callum said, looking around the area. "Damn it, damn it, damn it!" He kicked the loose boulders and thrashed his hands in the air, cursing the sky.

I counted the heads and realized we were missing one. *Eric.* I looked around frantically, not wanting to care about him, but deep down, I knew he was family. and I was supposed to keep him safe. I at least owed him that.

"Where is he?" I turned to the others and continued to search through the rubble that remained. Jaxon turned toward the remains and lifted the large pieces into the air, trying to search with me.

"He went with them, Freya." Haven grabbed me and started to shake my angrily. "He left with them. He betrayed us." Haven grabbed my face and made me focus on her words. "He betrayed us." I stared at her in disbelief. Her cheek has a large cut from her ear to her lower lip. I stood, shaking my head as I stared. I didn't start to believe her until I saw the tears roll down her face.

"No, he wouldn't." Anger spewed through me. "He—" I couldn't accept that. Not after the recent good he had shown me. I just couldn't accept that.

"Come on, we need to get out of here. We need to get out of Crystal Rock at this point." Jaxon grabbed my arms and pulled me closer to him. "It doesn't matter whose side he's on at this point, Isadora consumed the souls. We have no power against her. All of the witching world is in danger now."

"He wouldn't." I stood, dumbfounded at what had just happened over the last few minutes. Things were finally looking up, and now everything just came crashing down. "Fuck!" I screamed and threw my hands into the air, my overwhelming new magic needing to be released from deep inside me before it made me explode. I screamed louder and dropped to the ground as the tears started to roll down my cheeks, matching Haven's heartbreak.

This power was too much, and I wanted to combust. *How can Isadora take on so much magic?*

Angrily, I started to lose it. My magic started to take over my emotions, and I was ready to break. "Fuck!" I screamed again as a dome of magic exploded from my chest, knocking everyone back, sending them further away from me.

Not caring who was in my way, I was going to kill her, Ragnar, and Eric. Tonight.

"Ember, get me to my dad. Now!" I demanded, as I looked around and realized she wasn't within earshot. She was standing next to Jaxon who was hovering over someone laying on the ground. I ran to them, realizing what I had just done. Breathing shakily as I tried to reach them, I froze as I saw Callum laying there motionless on the ground.

"No." I gasped, as I reached him and tried to find a pulse. Jaxon ripped me off him and started CPR while I stood back and watched frantically. "Oh my god. No. Please, I didn't mean to." I stood with my hands covering my face, in shame and regret.

I did this. What have I done?

Jaxon stood up and turned toward me, pushing me back and throwing me down on the ground. "You. Need. To. Calm. Down." His tears matched mine while he struggled with my arms, as I thrashed out of his grip. His jaw clenched hard as he was holding back his own rage. I gave in and let my body become still, trying to wrap my head around how big of a shitshow we were in and how I just made things worse.

"Jax, I—"

"I promised my mom he would be safe." Jaxon stood up and released me from under his grip wiping his tears. "Freya. Damn it." He stepped back and shook his head, pacing back and forth before crouching to the ground and covering his head and his pain.

I laid on the ground before my knees buckled from

underneath me, trying to catch my breath and wrap my head around what I had just done. I didn't mean to. I just lost it. I was just so angry. Everything went to shit, and there was nothing I could do about it. Haven should've had her healing magic at the hospital while I was here to protect the souls. But instead, I had to be in two places at once. *Impossible.*

Ember squeaked behind me, "Hey. Are you still you?" I leaned up on my elbows and looked up toward her, nodding behind tears, wishing I wasn't me anymore. She nodded. "I'll be right back." She disappeared into thin air. I looked back to where she had been and panicked when she reappeared as fast as she had disappeared. "I just wanted to check on my mothers. They're okay." She half smiled as she looked around at the damage here. "For now. She knows I'm helping you all now. That isn't good."

I laid back down and covered my head, trying to come up with a better answer than running. Jaxon would never forgive me for this. My stupid temper just ruined my future with the only man that had ever held my heart. I did this. I killed Callum, and there was no going back from this. I ruined everything. Now I was nothing but a vengeful witch with magic inside me that was too powerful for me as a newbie. I chose my own destruction over our safety. All because I was too angry to analyze the situation and then take action. Having Haven's magic on top of mine was too powerful for me. I didn't want it. I didn't want any of it anymore. I just wanted to be normal again. I just want to go back in time and reverse ever awakening my Mark.

Deep down, I didn't want that at all. If I wouldn't have found out about being a witch, then Jaxon would not have swooped back into my life and pulled me back up. Haven would've been a distant stranger to me that I would never have run into, purposefully by my Aunt Clara, who I would not have met, either. My mother would not have come back into my life and mended my father. My father would still be my father, but to know that he was harder to kill than I thought was a nice safety net to have in a supernatural world. I took a deep breath and thought of all the good that had come the last few months and weighed it out with the bad. I had to think of this day by day and stop looking so far into the future. I exhaled slowly and just let my brain sort through the files in my head and decide on the next best plan. We just needed more time to figure out what the best option was. More time to train my dad. More time to get Haven's Mark back. More time to plan anything. We all just needed more time.

Time.

Thyme.

A thyme spell? Is that even possible? Could we fix all of this?

We had extra help tomorrow night under the red moon. We could harness its power. Just like in the dagger world. This could work. Couldn't it? I sat up quickly, trying to clear my head for a minute and give my brain time to think things through.

We would need to go back to the hospital before everything went to shit. I kept my hands over my eyes and thought about the exact moment where we could fix this. Before the souls were taken. Before Callum was killed by my stupidity. Before Eric betrayed us. Before Haven carved out her own Mark. Before Jaxon released Ragnar. Before Isadora took Haven.

Wait. There.

We could change the course at JFK. We knew exactly how that played out. We were all there. If we could replay that exact moment, knowing what her true intentions were. She didn't need Aisling that day, she was able to use Jaxon. She didn't need me that day, either. She just wanted to eliminate me as a threat. Aunt Lynn would be there for us to take back too. We needed to set the thyme spell for that exact time and replay it. Only this time, we would be in charge with the upper hand.

I looked down and saw a penny face up and took it as a lucky sign that this could work. I picked it up and put it in my pocket before calling out to Haven. I wiped my tears and didn't dare to look back at Jaxon or Callum while I planned to save his dad's life in my head. She walked over to me, feeling defeated herself. I looked at her face and remembered that I could heal that wound. I lifted my hand to her cheek and willed the vines to come out and heal. "Hey, how much do you know about thyme spells?" Haven looked over to me and smiled.

"The thought came to mind back when Aisling was taken and then again before I cut my Mark out." She winked. "I figured we could have a do over if the universe lets us, and maybe get everything back. How far back are you trying to go?"

"Far enough to fix all of this."

She looked over to Callum and pointed. Looked like he had an Anchor, after all. Callum sat himself up and groaned at his aching body. Jaxon ran to him and helped lift him off the ground.

"Dad?" He wiped off Callum's shirt and helped steady him. "How?"

"Well, damn, son, it's good to see you too." He laughed and slapped Jaxon's back. "You really think your mom would leave me unprotected and in charge of souls with her crazy family around?" He raised his arm and showed off his bracelet. "I'm no Anchor, but I have a brilliant Immortal for a wife."

I released the breath that I had been holding and ran to him. "Callum, I am so sorry. So, sorry. I didn't—"

"Oh stop. Now if you can just use that power against Izzy, then we might have a chance." He pulled me in close and hugged me.

"Yeah, the only problem is, it's not just Isadora anymore. Eric went with her, and Ragnar can't be far from them," Jaxon added.

Callum frowned as he looked around at who was left standing, "Huh." He exhaled slowly. "Well, now that is an issue."

I stood silently as I heard his hope fade quicker than it should've.

"I might have an idea," I said quietly to him, not wanting to get anyone's hopes up. I whispered the thyme spell theory in his ear.

He pondered the idea for a minute and let his brain tick through each scenario. "Freya, if you do this, there will be consequences. Manipulating time always comes with a price. A price that is not always wanted to be paid."

"I don't think we have another choice at this point."

He looked around at all of us that had gathered now and studied each person's expressions. Haven, smiling, knowing the plan could work. Ezra, shocked that he actually had great magic of his own. Aisling, ready to take down the Immortals that have hurt her family one too many times. Declan, pissed that Eric left without warning. Jaxon, ready to defend his mother's broken heart. Ember, ready to be free. Then me, ready to accept the consequences for whatever we had to do to make this right again. Jaxon grabbed my hand, and in that moment, I knew that we would be okay. Eventually.

"Call the others and have them meet us at Swig and Jig. And someone let the others know the plan. I need to figure out how to use this twin magic before I hurt someone unintentionally again," I said, as I processed exactly how our plan needed to go for this to work. Only this time, we were going to win. At least, I hoped so.

Chapter Forty-Eight

Haven Vine

The bar was just as we had left it. The closed sign was still on, and I was sure locals were pissed that their favorite hangout had been closed due to supernatural issues and being short staffed with everyone that owned the place in danger. We waited until everyone was here before sealing the bar. Only this time we weren't taking any chances, and Ezra used his shielding dome to completely close us off. Watching him use his magic was the most amazing thing I had seen with him, and the happiness it brought him was everything. I knew he felt closer to his mom while using it, and I didn't think he would ever let it go again.

Ezra looked over to me as I was admiring him finishing the protection seal. Now I felt like the powerless one next to him, but that was okay because I was going to get my magic back. We needed to plan this out exactly right, down to the last second, otherwise the Immortals would know something was off. I looked down at my phone and realized it was almost dead. Not that I needed to call anyone outside of this bar, but I felt better knowing I had a fully charged phone just in case.

"Hey, is there a charger here?" I waved my phone in the air.

Freya pointed to the office and said, "Bottom drawer to the left, most likely under a stack of applications now."

Our dad laughed as he nodded in agreement. "What would I do without you?" He smiled at her, and she shook her head, smirking. They must have an inside story about that one.

I walked to the office and opened the drawer, only to freeze when I saw an envelope with blood smeared on it and Freya's name written in big letters. I grabbed the letter out and examined it closely. This was not the normal piece of mail that anyone would keep. I held it up and looked through the light trying to see what it was.

ERIC signed in large print at the bottom. Talk about being signed, sealed, and delivered.

I gasped when I saw his name at the end of the paper. I hesitated on opening it myself or bringing it to Freya in front of everyone else. Then, I decided this was planted here secretly. It was not on the counter in plain sight. He wanted her to find it on her own. This was meant to be her eyes only.

"Hey, Freya," I yelled. "I can't find it." I lied, already gripping the charger in my other hand.

"Okay, coming. But I swear if Dad moved it to another spot, he will be in bigger trouble."

"Close the door," I said, as she walked past it.

She closed the door and looked back to me with questioning eyes. "What's going on?"

I held up the sealed envelope. "This is from Eric. We can either burn the lies or read them. What do you want me to do with it?" I grabbed a lighter that was sitting in the open drawer and held it close to the envelope, ready for her decision either way.

She stood, staring at the letter, burning her own hole through it. "Burn it. He's dead to me," she answered and looked away.

I flicked the lighter and froze myself.

"Don't hesitate. Like you said, lies either way," Freya said, disgusted.

"I know, I just… " I exhaled shakily.

"You're afraid that we might miss something?" she finished my sentence.

I nodded. "I'm a planner. My brain doesn't like to miss information, even if it's a lie. I have a need to analyze. My brain likes to pick apart each detail and let me decide the truth."

"Okay, fine. Open it." She inhaled sharply and waited.

I scanned the letter once, then twice, then a third time. I looked back up at her and handed the letter over for her to read for herself. She walked over and took it from me.

Freya,
Family always comes first. You have reminded me of that. I will forever be grateful for the hope you gave back to me. I know you think I betrayed you. I left to

save your family. So, now please save mine. Please tell my brother goodbye. Get a head start and get out of Crystal Rock. I will cloak you as long as I can. Maybe one day we can have that Thanksgiving dinner together. Either in this life, or our next. I promise next time I will be better at this family thing.

-Eric

Freya looked up from the letter, and I could tell that now she wished I would've burned it too. She shook her head and scrunched the letter together, raising it to her forehead in frustration. Then, she unraveled it and read it again only this time outloud.

"I promise next time I will be better at this family thing," she huffed and balled up her free hand into a fist. "We're not running from her."

"I agree."

"Eric's family, Haven. We need to free him of her."

I nodded, knowing that the letter hit a soft spot in her and the only plan we could go with now was the thyme spell. Whatever the consequence was, I didn't think either of us cared at this point.

I thought of Eric sitting next to Isadora and explaining to her where he had been the last few weeks, and my stomach turned for him. What would she do to him knowing that he'd been with us? Would he lie and pretend that he was infiltrating us? Would he say he was with Lynn or Declan? Would Ragnar kill him for betraying his daughter over the years? Did the souls talk in the prison world? Did Ragnar know Eric's true intentions? Now I couldn't stop thinking about him. I was no longer worried about my Mark or the thyme spell. Instead, I was worried about Eric's wellbeing. If that wasn't family, then I don't know what was.

"Haven?" Freya was saying my name, trying to get my long-lost attention. "Hey."

I looked up at her and just nodded. "Yes, we need to save him too."

She smiled as she walked next to me behind the desk. Grabbing a notepad and pen, she started to jot down a timeline, circling JFK. I thought through every moment at JFK, including the exact moment when I realized that Jaxon was getting too close to the devil. Then, I blushed when I thought about Jaxon's lips on mine, realizing that both Freya and Ezra watched that too.

"Hey, I'm sorry about that kiss."

Freya laughed, "I told Jax he needed to convince her, and what better way than an intimate moment? And it worked." She smirked and looked back down at the paper. "Don't worry, I won't kiss Ezra to make it even."

We laughed as a light knock on the door made us jump. Our dad peaked his head in. "Hey, did you find it? I swear I didn't move the charger."

I held it in the air and smiled. "We got it."

He walked over toward us, closing the door behind

him. "So, what are you planning behind our backs?"

"Not planning behind your back. Just making sure it will work before we present the plan to everyone," I said. "Hey, Dad," I hesitated for a brief moment before asking. "You don't think Eric would really betray us, do you?"

He thought about it for a minute before looking up. "My brother was one hell of a fighter back in the day, but his word meant something. Now, it's been a long time since I've been around him, but I do believe he is on our side."

That was the final proof I needed. Maybe we had more in common than I thought. "Okay, then let's do this." I turned to Freya and smiled.

She nodded and called the others to come in to go over the exact plan.

Chapter Forty-Nine

Jaxon Oakes

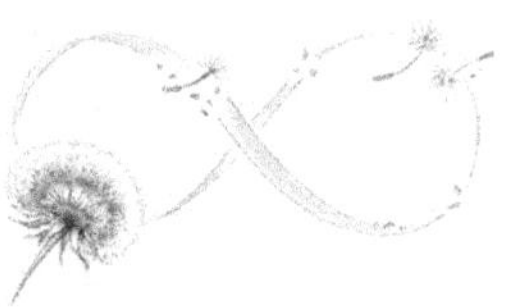

The plan seemed legit enough. I thought of each scenario that could happen and decided it was the only shot we had at trying to get the souls back and having a better advantage at this point. I didn't like that we didn't know the consequences of this spell, and I was nervous that the price would be greater than the reward. But I supported Freya with this one, and no matter what, if we lived through tomorrow, then I'd think about the consequences for the future after.

We were going to need to crash here for tonight. I looked around the bar and was thankful for the space, and even happier that I knew I mopped the floor just recently before we had to have an emergency closure. My hand went to my abdomen and felt the scar that was left from Isadora the last time we were in here together. I rubbed the raised area and decided that was my reminder of what she was capable of just for her own pleasure.

I sat down and leaned against the bar wall. Jim saw me sitting and walked over by me.

"What's running through your head, kid?"

"Nothing." I shrugged.

"Liar," he scoffed. "I know you better than that. I can see the concern written on your face." He looked out toward his daughters and smiled. "They will be okay."

"I hope so, manipulating time is not something we're supposed to mess with. I know firsthand." I froze as I realized I said too much. Jim looked back toward me and waited for more of the story to be told. "Two years ago, after the accident. I tried everything possible to reverse time itself to avoid the accident from happening. I did not want to be taken away from her. My mom had kept me in the dark, so I had no idea how much bigger all of this was. I wanted to let our futures intertwine again, but nothing worked. Then, one night, I added my blood to the spell and was able to get a glimpse into the past. It was not a set course to be changed but like a dream of scenarios. And each time when we were driving and I attempted to change the course, the universe stopped me. A woman's voice of warning came to me and pleaded with me to stop. That destiny had a plan, and if I did this now, then our magic world could crumble. Had I known then what I know now... that she was a syphon and healer twin, then it would've made more sense. But I was selfish. I didn't listen to the warnings. I continued to attempt to change the future anyway. As Freya and I were in the car, the second scenario from the real one, you were with us and driving before the semi hit us. Then, I tried a third time, only this time Alex was driving. It was another person added to our accident every time I attempted to change fate. No matter what I tried, we had the same outcome.

So, I finally realized it was selfish of me to try and keep her. The universe needed us to be split apart. Whatever was needed of her, whatever growth she needed to overcome was needed without me. So, that's when I stopped trying to change our past for a future together, and I started to accept that I needed to leave her alone and let her grow."

"Which is the real reason why you never came looking for her." Jim stared back at me with saddened eyes, nodding his head, realizing that I sacrificed time too. "You had to let her go to grow. The universe must've known she was meant for this very moment." He looked back at the twins, then back to me. "I guess we will see if she gets a warning too."

I nodded and sat back. "I know the thyme spell will work. It's the same one from my mom's book. The one ingredient I was missing for it to be successful was a twin Anchor's blood. I was able to see scenarios, but to change the actual course was impossible for me. It takes two Anchors to set a new course. Two sacrifices. I just hope that the sacrifice is not greater than their lives."

"What did you lose by trying?" Jim asked.

I looked back to Freya and smiled as she caught eye contact with me. "Jim, I lost everything for two years. As did she." His eyes followed mine, and he grimaced at the past.

"Luckily, you guys will have a lifetime to make up for the time that was lost."

"I hope so."

Jim put his arm around my shoulders and pulled me toward him. "I promise, you will. I will make sure of it."

We both laughed, knowing that there were no promises

that could be kept right now. "Thanks, Jim. And I promise to replace your Camaro someday."

He laughed. "Now that will take a miracle." He stood up and waved a flick of his wrist in the air. Cots with pillows and blankets appeared throughout the bar. I stood, amazed, as everyone gasped.

"Dad, how—" Freya raised her hands to her head. "How did you do that?"

Jim smiled and winked. "I've been studying. Well, and my brother reminded me how to do simple spells again."

"This is simple?" Freya asked.

"I mean, I hope they last through the night, so everyone doesn't fall to the ground mid sleep." He laughed as Alex walked over to him and hugged him from behind. He turned around and kissed her.

"They will hold up." She smiled and kissed him again.

We each grabbed a cot and moved them around. Tomorrow was going to come fast. Everyone was sound asleep the minute they laid down, or at least, they were pretending to be. Freya and I were facing each other on separate cots as her hand continued to lightly rub my arm. I kept my other arm underneath her head, trying to keep her as close as I could.

"Can I try something?" I whispered. As she sat up, confused, but nodded.

I looked over to Ember and waved her to come over to us.

"Close your eyes," Ember said, as she grabbed both our arms and teleported us.

I opened my eyes once we were standing where I asked her to bring us. I mouthed, "Thank you," to Ember as she winked and walked away. I rubbed Freya's arms. "You can open your eyes now."

Freya opened one eye at a time and gasped while she jumped into my arms, panicked that we were now outside and up high on our rock at Wyalusing State Park. You could hear the river crashing against the banks as the cold weather had started to freeze portions of it. This was her thinking space, and I needed her to clear her head.

"I figured you could use some fresh air."

She pulled back from me and looked up into my eyes. Laughing, she pulled my lips down to hers and raised up on her tippy toes to let our lips meet. She tugged on my hair as I pulled her closer into me, to keep her warm. Her kissing slowed as she lowered herself.

"Thank you," she whispered while looking out toward the river. She sat herself down on the rock, pulling her knees into her chest for warmth. I pulled the blanket out from behind me that I brought with us through our travels. I wrapped it around my shoulders and sat down next to her, pulling her into my arms and under the blanket.

"It's been a while since we were last here," I said, listening to the river. The crashing waves were soothing, and I could see why this place let her think. It was silent and loud all at the same time.

She smirked and leaned closer into me. "It's hard to believe that a few months ago my life was so normal. If normal can even be used to describe my life." She inhaled sharply and let it go slowly. "Now—"

"Do you wish I never would've showed up on your birthday?"

She turned her head up and scoffed. "I do not regret

that for a second. I just wish being where we are today didn't come with so many evils. If that makes sense." She shrugged. "There's been a lot to take in. My dad is a thousand years old, like what?" She laughed. "How does that even happen and go unnoticed?"

Laughing with her now, I had no answers for her.

"Am I missing anything for tomorrow?"

I shook my head, "I think you have it down. We just need some of her blood." I ran through the plan once more out loud. "She will be at the parade tomorrow. Everyone goes. We are going to pretend that it's business as usual. Ezra said he will get the sample. You and Haven will start the thyme spell as soon as the parade is over back at the bar. Then, Aisling, Declan, and Ezra will be at JFK waiting for time itself to start." I exhaled slowly. "As soon as she enters the field, then the time will start ticking. She will be brought back to the moment where she is walking in with Lynn. We won't have long once the sun starts to set and the red moon rises. The spell only lasts a few minutes before the timeline changes course, or we are sent back to the present with who knows what consequences. So, we have one shot. No pressure or anything."

She laughed, I looked down at her, and I could see she was nervous about the pressures of the world on her. With Isadora having the souls, there was no other way. We could not let her be that powerful.

"We need to keep that pointy end of the dagger far away from you and Ais."

I nodded. "I think I have an idea for that." It was a long shot, but it could work. If anything, it would help be a failsafe. She looked up at me and waited for more. I shook my head. "I need to keep it to myself. Just in case anyone gets into that pretty little head of yours."

I pulled her closer and kissed the top of her head.

We sat quietly staring out toward the river, and at this very moment, I was thankful for meeting her up here a few months ago. Even though bringing her back into this world may have started all of the danger, I kept telling myself that this danger would have still happened regardless of being back with her. She could be going through all of this alone, and I would never let that happen.

I stopped thinking and let my mind become silent. Freya's body became more relaxed and leaned into me further, making me realize that she had fallen asleep next to me. I smiled as I held her closer for a few minutes longer. I turned around and saw Ember waiting in the parking lot. I nodded toward her as she teleported next to us.

"You ready?" she whispered.

"Thank you for this."

She smiled as I stood, lifting Freya into my arms. She teleported us back to Swig and Jig, and I laid her down gently on the cot next to mine.

"Thank you."

"Anytime," Ember said and walked toward the window, staring out into the moonlight. She wasn't going to sleep tonight, and it made me wonder if she ever slept. She was one hell of a sweet person, but she was made of pure magic, and she had so much more to her than even she realized.

I walked to the office, closing the door behind me. Pulling out the dagger from the sheath I had been holding onto, I laid it flat against the wooden table. The obsidian blade glimmered back at me.

"Please work." I waved my hand over the dagger and my other hand over the stack of paper sitting next to it. "When in time, two is needed. Let this blade replicate, succeeded," I whispered the words and closed my eyes, willing the object to double. Behind closed eyes, I could see a light glowing, and the earth rumbled for the slightest moment that it could easily go undetected by anyone not waiting for it. I opened my eyes to see the stack of papers disappeared, and instead, a second blade was laying on the table. I lifted both and smiled when I realized the dagger double was as heavy as a stack of papers. It was an optical illusion. It would work, though. I took both daggers and sheathed the real one before hiding it back under my shirt in the leather harness. A simple magic trick could make a world of difference. I whispered to my ancestors for the extra help, "Thank you." I studied the blade, and I hoped that it would give us the extra minute we might need.

Chapter Fifty

Freya Chamberlain

The sun was brighter than I had expected. I didn't remember falling asleep, but I was glad I did. I needed whatever energy the sleep gave me. I looked around the bar and saw that I was the last one sleeping. The adults were all gone, and it was just us younger witches left.

I sat up quickly. "Where is—"

Jaxon answered, "They are heading back now. They brought my parents to the rubble of the house. They are preparing it to be whole and ready for the souls once the thyme spell is complete."

I nodded and looked at the wall thermometer, realizing that it was unusually warm for Halloween. But I was thankful that we wouldn't have snow this year.

Aisling was drinking coffee at the table with Declan. I walked into the office and grabbed the small present that was supposed to be in the drawer. I exhaled when I saw the wrapping paper was still intact with the bow on it. I walked back to Aisling and set the gift down in front of her. She looked up, surprised and shocked.

"I thought we would celebrate another day, after we save the world," she said.

"Just open it." I smiled and pushed the gift closer to her, sitting down next to her.

She giggled like a child and ripped the paper off the small box. She opened it slowly as she pulled out a small clear globe. She looked back at me confused.

"Place it in your palm," I said. She did just that, and her confused eyes turned to amazement as the globe started to fill with green smoke. Then, within seconds, the smoke cleared, and her parents appeared, laughing and smiling from across the world on their business trip. I knew that they weren't going to be home in time for her birthday, so I wanted to give her a gift that would include them.

"Hi, honey, happy birthday!" her mom said, and her dad waved, blowing her a kiss. "Freya said this thing is the new video call. It's so clear. I feel like we are right there with you. So now we're cool technology parents."

"It's live?" Aisling smiled and laughed. "Hi, guys, I miss you."

"We miss you too. We will be home soon. This deal is almost done. Hopefully, Lynn is treating you well."

"She always does." Aisling smiled, and I could see the strain in her emotions, trying to hold herself together.

"We have to get going, it's late over here, and the red moon is amazing. Be sure to check it out tonight."

"Oh, we will for sure." She laughed. "Up close and personal."

Her parents laughed. "My little spell caster," her dad responded, and Aisling's eyes popped a little wider as she remembered it was just a nickname he used to call her while she was little.

"Right." She laughed. "I love you guys."

"We love you more, have the best birthday ever. We will be home soon." They blew kisses through the globe and smiled before the smoke dissolved and the globe was clear again.

"Your aunt helped me with the spell. It's a locator globe. You can look at them whenever you want to as a one way or two way, no reception needed."

She looked up with a tear rolling down her cheek. "This is perfect and exactly what I needed." She leaned over to me and hugged me tight. "Thank you."

I hugged her back and looked over to Ezra. "Sorry, I didn't know it was your birthday too."

We both laughed. "I'll take one of those birthday hugs, though." He walked over and picked me up. Haven, Jaxon, Aisling, and Declan all joined us in one big embrace. We all laughed, and for a brief moment, I had hope that today would work and we would live for another day.

Ember appeared out of nowhere. "Hey, birthday twins." She smiled and walked toward us. "I just wanted to drop these off before tonight." She handed everyone a bracelet. "I'm going to be tracking each of you to know where I need to teleport to. If you need my help sooner, press this button, and I will be there faster than you can blink."

She passed out the bracelets. "Jaxon, that amulet is in your hands now. Remember it was designed for Izzy, do not let her escape this time. My mother's life is on the line without it."

Jaxon nodded. "It's part of the plan."

Ember smiled and nodded. "Thank you."

"You sure you don't want to join us for the parade?"

Ember shook her head. "My family is waiting for me to get back to spend the day with them."

I nodded and hugged her tight. "Thank you for helping us."

"I told you. You are important to our magic world. Plus, I like you." She winked and giggled before disappearing.

The town would've already been preparing the streets for the few floats that go through. It had been a yearly tradition for Halloween to go through the town passing out candy to everyone in the crowd. It was trick or treating, but in one place, and everyone left happy. Aisling had always believed it was for her birthday, and most of the town knew her and just agreed to celebrate each year with her. She was the Halloween princess in Crystal Rock.

Aisling stood in front of the wall mirror. I could tell she was disappointed that she wouldn't have a costume this year. Even though she was still as beautiful as always. I jumped when I heard a quiet knock on the door. We all froze as Declan stood and peaked through the blinds before hopping up and opening the door. Aunt Lynn was standing there with a box with a big bow on it and cupcakes underneath it.

"You're here!" Aisling squealed with excitement. "And you're healed." Aunt Lynn set the boxes down and hugged her tight, smiling.

"I'm me again and very mortal, and you're crushing me with your superpower strength." Aunt Lynn gasped as Aisling squeezed her tight.

"Ope, I'm sorry. I'm just so happy to see you."

They stepped apart from each other as Aunt Lynn grabbed the box with the bow. "Just a little something for today."

Aisling lifted the top off the box and pulled out a dress that looked as if it was from a different time. Which it probably was. She lifted it up in front of her and admired the navy blue, bedazzled lace top and frilly bottom that was screaming her name. Aisling brought it back down and had tears forming.

"It's perfect," she said, as she choked back tears. "Thank you."

"Anything for you, child. Happy birthday." They hugged again, gently this time. "You can still use that glamour spell I taught you, if you'd like."

"I have an idea." Aisling spun around as the dress formed to her body and her hair started to twirl in the air. A Viking updo and black ash patterns across her eyes with two small triangles between her brows formed as she stopped spinning.

I stood next to her, amazed at her beauty, glamour spell or not, she was beautiful. "Viking witch this year. Fitting really," she said, as she smiled.

I laughed and agreed.

Then, she pointed to me, "You, close your eyes." She motioned for me to twirl. I closed my eyes and spun, feeling sheepish.

"Stop."

I did as instructed and opened one eye to peek at the mirror. Then, opened both eyes in amazement. "Oh my god, Ais!" I turned and gasped at the purple bedazzled lace dress and frilly skirt, sequined to match hers. My hair was curled, the top half was braided and the bottom had loose curls. It was longer, definitely longer than my hair had just been a minute ago. With matching black ash across my eyes and a small Unalome symbol with my endless knot between my brows. It was beautiful. I was beautiful. I stood in awe. "Glamour spell." I pointed to myself and laughed.

"No, this is just you." Jaxon walked up behind me, kissing my neck, making me blush in the mirror. "You are always beautiful. But this costume is now my favorite one. Can you keep this one?"

I laughed, turning around and pinching him. "What are you going to be?"

Aisling stepped up next to him, "Close your eyes—"

"Nope, no. I'm good." Jaxon put his hands up and walked away by Declan. "Do not let her dress you up, Declan. I swear, she will put you into a Viking skirt or something." They laughed, and Declan put his hands up in defense, shaking his head too.

"We will be in the crowd, not the parade. We want to be the bodyguards." Ezra stepped in, laughing.

Aisling looked annoyed, but then turned toward Haven, who was sipping her coffee. "You, get over here." She smiled, and Haven shyly shook her head.

"Can't I just be me this morning? Later, I will have to be Freya again. Not that that is a bad thing or anything. I just want to be me."

Aisling scoffed, but nodded. "Fine, you're beautiful either way too. It's just fun to play dress up. Better to make the best of my possible last birthday." She half smiled.

Declan sighed and walked over to her, pulling her back

into his arms. "You, my love, will outlive us all." He kissed her forehead, just missing the ash designs. She pulled his lips down to hers as he lifted her up.

I blushed as I stepped outside, Jaxon joining me.

"Hey, you stay with Ais on the float and pass out candy until the end, no matter what. We can handle the sidelines," Jaxon said.

I nodded. "When the parade is over, I will have Ember teleport me and Haven back to the bar and start the thyme spell. Then, you should be waiting under the tree at the field. We need to keep things similar to how they were, otherwise she will get the déjà vu sense too soon and run. Haven's Mark will be back as soon as the thyme spell starts, and I plan on keeping it with her this time."

Jaxon smiled. "Yes, the only timelines we are messing with are Isadora's, Haven's, and Lynn's. Their blood will be the only blood in the one mix. I wish I knew the consequences of this spell. My mom doesn't remember ever using it before. So, we are playing fire with fire right now."

"But it's the only way."

He nodded. "I agree."

Chapter Fifty-One

Aisling Meadows

We could do this. We had to. Declan held my hand tight as we sat next to each other in the booth with Aunt Lynn across from us. We sat quietly and enjoyed the cupcakes before we were either going to survive or the world would end. I hoped survival was in our cards. I was happy to see Aunt Lynn feeling better and the unlinking that worked. She said she felt free for the first time in nearly a thousand years. So, at least we knew that part of the plan was a success.

Freya walked back in and said it was time to go. I inhaled deeply and stood up. At least I made it to nineteen. I walked toward the door as Jim and Alex walked back in.

"Wait a minute there," Jim said, pulling me in for a hug. "Happy birthday, sweet Ais."

Alex was waiting for him to release me before she grabbed me too. "You are so grown. Happy birthday." She kissed my cheek.

"When this is all over, we will have cake at my place." I laughed, and they nodded.

We walked toward the crowd gathering two blocks away from us. I was happy we would be there, both to protect the crowd of people in case Isadora decided to kill the whole town and two because I really loved being here for this.

"Happy birthday," friends in the crowd yelled, as they saw us walking by. Some came up for hugs while others waved. It felt like when I was a child again, and my parents swore this was all for me. Even though it wasn't. But I always liked pretending anyway.

Then, I saw her. Isadora was standing in the back of the crowd with Eric. I scanned around them and saw Ragnar's scar face glaring back at me. I grabbed Freya's hand and squeezed it hard. I pulled her to climb to the top of the float. Jaxon, Declan, and Ezra blended into the crowd and disappeared. Haven stayed back at the bar with her parents, making sure the thyme was completely dried and the other ingredients were being mashed together and ready for the blood drops to complete the spell.

Freya met my gaze once we were on top, and she nodded. She had seen them too.

"Did any of them look at you?" I asked.

She shook her head no. I could visibly see her body start to shake from her adrenaline rising. I grabbed her hand again and squeezed it tight.

"Hey, we've got this," I assured her.

Her hand stopped trembling. She smiled and grabbed the candy dish and readied it in the nook of her arm. "Yes, we do."

The float was made of orange and black streamers, and an oversized cauldron was bubbling at our feet. The bubble machine inside it stopped working, so I quickly waved my hand over the machine and got it to start spinning again. The group of dancers ahead of us started the music, and the parade began. I kept my eyes in the direction of the Immortals and watched carefully as Ezra was inching his way closer to them. Eric started to walk through the crowd, separating himself from her and walking toward Declan. My own body froze when I saw how close he was getting.

Freya noticed my shift in attitude and shook her head. "Toss the candy. He's with us."

I wanted to believe her, but something didn't feel right.

I grabbed handfuls of candy and started to toss it off the side to the kids. Freya mimicked me and did the same. The giggles and excitement brought me back to the reason why I loved doing this to begin with. They were all so happy. We would go through at least forty bags by the end of this. We smiled and laughed and tossed more.

Eric walked past Declan, checking his shoulder and moving toward Jaxon. Then, I saw Freya freeze. Declan looked down at something on the ground and picked it up. He was frozen in place. I continued to throw the candy out but carefully studied his expression. He finally looked up, nervously. He ran toward us on the float and jumped up. He quickly grabbed candy and started to toss it behind us toward the kids that may have been missed, trying to blend in with us.

"It's Ember," he whispered. "Isadora leveled the casino, and she couldn't find her mothers. I guess Oxana refused to help Ragnar get his magic back."

I gasped as did Freya, as soon we heard the news. Isadora was standing on the side smirking at both of us. Her smile was intentional to piss us off. Freya flinched to jump off the float.

"Stop," I said, grabbing her arm. "This is what she wants. She wants a reaction. Don't do it. We have a plan, and now we know Ragnar is powerless."

Freya's breathing sped up as she tried to calm herself down. The magic inside her was trying to escape, her emotions were pumping too fast for her. I scanned the crowd for Jaxon. Then, I saw Ember appear in the back of the crowd. She was furious, tears streaming down her face. She made eye contact with Isadora who started to mockingly wave to her. Ember flipped a switch and disappeared, then teleported behind Isadora. Isadora's chest rose as if something was touching her back. Ember was threatening her. No. She would ruin our plan. We needed Ember to help us. We could fix this. This just happened. We could reverse this. I think.

Isadora started to turn around as Ezra ran into them, grabbing Ember and disappearing. Isadora scanned the crowd, irritated. She was looking for them. Freya and I stood frozen trying to figure out what the hell just happened. Ezra didn't get her blood. The plan wouldn't work without it.

"Where's Eric?" Freya asked.

I scanned the crowd again and spotted him. He had Jaxon in a headlock to our left as Isadora was on our right. That was it. Freya lost it.

She jumped off the float and lifted her arms up and forced her fire to aim toward Eric's head, making him release Jaxon. The entire crowd screamed in excitement, thinking it was part of the show and then they started to disperse once Freya jumped off the float with her hands still ignited, pushing her way closer to Eric. She grabbed him with Haven's vines and lifted him into the air, tightening them around his neck.

"You traitor," she screamed, lifting him into the air and throwing him down into the gravel, then lifting him again. "Never betray your own blood." She lifted him again and pinned him against the building behind him two stories in the air. Isadora watched lavishly, loving every minute of torture Eric was being given.

She started to walk toward Freya's back, so I did what had to be done. I jumped between them and threw my arms up, whispering, "Ventus," forcing unnatural gusts of winds. Pinning her against the opposite wall, as the rest of the crowd safely left the street. We definitely had to do the thyme spell now or these poor people would remember that some of the town was no longer mundane.

Jaxon grabbed Freya and tried to bring her arms down, but she used her other hand and wrapped vines against him too. Eric was thrashing in the air and trying to escape her grip. Freya stepped closer as she continued to keep the two separated from her and each other.

"You don't deserve to live any longer," she yelled.

"Freya," Eric gasped, trying to bargain with her, his face becoming red as the oxygen was being depleted quickly. "Freya, stop."

"Do it," Isadora yelled. "He's a traitor. Kill him now."

Freya froze and turned toward Isadora as I held her up with forced air.

"Why are you pretending that Aisling can hold you back? Show me your power," Freya yelled.

Isadora laughed and whipped her hand in front of her, releasing the grip that I had on her. She continued to laugh as she straightened her coat and walked past me.

"Kill him, then you will be no better than me," she said, watching Freya cautiously.

"I am better than you. I will kill you both. Rid you both of this world." She released Jaxon and waved her arm toward her, forcing the vines to grab her neck and hold her back. Isadora gasped for a moment out of shock and tried to syphon the vine's magic, but failed. Ragnar watched intently before taking off and running down the street. I thought about grabbing him and realized that if things went as planned then he would be back in the dagger. So, I let him run like the coward he was. Isadora glared at her father's back and then turned back to Freya before finally getting the hold to slightly loosen. Just enough time for Jaxon to get behind her and snap her neck.

She fell to the ground motionless.

Freya released Eric as he tried to catch his breath.

"Damn. Freya. That," he coughed and rubbed his throat, "was too real." He looked up to Freya and grabbed her hand as she helped lift him up.

"Sorry, I had to make it look real."

"So, you got my letter?" he asked and smirked. She nodded.

"Only doubted you for a brief moment." She winked at him.

Eric looked behind them and stared at Isadora. "What's next?"

Jaxon grabbed a vial of her blood, "Let's get her back to the bar."

Eric nodded and picked her up like a rag doll.

"You think Ragnar will be back?" Freya asked.

Eric looked down the street at the empty road. "I think he's one selfish bastard and won't be back until he has his magic. Maybe this time we can keep him contained in the dagger world."

"Right. We need to get going," Freya said and headed toward Swig & Jig.

Chapter Fifty-Two

Haven Vine

I grabbed the dried creeping thyme and added it to the grinding bowl with the other ingredients. The last thing we needed would be three drops of blood from each of us. My mom walked up behind me and rubbed my shoulders.

"How are you doing?"

I stopped grinding the thyme and faced her, half smiling. "Should I lie and say I'm fine?"

She smiled and shook her head. "Oh, honey. None of this is okay. I am happy both my girls found their magic, but I am sad that you are growing up in a world with so much danger aimed toward our kind right now. When I was a child, my mother, your grandmother, taught me how to heal plants. I couldn't keep them alive for the life of me, and she showed me how to replenish them and let them grow beyond belief. Something so simple and small made all the difference in my life. I didn't see it then, but now that I look back, it was the simple magic that made me the happiest and far less drained."

I laughed as did she. "Healing succulents that I had overwatered were definitely my easy days." I started grinding the ingredients again. "Mom, promise me that we will all be together again. The fishing float seems so far away, but that was one of the best family moments I have had in a long time. Don't get me wrong, Aunt Clara and Ezra have made me very happy. It's just that all four of us being together was something different. I felt whole."

She smiled and pulled me into her side, kissing my head. My dad was listening to us as he walked over to us.

"Haven, you are my sweetest daughter with the kindest soul, and I will forever regret not being able to keep my family together over the years. But after tonight, we will have forever to make up our lost time."

"You promise?" I asked him, knowing that promises of today could not be kept when none of us knew how the night would end.

"You betcha, kid." He leaned in and hugged us.

"What was our grandmother's name?" I asked out of curiosity.

"Helen. Helen Day, and you, my sweet child, remind me so much of her. If souls are reborn, I swear you were lucky enough to gain hers."

I smiled as I looked down at my scarred arm where my Mark should've been. "What was her specialty?"

She inhaled sharply, "Surviving. She loved deeply, and she was one badass witch. She had a hard life before becoming a mother. Magic kept her alive in the hard days. She outlived all of her enemies and lived just to love and nurture all."

"She sounds wonderful."

"You would've loved her," she said, as the door opened and the others joined us.

"Now. We have to do the spell now," Freya yelled before they even made it in the door, as Eric walked in carrying Isadora in his arms following behind Freya. "Jaxon broke her neck, but she will be coming to shortly."

"We need Ember," I said, counting heads, realizing we were short two. "Where's Ezra?" I panicked as my breathing sped up. When no one answered, I asked again. "Where is he?"

"Ember, well—" Jaxon started. "The casino was leveled, Isadora went after Ember's family. Ember freaked and went after her in the middle of Main Street. The town saw everything. Then, Ezra tried to contain her panic, and she teleported away with him. We keep pressing our bracelets, and she's not responding."

"Were her mothers inside for sure?" I screamed, panicked, wondering where the hell my man was at.

"We're not a hundred percent sure." Jaxon looked down and fidgeted. He exhaled heavily as the weight of our plan was becoming more intense.

That was it, anger coursed through my veins. "Well, damn it. Someone better find them and find them now."

I grabbed my phone and dialed his number, praying that he answered. The ringing continued, and my anxiety started to grow. *Damn it.* The line connected.

"Hey, babe, we're on our way," Ezra's voice answered, breathing heavily.

I exhaled and sniffled. "Okay."

"Can you make Ember some overload tea? Her head is

spinning right now, and I'm afraid she will be a danger to everyone."

"Yes, just get here."

"On our way."

The line disconnected.

"Mom, can you make Ember some tea? They're on their way." As soon as the words left my mouth, they appeared in front of us. Ember was in tears in Ezra's arms. He was carrying her like a child. She was broken. Oh no. We needed her head clear.

I walked over to her as Ezra set her down in the booth.

"Ember?" I grabbed her hand and rubbed it. "Hey, listen, we can fix this. It just happened. We can get them back." Ember looked up to me and just bawled.

"No, we can't. The amulet is here. She wasn't wearing it."

"Perfect, that amulet was hers so we will add it to our course changing bowl for safe measures. When this works, then Isadora never would've taken the souls that made her powerful enough to do what she did to your mothers and the casino. Once we change this timeline, anywhere Isadora has been the last few days will be irrelevant. As if she did not exist. Do you understand what we are doing?"

Ember sniffled and wiped her face. "You promise?"

I froze. A promise on something that I wasn't even sure of myself made me hate myself for agreeing to it. "Yes."

My mom walked out from the kitchen with the tea and handed it to her. "Drink this."

Ember grabbed the steaming cup and gulped it. "Whoa, what was that magic?"

I laughed lightly. "It's helpful for emotions." I hesitated, knowing we needed her for this to work. "Will you help us?"

Ember looked around the room at each and every one of us with her. She inhaled heavily, letting her entire small body shiver, before wiping her tears and sniffling. "I have nothing left to lose."

I hugged her tight and watched as Eric laid our enemy's body down next to the spell.

Freya was the one to break the silence. "Okay, I need a drop of everyone's blood, if you want to keep your timeline from changing, then I need it now. Unless you are in need of a do-over."

"I don't want to lose my mom's magic." Ezra said, as he stepped over and pricked his finger.

Declan followed suit, nodding toward Ezra as he walked to me and did the same.

After them, everyone followed suit and pricked their finger to stay aware of the last few days. I wished that I could remember everything that had happened, but I knew that I needed my Mark back more. I looked down at my carved out Mark and grimaced.

"This will work," Freya assured me, as I stepped back from the blood donations.

"I know it will." I was just worried that Isadora would find another loophole.

Once Freya collected from everyone except from myself and Aunt Lynn, she took the droplets and added them to the granite mortar and crushed them together with the pestle and a handful of forget-me-nots to keep their past few days on the same timeline.

I took a deep breath, hoping that this was for sure going

to work. The weight of what Ezra and Declan could lose was terrifying. We didn't know how the souls that have departed worked in with a spell and we didn't need to take any chances.

I grabbed the other mortar made of marble that I had started with and added Isadora's small vial of blood for safe measures in case a drop may not be enough. Then, I grabbed Lynn's and added a drop of my own to the marble bowl. Freya inhaled sharply and waited for the next step.

"Where's Ragnar?" I asked.

"He ran."

I inhaled sharply, "Well, let's hope that both him and the prison world get sent back to how they should've stayed."

Freya nodded. "Let's hope."

"It's time. I need you to get everyone here to our field. I want everyone in place before we start this spell. I'm not sure if the forget-me-nots will interfere with them being transported there."

She stood up and nodded.

"Eric and Lynn, you need to drink this for the unlinking from Isadora. Lynn, when this spell starts, you will be relinked to them and Jaxon will have to unlink you quickly at the field." I handed them the mugwort and sage mix and watched as they downed it without questions.

We all stood in a circle and looked at one another. "Everyone ready?" Freya asked.

The nods started and then I blinked, and they were all gone.

Ember reappeared.

"Hey, Ezra wanted you to hang on to this." She handed

me a small pouch that I opened and a Jasper stone fell out into my palm. I stood and stared at it, turning it around after feeling an ident on the other side. I gasped when I realized what it was. The other half of the Jasper fossil.

"Where did this come from?" I asked her.

"Let's just say that our little teleporting field trip triggered a memory for him." She shrugged. "He asked you to hold it for safekeeping."

I smiled and put it in my pocket. "Thank you."

Ember disappeared again.

"Is that the other half of the fossil?" Freya asked, eyes wide.

I nodded.

I looked over to Freya, and it was just her and I left. "Yes, Ezra has been trying to find it from his memories as a child. Looks like they succeeded."

"A little extra magic never hurt anyone. Right?" We laughed together, and I smiled.

I grabbed the grinding bowl and placed it near the window where the sun was setting, and the moon could be seen at the edge of the earth.

"Are you sure about this?" I asked Freya one last time.

"No fucking clue, but we don't have another choice."

I agreed and nodded. "Hey, just a small note before I forget anything that might be valuable to us." I inhaled sharply and released it. "Isadora wasn't technically after releasing her father. More so, that he trapped her mother's soul in the dagger and she wanted her back."

"Huh," Freya gasped. "Well, that's new information. So, her mother is still trapped?"

"I guess so. He left her there the first time. Maybe we

can search for her when this is all over. We can talk to Margo about her after this is done."

Freya nodded.

Grabbing her hand and slicing her palm, then mine, we interlocked our hands together and raised them over the two bowls. I read the incantations that Jaxon had written down from his book and waited to see the flame ignite in both bowls.

"Here we go," Freya whispered, as the fire turned purple and raised to the ceiling as everything around us vanished and we stood in the dark. Then, a power gripped me and pulled me far away from the world, and I was utterly alone in complete darkness.

Chapter Fifty-Three

Freya Chamberlain

I frantically searched my surroundings in the dark and could not see or feel anything around me. I was standing completely alone. "Haven?" I whispered, too afraid to speak loud and destroy whatever fragile place I was standing in. "Haven, please?"

What have we done?

I closed my eyes, even though the darkness matched them being open and waited in silence for anything to catch my attention.

"Do you know what you are doing?" a woman's voice asked.

I opened my eyes and gasped as a woman was standing across from me, only she was not human. She was almost transparent and glowing, brighter than the sun. I squinted my eyes, trying to dim the brightness as she moved closer to me.

"Who are you?" I stepped back slowly, trying to see where I was.

The glowing woman laughed. "Oh, child. I am the

keeper of magic, the universe, the power source. Whatever it is you call me nowadays. I am the voice making sure that you understand what you are giving up by performing this thyme spell. Do you understand?"

"I know there will be consequences, but I do not know what kind," I answered honestly.

The lady smiled but with sad eyes. "Freya Chamberlain, your power is meant to be the greatest of your time, and you are willing to sacrifice it for a broken Immortal's mistakes? Are you sure there isn't another way?"

I stepped back and froze. "What do you mean, sacrifice my power? I will lose my magic?"

She nodded.

"Is there another way?" I asked.

She sighed as she floated closer toward me, circling me. "Child, you must decide what is most important to you. But any choice will come at a price that you must be willing to pay. Manipulating time could shatter all worlds. There needs to be balance, and a spell like this needs great power."

"But the moon—"

"The moon isn't enough," she interrupted.

"I have to remove Isadora from our world. I don't have another choice."

The woman stopped circling me and stood, gazing into my soul. "Such a big job for that young soul of yours. Do not taint your soul with blood. Afterlife is not keen on those that take lives. Isadora will pay her own price."

"But she has killed so many others. She is a danger to the world."

"Ah, yes. Or maybe she is just broken. You need to

decide her fate and yours, child. Whatever you decide, you must choose fast."

"Have you seen this happen already? Do we win?"

She smiled as her glow started to dim. "Depends on what you think is winning. Your timeclock will begin to tick in three, two, one."

The bright light surrounding the translucent woman grew brighter, and the entire room was a whiteout. Then, the woman disappeared, and Haven came into view, standing across from me with her eyes closed.

"Haven?"

She opened her eyes, one at a time, and smiled when she saw me.

"Oh, thank goodness. I thought I was going to be alone forever in the dark. What is happening?"

"We're doing a thyme spell, and we're heading back to JFK. Just go with the flow and keep the dagger away from Isadora at all costs."

She nodded, confused but didn't ask questions.

So, she didn't see the lady as I did. That made me even more nervous. What was I supposed to choose now? I looked down at my Mark, finally healed, and grimaced at the idea of living magicless again now that I had just learned of my gifts not that long ago. I would have to do what was necessary. Isadora was a danger to us all. We needed to lock her in the amulet if we had the chance, or we needed to unlink her and kill her. We have one chance to end her wrath on our world. We must rid her of this world and see what fate had in store for me today.

I looked down at Haven's Mark with vines wrapping around her forearm and glowing. I stared and pointed to it.

Haven glanced down and smiled when the vines started to unravel and her Mark was completely healed.

"It's back." I smiled.

"Back? Oh, things really got bad." She inhaled as she lifted her palm up and let a small pile of dirt grow and an orange lily grew from the center of the pile, whimsical and beautiful. I stared in awe at the moment, before grabbing and embracing her.

"It's time," I said, as she nodded.

I reached for her hand. "Focus on JFK, the moment under the tree. We need to get to the exact moment before she shows up to the field with Aunt Lynn."

Haven stared at me blankly before I realized her blood was not in the bowl of forget-me-nots. This was all happening in real time for her.

The kiss, I thought. I better at least give her a heads up.

"Hey, when Jaxon kisses you, just go with it. It's part of the plan."

Haven's eyes widened as she looked down at her Mark. I could tell she felt uncomfortable, but it was the part of the plan that had to happen for Isadora to believe it.

"Trust me," I whispered, as I rubbed her shoulder.

She nodded.

I looked at her one more time for reassurance that we could do this.

"We need to get into place. Haven," I hugged her one more time. "Please, keep Jaxon safe for me. We know her true intentions this time. Don't worry, Jaxon and Aisling should know too if the spell is working right. We will all be there."

She seemed confused but smiled anyway. "Okay, I promise."

I wasn't sure if she was promising me his safety or if we had the upper hand, but either way, I felt better about going into this moment than the last time we were there.

She nodded.

We grabbed hands and closed our eyes. I could feel the surroundings changing and a pulling feeling made my stomach turn. I opened my eyes as we were teleported to the field. The spell had started.

The nausea soared through my body as I tried to steady myself from the fast movement. I looked around and saw Jaxon waiting under the tree. Haven was next to him, catching her own breath. Aisling, Declan, Ember, and Ezra were at the edge of the trees. Everything looked like it did the last time, only this time Ember would be here to help us and she could get the elders when the time was right.

I walked over to the trees as Ember and Ezra teleported next to me, and we waited for Isadora to make her way to the clearing. I looked over at Aisling, who had the dagger in hand and was ready to walk out to her. The dagger shimmered a strange green glow, and something about it felt off. Ragnar must be back in it. At least, I hoped so.

I looked across the field and watched as the red moon was rising, leaving the field with an eerie fiery orange lighting. I thought about what the woman had warned me about, and I knew there was no other way. I watched as Jaxon and Haven sat under the tree, leaning into each other, and I knew what would happen next.

"What is the sign? When should I grab the others?" Ember whispered, pulling both mine and Ezra's attention away from the kiss that we were both dreading but neither of us said anything. This moment was too important to all of us. The souls, Oxana and her wife, Haven's magic, and Isadora's father in the dagger. This moment was literal life or death for all of us, including Ember's mothers.

"As soon as Isadora reaches for the dagger, teleport me and Ezra in between them. Then, grab the elders."

"Easy enough," she said in the most serious tone I ever heard from her.

I half smiled. "Yeah, I hope so."

I looked back at them under the tree and saw Isadora walking into the field with Aunt Lynn trailing behind her, floating in a trance. I felt my body tense as I knew minutes were left before we tried to change the course of time. It was either it worked, or everything went back to how we were half an hour ago: doomed.

Aisling walked out, dagger in hand, and reached them. I braced myself as I watched for the exact moment.

I put my hand in front of Ember, Ezra mimicked me on her other side. She grabbed our arms, and we braced ourselves.

"Now."

Chapter Fifty-Four

Freya Chamberlain

The moment happened so quickly I had to refocus my brain on my surroundings. Thankfully, Ezra was more prepared than I was and immediately threw his shield up, blocking the dagger from piercing Jaxon's body. Only this time, the dagger still shattered. I stood under the dome with Ezra and watched as the dagger hit the side of the dome and exploded into paper, flying across the field. Isadora stood in shock at her empty hands and then looked back up to us, rage filling her face. My shock matched hers as I realized the dagger was a decoy. So, where the hell was the original one?

"What have you done?" she screamed and charged into the dome. Losing our safety net as it dissolved, it left us open to her destruction.

The moment of chaos began as Isadora grabbed my body and pushed me hard against the tree. My tree. My field. My time. *This is my game now,* I thought, as her fist came toward me with force, just missing my face and crushing the tree's bark instead.

"Go," I yelled to the others. They had their own jobs that needed to be fulfilled, and I could take care of myself. She had no souls with her right now. We still had a chance.

Jaxon froze as he was torn on what to do. Then, he ran toward Aunt Lynn as Ezra shielded them. He started the unlinking spell again. More confident that he had already done it once and he wasn't fighting Isadora's beating. Ember reappeared with Eric, Aunt Clara, and my parents as Declan reached us in the field.

"You! What did you do to my father?" Isadora screamed into my face. "Where is the dagger? What have you done?" She lifted me with an unnatural strength away from the tree and high into the air.

I grabbed her body and tried to syphon her own strength from her. When she realized what I was doing, she pushed me away. My body reacted to the free fall, and I knew I couldn't fly to save my life. I tried to grab for the earth or water or anything to slow my fall, but I had nothing. I was free falling faster toward the ground. I continued to try and pull my magic from anywhere to slow me down but couldn't stop myself. I was going to hit the ground and die before all of this was over. I closed my eyes, the ground closing in on me, and I waited for impact.

A cool breeze of water flowed underneath me as Declan stood by me, pulling from the Mississippi, his eyes bluer than the ocean, saving my life with a wave of water catching me before the ground could. Relief was an understatement. I inhaled sharply and got back up, facing Isadora again, who had reached the ground gracefully. She looked as if she was debating on running or staying. I began to advance on her, then froze as I studied her movements. *Why is she just standing there?*

Eric walked up between me and Declan and smirked. My dad met me on the opposite side with Haven, Aunt Clara, and my mom. Aisling walked up next to Declan, grabbing his hand. We had an army up against her, and she had nothing. I smiled when I realized she was afraid. Jaxon and Ezra met us at the line. I turned around and watched as Ember teleported the unlinked Aunt Lynn safely out of the field back to the soul house with Callum and Margo.

Ember reappeared next to us. "Ember, now." We all grabbed hands as Ember teleported us directly into a circle around Isadora, making sure every inch was blocked for her to be unable to try to escape.

Isadora stood and circled us, trying to debate on who was the weakest link. Haven's vines were hers again and started to grow around us all for protection as Ezra contained us in a large dome, to keep her from trying to get free.

"It's over, Izzy, come on. The madness has to stop," Eric said.

"I always win," she said, as she frantically looked around at her options. "You are all fools. You cannot beat me. None of you can."

"It's time for you to leave this world," I said, pulling out the amulet. "Either willingly or forcefully." I left the link of hands and let them reconnect without me.

Shocked, she asked, "Thyme spell?" For a brief moment, I felt like we had an upper hand, then she laughed. "I should've known. I could smell desperation in this field. Things were too familiar. That means that I succeeded in my plans, and I was too powerful for any of you." Her laughter started to echo through the dome, and my stomach started to turn. "I've already won. I just need to waste time now. Because as soon as this spell is over, then everything goes back to me winning. And I always get what I want. Don't I, Eric?" She smiled at him, blowing him a kiss. "I must've made a mess out of things for you to go this far."

"Izzy, it's over," Eric said.

"Shut the hell up. You worthless Anchor."

Eric glared at her.

"Speaking of Anchors, where is my lovely sister? Afraid to fight the big bad wolf?" She snickered as she crossed her arms.

"That's enough," Eric growled as Jaxon tensed, ready to advance before my dad gripped his arm harder, keeping him in place.

"And now you have little Miss Ember on your side." She pointed and laughed. "What's happened for you to join Eric's side over mine?"

Ember's tears started to form as she tried to steady her breathing.

"Oh poor little Ember, go cry to your mommies."

Ember screamed before breaking the circle and charging past me, hitting Isadora back against the circle.

"You killed them," Ember yelled, as she electrocuted her.

Isadora pushed Ember off of her and threw her across the circle, spitting the blood that Ember had caused. "I would never hurt Oxana."

Ember froze and then teleported in front of her.

"Where are they?"

"Hell if I know, thyme spell, remember? At least some of you do," Isadora huffed. "Tell you what, bring me Margo, and I will find your mothers after this is over."

"Ember, don't, she's lying," I yelled, trying to grab her arm to stop her, but I was too late. Ember disappeared and reappeared with Margo in her arms.

Margo stood in shock, staring at all of us.

Fuck. Change of plans. Margo couldn't be here.

Jaxon let go of the circle and tried to reach his mom, falling back as his own whirlwind of gravel started to push everyone off balance on the ground. Jaxon was losing control.

I was stuck in the middle of chaos.

"Hey little sister, time for you to be useful again." Isadora smirked as she grabbed a hold of Margo. "Here, let me do everyone a favor. I'll unlink Eric, willingly." Her grip let loose as her arms flew up crisscrossed, then released an energy that pushed all of us harder against the dome, leaving Margo and her untouched. The ground stopped shaking as Jaxon tried to steady himself again. She was forcing us further away from them as the dome expanded to hold us against the edge.

She whispered incantations and marked an 'X' across her Mark as it started to smoke black as one triangle disappeared. She grabbed a hold of Margo, who dropped to her knees in front of her as Eric fell to the ground, writhing in pain. His body desiccating, as she truly was unlinking him and Anchoring back to Margo. I looked back at her and tried to reach her as she continued to force us away from her.

"I can't hold her," Ezra yelled.

I turned back toward Eric and watched as his Mark started to ignite and burn on his forearm. His pained face would haunt me forever.

"That's it," my dad yelled and let go of the circle and charged toward Isadora, pushing past Margo and knocking Isadora backwards. He took her and lifted her with a strength I didn't know even existed. "Leave my brother alone."

"Brother?" Her eyes grew wider as she started to connect the dots.

"Dad, syphon!" I yelled, realizing he may be the best match against her.

He started to syphon her magic and then froze as Eric started to yell louder.

"Unlink. Me," Eric yelled louder, as his Mark started to fade faster than mine had.

Isadora laughed again. "Yes, syphon from me, syphon from him, big brother Jimmy."

Jaxon ran to Eric and started the unlinking spell. "Jim, I'm going to need you," Jaxon yelled. Needing to link Eric to another Anchor and fast, Jaxon began to whisper incantations.

That was all it took: one second for my dad to look away before Isadora gained her advantage back. I followed her eyes as I saw the glimmer of the dagger hanging out of the bottom of Jaxon's shirt as he bent down to help Eric.

She grabbed my dad by the throat and lifted him, throwing him against the shielded dome, making it crumble as our circle was broken and everyone was dispersed in separate directions.

"Change of plans," Isadora yelled, as she ran toward Jaxon, pulling the dagger from behind him and running toward Aisling too fast for any of us to reach her. She gripped the dagger and sliced it into the air at Aisling, plunging the true dagger into her abdomen. Declan pushed Isadora off her and caught Aisling before her wide eyes looked down at the damage. Ezra became enraged as he threw a protection shield over Aisling and rushed toward Isadora, pinning her hard against the ground, beating her face in before being thrown off by a force that was unnatural. I needed to move quickly. I looked up as the sky eerily changed, knowing that in either outcome Ragnar was out now. Then, the red moon began to move at a faster pace, letting us know that our time was running out to change the course of fate. *Amulet or death. What's it going to be?* a voice whispered to me. But both would ruin Eric's existence, which would ruin my dad. I glanced over to Haven, who started to shake her head.

"Don't even think about it," I yelled, as Haven ran toward me, grabbing my hand and letting our magic flow between us. She was trying to force her magic into me as I did the same to her. Neither of us were willing to take the other's.

Our bodies started to glow and rise off the ground. I could feel her healing powers coursing through my syphoning as they began to mix. I looked down at my Mark and was astonished when it glowed brighter than the sun. I looked at hers as it matched mine. We were not consuming one another but instead strengthening ourselves. *Together.*

That was it. Anchors were stronger together than apart.

The others were busy fighting Isadora with their own strengths. It was a battlefield. No one had noticed Haven and I mixing our magic. She looked over to me and nodded. "Together," she said, as we touched the ground again.

The ground beneath began to shake, and I realized we were running out of time. The course of time needed to be changed now. We didn't have another minute to wait.

Haven grabbed my hand, and we advanced on Isadora, palms up as earth, fire, and vines combined and started to release from our palms. The battlefield froze as Isadora stood and attempted to push against us with her own strength.

Everything happened so fast that every minute that went by felt like seconds. Eric sat up with a new Mark on his forearm as my dad grabbed his shoulder, and they charged toward her. Aunt Clara and my mom joined hands and let their elemental magic mix. Then, Jaxon and Declan followed suit with earth and water. Ezra stood and grabbed Aisling's hand as their strength together expanded. All the Anchors were together, and we were all ready to finish this. Margo ran behind us, fleeing from the battlefront.

Isadora stood in the middle, waiting for us to meet her. Anchorless. The look of defeat finally met her eyes, when she looked down and saw her Mark gone. She tried to pull Margo toward her, but Haven and I reached her as the others circled her again. I looked up at the red moon becoming a thin sliver, meaning we had thirty seconds or less to finish this. I grabbed the amulet and advanced on her, forcing the 'X' we needed against her heart as she ripped it from me and forced it back on me, aiming straight for my heart. Haven pulled me back and jumped in front of me, as the sharp edge of the pendant came toward her. Only our dad jumped in front of it as it slashed his back, while holding Haven protectively. I stood and watched as the two of them vanished from in front of me. And we all were thrown backwards as a beam of light exploded from the amulet before it disappeared along with them.

"No," I screamed.

My mother's blood curdling scream escaped her throat.

I frantically tried to get to my feet as Isadora jumped up and stared at her empty hand, trying to put the pieces together herself. This was it. We were out of time. She charged me and lifted me up by my neck into the air.

"You're dead," she screamed.

We were out of time, and we only ruined ourselves further. I put my hands down, defeated, as she dragged me through the air. My dad and sister were gone. The amulet was gone. The souls would be imprisoned with her. The dagger prison world disappeared with my dad. Ragnar was free. We had nothing. The thyme spell only took more away from us. She began to syphon the magic I had left in me as I realized we lost everything.

My hand fell to my side, hitting my jacket pocket. I saw the fiery orange moon with only a slither left as I felt the side of my pocket and froze at the object there as we flew higher into the sky.

Squid ink.

Haven's conversation with me from the first time came to mind.

"Hey, Haven, how much do you know about this stuff?"

"The ink. Hm, are you thinking what I'm thinking?"

"Magic eraser for an Immortal?"

.   .   .

There was nothing left, and we were out of time. I grabbed it from my pocket and flicked the top off as I silently prayed for the souls that may be gathering back inside her to find their way back home. *I'm so sorry.* I grabbed the bottle and shoved it down her throat. She threw her head back and began to choke on it, spitting half of the black swirls of the galaxy colors back on me. Her veins became black as the poison filled her and me, making our magic disappear. Her grip loosened as she rubbed her throat with her free hand, continuing to choke. Her eyes met mine midair with fear for the first time in her thousand years. She looked down, and realization finally hit her as we began to free fall to the ground.

"Now we're both dead." I smiled as I realized the sacrifice was not just my magic, but it would be my life too.

My energy had finally left from inside me as we fell. I closed my eyes and felt hands wrap around my waist as we waited for the impact, knowing Isadora was just as scared as I was, but neither of us admitted it. We just held on and let our bodies fall.

The fall seemed endless as a loop of time continued. A ticking clock grew louder as it counted down our thyme spell to its end, and at the final tick, I opened my eyes to the sound of a woman's voice that I recognized but was not expecting. It was just me and the transparent woman standing in oblivion. "Well, child, you chose her fate, and you sacrificed your magic. Is that what you wanted?"

"I wanted everyone to live. No matter the cost."

"Isadora too?" She watched me intently, and I realized

when Isadora grabbed onto me as we fell that she wanted nothing more than to live too. It was as if her humanity switched back on for the first time in centuries.

"I just want the evil gone." I looked down and closed my eyes, as I kept waiting for the impact.

"Well, both the twins' magic has been either transferred or destroyed, so the mission is over, and the contract is now void. Isadora's immortality will be gone, and the world can re-balance. And for that, I am grateful. The town's memories of the parade's magical mishaps of today have been erased, and life can go on as normal again. You sure did really bring it down to the last second. But thank you for balancing the magic world."

I looked up, not expecting anything. "What about my sister and dad?"

Her illuminating body floated closer toward me. "They, I can do nothing about. They seem to be off my map."

"Are they," my stomach turned at the thought, "dead?"

The woman smiled.

"Please," I whispered, as I looked into her soul.

"I cannot say. But I do have a favor to ask you. Ragnar's escape has put many others in danger. I need you to contain him."

"I am magicless. Worthless."

"Oh, child. You are so much more. You will find your way." She smiled as her light grew brighter, and I could no longer see anything surrounding me. Her voice whispered back to me, "Eric is good at erasing things."

I stood silently in the bright light wondering what she meant by that. I felt as if I should've hit rock bottom by now as I pondered what was to come next.

Chapter Fifty-Five

Jaxon Oakes

I looked up and watched the two of them free fall, waiting for Isadora to do something. When she did nothing, I realized that something was wrong. "Ember, save her!" I yelled, as I watched them speeding for the earth.

She teleported and reappeared in front of me with them. They both had their eyes closed.

"Freya? Hey, Freya, look at me." She didn't open her eyes. She was breathing but wouldn't respond. "What happened? Eric? What's going on?" I pulled her against me and rocked her body, waiting for an answer. "Freya." I could feel tears start to build and I was trying not to let them fall, but damn. This was my Freya.

The others surrounded us as Isadora opened her eyes and sat up.

"Stupid girl." She started to cry as she threw the bottle down onto the ground, smashing it.

Clara walked over and grabbed the glass shards, "No." She looked back to Freya and shook her head. "The squid ink."

Alex gasped as she came down by her. "Her magic is gone. She's exhausted herself from the spell and has no magic to recover from it." She brushed Freya's hair out of her face and started to cry next to me.

My mother joined us and watched her sister carefully before studying Freya's state.

"Will she be okay?" I asked, frantically, trying to process what was going on.

My mother bent down next to us, "In time."

Eric growled as he grabbed Isadora and pinned her against the ground. She thrashed, trying to release herself from his grip. "You stupid bitch. What have you done?"

"What have I done? She just ruined me."

Eric spat next to her. "You were ruined the day you were born. Ragnar was right to want to kill you." He took her head and shoved it deeper into the ground. I watched as my mother grimaced and looked away. "That amulet was for you. Izzy, you don't deserve to live in this world."

Eric reached for the bloodied dagger. No one stopped him as he brought it to her throat. She whimpered and pleaded to let her live.

"You deserve nothing," he spat at her.

His hand froze when he looked back toward Freya who had started to stir in my arms. He pulled back away from her and sat back, watching as Freya opened her eyes. I helped her sit up. She half smiled at me before glaring at Isadora.

Eric stood, choking back rage and tears as he walked toward Freya. "What do you want me to do with her?"

I helped her stand as she walked over to Isadora and studied her face. *Fear.*

"Let her live."

I gasped as did the others as she made a decision none of us agreed with.

"Freya, that's not—" I said.

"Eric, erase her memories. I don't want her to remember any of us. I want her to live a lonely life without love and without friends. I want her to be nobody and clinging to the life she wished she had as she watches us all live out a happy life. I want her to wish for death and never let it come."

Eric watched Isadora intently and smiled.

"She has taken enough away from all of us, death would be too easy. I want her to suffer the loneliness she will forever have now."

Eric nodded and bent down to face his ex Anchor. "Without magic, you don't need an Anchor to live a miserable life. Here's to seventy years of misery, which is still a fraction of what you have caused everyone else. Call this mercy."

"Eric, no, please. You can't do this to me." Isadora tried to stand and push herself away from him, trying to pull elemental magic from anywhere. Nothing. He grabbed her arms and pinned her hard against the ground.

"Miss Izzy, you will not remember the good in the last thousand years of your life, only the pain and suffering that you have caused." When Eric's words began to flow, Isadora panicked.

"No, you are just like him. You are worse." She screamed, then became completely still and listened intently.

Eric continued, "You will not remember any of us, and

you will continue to search for a happiness that will never come. You will stay sterile and mourn your child."

Freya grabbed Eric's shoulder and added, "And you will forget about any love or happiness that has ever happened to you. You will never be able to take the easy way out. You will live and die alone."

They stopped talking, and Isadora blinked twice and grimaced as her head began to reroute her memories. Her body clenched, as her brain erased half of her life. I had never seen anything like it before.

Isadora stopped screaming and sat up quietly.

"Where am I?" she asked.

Freya sat down in front of her, brushing her hair from her eyes. "Oh, honey, you were in an accident. Your sister has offered to help you while you're on the mend."

Isadora shook her head. "My sister hates me."

"Exactly," Freya said, as Isadora started to cry.

My mother gasped, but stayed silent.

I grabbed Freya's arm, pulling her back into me. "I don't want her near my mother."

"Keep your friends close and your enemies closer," she whispered.

I exhaled and nodded. I looked at Isadora and stared as her body was bruised and not healing.

"What am I supposed to be doing?" she asked anyone who would listen.

"Take a painkiller. Welcome to the real world, you mortal bitch. Oh, and don't get hit by a truck," I said and walked away, pulling Freya with me. "Come here." I lifted her up and kissed her. Forgetting that our world was a mess still, I would forever be grateful that she was back in my arms.

I heard Alex's phone ring as she answered it, wiping her tears away.

"They're with you?" she asked, making all of us turn toward her with hope that Jim and Haven were teleported there. I held my breath waiting. "Good. We have another problem. It's Jim and Haven." My hope deflated when she said their names. "Yes, Margo is safe with us." She hung up the phone.

"The house is whole again, and the souls are safe there." She sniffled before the tears started to fall. Her husband and daughter were gone, and you could see the defeat across her face.

"We will get them back. You have my word." Eric grabbed Alex and held her tight against his chest, letting her guard come down as she fell apart.

Chapter Fifty-Six

Freya Chamberlain

Journal Entry:

It's been a while. The last few weeks have been a lot to take in. I haven't had the energy to pick up a pen, let alone get out of bed. I keep waiting for Haven and my dad to show up on the doorstep, but every time there's a knock on the door, it's never them. I know my mom is feeling the same way. If it wasn't for Eric and Jaxon staying here and forcing us to get up or to eat, we would've withered away in depression. Today is a new day, though.

I keep replaying what the lady said to me when I was free falling. I haven't told anyone yet about our new mission with Ragnar because I have zero motivation. If she would've just given me hope that my family was still alive, then maybe I would be moving faster. When I asked her about my sister and dad, she was silent. I wanted to punch the bitch in the face, but she was translucent and would've just floated away, making me stand there like the fool that I am. I just hope they are somewhere. Anywhere, but gone.

Isadora, well, she... UGH! I keep going back and forth in my head wondering if I should've just let Eric kill her, but a little voice inside me said to keep her at arm's length just in case. I haven't had the nerve to see her around Margo yet. But they are staying in Jaxon's old home with the souls, and more furniture now with Margo and Callum staying there to keep them safe. We saved the souls and ended Isadora's magic. Ember was reunited with her mothers and the casino was fully restored the minute the clock restarted. So, I guess we achieved something, but at such a great cost.

Aisling's wound healed, but with a wicked scar. Luckily, Ezra found his Mark to help keep her alive. She said she still feels like herself. I guess as soon as my dad disappeared, he must've brought the prison world with him instead of it being stuck with her. So, I guess that was another win. But now her and Jaxon have matching scars since the spell didn't

remove that one from him. I'm happy Jaxon is here with me. I just miss them.

~~**I know they are alive somewhere, but we just can't seem to find them. My magic being gone isn't helping. I can't even perform the most simple locator spell. Eric and Jaxon have been teaming up lately to be the dynamic duo to save our loved ones.**~~

I stopped writing and threw the pen across the room. "Fuck this." I took the journal and threw it toward the door.

"Hey, whoa." Jaxon dodged the journal while walking in and sitting down next to me on the bed. "Hey, what's going on?"

"What do you think? My family is still gone and so is my magic. I'm useless and I—" Saying the words out loud finally made me break. My emotions overflowed as did my tears. I just had no words left.

He grabbed me and pulled me onto his lap, like a child. "We will find them. Eric wouldn't be alive if Jim wasn't. He's linked to him. Remember?" He moved my hair out of my face and lifted my chin up to him. "They are somewhere. We just haven't located them yet."

The tears continued as my hope continued to deflate, and I buried my head into his chest. "It's been over three weeks." The ugly cry was real as he wrapped his arms around me tighter.

"I know. Why don't we go downstairs and at least eat something? After all, it is Thanksgiving." He continued to rub my arms, trying to help. But nothing was going to help my emotions right now, and there wasn't much to be thankful for.

I nodded, knowing that he wasn't going to take no for an answer. I slowly stood up and walked over to my desk and grabbed a hoodie, throwing it on before heading for the doorway. I stopped in front of the journal, bending over to grab it. I grabbed the newly written entry, ripped it out and crumpled it. "Happy fucking Thanksgiving." Jaxon frowned as I tossed it behind me and headed downstairs to face the other sad face of my mother.

I could smell the meal being prepared, but the thought of eating while my dad and sister were most likely suffering somewhere was pissing me off even more. Eric met me by the stairs, and I put my hood over my head and walked past him.

"Guess you got your wish. You're here for the holiday. Just not the right way," I sneered.

He grabbed my wrist and stopped me mid step. "That is enough. I let you pout and grieve but it's time to turn it off. We have work to do," he said sternly.

"Let go of me." I pulled at my wrist trying to release the hold. He squeezed tighter. "If I had my magic—"

"Well, you don't," Eric interrupted. "And if you stopped hiding in your sorrows, you would know that I will get it back."

I glared at him, "Why don't you get my dad back first?"

He pinned me against the wall of the stairwell, getting face to face with my attitude. Jaxon stepped toward us to get in the middle when Eric put his hand up to stop him. "They are my family too. Instead of sulking, you could be helping." He let go of my hands and walked away angrily. He stepped outside as Jaxon met my eyes.

"He's right, Freya. I know you don't want to hear it. But we need to get to work."

I knew he was right. I just didn't know where to start, and the sooner we started, the sooner the outcome would come to light. Whether it was good or bad. I just didn't know if I was prepared for a bad one.

"I'm sorry, babe," I said and felt more tears coming. But Eric was right. I needed to turn my emotions off and get my family back.

Jaxon frowned and pulled me in closer to him. "I don't need the apology. I think he does." He kissed me and pointed to the front porch. I nodded and walked to the front door, ready to bite my tongue at the words that I knew needed to be said.

I inhaled sharply and walked outside, letting the shiver from the cold and my nerves run through my body. Eric was standing silently in his pressed suit with his hands in his pockets. I walked up next to him and slid my hand through his arm and waited for him to look at me. When he didn't budge, I decided it was time to swallow my feelings and get back on track.

"I'm sorry. I know you are trying to help. I just—"

"You miss them. I get it." He stayed looking out toward the road.

"Thank you for being here. I never thought I would see my mom this broken. It's like reliving my past. Only it's reversed, like when she left my dad. I think that has a lot to do with my emotions right now. I've been here emotionally before, only this time it's my mom that's broken and the unknowing if we will ever see them again."

He turned and looked down at me, pulling his arm out of his pocket and putting it around my shoulders. It was a weird closeness that felt natural. A few months ago, I would've burned him alive for breathing near me. Now, his closeness made me feel safe. We had a weird family dynamic for sure.

"I'm going to get them back. You have my word."

"Please don't make promises you can't keep."

Eric turned me toward him and pulled my chin up to meet his eyes. "Freya, you have my word. I will not stop until they are back with you. No matter what."

I stared into his eyes and saw the determination was there. I half smiled and nodded. "Okay." I inhaled heavily, trying to hold back the tears I wanted to shed.

"Just trust my plans, okay?" he asked with a smile.

"I will," I agreed and finally smiled back at him.

I turned when I saw headlights coming from down the road. I held my breath until the car slowed and turned into our driveway. It was Margo and Callum. I exhaled quickly with relief.

They parked and stepped out of the car. The back door opened, and Isadora stepped out with them, heading for our house.

"Abso-fucking-lutely not," I sneered and took a step toward her. Eric grabbed my arm and held me back.

"I said trust my plans, and you agreed. Now play nice with our guests."

I turned back around toward him and glared.

Chapter Fifty-Seven

Haven vine

Journal Entry:

Well, here goes nothing. Journal entry #1. Weird. I don't see how Freya made this a habit. It seems kind of silly. But I guess there's not much else going on in this place. Maybe this will keep me sane. I'm sitting here in her room and using this journal with the infinity symbol on it. I swear I haven't read the other past entries. I'm just starting fresh in the middle of the journal.

Time runs differently here. Here, as in, I don't really know where 'here' is. But I'm assuming we're in the amulet, or maybe the dagger. With my dad carrying the prison world, I feel that the amulet and dagger world collided and created this space. The best part about this place is my dad is here with me. So, luckily, I'm not alone. The moon and sun set and rise in the same direction of the Mississippi. It's hard to tell how the clock works here. But it has been peaceful, though. It looks just like Crystal Rock, only no one is here. It's empty and quiet. Food never expires, and the sun doesn't last twenty-four hours. I've done the calculations, and it seems as though a few days or so go by in a normal twenty-four hours back home.

Home. I miss home. I miss my family. I miss Ezra.

I just keep replaying JFK in my head, and I just hope that the others are safe and that we won. Otherwise, if this is Hell and we didn't make it, then why would we be paired together? I always thought a personal prison world would be lonely. But this place is sturdy and standing and holding us both.

Dad's very happy. The other day, his old Camaro showed up in the garage. He was ecstatic to see it and has been practicing his magic to try and get it to start. He hasn't picked up a single tool, he's just been aiming his hands toward the engine and waiting for a miracle. I think it's fair to say that he needs some training. Starting tomorrow, his training will begin.

That's another thing, here I have my magic,

and my Mark is still intact so that has to mean something. We had to win something against Isadora. I just have so many questions, and I wish I could contact the others just for some reassurance that the world was still rotating. All I can do is hope, and hope is going to help us survive until we can be together again.

I guess this writing thing isn't too bad after all. With the days moving a little faster here, I might have to wait a few days before something exciting happens. Seems that not much will be going on in this world. I guess boring isn't so bad. Plus, I feel like I'm making up for lost time with my dad, and for that, I will forever be grateful.

If anyone ever sees this, just know that I love you guys and keep your head up. We're not too far away. At least, I don't think we are.

-Haven

How do villains become so evil?

Find out in the prequel
Eric and Izzy

For more information on the series check out the
author website for future updates:

https://stephanievorwald.wixsite.com/website

About the Author

Stephanie Vorwald is the author of the Witches & Immortals Series. She found her passion for writing long before she achieved writing 'The End' for her debut novel. She loves writing fantasy books where she can create her own world of magic in everyday, ordinary life. When she is not writing, she is a Registered Dental Hygienist. She loves being a mother to her kids and having family time.

www.ingramcontent.com/pod-product-compliance
Lightning Source LLC
Chambersburg PA
CBHW062108290726
48975CB00001B/152